HEARTBREAKER OF THE TON

Misfits of the Ton
Book Six

by
Emily Royal

ARE YOU SIGNED UP FOR DRAGONBLADE'S BLOG?

You'll get the latest news and information on exclusive giveaways, exclusive excerpts, coming releases, sales, free books, cover reveals and more.

Check out our complete list of authors, too!

No spam, no junk. That's a promise!

Sign Up Here

www.dragonbladepublishing.com

Dearest Reader;

Thank you for your support of a small press. At Dragonblade Publishing, we strive to bring you the highest quality Historical Romance from some of the best authors in the business. Without your support, there is no 'us', so we sincerely hope you adore these stories and find some new favorite authors along the way.

Happy Reading!

CEO, Dragonblade Publishing

Additional Dragonblade books by Author Emily Royal

Misfits of the Ton
Tomboy of the Ton (Book 1)
Ruined by the Ton (Book 2)
Thief of the Ton (Book 3)
Oddity of the Ton (Book 4)
Harpy of the Ton (Book 5)
Heartbreaker of the Ton (Book 6)
The Taming of the Duke (Novella)

Headstrong Harts
What the Hart Wants (Book 1)
Queen of my Hart (Book 2)
Hidden Hart (Book 3)
The Prizefighter's Hart (Book 4)
All I Want for Christmas is My Hart (Novella)
Haunted Hart (Novella)

London Libertines
Henry's Bride (Book 1)
Hawthorne's Wife (Book 2)
Roderick's Widow (Book 3)
A Libertine's Christmas Miracle (Novella)

The Lyon's Den Series
A Lyon's Pride
Lyon of the Highlands
Lyon of the Ton

CHAPTER ONE

London, August 1815

"I 'M PREGNANT."

Etty clenched her hands into fists as she uttered the revelation. The only sign that he'd heard was a slight hesitation in his arm as he raised the brandy glass to his lips. He drained the glass, set it aside, then leaned back, fixing her with his gaze.

"Is that so?"

"I've been wondering for some time now," she said, "but I realized this morning when my maid said that I'd not asked for extra…"

The ruby on his ducal ring winked malevolently as he held up a fleshy-fingered hand.

"I have no wish to know the details, Miss Howard. You may not have the breeding of a lady, but that's no reason to act like the commoner that you are."

The tone of his voice had hardened until it was neither the throaty, seductive drawl that he'd employed to persuade her into his bed, nor the strained grunts as he took his pleasure, his sweaty body heaving over her while the bedposts hammered against the wall.

Grunts that always served to turn Etty's stomach.

But momentary nausea was a price she'd been willing to pay if it secured her position as the Duchess of Dunton and thereby proving, at last, her worth to Mother.

And to Papa, of course. Mother might rule the family, but it was her father that Etty sought approval from. Mother had always valued Etty's beauty and social graces—Papa's approval was harder won, and therefore the more prized. But Papa only valued Etty's older sister—the ungainly Eleanor, whom the rest of Society derided. Yet Eleanor, as well as having secured Papa's love for doing nothing more than being her own, awkward self, had now secured the hand of the most alluring duke in England. Eleanor had succeeded where Etty had not. Which raised the question—what was so wrong with Etty such that a man of his quality preferred the *Oddity of the Ton* over her?

Etty placed her hand over her belly, pleading to the Almighty that it would be a boy.

Dunton poured another measure of brandy and drained the glass. "Well, I suppose that signals an end to my pleasure," he said.

Etty's heart fluttered with relief. If he left her alone until her confinement, so much the better. He could take a mistress for all she cared.

But it wasn't the done thing to tell the man she was about to marry that she found his body, his company—even the merest thought of him—utterly repugnant.

Instead, she curved her lips into a smile that her suitors had always described as *angelic*. It was a smile that, together with her beauty, had rendered her the most desirable woman of the Season, and had broken countless hearts.

But men's hearts were easily mended. A man's needs were simple—a pretty wife to adorn his arm, and a fat dowry with which to indulge in the pleasures that London could offer—in most cases, wine, gambling, and other women.

As to a *woman's* heart…

It served Etty's purpose best not to have one. Better to be the heartbreaker than the brokenhearted.

Heartbreaker…

It was a title she welcomed. Each broken heart she left in her wake strengthened the armor around her own heart, until her emotions had been numbed to the point of immunity.

Nobody would break *her* heart. Her objective wasn't to be loved. Love came hand in hand with betrayal. No—her one, defining objective was to become a duchess. A duchess was untouchable. She could live her life as she pleased, safe from the predators who resided in the waters of Society.

She only need play her part a little longer to secure her prize—the prize that sat before her.

She fluttered her eyelashes and widened her eyes. It was a gesture that had earned her countless suitors and filled her dance card.

"I am not so ungenerous, Your Grace," she said. "I understand the duties of an obedient duchess. I will not demand that you deny yourself the pleasure a man in your position deserves. Even if I'm carrying your heir…"

His eyes narrowed, and she caught her breath. Had she reeled the fish in before he'd been properly hooked?

"A man often wishes for more than one son, does he not?" she said.

He stared at her belly, and his tongue flicked out, moistening his lips. Nausea rippled through her once more—the sickness that had plagued her for almost a week now, together with revulsion at the memory of that thick tongue thrusting into her mouth, tainting her senses with the taste of sour wine and cigars.

Then he threw back his head and laughed.

She rose to her feet. "You would mock me, given the love we share?"

"Love? Ha!" he cried, not moving to stand. "Our difference in rank renders you so far beneath me as to be hardly worth my notice, but I will concede that we are alike in one aspect."

Why was he not standing? Throughout their courtship he'd been the epitome of gentlemanly grace—offering her his arm while they promenaded, barking orders at his footmen to fetch an umbrella for her when it had begun to rain, dismissing the same footman when he'd failed to show her due reverence. He'd even draped his jacket over a puddle to save her having to veer onto the wet grass.

So why, then, was he not standing in the presence of a lady?

"Are you not pleased, Your Grace?" she asked.

"Pleased?" he scoffed. "I ought to be affronted, but I am disposed to be amused."

Affronted? Amused?

And he was *still* sitting!

"Your Grace, I don't intend to amuse," she said. "Perhaps you should request an audience with my father."

"What for?" He laughed. "Do you wish me to commiserate him on his misfortune?"

"His misfortune?"

He leaned back in his chair and crossed his ankles. "The whole of London knows that Sir Leonard Howard's elder daughter is an imbecile, for all that she attracted the hand of a duke—out of pity, no doubt. And now, the younger daughter is proven to be a whore."

She recoiled at the insult. "How dare—"

"Spare me the indignation, madam," he said. "Do you think me a fool? Did you think I'd offer for you merely because you spread your legs and offered your cunny?"

Tears stung her eyes. "I-I did no such thing!" She blinked, and a droplet splashed onto her cheek. "You seduced me. You told me I was the most delectable…"

"Oh, spare me the tears, please!" he huffed. "A woman should know when to keep her legs open and her mouth shut. There's nothing more distasteful to a man than a slut who clings on like a leech."

"I'm not a…"

"By your own admission you *are*, Miss Howard," he snarled. "A filthy whore who, no doubt, thought she could entrap me into marriage by offering her body, then decided to up the ante and fuck her way through London in an attempt to appeal to my desire for an heir."

He gripped the arms of his chair, then heaved his body up until he stood before her. She cringed at the stench of sour breath and the distaste in his eyes.

"You'll find *me* the superior player, madam. I have no intention of shackling myself to an ambitious little slut whose lineage is tainted by the stench of the shop."

"My mother was a viscount's—"

"It matters not whose daughter your mother is," he said. "She tainted her family name by shackling herself to a commoner. I've no intention of tainting *my* name by doing the same. Now, I think it's time you left."

"But—"

"Leave, madam, or I'll have you thrown out like the blackmailing tart that you are."

"I'm no—"

"You spread your legs to entrap a duke into matrimony, hoping to establish some other man's by-blow as the future Duke of Dunton. Imagine what the gossipmongers would have to say about that?"

Her gut twisted in horror. "You wouldn't!"

He smiled, his eyes glittering in his fleshy, pasty face. "I'll be generous and refrain from warning my acquaintance of your sinful ways, provided that you leave now, and make sure that I never set eyes on you again." He sauntered toward the bellpull by the fireplace, his ungainly body rolling from side to side with each footstep. "I'll have Thomas show you out."

Thomas—the brutish footman who always lingered about Dunton's lodgings, whose eyes darkened with lust each time he looked at Etty.

"Thomas might be disposed to take my leavings," Dunton said. "What do you say? I daresay there's a shilling in it for you."

"You're disgusting!" she cried. "To think I'd take money for—"

"Ah, of course," he said, nodding as he reached into his waistcoat pocket. "How remiss of me."

He fished out a coin and tossed it to her. It struck her arm, then fell to the floor.

"For services rendered," he said. "Pick it up."

"I wouldn't sully my hands with—"

"I said. Pick. It. Up." His voice came out in a low growl as he stepped toward her. A ripple of fear coursed through her veins as he raised his hands. Those hands—those fat, fleshy hands—had already violated and ruined her. What else might they be capable of?

Trembling, she crouched and reached for the sovereign. Before she rose again, he tossed another coin at her.

"Consider that a little extra," he said, gesturing toward her belly. "To rid yourself of the bastard."

She palmed the second coin then rose to her feet. The world slipped sideways, and her vision blurred for a moment, then she righted herself.

"Of course," he added, "it's not my place to recommend anyone to deal with your...*little accident*—but I can instruct Thomas to take you to a bawdy house where there'll be plenty of whores who have availed themselves of such a service."

She caught her breath at another wave of nausea.

"Careful, Miss Howard, we wouldn't want you soiling my Aubusson rug, would we?"

Before she could reply, the door opened, and the thick-set footman entered.

"Ah, Thomas," Dunton said. "Do escort this"—he wrinkled his nose—"doxy out. Make sure she never returns."

"But..." Etty began, but the footman grasped her arm.

"Come along now, miss," he said. "There's no need to pester the duke anymore."

"The back entrance, if you please, Thomas," Dunton said. "I have my reputation to think of."

Waves of shame engulfed Etty as the footman steered her out of the parlor. Her life was ruined.

What would Mother say? Would she turn Etty out due to her failure to secure Dunton's hand? As for Papa…

Etty's heart clenched at the thought of the disappointment in her father's face. The chances of his being proud of her had always been slim, but nevertheless she'd harbored the secret desire that, one day, he might turn the same tender expression of love that he gave her sister each day onto her. But now, all hope of being loved—much less *liked*—by her father was gone.

The glittering future set out before her had crumbled to dust. In reality, that future had been an illusion. The rumors about Dunton had been true—that he relished debauching women, taking their maidenheads as trophies. In all likelihood, he kept the soiled bedsheets to mark his prowess.

Her stomach lurched at the notion—and at the metallic stench of blood that had beset her after Dunton took her for the first time, his chest puffing with pride as his lustful gaze settled on the smear of blood on her thighs.

As the footman shoved her out of the back entrance, she lurched forward, almost tripping on the steps. Her stomach finally succumbed to the nausea and she vomited over the pavement.

"Filthy whore!" the footman growled. "I s'pose I'll have to clean that up."

Etty pulled out her handkerchief and wiped her mouth. Then she straightened her stance and, with as much courage as she could muster, fixed him with a cold stare.

"Who else but you should clear up the evidence of your master's sins?" she said. "I daresay I wasn't the first, and I doubt I'll be the last woman he's ruined. I hope you take pride in your work, *Thomas*."

Then, biting her lip to stem the tears, she turned her back on him and fled.

CHAPTER TWO

Sandcombe, Lincolnshire, August 1817

THE LIFE OF a vicar was not, as many believed, one of peaceful contemplation. Instead, it was filled with the noise of people—so many people, with so many problems. And those people believed that most of their problems could be solved either by the application of an occasional prayer to the Almighty muttered at their bedside, or by weekly attendance at church. Better still if they declared their faith by singing a few bars of a hymn. Or *cawing*, in the case of Lady Fulford.

Andrew cringed at the memory of his patron's wife's voice. Why was it that those who lacked any talent for singing were always disposed to sing the loudest? But Lady Fulford was perhaps to be praised for her tenacity, if nothing else—spurred on by her friends, who described her voice as having a unique style of its own.

My friends tell me I have a unique style of my own, Mr. Staines, Lady Fulford had said on many an occasion when pushing herself and her equally talentless daughters to the forefront of a dinner party to entertain the guests and showcase their accomplishments—accomplishments that were expected to snare them a suitable husband.

A husband such as a vicar who also happened to be the younger son of an earl.

Yes, Lady Fulford believed that by inflicting her voice—and

her condescension—on the less fortunate souls in the village, she was affirming her superiority in the eyes of the Almighty, thereby effecting her own salvation.

The task of solving everyone else's problems—and the salvation of their souls—fell to Andrew himself. Like any vicar, he was considered the rightful property of his flock. Yet those members of the flock who needed him the most were the ones least inclined to demand his attendance. But he always allowed himself the indulgence of ensuring that the length of each visit he made was in direct proportion to need.

Which, by a lucky coincidence, meant that his visits to Lady Fulford were often very short indeed.

But, on occasion, he allowed himself to indulge in a morning to himself, to savor a moment's respite from the clamors of the people and their incessant problems—many of which could be solved by being a little kinder toward each other—and enjoy the solitude to be had from a stroll on the beach.

His favorite stretch of the coastline was at the south end of the village. That the rest of the population tended to avoid the area—due to the occasional riptide that rendered the water treacherous—was nothing but a coincidence.

At least, that was what he tried to tell the Almighty while engaging in his own nightly prayers when he begged forgiveness for wanting, and taking, respite from all the vestigial noise that people seemed to create.

He gazed across the sea—the shimmering blue adorned with ripples of light—and inhaled deeply. There was much to be said for the restorative properties of the sea air, which was why people flocked to resorts in their droves to take the waters, or enjoy a week or two's sanctuary from their otherwise unfulfilled lives.

It was why *she* had come to Sandcombe.

Eleanor—the purest, gentlest soul who walked upon the earth. A victim of her venomous sister's spite and a judgmental Society, Eleanor had fled London seeking solace in the country. And Andrew had fallen utterly and completely in love with her.

But Eleanor had been in love with another—the Duke of Whitcombe—who had followed her to Sandcombe, baring his heart and soul on bended knee to win her back.

Andrew ought to hate the man. Whitcombe was everything Andrew wasn't—handsome, powerful, and alluring, the sort of man who bedded his way through one half of London's women and broke the hearts of the other half. A firstborn son with the title, privileges, and admiration of the world that he considered his birthright.

And, most of all, Whitcombe was the man who had secured Eleanor's heart.

Lucky bastard.

Andrew flinched at the profanity and resolved to utter an extra-long prayer for forgiveness that night. Perhaps he might introduce a passage or two about the sins of envy—and cursing—in his next sermon.

Yes—he envied Whitcombe, and that envy had intensified the day Andrew read the notice of their marriage in the papers. But he could never hate the man, for he made Eleanor happy. Not because she was a duchess with, from what he'd gathered, a child already in the nursery and a second on the way. But because she was married to the man she loved—and who loved her.

No—Andrew's hatred, for which he begged forgiveness in his nightly prayers—was reserved for those who had striven to destroy Eleanor. Most notably her spiteful sister.

Miss Juliette Howard.

He curled his hands into fists at the mere thought of the woman.

Then he admonished himself. Why waste his efforts and thoughts on a creature he'd never meet? Hating her served no purpose.

Devil take me—I'll have to include a passage on hatred in a future sermon.

He drew in another lungful of air, his mind's eye picturing the sweet, clean sea air purifying his heart to combat his ill feelings. Then he thrust his hands in his pockets and turned inland. He glanced toward the cliffs that formed a horizon, and froze.

A lone woman was standing on the cliff edge.

The sunlight illuminated her hair—soft honey-blonde strands, loosened by the wind, glistened like gold. Her gown, a plain white muslin, billowed about her body in the wind, catching against her legs to reveal their shape. Her frame was so slight that she was in danger of being caught up in the wind and tossed into the air like a stray handkerchief.

Was she aware of the danger? One gust of wind and she'd be thrown over the cliff edge, her frail body dashed against the rocks below.

Who *was* she?

Even from a distance, an aura of despair seemed to shimmer around her—a lost soul staring out to sea, as if it might give respite from her pain.

Then she took a step forward, and Andrew's gut twisted with horror.

Sweet Lord—she was going to jump!

Before he could cry out a warning, her body stiffened. Then she turned and retreated, disappearing over the horizon.

Rather than take the longer path that wound through the sand dunes, Andrew sprinted toward the steps carved out of the cliffs and climbed them, pausing halfway to catch his breath. But by the time he reached the top, there was no sign of her. The landscape stretched before him—flat and empty save for the solitary cottage that had lain empty for almost a year since Eleanor left—and beyond it, the village, with its collection of red-bricked dwellings, overshadowed by the church spire.

Perhaps the woman on the cliff was a figment of his imagination, the archetypal lost soul he'd entered his profession to save.

As if to remind him of his duty, the church bell rang out seven times. Breakfast would be waiting for him at the rectory—as would those members of his flock he'd promised to call on today. There was no time to dwell on the apparition, no matter how lovely she was, or how much she'd touched his heart. In all likelihood, he'd never see her again.

CHAPTER THREE

T HERE WAS NOTHING so visceral—so *real*—as a mother's reaction to the cry of her child.

As soon as she heard it, Etty's gut twisted with the twin sensations of fear and the desperate desire to protect.

Did every mother experience the same? Almost from the moment Etty's child had left her body, the instinct to nurture had torn through the haze of pain and humiliation, and she had changed forever. She was no longer the disgraced, humiliated harlot who'd attempted—and failed—to entrap a duke, ruining herself in the process. She had become a tigress, driven by the feral instinct to protect her young.

Because, for the first time in her spoiled and pampered life, she had someone to love. Not the superficial desire for gratification that most of her acquaintance attempted to pass as love—but the raw, selfless desire to place the wellbeing of another at the forefront of her very existence.

Love had struck her with the force of a giant wave dashing her against a rock, smashing her former self, then reshaping her into a creature with a purpose. Not the purpose of the debutante desperate to outshine her rivals, but a woman destined to care for another living soul.

What a selfish creature she had been before! And not only selfish. She blushed with shame at the memory of how she'd treated others—her rivals on the dance floors of London's ballrooms, the servants who worked hard to maintain her coddled lifestyle, and…

Moisture pricked her eyes as she fought, and lost, against her mind, which drifted toward the one person who might have loved her had she given her a chance.

Eleanor. The sister with a heart as big as the sky that stretched toward the horizon, the gentle soul whom Etty had tormented merely for being different—a misfit.

Which is what I am now. A misfit.

But she had no right to complain about her lot. She was only reaping the rewards of her own spite—ruination, disgrace, and the bitter disappointment of her parents.

But there was one consequence of her sin that she never wished to be without. Her son—her beautiful, precious Gabriel. He may not have come from an act of love—his father might despise him, if he'd even deign to acknowledge his existence. But Etty loved him. More than life.

"I'm coming!" she cried as she ran toward the cottage.

As if in answer, his screams rose in pitch, and as she crossed the threshold, she saw him, his little body tangled among the blankets in the crib, his face contorted and red with anger.

"I'm sorry, my love—I didn't mean to leave you. I only wanted to look at the sea."

But, unlike an adult who outwardly accepted an apology with a polite nod, no matter their inner feelings, her child had yet to learn the dishonesty born of diplomacy. He merely screamed even louder.

She lifted him from the crib and pulled him to her breast. His cries lessened as his baby fingers curled around the muslin of her gown.

"Mama's here."

"Ma-ma…"

She smiled and kissed the top of his head, his soft, downy hair tickling her nose. "That's it, my love."

"Da-da…"

Moisture stung her eyes, and she blinked. "No, darling," she whispered. "Only Mama. But she loves you more than enough for two."

She approached the window and looked out across the landscape. The grassland stretched before her, falling away in a gentle incline toward the cliff edge and beyond, the expanse of the sea extending toward the horizon.

To think—her own father was, even now, beyond that horizon, enjoying the freedom that was the exclusive province of the male sex, on a quest to procure another shipment of the brightly colored silks that had made his fortune and rendered Etty the envy of her rivals during her first, and only, Season. She had always wanted to travel with him, but Mother had forbidden it, saying that a young lady's place was in London, dazzling Society with her beauty.

But beauty—though it had made her the envy of the world— was a curse. Perhaps if she'd been less beautiful, Papa might have loved her more.

And Dunton would not have seduced her.

"But then, I'd not have *you*, would I?" she whispered, kissing her child once more. She turned the child so he faced the window. "What do you think of our new home, Gabriel?"

The little boy reached toward the window and placed his hand on it. "Doh-doh."

She smiled. "Window, my love. It's a *window*."

"Doh-doh."

He removed his hand, leaving a palm print in the thin layer of grime on the glass, and she caught his hand before he put it in his mouth.

"No," she said. "Dirty."

"Dir-dir."

"That's right—and you'll be sick if you eat it. We'd better get you cleaned up." She glanced over her shoulder at the parlor. "You *and* this cottage."

She had arrived last night under cover of darkness, having

fled London with the aid of Mr. Stockton, the solicitor who, while he tutted his disapproval, did nothing to prevent her flight. Most likely he expected her to return to London within a sennight, penitent and subdued, given that her stipend was only three hundred a year. Like all men who viewed her as a frivolous young lady who cared for nothing but fine gowns and glittering parties, he'd expect her to succumb to the temptation of taking a husband to release her dowry. But a fortune of twenty thousand wasn't enough compensation for sacrificing her freedom. As Mother had made plain, Etty's chances of a glittering match were now gone. It would take an extraordinary man indeed to take on a ruined woman with a bastard clinging to her skirts, even for such a sum. The best she could hope for was a fortune hunter who'd most likely drink and whore his way through her fortune—gone was the prospect of finding a man extraordinary enough to *love* her.

But extraordinary men did not exist, other than in fiction.

Men didn't marry for love. They married for three reasons— to best their rivals by securing the prettiest girl in the room, to increase their coffers, and to enhance their status in Society.

No—a life of solitude in a dusty, abandoned cottage was preferable to a life of imprisonment and misery, and preferable to the rivalry and vindictiveness of the *ton*, thinly disguised under a veneer of elegance. And dust could always be wiped away. Some stains—if not all—could be removed.

"We'll be happy here, my love," she said. "Just you wait and see. And you'll grow up to be a better man than your…"

Unable to voice the words, she let out a sigh, her breath misting on the window. She had no time for despair—there was simply too much to be done. Occupation, and her responsibility for another life, would stave off any selfish melancholy at her situation.

As she continued to look out of the window, her breath hitched as a man appeared on the path, rising from the cliff edge. He paused for a moment, glanced over his shoulder toward the sea, then continued along the path.

"Who's that, Gabriel?" she whispered.

It was the same man she had seen on the beach earlier, ambling along the shoreline, moving toward the water, then leaping back to avoid the waves. Until he'd glanced up and turned his face toward her.

Dressed in an olive-green jacket, cream breeches, and polished brown boots, he looked every inch the gentleman. A thick white cravat covered his neck, giving him a distinguished air.

She shrank back, her heart rate increasing. Mr. Stockton had said there were no gentlemen living in the village—other than the squire, who, in his sixties and with three grown-up daughters, was unlikely to pose a threat. It was what had attracted her to Sandcombe—that and Eleanor's account of the village in her letters.

The irony was not lost on Etty, that she was now residing in the same cottage her sister had fled to after Etty attempted to destroy her. But perhaps that was part of the symmetry of fate. The perpetrator of sin was reaping the consequences to better understand the suffering of her victim.

"We don't want him to see us, do we, my love?" she whispered, kissing the child. "Your mama's not receiving visitors today."

The path came past the cottage before veering toward the village. Soon, the man would be within six feet of her. Cradling her son, Etty stepped to the side of the window, to watch him unobserved. His gait was determined, swallowing up the path in long, even strides. The church clock pealed in the distance, and he quickened his pace.

Perhaps he was a visitor, taking a vacation, staying at the inn with the sign depicting a ruddy-faced sailor she'd spotted from the carriage last night. Perhaps, like her, he craved a moment's peace from the world and had taken a solitary constitutional before breakfasting with his family.

He neared the cottage, and as his pace slowed he glanced

toward the window as if he sensed he was being watched. Etty's breath hitched as she caught sight of his face—a high, domed forehead, straight nose, and full lips. And his eyes—a warm chocolate brown, wide and expressive. He ran a hand through his hair—thick, dark-blond locks that curled at the ends.

Then the child in her arms let out a wail, and the man stopped.

"Hush!" Etty whispered. "Mama needs you to be quiet."

She stepped away and held her breath, rocking her son to and fro. The boy quieted, issuing little mewls of contentment, and she moved forward again, then froze.

The man was staring directly at her.

He tilted his head to one side and narrowed his eyes. Then he shook his head and resumed his journey toward the village, and her stomach fluttered with relief.

He hadn't seen her.

She smiled to herself and kissed her child once more, and he cooed in response.

"Sometimes, Gabriel," she said, "dirty windows are a blessing."

CHAPTER FOUR

"WOULD YOU LIKE me to tell you the news, vicar?"

Andrew set his teacup aside. "By all means, Lady Fulford."

Why the woman deigned to ask the question was beyond him, given that she'd always say her piece whether anyone liked it or not.

She straightened her back and gave the self-satisfied nod of the gossipmonger eager to demonstrate her prowess by being the first to impart some salacious piece of news. Next to her—sitting in order of age and therefore the order in which she wished them to marry—were her daughters. The eldest—twins—were barely distinguishable from each other, save for the nose of the elder being a little longer than that of the younger. The youngest barely lifted her gaze from the floor. Three young women with no qualities of note other than their overinflated opinions of themselves and their overly ambitious mother.

Oh dear, that's another sinful thought for which I must pray forgiveness.

Though it was not the kind of sinful thought that rendered a man stiff with need. One look at the Fulford girls was enough to make one's manhood shrivel in fear.

Andrew always found a wicked voice in his mind whispering of the benefits of the Fulford girls being struck dumb. In that particular wish, he doubted he was alone. Last week, after dinner,

Mrs. Lewis, for all that she was Lady Fulford's particular friend, had visibly flinched when Elizabeth and Sarah Fulford were invited to sing a duet, Mr. Lewis was taken with a sudden turn of colic, declaring the necessity of a visit to the privy before almost sprinting from the room. The man was to be commended for his ingenuity.

"Shore Cottage is let at last!" Lady Fulford cried, returning Andrew to the present.

"Is that so?" he asked.

She set her teacup down with a clatter. "Oh, vicar—is that *all* you can say?" She turned to her daughters. "Is that all he can say, girls? What say you, Mrs. Lewis?"

"Have you met the occupant?" Mrs. Lewis asked.

"Perhaps it's a young man," the eldest Miss Fulford said, her eyes widening with anticipation.

"Now, Elizabeth," Lady Fulford said, "you mustn't speculate."

"A young man would be such a benefit to the village!" Mrs. Lewis said. "To think—that poor cottage has been left empty for so long, after that dreadful woman left."

"That *dreadful woman* is now the Duchess of Whitcombe," Andrew said.

Lady Fulford arched an eyebrow. "Far be it from me to speak ill of a duchess, but that woman played us all false— masquerading as a widow, when we all knew what she was about."

"Quite so," Mrs. Lewis added. "Surely, vicar, you don't condone such deceit. Does the Almighty not tell us to abandon all thoughts of deception?"

"I wouldn't condone deception when there's malice intended," Andrew said, "but Eleanor"—Lady Fulford drew in a sharp breath—"*the duchess*, came to Sandcombe with no intent to harm us. We should show more compassion to those who might act out of necessity rather than for personal gain."

"That's very charitable, I must say," Lady Fulford said, her voice sharpening, "given how she led you astray."

"She hardly did that," Andrew said, laughing.

"I beg to differ, Mr. Staines. Did she not lead you to believe that she'd accept your suit when she was, in fact, pursuing another man?"

He flinched as her arrow hit home.

"In fact…" Lady Fulford continued, but the youngest Miss Fulford leaned forward.

"More tea, vicar?"

"Caroline!" her mother said sharply. "It's most unseemly to interrupt your mother when she's—"

"Thank you, Miss Caroline, that's most kind," Andrew said. The girl rose, blushing, and took his cup.

"Has the new tenant taken residence?" Mrs. Lewis asked.

"I believe so," Lady Fulford said. "Mrs. Gadd said she'd received an order for a hindquarter of pork to be delivered to the cottage on Saturday, and young Thomas Ham told our stable boy that he saw a carriage outside there last night."

"Whoever it is must be someone of means if they can afford a carriage," Mrs. Lewis said.

"Perhaps it's a family," Caroline said, pouring tea into Andrew's cup.

"A family? In a hovel that's barely large enough to house one?" Lady Fulford exclaimed. "Don't talk nonsense, child! A family of means would never stoop to live in such a place!"

"Then perhaps it's a young man on vacation, Mama," the eldest Miss Fulford said, pulling a face at her sister.

"A single man," Sarah Fulford added.

"What do *you* think, vicar?" Mrs. Lewis asked.

"My hopes are pinned firmly on the newcomer being a young man," Andrew said.

Preferably one in search of a wife. Perhaps then the attention of Lady Fulford and her unmarried daughters might turn toward that unfortunate fellow—another poor carcass for the crows to pick over.

"The place is hardly fit to be lived in," Mrs. Lewis said. "The garden is overgrown with weeds. There's nobody to tend to it since Mrs. Legge's father passed, God rest his soul."

"The garden didn't seem so badly overgrown this morning," Andrew said.

Five pairs of eyes focused on him.

"You've been to the cottage, vicar?" Mrs. Lewis asked.

"I passed it on my morning walk."

"And did you see the tenant?" Lady Fulford's thin-lipped mouth curved into a smile. "Vicar, you've been teasing us, have you not? Have you called on him? Is he a man of means?"

"I'm sorry to disappoint you, but no," Andrew said. "The cottage looked unoccupied."

And it had, save for the shadow he'd seen at the window. And he could have sworn he'd heard a cry—high pitched, like that of an animal, at which point the shadow had moved, then disappeared. He'd dismissed it as an animal—a fox, perhaps, seeking refuge from Mr. Fulford and his hunting dogs.

But what fox stood tall enough to look out of a window?

Perhaps the apparition he'd seen at the cliff top hadn't been a ghost.

CHAPTER FIVE

WHAT COULD BE more uplifting for a weary soul than a song? And though Etty had always preferred the Italian airs heard in London's drawing rooms to a hymn, the enthusiasm of the congregation as they sang the chorus in unison couldn't fail to lift her spirits.

Even if their enthusiasm could not always be matched by their ability. The family standing across the aisle, well turned out in their Sunday best—clothes that were ill fitting and eliciting discomfort in their expressions—were tolerably talented. The man had a rich, deep voice, his wife a clear alto. Their children sang more softly while they clutched their hymn books, and Etty recognized their son as the polite young man who'd delivered the joint of pork yesterday. A family of pig farmers would never be welcomed into Society, but had they been gentlefolk, their singing talents would have made them the toast of London's drawing rooms.

Etty glanced about the church. The building was smaller than the churches she'd been used to in London, but its size rendered it less imposing. Light filtered through the windows, dotting the interior with jewels of color, and she let her gaze wander, following the beam of light that stretched along the church.

At the very front sat a family of five—a gray-haired couple and three daughters who looked to be of a similar age to Etty. With their stiff backs and elegantly tailored attire, they must be the principal inhabitants of Sandcombe. The local squire, Mr. Stockton had said so. They had arrived late for the service that morning, while the rest of the congregation remained standing. After casting a cursory glance at Etty, at which point the matriarch wrinkled her nose in a sneer, they'd glided along the aisle, issuing the occasional nod to the congregation, in the manner of royalty acknowledging the subjects they despised.

They now stood, clutching their hymn books, stiffened bodies exuding arrogance and self-importance.

Two years ago, Etty had been exactly like them.

Except perhaps in respect of their singing talents. The man's voice was tolerable, but the woman reminded her of a gang of laborers sawing wood in unison. The daughters were no better. A flock of angry seagulls fighting for fish scraps would earn greater applause, and cause less pain to the ears. But, doubtless, no creature in the village—perhaps not even the squire himself— would dare give an honest opinion regarding the quality of their voices.

Etty smiled to herself. Perhaps there was one benefit to her ruination—that she'd never again be invited to the sort of dinner party where she was required to endure the caterwauling of some conceited debutante or her mama, and applaud their "singing."

Stop it! a voice inside her mind admonished her. How many times had Papa warned her of the sins of spite?

And of jealousy. For was she not jealous of the family standing at the front? They had respectability, and were most likely admired for their position in the world—even if their world was this little, obscure corner. Sandcombe might only be a day's ride from London, but it might as well have been across the ocean that her new home overlooked. And it was ruled by the family standing at the front of the church—the family who had wrinkled their noses in disdain when they set eyes on her, as if she were nothing.

And I am *nothing now.*

The hymn concluded, the last echoes of the voices disappearing into the ceiling. At a word from the vicar, the congregation sat. Etty placed her hymn book on the pew, then adjusted the shawl that held her son close. He stirred in her arms, then stared at her with his deep-set blue eyes.

"Mama."

"Hush, sweetheart," she whispered, as a woman in the pew in front turned to glare at her, before resuming her attention on the vicar climbing into the pulpit. The murmur of whispers faded, punctuated by the occasional cough. A brief moment of silence descended, as if the congregation held their breath in anticipation. Then the sermon began.

Gabriel let out a gurgle, and his forehead creased into a frown. Etty recognized the precursor to a bout of crying. No doubt he was hungry, given the voracity of his appetite—yesterday he'd eaten enough of the stew for a boy twice his size.

He let out a low cry, and the woman glanced over her shoulder once more and issued a sharp sigh.

Why was it that children always grew distressed when they needed to remain silent? The woman—and, most likely, the family at the front of the church—believed that children should be hidden away, lest their spontaneous, improper, and uncouth noises tainted the sanctity of a church building.

With luck, the sermon would be short. Unlike Reverend Gache's sermons—*he* clearly believed that the number of souls he saved during a service was in direct proportion to the length of his speeches. With even greater luck, today's sermon would be a little less righteous than Reverend Gache's pontifications. He had been willing to baptize Gabriel—doubtless due to Papa's generous donation to the church—but accompanying the service had been a lecture on the sins of women, from Eve, the original sinner, to the women who tempted righteous men to stray. Of course, being a man himself, the reverend had said nothing of the men who ruined women for nothing more than their own gratification.

Gabriel let out another cry, and Etty flinched at a ripple of tuts from the surrounding congregants. She held up her forefinger to her son's face. His mouth creased into a smile as he grasped her finger, curling his fingers around it.

"We are all sinners in the eyes of the Almighty," the vicar said, his voice echoing through the building.

Sinner.

Yet another pious man resolved to judge those he deemed unworthy.

Would she be forever condemned as a sinner?

"And it is said that we must repent of our sins."

Some sins, perhaps. Etty cringed at the cruelty with which she'd treated others, including her own sister. But as she cradled the product of her greatest sin in her arms, her heart rebelled against the vicar's words.

"After all," he continued, his voice rich and warm, "is that not why each and every one of you is here today? To seek absolution from your sins?"

Etty's cheeks warmed. Were his comments directed at her, the sinner in the back row?

"What is absolution?" he asked. "Can it be earned merely through an hour's worship on a Sunday? Do we emerge from the service cleansed of our sins in the knowledge that we might sin again? Or should we set aside time to reflect upon our sins—the consequences of our actions, not just on ourselves, but on those around us?"

A cough erupted from somewhere near the front, followed by a volley of shushing.

"If a man beats his son on Friday," the sermon continued, "then repents on Sunday, does the Almighty give him leave to beat his son again? Or a woman, who passes by a less fortunate soul without offering help—is she a worthier soul by virtue of attending the service today? When a sinner prays, what is he asking of the Almighty? Does he expect, through the act of prayer itself, to be absolved and given the freedom to sin again? Or should he be asking for something more, the strength to atone for his sins, to understand the suffering of those he—or she—has sinned against? Who is the worthier, the congregant who prays for forgiveness, or the heathen who takes action to mitigate the consequences of their sins?"

Etty glanced up at the figure in the pulpit. *Heavens!* Was the vicar casting judgment on his congregation—on the overly righteous creatures who believed themselves worthier individuals merely through attending church? What extraordinary words for a man who was, no doubt, living under the patronage of the very people he sought to criticize.

As Etty studied the vicar's features, her heart gave a little jolt.

It was the man from the cliff path.

From his elevated position in the pulpit, a beam of sunlight illuminating his features, she could see him more clearly. His blond hair shimmered in the light like a halo as he turned his head to gaze across the congregation. His chocolate-brown eyes bore an intelligent, searching expression—as if he could see into a person's soul at a mere glance, their sins laid bare.

"And what of the sinner who the more righteous among us believe to be beyond retribution?" he continued. "Should they be condemned forever, or should we ask for the strength to understand them? There are those of us driven to sin through necessity, or the persuasion of others. Those whom the more fortunate might condemn as having weak souls, but..."

He paused as his gaze settled on Etty. His eyes seemed to darken as they focused on her, searching her soul for its weaknesses.

And he would find many. For whom, among the congregation, could possibly have sinned more than she?

For a heartbeat the two of them stared at each other, the rest of the congregation seeming to fade into the background, blurred and indistinct, as if they were the only two creatures in the church.

He dipped his head a fraction, as if to acknowledge her presence, and her cheeks warmed at his scrutiny.

Why did he not continue?

The silence seemed to stretch, and she held her breath, tensing her body in anticipation for…

For what? Condemnation? Would he single her out as the ultimate sinner—yet another man to condemn a woman for a moment of weakness, declaring that, no matter how fervently she prayed for forgiveness, her tenancy in hell was already secured?

The child in her arms began to cry as she tightened her embrace with the instinct to protect him from the condemnation of the world.

Bastard. By-blow…

Words she'd heard before—hushed whispers from the doctor who'd delivered her son, leaving her bleeding and in pain so that he might return to his worthier patients as quickly as possible. Reverend Gache's protests of allowing sinners into his church, which were abruptly silenced by the clink of Papa's sovereigns.

Tears pooled in her eyes as she clung to her son. He let out a wail that echoed around the church, and a volley of tuts and hisses filled the air. The family at the front turned their heads in unison, the bright, wide-brimmed hat of the squire's wife almost knocking off her daughter's bonnet.

"Well, *really!*"

Etty cringed. How she longed to yell back at the woman—to ask her whether she believed there to be no sin greater than a child crying! But she had come to Sandcombe to hide away from judging eyes. To be left alone.

"Hush, my love," she whispered, rocking her child to and fro. But his cries persisted. Perhaps, if the vicar continued his sermon, the congregation would ignore her and resume their attention on him.

She looked up. He was still staring at her, but the soft, searching expression in his eyes had gone. Instead, they had darkened with anger. His hands, which he'd been gesturing with while he spoke, now clasped the edge of the pulpit, the knuckles whitening.

Perhaps that was what his sermon was really about—that there were some sins which could never be forgiven.

Etty stood, cradling her son in her arms. The vicar's eyes widened and he leaned forward, as if to see her better.

She slipped out of the pew then retreated toward the door. The vicar opened his mouth as if to speak, and she grasped the door handle and turned it, wincing as it creaked open. She exited the building, the door swinging back with a bang. Then, clutching her son, she ran through the churchyard, only slowing once she was out of sight of the church.

CHAPTER SIX

"A MOST *INTERESTING* sermon, vicar," Lady Fulford said as she exited the church, arm in arm with her husband.

"Thank you, Lady Fulford."

Andrew bowed his head in acknowledgment, awaiting the admonishment. Lady Fulford always described something she found fault with as *interesting*. It was her way of acknowledging the efforts of those she considered lesser beings, while also explaining how they must do better next time.

"Though I fail to understand," she continued, her nasal whine set at just the pitch to scrape against his nerves, "why you saw fit to ask so many questions."

"A vicar does not exist to instruct his congregation on what to do, Lady Fulford," he replied. "His role is to present his congregation with questions on pertinent issues."

"Nonsense!" she scoffed. "What's a vicar's purpose if not instruction? You are responsible for the moral and spiritual welfare of your flock, Mr. Staines. A shepherd must instruct his flock to prevent them from straying."

"My flock consists of men, women, and children, Lady Fulford—not sheep," Andrew said. "The Almighty has gifted us with the free will to decide for ourselves what we must do. We should therefore be given the empowerment to make our own decisions. An act of goodness has little merit if it's undertaken under coercion or instruction. But if it's undertaken with free will, gladly and joyfully, then it has greater merit."

"Free will is all well and good, vicar, but if all of us had free will, the world would descend into chaos," she said. "Would it not, Sir John?"

Her husband nodded. "Quite so, my dear. Not all of us are the same. Consider the difference between men and women, for example. Men are stronger and more capable of directing the world. That is why a woman vows to obey her husband—so that she might act upon his instructions. And then"—he gestured toward the other people milling about the churchyard—"there's the distinction of rank. The lower classes rarely know what's best for them, and are in need of instruction in order to survive."

"Instruction from men such as yourself?" Andrew couldn't help asking.

Sir John narrowed his eyes, and Andrew suppressed a shudder at the flicker of spite in their expression—the pale blue the color of ice. Almost involuntarily he glanced toward Mr. Gadd, who stood less than ten feet away. The farmer watched them, apprehension in his eyes, his youngest daughter standing beside him. Then he touched his cap and bowed his head.

"Sir John," he said.

The squire glanced at the farmer, then took his wife's arm and strode out of the churchyard.

Andrew lifted his eyes to the sky for a moment, uttering a silent prayer for the uncharitable thoughts that always entered his mind when he spoke to the Fulfords.

And for the ungodly degree of anger that had gripped him during the sermon when he'd overheard Lady Fulford voicing her disapproval of the crying child.

God's house is not for screaming brats.

The crying had come from the back of the church, where Andrew had spotted a golden head illuminated in the sunlight. His breath had caught, and for a moment, the sermon forgotten, he'd lost himself in a pair of soulful eyes the color of cornflowers gazing at him from across the nave.

It was the woman from the cliff top, cradling a child in her arms. She'd wrapped a shawl around herself to secure the child to her body, which in itself was nothing of note, except for the shawl. It was not the rough, homespun garments in muted greens and browns that most villagers used. It was a rich blue, the color of pale sapphires, that caught the sunlight and shimmered as she moved, emphasizing her eyes—the most beautiful pair of eyes he'd ever seen.

He'd wager his tithes that the shawl was silk. It wouldn't look out of place in the finest establishments of London's premier modistes. Not that he had any experience of modistes—or of women.

Unlike Robert. But then, Andrew's brother, being the eldest, and therefore the heir, had amassed, in the years since leaving Oxford, considerably more experience of modistes—and life in general, particularly *women*—than Andrew could hope to achieve in a lifetime.

Robert would have known what to say to her, the beautiful creature sitting alone at the back of the church. He possessed that easy grace that could charm their nanny into giving him an extra sweet bun, his tutors into forgiving his lack of prowess at Latin and mathematics—and each woman he met into welcoming him into her bed.

Or, if Robert's tales were to be believed, not just their beds, but all manner of locations—a secluded corner of a garden, over the desk in a library, up against the wall in a hallway…

And even on the beach, which, were it not for the sand he'd spotted on his brother's breeches after returning from an afternoon stroll with his latest paramour, Andrew would not have believed possible.

To think—what must it be like to make love to a woman and revel in the glorious release, unencumbered by guilt or remorse? What must it be like to make love to a woman on a *beach*?

Andrew shifted position as his breeches grew a little too tight at the image of a pair of vivid blue eyes widening in pleasure at his touch.

Oh, heavens! That was another item to add to his nightly prayer for forgiveness.

It's no sin to make love to a woman, Drew. You only need hear her cries of pleasure to understand that.

Perhaps Robert was right about love not being a sin. But envy *was*. Sometimes Andrew struggled to conquer his envy of his older brother, no matter how much he loved him. What might it be like to have Robert's lust for life and pleasure, unencumbered by conscience?

And what of the countless women he bedded? Granted, Robert ensured each woman was willing and well compensated for her trouble, but what of the consequences that Robert never bothered himself with?

Such as unwanted children.

Andrew glanced across the churchyard to where Mr. Gadd stood with his wife and children. The farmer stared at Sir John Fulford, his usually mild expression twisted into dislike. Then, after the squire and his wife passed through the lychgate, the farmer resumed his attention on his family and shepherded them toward Andrew.

"A fine sermon there, vicar," he said. "My Peg was remarking on it just now, weren't you, love?"

Mrs. Gadd wiped her eyes. "Aye, that's right, vicar," she added, nodding to her son. "You thought so, didn't you, Jimmy?"

The lad nodded unsmilingly. What had happened to his usual cheery demeanor? Most days when he came to the vicarage with a delivery, he could be heard whistling a merry tune even before he approached the door.

"That's very kind Mr. Gadd," Andrew replied, "and Mrs. Gadd, of course." He lowered his gaze to the young girl holding the farmer's hand. "And how are we today, Frances?"

The girl colored and gave him a shy smile.

"Answer the vicar, Frannie, love," Mrs. Gadd said.

"There's no need to rush her, Mrs. Gadd," Andrew said.

"There's plenty of time. After all, it's a day of rest, is it not? No need to be making haste or saying more than we care to."

The girl looked up at him, unblinking. "It's my birthday today. I'm twelve."

Andrew's gut twisted with shame, and he drew in a sharp breath.

August the thirteenth.

Sweet Lord—how could he have forgotten the date?

He exchanged a glance with the farmer and his wife—Mr. Gadd's expression bearing the veneer of stoicism, Mrs. Gadd's eyes bright with unshed tears. Then he patted the girl's head.

"Oh!" he said, overly brightly. "A-are you doing anything special?"

"Mrs. Ham's bringing a fruitcake round later," Mrs. Gadd said. "Isn't she, Frannie, love? That's right kind of her, seeing as she's always so busy with those lads of hers—they're such a handful, especially that Tom."

"Aye, they're that," Mr. Gadd said. "But they're good lads, really—just like our Jimmy. They'll grow into fine young men. Children are a blessing, Peggy, love—I'm sure Mary Ham would sooner have them than not. I…"

His voice wavered, and he tightened his hold on his daughter's hand.

"I understand," Andrew said, quietly, before resuming his attention on the girl. "You're lucky to have one of Mrs. Ham's cakes, Frances," he said. "They always win at the village festival, and no matter how often my cook asks, Mrs. Ham won't reveal the recipe."

"Would you like to come for tea and have some cake, vicar?" the girl asked.

Andrew shook his head. "I'd love to, but I think today's a day for your family. You'll not want me intruding on your day."

"Do come," Mr. Gadd said, "unless you've other parishioners to visit—we wouldn't want to take you away from your duties now. There's that new lass at Shore Cottage—Mrs. Ward, her name be, the one with the young 'un who, I daresay, is needing a spot of help. She seemed distressed during the service today, and she's all on her own, at least from what I can see. And Shore Cottage is so out of the way, there's no folk nearby to call on."

"She might like it that way, William," Mrs. Gadd said. "Not everyone wants to surround themselves with folk. I'll admit it's hard with a little one even if you're not on your own. But she seems pleasant enough. A widow, or so I heard—her husband passed before their son was born. But he's left her a stipend to live on."

"Have you called on her, Mrs. Gadd?" Andrew asked.

She shook her head. "I only know what Mrs. Ham told me. Our Jimmy took over a hindquarter of pork yesterday. Paid in advance, it was, too. Said she had the voice of a lady, didn't you, Jim? All airs and graces, you said. But for all that, she was very civil."

The lad shrugged. "She thanked me, that's all."

Which, if she had a genteel background, made her stand head and shoulders above the likes of Lady Fulford, who Andrew had yet to hear utter a word of thanks to anyone. In fact, ladies rarely thanked anyone they considered beneath them.

Which made the mysterious woman all the more intriguing.

"We shouldn't be keeping you, vicar," Mr. Gadd said. "We're taking Frannie to Skegness today—after we've visited our Freda, of course. We should be back at the farm around six if you're wanting a spot of tea. It'd be a great comfort to us if you visited, wouldn't it, Peg?"

His wife nodded. She opened her mouth to speak, then she closed it again, and a tear splashed onto her cheek. Their son drew her close, and she let out a soft sob.

"Perhaps I'll visit later, then," Andrew said, then he touched her arm. "She's in a better place, Mrs. Gadd," he said quietly.

"Aye," she whispered. "B-but I'd rather she were…"

"I know," he replied. "Some wounds can never completely heal, no matter the passage of time, whether a year has passed or twelve."

He spotted Mrs. Lewis approaching, a determined look on her face, and sighed to himself. No doubt she had some demand to make, or some ill-thought-out idea that only served to create more work for him—work for which she would claim the entirety of the credit herself.

Oh dear—that's another sinful thought to ask the Almighty to forgive in my prayers tonight.

"Mrs. Lewis," he said, forcing a brightness into his voice. "Is there something I can help you with?"

Mr. Gadd took his wife's arm. "Come on, Peg, love—Freda won't wait for us forever."

A funny turn of phrase, particularly given that Freda would be waiting for eternity, but nevertheless, Mrs. Gadd gave him a watery smile, and the family set off through the churchyard. Mrs. Lewis glanced in their direction and wrinkled her nose into the sneer always adopted by women of her class when they set eyes upon individuals who worked for a living.

"Now, vicar," Mrs. Lewis said before he could draw breath, "I had one or two ideas about the flowers for the harvest festival I'd like to share with you. I know it's some weeks off yet, but one cannot begin planning these things too early, particularly if we want the church to look its best. I won't have it said hereabouts that Sandcombe is shabbily turned out compared to Havens Heath. My sister was boasting only last week that…"

He let her rattle on, nodding and smiling at the appropriate places so as not to cause offense, silently praying that a nod was not taken as a declaration of commitment to whatever scheme she had planned to outdo her sister and the ladies of Havens Heath via competitive floristry. At length she finished, and, seemingly satisfied—though most likely more with herself than anything he'd said—she strode out of the churchyard, leaving Andrew to return to the church building to join his curate.

After pausing at the door to glance toward the spot at the far end of the churchyard where the Gadd family had gathered,

Andrew returned inside. His gaze wandered to the back pew where the mysterious woman had sat. The woman with a child, an expensive silk shawl, the voice of a lady, and a stipend from her late husband.

He closed his eyes, relishing the image of her face in his mind's eye. She was exquisitely beautiful with her delicate features, soft blonde hair, and expressive blue eyes. If she were a lady, she'd be the toast of the *ton*, with men like his brother vying for the opportunity to court her.

Why in the name of the Almighty had she chosen to live on the outskirts of a country village, among strangers? And though, as vicar, he had every right to call on her, she may not welcome the intrusion.

And then there was the temptation—the merest thought of her set his pulse racing, as if he feared that her presence would tempt him into sin.

But oh, what pleasure might he find in such sin!

Next week. He'd summon the courage to speak to her next week, after the service. Perhaps by then he'd have conquered the unfathomable need that ignited deep within him when he first caught sight of her on the cliff top. But if not…

Oh, Robert—if only I could be more like you. You'd know exactly what to do.

Yes, sometimes Andrew envied his brother. And envy was the one sin that a second son—especially the second son of an earl— could never be free from.

CHAPTER SEVEN

"**W**HAT IS, LOVE?"

The sermon began and the congregation fell into a hush.

Etty settled Gabriel on her lap and ignored the sharp glance from the woman in the row in front of her. It was the same woman from last week, whom Etty now knew to be the squire's housekeeper. Clearly the parishioners took a proprietorial approach to their seats in the church. Everyone seemed to be sitting in exactly the same position as last week—the innkeeper and his wife, who'd seemed pleasant enough when Etty passed the inn on her way to the market during the week, and the farmer and his family, including James, the lovely young man who'd delivered the leg of pork.

And, of course, the squire and his stiff-backed family, right at the front in their position of prominence.

Sir John and Lady Fulford, the innkeeper's wife had said when Etty asked their names, uttered in the hushed tones of the subservient villager. Clearly the Fulfords considered themselves superior to the rest of the village.

What might they have done had Etty stridden to the front and occupied their pew, rather than hiding at the back again?

"Love thy neighbor," the vicar declared. "We have all heard that spoken many times. But how many of us have paused to ponder the meaning of love, and the many forms it takes?"

Etty sighed. *Every waking hour, vicar.*

Her definition of love had undergone such a change in the past two years, from material desires to selfish needs, until it finally settled on her son. The love a mother bore her child—a mother who would die for him if fate required it.

She settled Gabriel on her lap and kissed the top of his head.

"Mama," he said softly.

"Hush, my love," she whispered, pulling him into an embrace.

"For many of us, love can be selfish," the sermon continued. "What we may describe as love is often, in fact, a selfish wish for our own gratification. We might express love for another person only because we *desire* them."

The squire and his wife stiffened. Doubtless they considered the subject of *desire* unsuitable for the vicar to discuss in public.

"Or we may express love for an object merely because we find it pleasing, or because we believe that our lives are the better for owning that object. In which case, what we believe to be love is merely envy and pride. Who among us here today has committed such sins and sought absolution by convincing ourselves, and others, that we have acted out of love when, in fact, we have acted out of a selfish desire for our own gratification?"

The vicar cast his gaze over the congregation, and Etty cringed.

He might as well have been speaking about her—*to* her.

"But desire is not the only form of love." His voice softened. "The purest form of love is that which we harbor for others— where we place their welfare above our own convenience. That is the embodiment of love, where we seek to perform acts of kindness and devotion—not for reward or consequence, but for the simplest of reasons." He paused, and his lips curved into a smile. "Because it's the good thing to do. Not what is *right*—for being right implies a sense of superiority, of following rules and traditions set by others—but what is *good*."

A murmur of whispers rose, and the vicar's smile broadened as he raised his hand.

"Permit me to explain," he said. "While I would not, of course, condone acting in a manner that contravenes the law of the land, or disrespects the long-held traditions that we hold dear, I would ask you to always look into your hearts and question whether your actions would stand the ultimate test—the test of whether those actions would better serve the word of the Almighty, who asks us to love one another without condition or desire for reward."

Etty's cheeks warmed with shame. Most sermons were delivered with such harshness, as if the man in the pulpit had declared himself to be both judge and executioner upon the souls he preached to—and ordered them to comply with his instructions, lest they face an eternity in the fiery pit of hell. Such sermons had only ever given rise to anger and indignation within her heart, against a mortal man who wished to wield his power over others. But this man before her now, who spoke with such gentleness and warmth of spirit, was making no demands of his flock. He was merely asking the congregation to be kind to one another.

And it was his very kindness that spoke to her soul, laying it bare for her eyes to see, and opened her eyes to her own cruelty.

She glanced up to find him looking directly at her, understanding in his expression, as if she'd also revealed her soul to him.

"We hear tales of the great deeds of men," he said. "Deeds that further the cause of our world, or accomplishments in remote lands, such as Waterloo, that defend our countrymen against the tyranny of our enemies. But what of the deeds undertaken at home, deeds that go unobserved and unacknowledged? All of you—young or old, men or women—have the power to change the world. The smallest act can be the purest if delivered with selfless love. And, if it ignites a spark in one heart, it can bring forth a flame to light the whole world. To bring light to the world, we do not need to ride to war. An act of love could be delivering alms to the needy, or taking time from your busy lives to comfort another. Or it may be as simple as tolerating a crying child in church."

Etty's heart fluttered as she clung to her son. *No—it must be a coincidence.* He couldn't be referring to last week—could he?

But his gaze remained fixed on her.

"Children should be cherished," he said. "And we must always listen to them. Most of us abide by the rules of the society in which we live—we might refrain from speaking for fear of causing offense, or we inhibit our feelings for fear of retribution. We restrict our natural responses to the world around us. But children—in their early years, when their souls are pure and untainted—have yet to learn such inhibitions. Children express themselves freely. When a child cries, they're telling us that something is wrong. Those of us who disapprove of, and shush, a crying child are placing our own comfort, and our wish to conform to society, over the need to right that wrong."

Moisture stung Etty's eyes, and she leaned forward to kiss her son's head. The vicar smiled and inclined his head, as if in recognition.

"And so, rather than merely invite you to ask questions, I would have you consider the merits of this one instruction..."

He paused and glanced toward Sir John and his wife in the front pew.

"Love thy neighbor," he said. "Go forth and act with consideration toward another, whether they be a friend you've fallen out of favor with, a subordinate in your employ, a relative you've been meaning to write to but have yet to find the time, or..."

He resumed his attention on Etty.

"Or a stranger in need of a friend."

Gabriel fidgeted on Etty's lap, then tried to climb to the floor.

"Not yet, sweetheart," she said, pulling him into her arms. "Mama will take you outside in a moment."

When he'd settled, she glanced up again. The vicar had stopped speaking, but was still looking at her. When she met his gaze, he continued.

"I will always lend an ear if you wish to discuss what it is to love—to do good. And for those of you in need, who have none other to turn to, then I am at your disposal."

Etty's vision clouded. She blinked, and a tear splashed onto her cheek. The vicar smiled again, and she looked away, unable to conquer her shame.

His words were for *her*—the stranger in need. The misfit. The pathetic creature with no one to turn to. Was that how he viewed her, a lost soul to be pitied?

Then he resumed his attention on the rest of the congregation and the sermon continued. But this time, when Gabriel let out a cry as he tried to snatch Etty's hymn book, the volley of tutting she'd expected was conspicuous in its absence.

When the service concluded, Etty slipped out of the building. Gabriel wriggled in her arms, squealing with excitement, and she placed him on the path and took hold of his leading strings.

"Stone!" he cried, toddling toward the gravestones.

"No, sweetheart, we can't play on those," Etty said.

"Stone! Stone!"

She glanced over her shoulder at the main entrance to see the vicar emerge chatting to the squire's wife. The woman's nose twisted in contempt as she glanced at Etty. The vicar might have delivered a sermon on being tolerant of noisy children, but Lady Fulford—and, most likely, half the congregation—would have already let go of any resolution to live by the principles he'd spoken of. For them, it was the mere attendance at church that rendered them superior to others—there was little need to sully themselves with any of the activities that the vicar had described as *good*.

"Come on, Gabriel—let's take a look at the stones around the back."

Etty picked up her son and carried him along the path that ran alongside the church building, where he could explore the gravestones away from Lady Fulford's disapproving stare. Once out of sight, she set him down and approached a statue of an angel covered in moss.

"Stone!" he cried, toddling forward until he reached the limit of his leading strings. Etty gave them a gentle tug.

"Come and look at this angel, sweetheart."

"Stone!" he cried again. "Stone, stone!"

"No, Gabriel, let your mama take a look…"

He let out a wail and rolled onto the ground.

"Gabriel, please!" she cried.

"Stone!"

With a sigh, she approached him and set him on his feet. "Which stone do you want to see, sweetheart?"

He toddled toward a headstone near the edge of the church-yard, fashioned from soft gray stone, patched with lichen, as if someone had dropped great splashes of yellow and green paint on the surface. At the foot was a posy of flowers, a mixture of wildflowers, grasses, and a single rose. The wildflowers had already withered, their petals clinging limply to the stone, but the rose still held its color—a soft pink, one petal turning brown at the edges.

Gabriel reached for it, but Etty pulled him back.

"No, sweetheart, it's not yours. It belongs to another." It belonged to the poor soul whose body lay in the ground beneath the stone.

Etty crouched beside the headstone and read the inscription.

Here lies Freda Gadd
beloved daughter
b Dec 25th 1789
d Aug 13th 1805

"Beloved daughter…"

Etty's heart ached at the simple inscription, and she drew her son into her arms. Somebody's child lay in the ground before them. Of all the pain a heart had to endure, none was greater than that of losing a child.

A twig snapped behind her, and Etty leaped to her feet and turned to see the farmer's lad standing in the center of the path, his hands in his pockets.

"Are ye all right, Mrs. Ward?"

"Y-yes, I'm sorry, James," Etty said, wiping her eyes. "It's just…" She gestured to the headstone. "I know children die all the time," she said, "but to see it carved into a stone makes it more real. I-I've never known anyone to die, except my grandfather, warm in his bed. But this girl was just fifteen years old."

"Aye." He nodded and let out a sigh. "That she was."

Etty glanced at the headstone again.

Freda Gadd.

"James Gadd," she whispered. "Sweet Lord—she was your *sister?*"

He nodded. "Aye. Twelve years ago last week. Ma still cries for her. Not even our Frannie…" He hesitated. "It matters not."

Etty touched his arm, and he flinched. "It does matter, James," she said. "It matters a great deal. When you lose someone you love, a piece of your heart goes with them. And the pain may fade, but it'll never truly leave you. But you wouldn't want that, for then you might forget them. And Freda deserves to be remembered."

He nodded. "Aye, that's what Pa says. We always mark the day so we can remember her. Do you remember Mr. Ward?"

Etty opened her mouth to ask who Mr. Ward was, then checked herself. "Only a little," she said. "He…left us before Gabriel was born."

"Forgive me, Mrs. Ward. I didn't mean to pry."

She smiled. "It matters not. What matters is that your sister is at peace, knowing that she's not forgotten."

The lad sighed again. "She died before I could tell her that I loved her."

"I'm sure she knew."

He shook his head. "We always fought. She used to tell me

what to do, and I didn't like it. She was five years older than me, you see."

"Brothers and sisters always fight," Etty said. "It doesn't mean they don't love each other."

She fought to restrain her conscience at the memory of how she'd tried to ruin her own sister.

"Do you have a brother, Mrs. Ward?" he asked.

"I have a sister," Etty said. "But I was unkind to her."

"Are you sorry for it?"

"More sorry than you can imagine, James."

"Then tell her," he said. "Make your peace with her, before it's…" His voice wavered then trailed off. He averted his gaze and wiped his eyes.

"Forgive me," Etty said. "I'm intruding on your grief." She took her son's hand, but he pulled free and reached for the rose. "No, Gabriel," she said, catching his arm. "I've told you already, it's not yours."

"Take it," James said, bending to pick up the bloom. "Freda would want him to have it. She loved children. If only she'd lived to see…" He shook his head. "You mustn't mind my rattling on, Mrs. Ward." He held out the rose. "Mind the thorns—you might want to remove them before giving the rose to your boy."

Etty curled her hand around the stem, ignoring the prick of the thorns. "You're a kind lad," she said, recalling the vicar's words. "A *good* lad. Your sister would have been proud."

Her words seemed to increase his distress. "I couldn't protect her," he said.

"You must have been very young when she died," Etty said. "I'm sure you did everything you could."

"But it wasn't enough."

"What's all this?" a voice asked.

Etty turned to see the vicar standing behind them in the middle of the path.

He glanced at the rose in her hand and frowned. "Is anything the matter, James?" he asked.

"No, vicar," the lad replied. "Mrs. Ward was just looking at Freda's headstone."

"So I see."

The vicar's eyes, at close quarters, were a deep amber color, warm and rich. Their expression hardened as he continued to stare at the rose. He blinked, and a flicker of judgment shimmered in their depths.

How dare he judge her!

Etty took a step back, then held out the bloom to James.

"No, keep it, Mrs. Ward," he said. "It's a gift from Freda."

The vicar raised his eyebrows.

"Thank you, James," Etty said. Then she nodded to the vicar. "Good day, *vicar*," she said, coldly. Then she retraced her steps along the path, pausing to smile at Mr. and Mrs. Gadd as she passed through the lychgate.

Love thy neighbor, the vicar had said from his pulpit not fifteen minutes earlier. But clearly he believed that only the worthy were deserving of love.

Which excluded her.

CHAPTER EIGHT

I N THE DAYS since Andrew last ventured near Shore Cottage, the place had been tidied up, though it had yet to return to the beauty of its former life. But now, someone had evidently tried their best to at least make the place look habitable, if not welcoming.

The trailing rose surrounding the front door had been clipped. Not tidily—were he alive, Mr. Legge would have had a fit of apoplexy at the manner by which the stems had been hacked back. But roses were hardy plants and could weather all manner of harshness.

Unlike the occupant of the cottage, given what Andrew could hear.

As he drew near the front gate, high-pitched wails filled the air, together with pleas for mercy.

"Please desist, sweetheart—I cannot bear it!"

The screams only increased.

Sweet heaven—it was almost as bad as the shouting he'd heard from the Smiths' little cottage earlier. Though in that case, the shouts had been uttered in Ralph Smith's slurred voice, followed by his wife's gentle pleas for mercy while their newborn child, who'd not yet learned the need to be quiet to placate its father's temper, wailed in distress.

But Loveday Smith was a survivor, and though the birth had been difficult, she had assured Andrew that she'd soon be well enough to return to her position at the Fulfords' house, which would both placate her husband's temper and ensure she spent the majority of her time out of his way—at least, until she quickened with her next child.

Why was it that men of the world had been given leave to rule it, whereas women, who were considered the rightful property of their husbands, could only hope to survive it?

Even little Frannie Gadd would soon have to learn the rules of survival. At twelve years, she was old enough to be sent out into the world to earn a living. But it was the way of the world, both among the highborn and the low. Sons inherited estates, or worked the farms, or sought professions of their own, and daughters were sent into service—as wives or maids.

Perhaps he should consider that as material for his next sermon—rouse the women of Sandcombe to take charge of their lives and resist their husbands and parents. The bishop would just *love* that.

But the world could be changed with small steps. And if he could not change the world for everybody, then at least he could change it where it was within his power.

Andrew approached the door and another wail came from within, followed by sobbing.

What had driven the woman inside the cottage to come to Sandcombe? What had *she* survived?

He knocked on the door, and her sobbing stopped. The child's wails continued, and Andrew knocked again.

"Mrs. Ward?" he called out. "It's Mr. Staines."

More wailing.

"The vicar," he added.

"Oh!" a voice cried, and footsteps approached. Then the door opened and she stood before him.

His heart skittered at the sight of her—as it had done only that morning after the service, when he'd come upon her in the graveyard.

From a distance, she was beautiful. At close quarters, she was breathtaking.

Her delicate, perfectly proportioned features were reminiscent of the angels he'd seen in portraits—porcelain skin giving her an almost ethereal quality. Honey-blonde hair framed her face in soft waves, the curls coming loose about her shoulders only serving to soften her beauty. As for her eyes, he'd never seen a blue so vivid, the unshed tears enhancing their color, as if he stood before an exotic ocean into which he longed to dive.

But what clawed at his heart was the raw anguish in their expression—as if she'd surrendered her defenses until her soul was laid bare for him, exposing her desperation.

"Mrs. Ward…"

"How do you know my name?" she asked, her eyes widening. "Wh-why are you here?"

"It's my duty to visit all my parishioners," he said, "to tend to those in need…"

She drew in a sharp breath, and the expression in her eyes hardened. "I have no need of charity, vicar."

"Mr. Staines, please," Andrew said. "And I apologize if I gave offense."

"I can take care of myself."

"I'm sure you can, Mrs. Ward, but there's no shame in accepting a little help."

"I'm in no need of any—"

"*Service*, then," he said. "Not charity. A vicar exists to serve his congregation, and, as you have attended church since your arrival at Sandcombe, I consider you one of my flock." He extended his hand. "May I offer my service, if nothing else?"

She glanced at his hand, then another wail rose from within the cottage. She slumped against the doorframe and closed her eyes. When she opened them, a tear splashed onto her cheek.

"Let me at least assist you with your child," he said.

"I'm in need of no—"

"I beg to differ, Mrs. Ward," he replied, smiling. "Let me help—for the sake of your ears, if nothing else."

She frowned at his weak little joke.

"A child can be hard work," he added. "Especially if you're on your own."

"How would *you* know?" she snapped, her body stiffening with hostility.

"Granted, my sex gives me no right to speak from experience," he replied, "but many of my parishioners are women on their own, and I strive to understand their plight and help where I can."

"And why should I entrust you to help me?"

"A vicar is a most tenacious of visitors," he said. "He'll not take refusal lightly, and will always insist on visiting his parishioners, even those who do not welcome his visits. In that respect, he's akin to a village busybody."

"The village busybody?"

"Yes," he said. "We all know her—she considers the residents of the village to be her subordinates and will push herself into their homes, uninvited or not, to exhaust their defenses until she's persuaded them to help her with the village fete, her latest charitable drive for the needy, or the collection for the church roof, for which she will take all the credit herself."

"Is that not what a vicar does?"

"Certainly not," he said. "Unlike the busybody, the vicar only wishes to serve, not *be* served."

Her expression softened and the air of hostility diminished as she let out a sigh, most likely of resignation. Then she stepped back and gestured inside.

"Very well," she said. "There's little point in exhausting my defenses if you're going to admit yourself anyway."

He let out a laugh. "That's the most honest invitation I've had since my ordination. I daresay most of my parishioners consider me a necessary evil rather than someone to be welcomed into their home."

"Then why do you do it?" she asked. "Because it's the right thing to do?"

"No," he replied. "It's because it's the *good* thing to do."

The corner of her mouth twitched.

"Ah!" he cried. "Do I see the beginnings of a smile?"

Another wail.

"What can I do to help?" he asked.

"I don't need—"

"I didn't ask whether you needed anything, Mrs. Ward," he said. "I asked what I could do."

She led him through the hallway and into a parlor overlooking the sea. The room looked as he remembered it when he'd visited Eleanor, except for the dust on the windows and the cobwebs clinging to the ceiling…

…and the crib in the center, where a toddler stood, clinging to the sides, mouth open, wailing.

As Andrew entered the room, the child paused, sea-blue eyes widening as they focused on him.

"Sweetheart, we have a visitor," his mother said.

The child stared at Andrew, then resumed attention on its mother, opened its mouth, and let out another wail.

"Gabriel, no!" She rushed toward the cot and lifted the child into her arms.

"And who might this be?" Andrew said brightly.

"My son," she said. "Gabriel Leonard." She kissed the top of the child's head and sighed. "Gabriel, because he's my angel."

"And Leonard? Is that Mr. Ward's name?"

"No," she said sharply, and the boy let out another cry as she tightened her hold on him. "It's after my father."

"I apologize. I meant no offense," Andrew said.

She blinked and another tear splashed onto her cheek. "It matters not."

"Are you—forgive me—a widow?"

She let out a sigh and turned toward the window, the sunlight illuminating her profile. "Mr. Ward is no more."

"I am sorry for it."

"Don't be." She leaned against the window frame, her gaze

fixed on the view outside.

Yes. She was a survivor.

And she was exhausted. Though she clung to the child with the ferocity of a tigress protecting her young, her body trembled as if her legs could no longer hold her thin frame. Dark rings circled her eyes, in stark contrast to her pale skin.

"Here, let me," he said, offering his arms. "I can take the child for a moment."

She opened her eyes and frowned, her gaze unfocused, as if she'd forgotten who he was. Then, as he stepped forward, she gave a nod of resignation and handed the child over.

The boy's cries increased at first, then, as Andrew held him in a firm grip, he settled, his wails lessening to soft sobs.

His mother frowned and shook her head.

"I can't understand it," she said. "He's not settled since we returned from church—no matter what I've tried—yet as soon as you take him, he quietens. Do you perhaps come endowed with the power of the Almighty?"

"I think, perhaps, your son was crying because he *could,*" Andrew said.

"He's hungry," she said, "and he always cries when he's hungry. But he won't…"

Her cheeks flushed and she averted her gaze.

"Won't what?"

She approached the crib, picked up a shawl, and draped it over her shoulders, her blush deepening. "It matters not."

Andrew's own cheeks warmed as the realization hit him— he'd noticed a stain on her gown, just below the neckline.

"Won't he nurse?" he asked gently.

She shook her head, then closed her eyes and lifted her hand to her mouth, a small sob escaping her lips. "I-I cannot speak of it."

"Because propriety dictates it? I promise you, Mrs. Ward, a vicar is taken into his parishioners' confidence as much as, if not more than, a doctor is by his patients."

"And what does a vicar have to say to a mother who is failing her son?"

"I see no failure, Mrs. Ward."

"Then what do you see, vicar?" she asked, her eyes bright with tears.

"I see a woman all alone in the world," he said. "A woman who has overcome adversity with a determination to survive. A woman who understands the meaning of love, who wants to do the best for the child she cherishes above all."

The tears spilled onto her cheeks. "Do not be kind to me, vicar."

"Mr. Staines, please."

"Do not be kind to me, Mr. Staines. I deserve no such consideration."

"We are all deserving of consideration, Mrs. Ward."

She shook her head. "Not I. I cannot even give my son what he needs."

"From what I can see, your son is a perfectly healthy boy, and has everything he needs," Andrew said. "If he no longer wishes to be"—he hesitated—"nursed, it's because he's growing up. I take it he has a healthy appetite?"

She nodded. "I tried him with the stew last night, and he seemed to enjoy it, though this morning…"

She wrinkled her nose, and Andrew grimaced. He could just imagine the consequences of a child taking solid food. The stench in Mrs. Biggs's cottage after her first child digested his first solid meal had been enough to flatten a herd of cattle.

She averted her gaze. "There's so much to do just to keep him clean and tidy that it leaves me little time for housekeeping." She gestured about the parlor. "What must you *think*! I'm ashamed to admit anyone."

"I think you're working as hard as you can with no help," he said. "But we must all make time for ourselves, to reflect and to enjoy the moment After all, is not life there to be lived?"

"That's an easy argument for you to make, vicar."

"Mr. Staines, please. Or, if I may be so bold, you could call me Andrew."

Her mouth twitched into a smile. "Mr. Staines." She gestured to the boy in his arms. "He likes you, at least, but a child is permitted more freedom when it comes to intimacy. And I suspect he's the principal reason for your visit."

"You wound me, madam," he replied. "I came to see you. Your son has everything he needs—a loving mother. Whom do *you* have, Mrs. Ward?"

"I have no one."

"I beg to differ," he said. "You have me. And if I may be so bold as to make a suggestion, I think I have the very person who might be able to help you."

She arched her eyebrows, and he caught a glimpse of another woman in her expression and the way she held herself—a lady, reigning over the ballrooms of London.

A mystery surrounded her—who she was, and why she was in Sandcombe.

She was a lost soul, out of her world, and her allure was not merely due to her exquisite beauty, or the sorrowful expression that tore at his heart. It was in the fierceness with which she cared for her son, the purest expression of love, even though she believed herself to be inadequate. Never had he seen such strength of love in another living soul.

What might it be to be loved by such a woman?

He held out his hand. "I know I have no right to demand your trust, seeing as you hardly know me," he said, "but I ask it nevertheless. Let me help you—and I will ask nothing in return. You have my word."

She lowered her gaze to his hand, a flicker of astonishment in her eyes at his declaration. Yet she remained still.

"Are you so alone in the world that you believe it impossible to find another living soul whom you can trust?"

"Trust must be earned, Mr. Staines," she said. "I know from experience the folly of trusting another. There is no service that can be offered without expectation of something in return."

"Then I shall do everything in my power to earn your trust," he said. "Take my hand as a gesture of faith, if nothing else. I give you leave to sever it from my body if I prove myself unworthy."

The corner of her mouth twitched into a smile again. "I fear I'll be unable to administer your punishment should you betray me, Mr. Staines. My kitchen knives are in sore need of sharpening."

"Then the first task I promise to accomplish shall be to sharpen each and every knife in your kitchen."

She met his gaze. Through the despair that seemed so much a part of her, he caught a flicker of mirth in her expression, and a ripple of warmth rushed through his blood, pooling at his center.

Then she stepped forward and took his hand. The air seemed to crackle as their fingers touched, and he caught his breath at the burst of need deep inside his body. His breeches seemed to tighten, and he shifted his feet to ease the thick ache in his groin.

Dear Lord! His body had never experienced such a powerful reaction, not since he'd first entered manhood and, as a callow youth, had pleasured himself to secret dreams of the women that Robert regaled him with tales of—painted peacocks capable of wringing every last drop of exquisite pleasure from a man. Then he had set such sinful urges aside when entering into his vocation. But, as his older brother had always said, a man had needs, and no matter how many prayers he might utter, those needs always simmered close to the surface, ready to burst forth when the right woman presented herself.

In Robert's eyes, all manner of women had claimed that particular title. But Andrew had accepted the opposite of his brother's rakehell lifestyle in the belief that only one woman existed upon whom he could bestow the title of the *right woman*.

And the deep tug at his soul told him that the right woman was standing before him here and now.

SWEET HEAVEN—THE EXPRESSION in the vicar's eyes was almost enough to restore her faith in others.

Almost, but not quite.

Resisting the visceral urge to pull herself into his arms—arms that looked strong enough to weather the burdens of the whole world, let alone hers—Etty released his hand, her soul shivering at the momentary sense of loss.

He might be a vicar, having delivered extraordinary sermons that spoke of a more *liberal* nature. He might have delivered a pretty speech with his strong, yet equally gentle voice, his warm brown eyes that threatened to claim her heart. Yet those same eyes had cast their judgmental gaze on her that very morning, and he'd assumed the worst when he saw her with the rose in the churchyard.

She was done being judged by others, and she was done trusting those who only sought to take advantage.

And, for all his pretty speeches, the vicar was a man. And men were not to be trusted.

Except perhaps Papa—but, even then, all Etty's father had ever given her was his disappointment.

The vicar's eyes narrowed, then he nodded, as if in resignation. Still cradling Gabriel in his arms, he stroked the boy's hair gently, his body athletic and powerful, yet tender and caring at the same time.

Gabriel's own father would refuse to acknowledge his existence, and no man in Society would want to take on a sullied creature such as herself, not to mention another man's bastard. Even Papa had hesitated to show any affection for the boy, unable to hide the flicker of dislike in his eyes—dislike for the lecherous man who'd sired him, and disappointment in the daughter who'd ruined herself.

Yet the man standing before her—who, given his vocation,

was the most likely to cast judgment on her—cradled her son in his arms as if the task came naturally, with the easy affection of one who did not judge, but who merely loved.

"He likes you, Mr. Staines," she said.

He smiled over the top of Gabriel's head. "He's a delightful little boy, and a credit to his mother," he replied. "But I'll wager he can be something of a handful. I can see a resoluteness about him. But perhaps that is to be expected when his mother is resolved not to accept the help of others."

"Are you here to remark on my character, vicar?" she asked.

"I'm here to offer help," he replied. "And to apologize."

"Apologize? What for?"

"For misjudging you this morning, after the service," he said. "In the churchyard. I fear I disapproved of you without cause and made my disapproval known. And for that, I am sincerely sorry."

Could he read her thoughts?

"You see," he continued, "I care a great deal for the Gadd family. Their daughter Freda's passing was a great loss."

"And you think I'd be insensitive to the grief of others merely because I'm a stranger?"

"I have no wish to excuse my conduct," he said, "merely to present you with a reason, though that reason be unjustified. And, of course, you will have known grief yourself."

"I?"

"Your late husband."

She nodded, then turned away from his gaze. "Would you like some tea?" she asked. "I'm sure it's expected when the vicar calls. I-I think I have some in the kitchen, if you could mind Gabriel for a while."

"Perhaps another time, when you are less busy," he said. "And I meant what I said—I have the very person in mind who can help you."

"Are you about to foist a village busybody on me?" she asked.

He let out a laugh. "No, a young girl in need of work. She's old enough to be sent into service. Her family need the money, but they would be heartbroken if she were to leave Sandcombe. So, you see, you'd be doing them a favor, and gaining a helpmate and companion in return."

Etty shook her head. "I relish the quiet too much, vicar, and wouldn't want a stranger in my home. Please understand—I am not one to welcome prying eyes."

"Yet you admitted me."

"Only because you threatened to erode my defenses."

He laughed again, and her heart tightened at the natural mirth in his voice—not a laugh given by a suitor desperate to ingratiate himself with the prettiest debutante in town, but the genuine laugh of an honest man.

"You are at liberty to refuse, of course," he said, "but the person I have in mind is Frannie Gadd."

"James's sister?" Etty shook her head. "She's just a child. How old is she—fourteen, at most?"

"She's twelve," he said, "and therefore old enough to go into service."

Twelve? Was a girl really considered old enough at twelve to be sent away to toil day and night, at the beck and call of others?

Others such as myself.

How old had the servants at Papa's townhouse been? The housekeeper was a widow in her forties, whose barked orders could always be heard throughout the house, particularly in the early morning, just before dinner, and each time visitors were due and there was work to be done. Etty's own maid had been only a year or two younger than Etty herself. But what of the scullery maids and chambermaids, the servants who were kept downstairs lest the sight of them offended the family they served? Yet Etty had always indulged in the fruits of their labors, such as the fire that always blazed merrily in her bedchamber when she retired. Perhaps a child of twelve had been the one to scrape out the ashes, choking on the clouds of soot, before laying the coals and lighting them then scuttling away in fear of a beating were Etty to catch sight of her and be offended by her presence?

What a spoiled, selfish creature she had been! Perhaps she still was. But, at the very least, Etty could help another young girl to atone for the many other young girls whose toil she'd taken for granted in her former life.

For, if she'd learned one lesson from her ordeal, it was that Etty Ward was going to be a better person than Juliette Howard.

And the first step was to do something good. Not right, but *good*.

"Mrs. Ward?"

Etty blinked, and a tear splashed onto her cheek as the vicar's concerned face swam into view.

"You must forgive me," he said. "I did not mean to offend or pain you."

"You make me quite ashamed, Mr. Staines," she said. "I should be glad to employ the girl if she's willing, and if her family trust me to care for her."

"I think they would," he said, smiling. "Their son spoke highly of you, of what you said to him this morning in the churchyard. He said you gave him great comfort."

"I only said what anyone would say to a young man grieving for his sister," Etty said.

"That's where I beg to differ, Mrs. Ward. Not everyone would do such a thing. Only those who understand loss, and who are kind enough to wish to ease the pain of another." He smiled, the warmth of his eyes intensifying. "And Jimmy Gadd would not gift his sister's rose to just anyone. I should have recognized that, and I apologize for not doing so."

Gabriel stirred in his arms and let out a yawn.

"Ah," he said, "I see your son is a congregant in the making, for he struggles to stifle the urge to fall asleep at the sound of my voice. He only needs to learn how to sleep without his snores echoing around the church building. Unlike old Mr. Penny." He winked at her. "I daresay Mrs. Penny's blushes would be spared if my sermons were a little shorter so as to maintain her husband's attention."

"Well, I for one would not wish to have your sermons cut short," Etty said. "Not when you are encouraging your congregation to question themselves and to think. Far better that than a vicar who merely orders his congregants to do his bidding. I particularly enjoyed your sermon today on the need to tolerate a noisy child in church."

"Did you?"

She nodded. "Few sermons are so…considerate."

"Then I consider my objective achieved," he said, "for I believe I thought of you when I wrote it."

He approached the crib and placed Gabriel inside. The boy struggled to his feet, gripping the sides, and watched the vicar with his wide, expressive blue eyes—which, thank the Almighty, reminded Etty of her father's, rather than Dunton's.

"Shall I send Frannie to you tomorrow?" he asked. "I'm sure you'll like her, but if not, I'll pledge to clean the cottage myself. Though I might perhaps stop at sharpening your knives."

"You're too kind."

"It's not kindness," he said. "It's a pleasure."

His smile broadened, and his eyes gleamed with the earnestness of an innocent youth eager to please.

Then she saw it—the quality that set him apart from others.

His innocence.

In her life, Etty had only ever known one other truly innocent soul. Eleanor—the sister she had almost destroyed with her spite and jealousy. Eleanor—who had fled to this very cottage. Perhaps they had been friends, this kind, insightful man and Etty's gentle sister.

If only Etty had been courted by a man such as him during her Season instead of making a fool of herself, trying to entrap a duke, then falling into ruination. The vicar might be a fully grown man who would have experienced life and an education, but he was, essentially, an innocent—more innocent than she. He had yet to shed the purity of youth and become the predatory male.

And yet there was a strength about him, a strength of character radiating from his eyes. He had no need of experience, for he had insight—the ability to understand a person merely by observation.

Andrew, he'd said his name was. A rather intimate introduction, given it was the first time they'd spoken. But the name suited him.

It meant *manly*.

Yes, he was that, all the more for his tenderness he showed toward her son. For who but the strongest of men would have the courage to display such gentleness in the presence of a stranger?

"I have intruded on your time for too long," he said. "I'll bid you good day, and send Frannie over tomorrow. But if I might make a bold request, may we part today as friends?"

He extended his hand once more, and, before Etty could resist, she reached out and took it. This time she was ready for the rush of longing as her skin touched his, but she still caught her breath as his long, lean fingers curled around hers. Gentle, tender, sensitive fingers, made to give comfort, rather than the coarse, fleshy fingers of another that had only ever made her skin itch with the need to cleanse herself.

"Good day, Mr. Staines," she whispered.

"Perhaps, one day, you might call me Andrew."

His cheeks flushed a delicate shade of pink, as if he understood the intimacy of the address, yet had dared to utter it anyway.

"Good day, Mrs. Ward." He lifted her hand to his mouth and brushed his lips against her skin.

She suppressed a cry at the rush of need.

"Etty," she whispered, before she could stop herself.

He arched his eyebrows. "Etty?"

A flare of desire ignited in his eyes, and she withdrew her hand.

Then the desire disappeared, replaced by the warmth. He bowed, then retreated to the door.

"I look forward to seeing you in church next Sunday, Mrs. Ward."

He stepped outside and Etty watched as he strode along the path toward the village, disappearing among the trees without a backward glance.

What must he think of her being so familiar, offering up her name on a first acquaintance, like a harlot enticing a man to purchase her wares?

How could she have been so foolish! Hadn't Papa berated her on her lack of decorum that had thrown her onto the path of ruination?

A man such as Mr. Staines—*Andrew*—was not for her. A vicar had a position to maintain. He was revered by his parishioners as the moral ideal to which they must all aspire. And as such, a woman in Etty's position was not for him. He deserved an honest girl—an innocent, untainted by ruination or sin. Etty had long ago thrown away any chance of a life with such a man.

And yet for the first time in her life, she had, when their hands briefly touched, felt a connection, as if their souls called out to each other across a chasm, as if she had been waiting all her life for the one man to make her truly happy. Not a man to furnish her with jewels, lavish carriages, or a title, but a man to love her merely for herself.

Eleanor had once spoken of a single defining moment, when a person stumbled across her true soul mate. And, in her vanity and spite, Etty had ridiculed her sister, thinking her words to be the nonsense uttered by a simpleton.

Until now.

But the defining moment had come too late.

By a cruel twist of fate, Etty—who had once had her pick of suitors—only now knew what it might be like to desire a man's suit when all hope of finding a suitor had gone.

CHAPTER NINE

THERE WAS, PERHAPS, one way to determine whether another person was truly good.

Which was how they treated a crying child.

Etty's heart warmed at the expression on Frances Gadd's face as the girl lifted Gabriel out of his crib.

"Who do we have here?" the young girl cooed. "Such a handsome young man—you'll be breaking hearts before you're in your breeches, won't you?"

Etty winced at the memory of her former self and how she'd measured her success in Society by the number of hearts she broke.

Heartbreaker of the ton…

That was what Eleanor had once called her. And Eleanor had been right in that—and in all things.

"I sincerely hope not, Frances," Etty said.

The girl blushed and set Gabriel down. "Beggin' yer pardon, Mrs. Ward—I meant no offense, truly."

Etty approached the young girl, who stepped back, her eyes widening, fear flickering in her green gaze.

Heavens—did she think Etty was going to strike her?

"I-I'll do better, I promise, Mrs. Ward," she said. "Please don't send me back. I-I only meant that he was such a handsome lad, that he's bound to have his pick of sweethearts."

"That's very kind of you, Frances," Etty replied. "But I would hope my son grows up to be a kinder man than the sort who'd break a girl's heart. I want him to be a better man than…"

She hesitated.

…*than his father.*

Which, given Dunton's cruelty in his disregard for her and his treatment of his subordinates, was unlikely to be a challenge. Gabriel would grow up to be a fine man. A good man who cared for, rather than judged, the sinners in his midst.

A man such as Mr. Staines.

"Mr. Staines has been ever so kind," the girl said.

Sweet Lord—had Etty spoken out loud?

"Oh, has he?" she asked.

"Yes, ma'am. It was him what sent me here today. He told Ma he'd found me employment here in Sandcombe, and I couldn't believe my good fortune. But I don't want to let him down."

"I can't imagine your letting anyone down, Frances," Etty said. "I can see that my son adores you. And he's as good a judge of character as any."

"Then you'll take me as housemaid?"

Etty's heart almost broke at the desperation in the girl's voice. She was a mere child who had only one choice before her—to seek a wage to support her family.

At twelve years old, Etty had had no such concerns to trouble her. For as long as she could remember, she had outshone her older sister in elegance and beauty—and had a host of adults who never ceased to remind her of her qualities and the success she'd make of her life. At twelve years old, the prospect of toil had never entered her mind.

"Of course," Etty said.

"To live in?"

"Don't you wish to remain at home?"

"Oh." The girl's smile slipped. "It's just that Ma said I could earn…" She blushed and lowered her gaze. "Beggin' yer pardon, it's not done to speak of such things."

Of course! A live-in housemaid earned more than one who visited daily.

"I hear twelve pounds a year is a reasonable sum," Etty said.

The girl's eyes widened, and Gabriel almost slipped from her grasp. Then she tightened her hold on the boy and shook her head.

"No—no, Mrs. Ward," she said. "That's too much. It's what Mr. Smith earns at the Sailor, so my da says."

"The Sailor?" Etty asked.

"The inn," the girl said. "Not that you'd know. Da says he drinks most of it, leaving Mrs. Smith with next to nothing for the housekeeping."

"And you think I should pay you less than this Mr. Smith earns?"

"What Mr. Smith does is *man's* work."

"Does he work harder than you intend to work for me?"

"Oh no!" the girl cried, an undertone of pride in her voice. "Ma says I work twice as hard as anyone—and I'll work even harder for you, Mrs. Ward, never you fret about that."

"Then," Etty said, "if a woman—or in your case, a girl—works harder than a man, she should, at the very least, be paid the same. Perhaps this Mr. Smith expects to be paid more merely because he drinks most of his wages, leaving little for his unfortunate wife."

"Loveday Smith is able to make her housekeeping stretch ever so far—or so Ma says, though she'll be returning to her position soon, at the big house"—Frances hesitated, a flicker of apprehension in her eyes—"at least, when she's well enough."

"Your mother sounds like a gossip," Etty said.

The girl blushed. "It's not that, Mrs. Ward, but my ma cares ever so much for Loveday Smith. She's Ma's cousin, you see, and Ma says Loveday reminds her of our Freda. She has the most beautiful baby girl—she said I've looked after her ever so well. You can ask her yourself if you like, Mrs. Ward, ma'am, before deciding whether to take me on."

"I've already decided, Frances, dear," Etty said, her heart aching at the eager girl's expression, "and I'm sure Mrs. Smith wouldn't relish a visit from me. I am, after all, a stranger."

"Ma says Loveday Smith needs visitors, even if she don't like them. Mr. Staines visits her a lot."

"Why does she need visitors?" Etty asked.

"She's always hurting herself," came the reply. "She broke her arm last year and couldn't work. Mr. Smith was ever so cross about it. Then just before she had baby Anna, she fell down the stairs and sprained her wrist. She had an awful big bruise on her face when Ma and I visited her yesterday. Walked into the door, she said. Mr. Smith said she was a clumsy fool, and Ma got ever so cross with him before he left."

"He left?"

"Aye, he spends most evenings in the Sailor now the baby's here. Da says he should be at home tending to his wife like any good husband, but Ma said he's better out of the house. She said it's better for Loveday—but how can it be if she's always having accidents? What if she fell and her husband wasn't there?"

"Perhaps Loveday Smith has fewer accidents when her husband is not at home," Etty said.

"That's what Jimmy says," the girl said. "And Ma says she'll be all better once she's working again."

"You mean she has to *work*?" Etty asked. "When she's just had a baby?"

"Aye, she works at the big house helping out with the mending. Ma says it's better for her, though not by much, provided she stays below stairs. Loveday's ma takes care of her children," Frances said. "I asked if I could help, but Ma said I wasn't to visit her on my own. I don't know why. We were friends at school, until she left to work at the big house."

"She's your friend?" Etty asked. "And she has two children? Heavens above, how old is she?"

"Seventeen last summer, but Mrs. Swain taught us all just the same."

Etty shook her head. A young girl—barely out of childhood—and already with two children and a drunkard for a husband. But perhaps Frances was mistaken.

"How old are you, Frances?"

"I was twelve last Sunday," the girl said, pride in her voice. "Ma says that makes me all grown up."

"Did you do anything special to mark the occasion?"

"We visited Freda's grave like we always do, then Mrs. Ham from the Sailor brought round a fruitcake special. There's some left. I could bring you a slice."

"Do you miss Freda?"

"I never knew her," the girl said. "She died before I was born."

What had been inscribed on the headstone? *d Aug 13th 1805*

August the thirteenth had been last Sunday.

Which meant Frances had been born the day her sister died.

Something of a coincidence…or perhaps not?

"Jimmy misses her," Frances said. "Sometimes I hear Ma crying. I want to comfort her, but sometimes she looks at me as if she blames…" She shook her head, and her eyes glistened with moisture. "Forgive me for rattling on, ma'am."

She turned her attention to Gabriel. "What do you want, little man?" she asked. "Do you want to explore?"

"You can set him on the rug," Etty said. "I swept the floor yesterday. He likes to crawl about the house, and he's already walking, though he needs a little help."

"What a clever boy you are!" Frances said brightly. She placed Gabriel on the rug, then took his hands, steadying him while he took a teetering step forward. "We're going to have so much fun together," she said. "There's so much to explore hereabouts." She glanced up at Etty. "That is, if your ma allows it."

"Of course I'd allow it," Etty said. "The countryside is beautiful. I've never lived in the country before. It's so peaceful compared to London."

The girl's eyes widened. "You're from London? What's it like?"

"Too much noise," Etty said. "And too many people. All crammed together, wanting to know everyone else's business. Sometimes I felt as if I couldn't breathe. And I didn't want Gabriel growing up there. So I brought him here, where we could live away from prying eyes."

"There's plenty of prying eyes in Sandcombe," Frances said. "But you're out of the way here."

Etty nodded. It was no wonder Eleanor had come here seeking solace. Two sisters who had never been close, both fleeing the judgmental eyes of the world after ruination. Except, in both cases, that ruination had been brought about by Etty herself—her spite and envy.

"Have you been to the beach yet, Mrs. Ward?" Frances asked. "I could take Gabriel there. I'm sure he'd like to see the sea."

"How about we spend the day on the beach?" Etty said. "We could have a picnic."

"Oh!" Frances let out a cry of joy. "A picnic? Can we really?"

Etty smiled at the girl's enthusiasm over something so simple as a picnic. But perhaps, in her hard life, she had rarely experienced such a treat.

"We can have picnics as often as you like, Frances," Etty said. "What do you think of that?"

More tears glistened in the girl's eyes. "I think Gabriel is the luckiest child in the world to have you as his ma. I wish…" She shook her head and resumed her attention on the little boy. "I'm going to show you so much, Master Gabriel," she said. "You're going to love the beach, the feel of the sand between your toes. And paddling in the sea—you just wait till you try it!"

She glanced toward Etty again. "Of course, I won't shirk my duties, Mrs. Ward. Ma says I must work hard and keep house for you."

Etty lowered herself onto the rug beside Frances. Gabriel let out a gurgle, then toddled toward her, arms outstretched, and

Etty drew the boy into her arms.

"My darling," she said, kissing the top of his head. Then she smiled at Frances. "Life isn't all about hard work," she said. "We must also enjoy it while we can."

She closed her eyes, recalling a pair of warm brown eyes framed by soft blond hair. What had the vicar said to her yesterday?

"Life is there to be lived."

"That's what Mr. Staines always says," Frances said. "I like Mr. Staines, don't you?"

Etty nodded. "Yes," she whispered. "Very much."

"He's said some very civil things about you, Mrs. Ward. He said you'd be the kindest employer in Sandcombe and that you were in need of a little kindness yourself."

Etty couldn't be more ashamed. She had no need for kindness, not after the sins she'd committed. Yet if what this innocent girl said were true, there were other souls in Sandcombe whose need far surpassed hers—a young woman with a brutish drunkard for a husband, and a mother whose grief for the daughter she lost marred her love for the daughter she had.

And though Etty could never atone for the sin she'd committed against her own family, perhaps, in exiling herself to this remote little village, she had found her purpose.

She might lack the ability to change the world—Papa had always told her she was too selfish a creature to think of others. But if there were a handful of souls to whom she could provide some comfort, then perhaps she could earn her place in the world. Not merely to prove her father wrong, but because it was the *good* thing to do.

CHAPTER TEN

I T WAS MERELY a coincidence that Andrew's Sunday afternoon constitutional took him past Shore Cottage.

Or so he told himself as he approached the front door and knocked.

The cottage looked much as it did last week, paint still peeling off the door and window frames. But signs of occupancy gave it a welcoming air. The garden had been tended to, and Andrew caught sight of a rainbow of colors in the border running along the side of the building, the blooms no longer having to compete with the nettles that had previously overrun the garden. The windowpanes had been washed and he caught sight of his reflection in the glass, through which he could discern the interior of the building.

His heart fluttered as he spotted a shape moving about inside.

She might resent the intrusion. But it was not unusual for a vicar to visit his parishioners regularly, even those who'd not attended church that morning.

Especially those who'd not attended that morning.

Before the service began, Andrew had waited, like a good citizen, for the congregation to gather. But while the rest of the company waited for the principal family of Sandcombe to take their places at the front of the church, Andrew had been waiting for another congregant.

But he'd waited in vain. The pew at the back remained empty.

Little Frannie Gadd had attended, taking her place with her family, but before Andrew could think of a reason to speak to her, she'd bidden her parents farewell, hugged her brother, then skipped off toward Shore Cottage.

Yes—Andrew had every reason to visit Shore Cottage today. To visit Frannie Gadd, and to inquire after Mrs. Ward's health.

Etty.

During their last encounter, she'd said her name was Etty. She had entrusted him with her name. Might that give him cause to hope…

The door opened and Frannie stood in the threshold.

"Oh! Vicar," she said. "Are you come to visit Mrs. Ward?"

"Is she receiving visitors?" he asked.

"I'm sure she'll receive *you.*"

Andrew tempered the flare of hope. "Perhaps you should ask her first. I wouldn't wish to intrude if she's occupied. Or indisposed," he added. "She was absent from church this morning."

Frannie blushed. "Please don't think badly of her, vicar. Gabriel took ill in the night. He's better now, but Mrs. Ward didn't want to disturb him from his bed. I offered to take care of him for her, but she wanted me to go to church so I could see my family. She's right kind, she is."

"I'm no such thing, Frances," a voice said.

Etty appeared behind Frannie, and Andrew's heart fluttered.

How Robert would tease him over what could only be described as a boyish infatuation! But with Society beauties falling at his feet, Andrew's brother wouldn't cast a second glance at the widow hiding in exile in a tiny cottage with a child in tow and none but a farmer's daughter for company.

She moved out of the shadows, and Andrew caught his breath at the color of her eyes, which seemed to reflect the sea— shades of blue, shimmering and dancing with jewels of light.

"Are you come to admonish me for absenting myself from

church this morning, vicar, or is this merely a social call?"

Her voice carried an edge, as if she were preparing to defend herself against the condemnation of her soul.

"Neither," he said, cursing himself inwardly as he felt his cheeks warming.

For a moment she stared at him unsmiling, then she nodded. "In which case, you may come in," she said. "Would you like tea?"

"Oh yes, please," he said, stepping forward, before cursing his eagerness. He could just imagine Robert's teasing voice.

You've got it bad, brother.

Perhaps he did.

"Then, Mr. Staines," she said, "this *is* a social call."

"I hope you'd view my visits as anything but a *social call*," he replied. "Social calls are what one does when visiting the likes of Lady Fulford, where I'm expected to listen to what my hostess has to say and respond only when appropriate. And, in responding, I must say the right thing without saying anything at all."

The corner of her mouth twitched into a smile. "The right thing?" she asked. "Or the *good* thing?"

"Oh, very much the *right* thing."

Frannie's gaze moved between Andrew and Etty, confusion in her eyes, and Etty placed a light hand on the girl's shoulder.

"Frances, sweetheart, could you make some tea and bring it to the parlor?"

The girl bobbed a curtsey then disappeared into the rear of the house, and Andrew followed Mrs. Ward into the parlor.

The room had been transformed since his previous visit. Light filled the room, streaming in from the windows, framed by pale curtains. The layer of dust covering the floor had gone, as had the cobwebs that choked the ceiling.

She gestured to an armchair by the fireplace, then sat on a chair beside a small breakfast table as he took his seat.

"So," she said, "if this is *not* a social call, I should expect you to disagree with everything I have to say—that is, assuming that you intend to listen?"

She tilted her head to one side, and he caught a flicker of mischief in her expression.

Sweet Lord Almighty—did she know the extent to which she tortured him? A woman of beauty, who had endured hardship, was danger enough to the heart of a naïve man with little to no experience of the female sex. But one with wit and a sense of mischief as well…

He might as well prostrate himself before her feet and declare his adoration.

Or he would, if he possessed the courage.

"Forgive me, Mr. Staines…" she began.

"*Andrew*, please."

She blinked, and his heart soared as her cheeks flushed a delicate shade of rose.

"Andrew," she said, lowering her voice. "Forgive me—I understand how a vicar might lack the understanding to comprehend why one of his flock absents herself from church."

"You are under no obligation to attend," he said. "Neither are you obliged to explain yourself. I'm here out of concern for your welfare."

"I am well, as you see," she replied. "But my son was feverish and I had no wish to leave him. Frances offered to tend to him, but she's not seen her family for a week. I couldn't deny her the chance to spend time with them. And I couldn't rest easy being separated from Gabriel even for a moment. He's my whole world, you see."

"Yes," Andrew said, nodding. "I do see—and you are to be commended for it."

He leaned back in his chair, while in the background, merry singing came from the rear of the house.

His hostess smiled. "Frances is a dear child," she said. "How can one soul exude such happiness even under adversity? Her life cannot have been easy, yet in all the time she's been here, I've never once heard a cross word from her."

"Perhaps that's because she's a child," Andrew said.

"Not all children have such a disposition," she replied. "Take myself, for instance. Only now do I see how spoiled and pampered I was, expecting everything and giving nothing. Frances Gadd is the model of what every child should be. The purest of souls."

"You were raised in a different world, that's all," Andrew said. "I take it you come from Society? Your accent is London, yes? Did you perhaps have a London Season?"

Her smile disappeared, and she stiffened. "I…" She looked away, and her hands curled into fists, gathering her skirts, the knuckles whitening.

"Forgive me. Mrs. Ward. I have no right to pry," he said. "After all, this is not a social call. I'm not one to indulge in gossip." He leaned forward. "In fact, I'll wager you'd have enjoyed my sermon this morning, though I say it myself."

"Oh?" she said, her voice stiff.

"It was on the sins of gossipmongering—on how indulging in rumors about one's fellow parishioners is to be frowned upon." He turned as the door opened and Frannie entered the room with a tray of tea things.

"What did you think of my sermon, Frannie?" he asked.

"It was wonderful!" The girl nodded with enthusiasm. "I liked the bit you said about how grownups are worse than children, because they ought to know better, or something like that."

"Yes," Andrew said, nodding. "They ought to know better because they understand the speed with which rumors can be spread."

Mrs. Ward turned to face him. "And," she said, "they understand the hurt those rumors can cause."

"Precisely," Andrew said. "Perhaps you had no need to attend church this morning, Mrs. Ward, if you had nothing to learn."

"There's always something to learn, vicar." She rose to her feet. "Frances, dear, let me help you with that. The teapot looks awfully heavy."

"It's no trouble, Mrs. Ward," the girl said. "I filled it a little too much, that's all."

Etty gave Frances an affectionate smile, and Andrew uttered a silent prayer of thanks to the Almighty that He had delivered that sweet child to a home where she would be treated with kindness and not blamed for the sins of others—a sin she was party to, merely through being born.

"If you have concerns about your mortal soul, Mrs. Ward, I can always bring my sermons to you," he said.

"I wouldn't want to put you to any trouble."

"It's no trouble, I assure you," he replied. "I'd relish the prospect of engaging in a conversion about the principles of life with a member of my parish who has experienced something of life outside the village. Did you know that most of my flock haven't ventured further than ten miles from the village in which they were born? How is one to gain a wider understanding of the world if one does not experience it?"

Her smile slipped. "I wouldn't advocate a wider understanding of the world," she said. "The world is not a kind place— particularly for a woman."

"I understand that," he replied. "I—"

She raised her hand. "Forgive me for contradicting you, Mr. Staines, but you understand no such thing. Your sex prevents you from understanding the plight of a woman because you will never have lived the experiences she must endure in a world ruled by men."

Damn.

He allowed himself a silent curse—for which he'd pray for forgiveness tonight.

Just when she seemed to be warming to him, he had to open his mouth and reveal his ignorance of women.

"Perhaps you consider my life a privileged one because I had a London Season," she said.

So, she *had* been a debutante. Might Robert have known her, danced with her at some ball or sat next to her at a dinner party?

Lucky bastard.

Oh dear—another curse requiring the Almighty's forgiveness.

She let out a sigh, much like a disappointed parent, then met him with the full force of her gaze.

"I see the envy in your eyes… No, do not deny it," she said as he opened his mouth to protest. "In terms of material comfort, I'll admit my life has been easy compared to many of the women hereabouts. Wealth is noticeable. It exists on the surface, in silken gowns, bright jewels, and large townhouses—and the Society accents schooled by governesses through years of elocution lessons. To the casual observer, who fails to look beneath the surface, women in Society are masters of our fate. Yet, like *all* women, we are just as beholden to the men who own us."

His heart ached at the undercurrent of pain in her voice. Perhaps the late Mr. Ward had been unkind.

She paused, as if contemplating something. Then she shook her head and looked away.

"I expect no sympathy," she said. "I have not been so unfortunate as to have endured an unhappy marriage."

Her voice sounded strained, as if she recited each word with care.

Andrew's cheeks warmed with shame. How could he—a vicar, a man of moral standing—indulge in his desire for a woman recently widowed, with a young child, who still mourned her late husband?

"Perhaps, if you are looking for suggestions for material for your next sermon, Mr. Staines, you should consider the sins of men who believe their rank gives them the right to take advantage of naïve young women. Men who care nothing for the consequences, such as ruined lives."

"Or unwanted children."

Andrew spoke the words before he could stop himself.

She froze, and the warmth in her eyes turned to frost. But before she could respond, an explosion of crockery shattered the air, followed by a shriek.

She leaped to her feet.

"Frances!"

"Oh, ma'am!" the girl cried. "Forgive me—I'm ever so sorry! *Please*, I didn't mean it!"

Andrew turned to see Frannie cowering beside the table, shards of crockery at her feet, a dark brown stain spreading across the rug.

"Oh, Frances, what have you *done?*" Etty rushed toward the girl, who cringed, and Andrew leaped to his feet, ready to defend Frannie against her mistress's wrath.

But there was no need.

Etty rushed toward Frannie, arms outstretched.

"You've spilled tea over your gown!" she cried. "Have you scalded your legs? Your mother will think I've taken such poor care of you if you've hurt yourself."

Frannie sniffed and shook her head. "It missed my legs, Mrs. Ward, ma'am. But your carpet, and the b-beautiful teapot! You told me it was your grandmother's. Oh, ma'am, how will I ever make it up to you?"

"A teapot can be replaced," Etty said, "but *you* can't."

"What will you d-do with me?"

Andrew's heart ached at the fear in the girl's voice.

"I have the very thing," Etty replied. "You must help me choose a new teapot at the market. Can you do that for me?"

Frannie continued to sniff, but she nodded. "You're not angry?"

"Of course not!" Etty said. "Why would I be? I'm only relieved that you didn't scald yourself. It's my fault—that teapot always was too heavy when full. I should have realized."

"N-no, it wasn't that," Frannie said. It was..." She glanced at Andrew, her lip wobbling. Then she burst into tears.

"Hush now, sweetheart!" Etty said. "There's nothing to cry over. Now, what say you to a glass of milk and a slice of cake? You can take it in the garden—or in your room, if you prefer."

"B-but the mess. It needs clearing. I—"

"I'll see to it," Etty said. "You've had a fright. My papa…" She hesitated, closing her eyes for a moment. "My father always said there was nothing better than a slice of cake for a young lady who's distressed. Of course"—she cast a glance at Andrew and smiled—"he also advocated a glass of brandy, but I daresay your mother would object if I turned her daughter into a toper." She took Frannie's hand and patted it. "There!" she said. "All better. Now, let's get you settled upstairs. Mr. Staines, would you excuse us?"

She exited the parlor, taking Frannie with her, and Andrew heard footsteps on the stairs as their voices receded.

Steam rose from the tea stain on the carpet. Andrew rose to his feet and made his way to the rear of the cottage in search of a rag.

He found one in the kitchen, draped over the washbasin, and took it and glanced about the room. The kitchen was tidier than he recalled from the last time he'd entered it. The wooden dresser had been polished clean and someone had placed a set of crockery on the shelves in neat rows. In the center of the lower shelf was a jar of flowers, wild blooms from a nearby meadow.

Andrew smiled, running his fingertips over the petals. Little Frannie always loved picking flowers, and he smiled at the prospect of her new mistress appreciating them.

And appreciating *her*—more than Frannie's mother appreciated the girl.

Not that Mrs. Gadd was to be blamed. She still grieved for the daughter she'd lost. She cared for Frannie, of that Andrew had no doubt. But the girl would always remind the family of the tragedy they'd suffered.

And though she was almost the image of Freda, a part of Frannie would always remind them of another in the slant of her eyes and the shape of her mouth.

Some women, like Etty, most likely took comfort from the echo of their child's father in their looks and mannerisms. But Mrs. Gadd…

No. Now was not the time to reflect on past tragedy. Frannie deserved better—and when Andrew looked into Etty's eyes, the tender affection with which they looked upon the girl was enough to convince him that he'd given Frannie the best life she could hope for.

He returned to the parlor, then kneeled on the carpet and placed the cloth over the stain, letting it absorb the tea. At least the carpet bore a bright pattern, rendering the stain less visible. In fact, from a distance, it would hardly be noticeable.

The teapot, however, was another matter. The lid was intact, but the body lay in four pieces.

He picked up a piece—white porcelain depicting two figures in a garden, leaning toward each other over a bed of flowers as if in conversation, surrounded by a border, an intricate design in gold and red, forming swirls and tendrils in the shape of feathers, or the fronds of giant ferns, perhaps. A second, smaller, piece included the base—a thick oval shape, banded with gold, still warm to the touch. He turned it over and inspected the underside, tracing the maker's mark with his fingertips.

K.P.M.—written in a cursive hand—and beneath, a pair of swords crossed.

He picked up the lid. The pattern—delicate images of flowers in myriad colors—was exquisite. He might be ignorant in regards to antiquities and fine porcelain, but he was not so lacking in understanding as to be unable to recognize quality when he held it in his hands.

"Whomever you may be, K.P.M., you're a master craftsman."

"It's Meissen," a voice said.

He glanced up to see Etty standing before him. "I'm sorry?" he asked.

"The teapot." She gestured to the shard in his hand.

"He's the maker?"

She shook her head. "Meissen is a town in Germany, where the pot was made. My mother has a collection of teapots from the Far East. But I always preferred this one."

She plucked the larger piece from his hand and smiled at the image.

"I always used to wonder what the figures depicted were talking about," she said. "Papa said that most likely they were asking each other how much longer they had to pose for the artist."

"That seems a reasonable assumption to make."

"Only if you consider the image literally," she replied. "But I never thought of them as models posing for an artist to earn a coin or two. I saw them as characters in a story. Were they meeting in the garden in secret? Why did the one on the left look so sad?" She set the piece on the table and sighed. "Fanciful nonsense, my mother said. I soon grew out of it."

"Not fanciful nonsense, but imagination," Andrew said, placing the other pieces on the table beside the first. "Without imagination, the world would be a poorer place. And your teapot's now broken. I'm so sorry."

"It's not your fault."

"Frannie didn't mean to drop it, I'm sure."

"It matters not," she said, a flicker of pain in her eyes. "Everything breaks eventually."

Then she fixed her gaze on him. "What matters more is what caused Frances to drop the pot."

"Her hand slipped, that's all."

"At the very moment you referred to *unwanted children*."

He opened his mouth to reply, and she raised her hand.

"Pay me the courtesy of refraining from deception, or denial," she said. "I have no wish to pry, and nor do I relish gossip. But Frances carries a secret, and given that she is a child living in my home—for all that the world expects her to undertake paid work—I feel some responsibility for her welfare."

"Frannie's hiding nothing from you, Etty."

Her eyes widened at the familiar address. "Perhaps not, but a secret exists nonetheless. I have no wish to distress Frances, please believe me. I only wish to ensure that I do not place her in any danger. I take it the secret has something to do with her sister Freda, and possibly Loveday Smith, whoever she may be?"

Good heavens! How could any creature possess such insight? "Loveday Smith is a young woman from the village with two children."

"And are her children unwanted also?" she asked, resuming her seat.

"Of course not!" he replied, and her eyes narrowed at the vehemence in his tone. "Loveday is the kindest, gentlest creature in the village—save young Frances, perhaps."

"Then perhaps it's Frances herself who's unwanted."

His cheeks warmed under her scrutiny. "Mrs. Gadd is a kind woman, and…she loves Frances."

"Young James, then?"

"She loves her son also."

She exhaled, then leaned back in her chair. "Interesting." The color of her eyes intensified, deepened by a sharp intelligence.

Why did he feel as if he were a schoolboy in his housemaster's study after having committed a transgression? Or perhaps a criminal facing a magistrate?

Imagine the world if women were permitted to execute the law. Heaven help the men who committed transgressions. But then, perhaps, a woman would be the best hope for a misfortunate soul seeking an advocate to defend them against an unjust world.

Souls such as Frannie Gadd.

"The plight of any misfortunate soul is interesting," Andrew said. "At least, I find it so, otherwise I would not have entered my profession."

"You misunderstand me," she said, shaking her head in the manner of a disappointed governess. "I meant it was interesting that you referred to Frances as Frannie, and James as Mrs. Gadd's son." She leaned forward. "Why was that, I wonder?"

"I wasn't aware—"

"Mr. Staines, if we are to be friends, you must pay me the

courtesy of refraining from deception. Of course, if you have no wish to tell me the truth, then say so. But I cannot abide falsehood."

"You're the last person I wish to deceive."

She raised her eyebrows, and he caught a spark in her eyes, a flicker of something—recognition, perhaps, as if her soul reached out to him.

Then she blinked and it was gone.

"If you intend to flatter me into changing the subject of our conversation, I'd prefer it if you simply told me you'd rather speak of…"

She broke off, then gestured to the window. "The weather is unusually clement for this time of year."

He flinched at the disappointment in her tone. "I care a great deal about Frances," he said, "and I have no wish to do anything to the detriment of her happiness."

"We are of one mind in that, at least."

"And many other things, I trust."

She paused, and the ticking of the clock on the mantelshelf filled the silence. He glanced toward it—an ornate timepiece with a white face bearing deep blue Roman numerals, and gilt hands that glinted in the light. The body had been carved in an ornate fashion, decorated in gilt. It seemed out of place in a remote little cottage on the outskirts of a village. But in a London drawing room, it would have fit in.

Like the teapot poor Frannie had dropped.

"Let me tell you what *I* see," she said quietly. "In Frances, I see a hardworking, gentle soul who yearns to be loved." She raised her hands when he opened his mouth to protest. "Please, Andrew, hear what I have to say before interrupting."

His breath caught at her use of his name, spoken with a sincerity capable of capturing his heart.

"I'm not disputing that Mrs. Gadd is a kind woman," she continued. "As an outsider in this village, I can perhaps view it with a more rational perspective than those who have lived here for generations. I'm not so blind as to have missed the judgmental stares of the people I have passed in the street—folk who believe the village belongs to them and who harbor nothing but suspicion toward incomers. But Mr. and Mrs. Gadd have been nothing but civil toward me and Gabriel. But sometimes..." She made a random gesture with her hand. "I cannot place it—sometimes, I see Mrs. Gadd look upon Frances with something akin to regret. At first I wondered if it were because Frances was a late child— she's several years younger than James."

"Many women have children later in life," Andrew said.

"Yes—women have no choice in the matter, do they?" she retorted. "A wife is considered a man's property, to be used as he sees fit, and *corrected* if she fails to satisfy him."

Sweet Lord—had her late husband *beaten* her?

"I'm not saying that Mr. Gadd seems anything but loving toward his wife," she continued. "But he, too, looks at Frances differently to how he looks at James. At first I wondered if it were because most parents value a son above a daughter—fathers in particular always wish for a boy."

"If you think Frannie is unloved, you're mistaken," Andrew said. "Surely Frannie's not said—"

"I believe they love her," she interrupted. "Frances has said nothing. It's more what she *hasn't* said."

"I don't understand."

"Naturally. You're a *man*."

He flinched at the bitterness in her tone.

"I've learned, to my cost, that people rarely tell the absolute truth, and one must therefore decipher what they say by considering the space between the words—much as an artist considers the space between the objects she paints. The blank spaces are as much an integral part of the message as the words and objects. But most people, men especially, tend to ignore them."

He couldn't help smiling at her words. Eleanor, the woman who'd resided in this very cottage, had once said the same about the pictures she painted. Perhaps Etty was right—women were endowed with the ability to look into the gaps between. Perhaps that explained their insight.

He leaned forward and offered his hand, an expression of trust.

"What has Frannie *not* said?" he asked.

For a moment she stared at his hand, then, her eyes glistening with moisture, she took it.

"That she bears responsibility for her sister's death. That she committed a sin merely by being born."

Her voice wavered, then a tear splashed onto her cheek.

Unable to fight the instinct, the need to ease her pain, he lifted his free hand and brushed the tear aside. His breath caught at the feel of her smooth skin beneath his fingertips. He placed his palm on her cheek, and she closed her eyes, shuddering as she inhaled.

"Etty, I…"

Her eyes snapped open, and his gut twisted at the intensity of their gaze, the color of a deep ocean filled with sorrow. Was she speaking of Frannie, or perhaps—

Sweet Lord…

Had her son been unwanted? No—that couldn't be. Her whole body radiated with the fierceness with which she loved Gabriel.

But perhaps the boy's father…

"Forgive me," she said. "I've no right to pry. But I wondered, perhaps, if Freda wasn't Frances's *sister* after all."

Surely she didn't possess the insight to…

"That, perhaps," she continued, lowering her voice, "Freda was her mother."

His gut twisted in apprehension.

"I see I am correct in my assumption," she said. "I take it the young man refused to offer for Freda?" Her expression darkened. "It happens. More often than the world would care to admit—children born out of wedlock, hidden away lest they taint the purity of those nearby."

Andrew shook his head.

"Does he live in the village?"

He shifted in his seat. Why must she continue with her questioning?

"Do I discomfort you, vicar?" The hard edge to her voice had returned. "Do you perhaps blame a young woman for falling in love and yielding to her lover's demands on her body?"

His cheeks burned as if they were on fire, and she withdrew her hand.

"I see," she said, nodding. "Like any man, you lay the blame at the feet of the woman. Do you blame the child also?"

"Freda was *not* to blame!" he cried, no longer able to suppress his anger. "Why must you continue to speak against the whole of my sex so? Not all men are cads who take an unwilling woman then blame her for their sins."

She recoiled.

"Shall I tell you why Mrs. Gadd, kind and loving as she is, struggles with her faith, and looks upon little Frannie with regret?" he said. "It's because each time she looks at her, she's reminded of the man who seduced her daughter and in doing so brought about her death—the very man to whom she is expected to curtsey and show deference to."

Her hand flew to her mouth and she let out a low cry. Then she stiffened and glanced at the door.

Had Frannie overheard?

But when he turned, the doorway was empty.

"Does Frances know that…"

"She's Sir John Fulford's bastard?" He cringed at the ugly word and shook his head. "Why add to her disgrace? A child out of wedlock is enough of a pariah. Few know the full circumstances of her birth. Outside her family, excepting the"—he hesitated, fighting the bile rising in his throat—"the *father*, none but myself and one other."

"Loveday Smith?"

Heavens—was she a witch in possession of the ability to read the mind of another?

He nodded. "And now you."

She turned her head toward the window, her face pale in the sunlight.

"Forgive me, I didn't mean to distress you," he said. "Freda was sent into service, as most young women are, but her master…"

She raised her hand. "There's no need to explain. A man in an elevated position in Society will, in my experience, always take advantage of those he considers beneath him. It was my fault for asking." She let out a sigh. "Poor Frances—to carry the burden of always reminding others of the man responsible for the death of her…*sister*."

"Perhaps now you understand the depth of Mrs. Gadd's gratitude when you agreed to take Frannie on. She had no wish for the child to suffer Freda's fate."

"Or Loveday Smith's, I presume." She resumed her attention on him. "Frances told me Loveday worked in the scullery at Sandcombe Place until she quickened with child. She's going back there when her baby's old enough. Her husband…" Her voice trailed off, and she stared at him. "Does her husband know that her child is another's?"

Andrew nodded. "He offered for her knowing she carried another man's child."

"And he's willing to have her work there?"

"They need the money."

"But—she's being placed in danger!" she cried. "Why is nobody doing anything to prevent it? Why aren't *you?*"

"By rights, she's the property of her husband," he said. "I do all I can to ensure her safety. Believe me, she's safer at Sandcombe Place. The cook is an understanding woman, and has promised to keep Loveday below stairs."

"Oh, of *course*," she said, a sneer in her tone. "It's the woman's responsibility to avoid the man who wants to seduce her—

just as it's her responsibility to deal with the consequences."

"Loveday loves her children, no matter who the father is," Andrew said.

"I wasn't doubting that," she retorted. "A mother's love is something you'll never understand. But nevertheless, Sir John's life is unaffected by his actions—a moment's gratification, then he can carry on as if nothing happened and forget about the woman he seduced. It's Loveday who pays the price, no matter how much she may love her children." She shook her head. "I thought *London* was debauched! I came here to the country to escape the depravity of the town, only to find it far worse here. How can you sit there and do nothing?"

"There's only so much I can do," he replied, swallowing his shame. "Each night I pray for the strength to help everyone in need. But I can't."

"I'm not asking you to help *everyone*. Just one person."

"And I have," he said. "I've ensured that Frannie Gadd is safe from harm, from…"

She drew in a sharp breath and wrinkled her nose in disgust. "Safe from being seduced by the man who sired her?" She shook her head. "What world do we live in that permits such vile acts? What is to be done?" She shuddered and she let out a soft sob.

He caught her hands and lifted them to his lips. "Hush, Etty," he whispered. "I beg you not to distress yourself. We live in a good world—I have to believe that. And we cannot fight all evils. Some battles are too insurmountable to win. The best we can do is choose those with which we have a chance of success, to help where we can be assured of making a difference."

"How can you say such things when you know such misery exists?"

"Because I must," he said. "It's what I have to do to prevent myself from giving up. A single man against the tide of the world is in danger of being dashed to pieces and drowned if he seeks to fight it. Do you not think I struggle every day when I see the injustice being heaped upon the people here at the hands of my patron? Do you not think that I struggle with my faith, my vocation, when I know that my bishop, despite his position in the church, would side with the very men who benefit from and perpetuate the injustices of the world?"

"You can fight them," she said.

"I am but one soldier facing an army," he replied. "In fighting openly I would be cut down at the first stroke—and what good would that do for the likes of Frannie Gadd and Loveday Smith? So I do what is within my power, to protect them as best I can."

Her expression of disapproval, mingled with deep sorrow, tore at his heart. More than anything he wanted her approval, even if he could never hope to earn her admiration.

Or her love.

He reached for her hands and gave an inward sigh of relief when she didn't snatch them away.

"Did someone hurt you?" he asked softly. "Is that why you care so deeply about Frannie?"

"Why must you assume that I must have been hurt in order to care about others?" she asked, the tightness in her voice increasing the pitch.

"I think you would care about others whether you'd been hurt or not, Etty. Kindness is a quality that few possess. It's ingrained in their souls, an instinct to nurture and love. It cannot be taught, or earned through suffering. It merely exists."

She closed her eyes, her chest rising and falling in a sigh, and his blood warmed with desire as she threaded her fingers into his.

"You're wrong," she whispered. "So wrong."

"Is your opinion of me that low?" he asked, the pain in his heart warring with his desire.

She shook her head. "Oh, no, Andrew," she said. "You're the kindest man I have met. But you cannot be more wrong about me. I am not kind—far from it. I have been cruel, and I have thought nothing of giving pain to others, even those closest to me. And it is only through experience have I learned that the world is in great need of kindness."

He lifted her hands to his lips and placed a light kiss on her knuckles. "You have a kind soul, Etty. Perhaps you were unable to recognize it until you suffered the unkindness of others."

She blinked, and a tear splashed onto his hand. He dipped his head and placed a kiss on her skin, tasting the salt of her sorrow.

"Do not be kind to me, Andrew," she said. "I-I couldn't bear it."

"Why?" he asked. "Because you believe you don't deserve it? Or perhaps you've learned, to your cost, that the appearance of kindness can be the precursor to cruelty?"

She let out a low whimper, and his heart seared with pain at her cry—its very gentleness evidence of the intensity of the pain she suffered. Unable to suppress his need, he pulled her close and brushed his lips against hers.

For a moment, she stiffened. A nugget of shame swelled in his mind, but before he could release her, she parted her lips in invitation. He flicked his tongue along the seam of her mouth, and she grew still, as if she waited.

But for what?

Robert would have known what do to. Andrew's brother— the master at seduction—would, at the touch of his hand, have rendered her open and ready, begging him to take her.

Surrendering to instinct, he slipped his tongue inside her mouth, relishing the warmth and the delectable taste.

Like honey.

The taste grew sweeter as he caressed her mouth with his tongue, and she let out a soft sigh and leaned toward him. Emboldened by her body's encouragement, he flicked his tongue along the tip of hers. The warmth in his body increased as she responded to his kiss, curling her tongue around his, drawing him into a dance more seductive than anything he'd experienced in a ballroom.

Then she stilled, and a swell of panic rose within him.

She was a woman of experience—what did she expect of him?

Perhaps more of the same.

He deepened the kiss, relishing her soft warmth, and his manhood surged with need at the prospect of the sweet warmth elsewhere—that sweetness his older brother had said could make a man go mad with want until he claimed it for his own.

Her soft mewls of pleasure threatened to unleash the torrent of lust building in his mind, hammering against his defenses, that primal urge all men fought to conquer…or satisfy.

She arched her back—almost imperceptibly, but enough to move her breasts close to his hands—so close that he only need move a fraction…

Ought he dare? Robert had always told him that a woman spoke more clearly with her body than with her words.

Unable to resist, Andrew shifted his hand and suppressed a cry as his palm met the swell of her breasts. Such soft sweetness hidden beneath a thin layer of muslin! Her chest rose and fell as her breathing quickened, and she curled her tongue around his, caressing it from root to tip, sending a bolt of lust into his groin. Then he curved his palm to cup her breast and she moved closer, pressing her soft flesh against his palm, until he felt it—a hard nub pressing insistently against his hand, as if it begged for his attention.

Heavens! His brother had spoken the truth, that there was nothing so delectable as a peaked nipple awaiting a man's attention. Awaiting *his* attention.

What might it be like to touch it with his fingers, without the barrier of a layer of muslin? What might it be like to *taste* it? All he need do was lower her neckline and dip his head…

Sweet holy Lord—what the devil am I doing?

He broke the kiss and removed his hand. For a moment, the woman before him remained still, like an angel, her hair coming undone in untamed wisps surrounding her face like a halo. As for her expression…

Her eyes had darkened into deep pools of pure, raw need. And, for the first time in his life, Andrew understood what his brother had meant when he said that a man would know when a woman was ripe for the taking.

Then she blinked and the desire vanished, replaced by distress.

But in that moment—that sweet, glorious moment—she had wanted him.

And he wanted her. Lord save him, he *wanted* her.

"F-forgive me, Etty…" He hesitated. "I mean—Mrs. Ward. I don't know what came over me. I didn't mean to…"

Curse it! Why could he not complete a coherent sentence?

"I-I mean," he said, gesturing to himself, "I've never…"

No—that wouldn't do. He'd drawn her attention toward that part of him over which he had no control. An inferno of shame raging through his cheeks, he crossed his legs to hide the bulge in his breeches.

"Are you a rake, Mr. Staines?" she asked, her voice steady.

Why was it that she was able to maintain her composure where he'd turned into a blabbering simpleton?

"I'd never take a woman unwilling," he said.

She tilted her head to one side. "That's not what I asked. Besides, there are many forms of *unwilling*. Most men choose to ignore them and use their ignorance to justify their actions."

"I'll confess my ignorance on such matters," Andrew replied.

Anger flickered in her expression. "To those who lack understanding, unwillingness takes one form," she said. "Struggles, pleas to stop, and cries for help. But, unfortunately for *my* sex, there exist the predatory creatures among *yours*, who take advantage of a woman's innocence of mind. Those who flatter and prey upon the need with which my sex is burdened in a world ruled by men."

He nodded. "The need to find a husband."

"You understand our plight, vicar. Perhaps you also understand that it places us at a disadvantage. It pits us against each other—we become rivals, often fighting each other to secure the attention of a man. It can also place us in a position of desperation if we are required to yield ourselves—much as a gamester with little capital will throw in everything he has to secure the prize, at risk of ruination to himself. It is this form of *unwillingness* in a woman that goes unnoticed—a desperate woman who dares not defend her virtue when placed under persuasion to yield."

"You make me quite ashamed," he said. "I'd never take such advantage of a woman. I wouldn't even know…"

A smile curled her lips and a glint of amusement twinkled in her eyes. She was laughing at him, at his naiveté.

He looked away, but she caught his hand. "Mr. Staines—*Andrew*—be not ashamed of your innocence. I asked whether you were a rake because I deplore rakes. The fact that you are not such a man is in your favor. It is something to be proud of, though I fear most men consider their…*inexperience* as something to be remedied as soon as possible."

"I have seen the impact a rake can have on a woman," Andrew said. "A woman not unlike yourself." He closed his eyes, recalling the image of Eleanor sitting in the very same chair Etty now occupied—a creature as innocent as he.

"Who was she?" she asked.

He shook his head. "It matters not. She's happy now—married to the cad. I hope, one day, he'll begin to deserve her. He certainly gave me cause to believe so, if such a man can be redeemed by the love of a good woman."

"Only if he loves her in return." She squeezed his hand. "Did you love her also?"

"I believed I did." He sighed. "I loved her enough to let her go—and I love her enough to be content that she is happier with another than she ever could have been with me."

She smiled. "That's the purest form of love—that which you harbor for another, where you place her welfare above your own convenience."

His heart leaped with recognition, and she nodded.

"Yes, Mr. Staines," she said. "I recall your sermon that first day, alone, at the back of a tiny church in a remote little village. It was the first time I truly understood the meaning of love—to place the happiness of others first."

"It's what *she* did," he said. "I remember sitting here in this very spot and telling her the same. You remind me a little of her."

She stiffened and drew in a sharp breath. "Wh-what do you mean?"

"Your kindness," he said. "She and I shared a friendship. There's no harm in a man and a woman becoming friends, is there?"

For a moment she stared at him, the haunted expression returning to her eyes. Then she stood.

"I should see to that tea stain," she said, gesturing to the carpet. "What must you think of me, letting my guests mop up after me?"

"The pattern is such that it won't be noticeable," he said. "If you soak it in water, the rest of the stain should come out. The trick is to soak it right away, rather than let it dry."

"Are you giving me household tips, vicar?"

"It's a poor man who's incapable of taking care of himself," he replied. "A bachelor—particularly a vicar who must live frugally—is almost as good a preserver of household items as any woman. Though I would ask you not to repeat that to my housekeeper. Mrs. Clegg is very particular about her duties, and though I aim to maintain a degree of self-sufficiency, like any unmarried man, it is my fate to rely on her to keep my life in order—until I have a wife, of course."

"And do you intend to instruct your wife in household tasks when you are married?"

He shook his head. "No, Mrs. Ward. First and foremost, I intend to love her. With every fiber of my soul."

Her eyes widened, then she nodded, slowly. "Yes," she said quietly. "I believe you will."

Her voice carried an undertone of sorrow. What had she known of love? It was plain that she loved her son and was growing to love Frannie Gadd, the child she'd taken to her heart.

But did anyone love *her*?

She seemed to believe herself undeserving—but everyone deserved to be loved. Even those who had committed the worst sins of all. Creatures such as Sir John Fulford—the product of a world ruled by men, a man who took what he wanted no matter the consequences. And creatures such as Eleanor's sister—the woman who'd tried to destroy an innocent to further her own ends.

But today was not a day to dwell on the undeserving—it was a day to give the deserving a purpose.

"Mrs. Ward," he said, "what say you to accompanying me on my visits to the poor of the parish?"

"Me?"

"There are many in the village in need of a little help—widows with no means to support themselves, new parents, struggling with a sick child…" He hesitated. "A new mother unwilling to return to service, yet fearful of angering her husband. You are right that I cannot help them all, but I do what I can, and I encourage others to do so, though few listen to me."

"And you believe *I'll* listen?"

"I believe you capable of so much more, Etty."

She colored and looked away. Why did she dislike compliments? A creature as beautiful as she—and a former debutante—must be used to praise on a daily basis. But perhaps she'd grown to recognize it for what it was—soulless flattery.

"If not for your sake, then would you consider accompanying me for mine?" he asked.

"*Your* sake?"

"I'd rather have *you* accompany me than Lady Fulford."

"So my most favorable quality is that I'm not Lady Fulford?"

"That is a quality all women share."

A smile twinkled in her eyes. "For shame, vicar," she said.

"Lady Fulford has been threatening to bestow her presence on my visits," he said. "Not for the purpose of soiling her hands with work, of course."

"Of course?"

"I'm afraid that she's taken to suggesting that her daughters accompany me, Mrs. Ward. They are of marriageable age."

Her mouth twitched into a smile. "Ah, I see—you wish me to protect you from predatory females?"

Put like that, it made his plight sound rather pathetic.

She let out a soft laugh. "I'm only teasing you, vicar." Then she paused, and her laughter died.

"Mrs. Ward?" he asked. "Are you well?"

"I was merely wondering when I had last laughed before today." She shook her head. "I cannot recall it. Not a genuine laugh, at least."

"That settles it," he said. "If only to hear your laugh, I insist you accompany me."

"Very well," she replied. "A vicar bent on tending to his flock is, I believe, even more persistent than a debutante's mama. But you must wait until I am satisfied Gabriel is fully recovered from his fever. I wouldn't want to leave him, and much as I trust Frances to take care of him, I'm unwilling to burden her more than necessary."

"Then it's settled," he said. "Perhaps next week."

He took her hand and lifted it to his mouth. She made no attempt to resist, and he brushed his lips against her skin.

Mrs. Ward carried a secret herself—a burden that had crushed her confidence and the value she'd placed on her self-worth. Or, perhaps, she had never been valued by those around her, like Eleanor before her.

But, unlike Eleanor, Etty had stirred a deep longing in his soul. He had loved Eleanor Howard—or, at least, *believed* that he loved her. But the woman sitting before him now, whom he'd known barely a fortnight, had touched his soul in a manner he'd never imagined possible, despite having read countless stories about miracles and revelations.

Etty Ward was not alone in having only recently realized the true meaning of love. The woman sitting before him, whose tiny hand he cradled in his, cherishing the privilege of being near her…

She had opened Andrew's eyes to what it meant to fall in love with another—a feeling he'd never experienced.

Until today.

CHAPTER ELEVEN

ETTY'S GUT TWISTED in fear as the sound of horses' hooves drew near, then stopped outside the cottage. By the time the knock came on the door, she was already in the hallway, smoothing down the skirts of her dress for what felt like the twentieth time.

Frances took her hand. "Wait in the parlor, ma'am, and I'll let your guest in."

Dear Frances—such a sweet, kind child! And courageous, given that Etty had been unable to stem the tremors in her body from the moment she'd read her father's letter announcing his intention to visit.

She let the girl usher her into the parlor, then waited, her heart hammering as she heard the knock on the front door, followed by the murmur of voices—Frances's light tones, together with the familiar rich timbre.

Then the parlor door opened to reveal Frances, her slight frame dwarfed by the man beside her.

A brown leather satchel in his hand, he looked resplendent in a dark-blue jacket and an understated silk-embroidered waistcoat that reeked of prosperity despite its muted colors. He was much the same as when Etty's had last seen him, though his mane of once-dark hair sported a little more gray. His skin was tanned, most likely from his travels, and the portliness had gone. He looked healthier, happier. And more prosperous.

Clearly Etty's actions had not completely ruined him, given that his knighthood had now been elevated to a baronetcy.

He stepped toward her, and her senses were overcome by the familiar scent of smoke and spice—the scent that transported her back to a time when she lived her life in blissful ignorance of the world. It was a scent she'd yearned to relive, yet feared it at the same time, for it came hand in hand with the man who wore it.

Etty rose to her feet, fisting her hands to disguise her trembling. Then she dipped into a curtsey. "Papa."

"Daughter."

She flinched at his tone. Why must he always sound so disappointed? Would he ever forgive her transgression against her sister, his undoubted favorite?

"Frances, sweetheart, would you mind seeing to the tea?" Etty asked.

The girl bobbed a curtsey. "Yes, Mrs. Ward." She turned to Etty's father. "Please, sir, take a seat. I'm sorry I don't know your name. I only know you're Mrs. Ward's father. We've been expecting you. Mrs. Ward showed me your letter."

Etty flinched at the girl's lack of decorum, steeling herself to defend Frances from her father's admonishment, but he gave her an indulgent smile.

"Thank you, my dear," he said. "My name is Sir Leonard."

Frances's eyes widened. "Oh! So Gabriel was named after you."

"Gabriel?"

"Gabriel Leonard, Mrs. Ward's child."

He drew in a sharp breath, and Etty flinched at the reference to her son—the child her mother had referred to as "the bastard that sealed our family's disgrace" before Etty fled London.

"Are you a *lord*?" Frances asked.

Papa resumed his attention on the girl and let out a chuckle. Etty's heart ached at the warmth in his voice—a warmth he'd never bestowed on her.

"I'm afraid not, child," he said. "I'm only a baronet, and before that, a knight. Unfortunately, not like the knights you read about in storybooks, who ride around the country protecting fair maidens."

"I can't read, sir," Frances said, "but Mrs. Ward is teaching me."

"*Is* she, now?"

Etty flinched as her father turned his gaze on her.

Frances bobbed another curtsey then disappeared. Etty gestured to a chair—the same chair the vicar had occupied days before—and her father approached it. He sat, placing the satchel on a nearby table, then glanced about the parlor.

"This seems a comfortable room," he said.

"I do what I can, Papa—with Frances's help."

He nodded. "She seems very capable for one so young."

"She's no younger than the chambermaids we had at home," Etty said. "If you're implying I'm taking advantage of a child, perhaps you should look to your own household before judging mine."

His eyes sparkled and the corner of his mouth creased into a smile—the smile he'd reserved, almost exclusively, for Etty's sister.

"I'm not here to criticize you, Juliette," he said.

"Then why *are* you here?"

He let out a sigh. "Would you believe it if I said I wanted to see how you were?"

"But when we last spoke, you said…"

He raised his hand, and she trailed away, beset by memories of admonishments meted out in his study. The unspoken words clung thickly to the air between them.

You said that you wished you were anybody's father but mine.

"I feel nothing but shame for what I said, Juliette," he said. "I spoke in anger."

"Is not that when we reveal the truth in our hearts?" Etty asked.

"Were you revealing the truth when you told your sister, in

front of a drawing room full of guests, that she was a whore?"

"Oh!"

A sharp cry rang out, and Etty glanced up. Frances stood in the doorway, a tea tray teetering in her hold.

Etty leaped to her feet and took the tray. "Oh, Frances, sweetheart!" she cried. "You mustn't carry so much. Let me take it. Why don't you take a turn about the garden? I can see to the tea."

She took the tray and set it on the breakfast table. Frances stared at Etty's father.

"Forgive me, child," he said. "I should not have said such a thing in your presence—or at all." He gestured toward the window. "Your mistress is right. It's a fine evening for a stroll outside."

Frances bobbed another curtsey, then fled, closing the door behind her.

Her hands trembling, Etty poured tea into a cup, followed by a splash of milk and two spoonsful of sugar. She stirred the tea, then handed the cup to her father, and he took a sip.

"You remember how I like my tea," he said. "Not even your mother..." He paused, then took another sip, while Etty poured herself a cup.

She resumed her seat, and silence filled the room, punctuated by the delicate tinkling of the spoon as he continued to stir his tea while looking about the parlor, his gaze falling on the mantel clock.

At length, he resumed his gaze on her. "I'm sorry."

Etty sipped her tea. "I assure you, Frances has heard much worse, and I doubt she caught your meaning."

He set his cup aside and leaned forward. Etty's heart jolted as he took her hand, his warm fingers roughed with toil interlocking with hers.

"No, daughter," he said quietly. "I'm sorry for what happened to you."

"It was my own doing. As you said."

"You may have been the one to…" He paused, as if searching for a polite turn of phrase.

Go on, Papa—tell me that I tried to ruin my sister out of spite, spread my legs for a lecher, and birthed his bastard. Go on—I dare you.

"It matters not what you did," he finally said. "What matters is where the true responsibility lies. There is only one person to blame. And that is myself."

Her hand slipped, and she winced as tea spilled onto her skirts. "Y-you?"

He frowned, a flicker of pain in his eyes. "Yes, my daughter," he said. "Forgive me."

He squeezed her hand in a gesture of affection she'd not experienced before.

"You were such a beautiful child, you see, that I believed you had no need of my help," he said. "We live in a world where beauty and elegance are valued above all else. Your poor sister has always been so painfully shy and awkward, so out of place in Society. You outshone her in beauty and grace almost from the moment you were born—*everybody* remarked on it. And so I believed Eleanor's need was greater than yours. And that was my greatest mistake. Her need was not greater—only different."

He glanced away, and she caught a glistening of moisture in his eyes.

"I failed you, Juliette," he said. "And for that, I am very sorry."

"Etty," she whispered.

He raised his eyebrows. "I beg pardon?"

"Juliette is no more," Etty said. "I have no wish to be reminded of my past. And"—she glanced toward the door—"Eleanor made many friends here. Friends who would rightly condemn me for what I did, if they knew who I was."

He patted her hand and smiled. "I understand. Eleanor came here to start again. It's only right that you be permitted to do the same. I'm no advocate for running from one's past, but everyone deserves a second chance."

"Even me?"

He flinched at the sharpness in her tone. "I think perhaps *I'm more in need of a second chance,*" He blinked, and Etty's heart ached to see moisture in the eyes of a man she'd believed incapable of emotion. Even when he'd condemned her for her actions, he'd delivered his lecture in his usual toneless manner, as if reading from a legal document.

"Papa…"

He lifted his hand to wipe away a bead of moisture on his cheek. "You see, Eleanor was mine," he said. "The quiet, serious child who rarely smiled and disliked company. You, on the other hand—bright, vibrant, with a smile for everyone—you were your mother's."

Etty flinched at the mention of the parent who had raged at her, delivering a tirade of admonishments. But her mother's rage she could weather better than her father's measured disappointment.

"How is…Mother?"

He patted her hand. "As well as can be expected. Her nerves still plague her, but we do the best we can. And, of course, she has a duchess for a daughter now, which gives her comfort."

"I daresay she's now claimed Eleanor as *hers*, given Eleanor's greater worth."

He frowned and let out a sigh.

"Forgive me, Papa," Etty said. "I did not mean to speak ill of Mother. I'm responsible for her…disappointment." She shook her head. "I know you'll never believe me, but I'm sorry for what I did."

"There's nothing to be sorry for," he replied. "I should have been firmer, done more to unite you and Eleanor. You're more alike than you may think, Juliette. I'm only ashamed that I never gave you the chance to discover your similarities rather than emphasize your differences." His lips curved into a smile. "Eleanor sends her love."

"Is she well?"

"She's entering her confinement, otherwise I suspect she'd have asked to come with me. You should write to her. Or you could pay her a visit. I could take you in the carriage."

Juliette's gut twisted with shame. "I-I couldn't, Papa. She must hate me for what I did—and I doubt her husband would let me near her."

"Your sister is too generous for that. As for Whitcombe, he's so smitten with Eleanor, he'd do anything she asked. He's a changed man since he married her. As soon as I returned to London last month, he invited me to dine with him at White's."

White's—the lair where Society's predators presided. Where…

She shuddered, hating herself for wanting to ask… "Was…*he* there?"

After a pause, Papa responded. "He's rarely seen in London. Whitcombe told me he's married."

Etty's heart ached. So, her former friend and rival had secured the prize.

"Juliette, there's nothing to hope for with regards to Dunton."

Etty shook her head. "I had no hopes for myself, I assure you, but Arabella deserves a better fate than to be his wife."

"*Arabella?*" Papa raised his eyebrows. "You think…"

"We may have parted on sour terms," Etty said, "but she was the only friend I had, shallow though that friendship was. When there are few true friends in the world, I must be grateful for the friends I have."

True friends—such as the vicar.

Andrew…

The memory of his kiss still lingered—his soft lips, teasing hers open, before his tongue probed gently, tentatively, as if he feared her rejection. An innocent, but all the more desirable, for his gentle touch was not born of design or stratagem—it was not the act of a lecherous rake wanting to prove his prowess by seducing a maiden into ruination. It was the purest act of all—an innocent soul seeking pleasure.

"Dunton hasn't married Arabella," Papa said, returning Etty to the present. "He's married her aunt."

"Her *aunt?*"

"Whitcombe arranged it—it seems as if Dunton disgraced himself by indulging in a little fraud over Lady Arabella's fortune. He's now living a quiet life in exile, with hardly any funds and fewer friends, while your friend is now the wife of a gardener."

"Arabella married a *gardener?* B-but she has a title!"

Papa grinned. "It's possible for a lady of rank to marry a commoner, Juliette."

"Forgive me, Papa, I didn't mean to impugn Mother's choice in marrying you."

"It matters not, my dear," he said, patting her hand. "Though I daresay Lady Arabella will be more satisfied with her lot than..." He shook his head. "It matters not. Whitcombe tells me they're very happy together. The man—Baxter, his name is—is redesigning the gardens at Rosecombe, and they're frequent visitors there. Arabella and Eleanor have become friends—would you credit that? I'm sure she'd like to see you again as much as Eleanor would."

"I'm glad for Arabella," Etty said, "but I no longer belong in their world."

"You're happy here?"

"As happy as I deserve to be, Papa. And I'm more fortunate than most."

"Dear daughter!" he said, and Etty's throat tightened at the affection in his voice. "Perhaps you can find peace by helping those less fortunate not only by helping others, but by giving yourself a purpose. There is much to be gained from knowing that you've changed the world for one individual, even if you cannot change the whole world."

"Oh!" she cried. "That's what Andrew—I mean, Mr. Staines—said."

"And he's right, Juliette." He tilted his head to one side. "Mr.

Staines—Eleanor has spoken of him. The vicar, yes? He was kind to her when she lived here. Does he speak of her much? I'm sure she wouldn't mind your passing on her good wishes."

Etty withdrew her hand, her cheeks warming. "H-he speaks much of her—and of his anger at the sister who tried to destroy her."

Papa's eyes widened. "Then…"

"He doesn't know who I am, Papa. Nobody does. I'm Mrs. Etty Ward—not Miss Juliette Howard. I have no wish to lose his friendship when he's the only friend I have."

"A friendship founded on deception will crumble eventually, daughter," he replied. "If you are to be truly at peace, then you must accept the truth—and let others accept it also. If they cannot give you their good opinion, then they do not deserve you. But it's your burden to bear and your confession to make, if you so wish."

Papa was right. A good opinion founded on deception had little worth.

But would she ever be willing to risk Andrew's good opinion by revealing the truth of her sins? Not when she valued his friendship more than anything.

Anything except…

As if he'd read her thoughts, a familiar cry came from Gabriel's chamber upstairs. Etty stood, her cheeks flaming. Her father's disappointment in her behavior must pale in comparison to his disappointment at being so loudly, and rudely, reminded of the fruits of her ruination.

He rose and caught her hand. "Daughter…"

She flinched, awaiting the sermon.

But it never came. Instead, a pair of solid arms drew her into an embrace. She clung to him, curling her fingers around the lapels of his jacket, inhaling the faint aroma of spices and cigar smoke.

"Papa, I'm…"

"Hush," he breathed. "There's nothing to say. Let your silly old papa hold you for a moment. I've missed you—my beloved daughter."

Moisture stung her eyes and she blinked. A tear splashed onto his jacket, disappearing into the fibers. At length, he released her and kissed the top of her head.

"Now," he said, "there's one thing I'm very much looking forward to—and that is meeting your boy. Gabriel *Leonard*, eh?"

"Do you mind?" Etty asked.

"That you named him after me?" A broad grin stretched across his face. "There's nothing that could make me happier. I only hope I prove to be a better grandfather to Gabriel than I ever was a father to you." He retrieved the satchel and pulled out an object. "Recognize this?"

It was a toy boat, carved from wood. The sails, fashioned from cotton, were threadbare around the edges, the material yellowing—but given its age, it was in excellent condition. And it had taken pride of place in Etty's father's study for as long as she could recall.

"Your boat?"

He held it out and she took it, running her fingertips over the body, the thin grooves carved in the shape to resemble the planks of wood. Her father had never let either of his daughters touch it, much less play with it. She turned it over in her hands, running her fingertips across the inscription on the side.

H.M.S. Howard.

"My father made that for me when I was younger than Gabriel," he said. "He always said that if a man was capable of making something with his own two hands, then he would never go hungry. A fine man, he was—and I grew up determined one day to have a ship that I could call my own. Poor Father despaired of me when I showed a singular lack of talent for shipbuilding, but he encouraged me to pursue my own business interests, and when I finally commissioned a ship of my own, I named it after him, in his honor—though he didn't live to see it. But he taught me to work hard, to take care of myself. This ship is a reminder of the man he wanted me to become."

Etty stared at the toy boat, her eyes misting with tears.

"I didn't know," she said. "I-I can't take this if it means so much to you."

"Yes, you can," he said, "precisely *because* I value it. It serves as a symbol of my father's—your grandfather's—determination to make a better life for himself and those he loved. It's a determination that has passed to you, dearest daughter, and I hope and pray that your son inherits it, and grows up to be as fine a man as my father."

He pulled her to him and placed a kiss on her forehead.

"And now I think it's time I met my grandson, don't you?"

Blinking back tears, Etty nodded, and, arm in arm, they exited the parlor.

CHAPTER TWELVE

"**S**WEET LORD—IS THIS it? Does Mrs. Smith live *here?*"

Andrew glanced at Etty standing beside him, a basket hooked over one arm. "This is her *home*," he said.

"But it's so small!"

"It's no smaller than the others we've visited."

"I know, but I can't imagine anyone surviving with so little space."

"It may not be as grand as the townhouses you grew up in, Mrs. Ward, but I assure you it's better than most. And I daresay your servants in London survived with less. A four-room cottage for a family of four is to be preferred to a tiny room in an attic shared with six or seven other housemaids."

Almost as soon as he'd uttered the words, his conscience pricked at him. She flinched, and raw shame flickered in her expression. He had no right to condemn her for having been brought up in luxury. Her cottage might be palatial compared to Loveday Smith's tiny dwelling, but it must be considerably smaller than what she'd been used to in London.

He reached for her hand. "Forgive me, I didn't mean to cast judgment."

"Did you not?"

She raised her hand and rapped on the door. Light, hurried footsteps approached and the door opened to reveal Loveday Smith's eldest child. The girl stepped back, her mouth forming an

O. Her sloe-black eyes widened as she stared at Andrew's companion.

"Oh!" She let out a cry, then glanced over her shoulder. "Oh! I-I…"

Andrew approached the girl. "Florence, child, we're here to call on your mother."

"Y-you…" The girl's voice trailed away as she glanced up at Andrew's companion, a flicker of fear in her eyes. She looked as if she'd turn and flee inside if Etty approached her, but Etty made no move.

"That's a pretty name, Florence," she said. "It means 'blossoming,' doesn't it? Is your mama fond of flowers, perhaps?"

"I-I…" The child shook her head.

"Florence, this is Mrs. Ward," Andrew said. "She especially wanted to meet your mother."

"Oh." The child hesitated, then dipped into a curtsey. "Pleased to meet you, ma'am. C-come in."

Andrew stepped inside, and the stench of damp assaulted his senses.

"Ma's restin', vicar," the girl said.

"Is she in her chamber?" Andrew asked.

The girl nodded. "I'll take ye—and the lady."

She led them up a narrow staircase that creaked with each step, to a tiny, uneven-floored chamber where the stench of damp mingled with the acrid odor of stale sweat. To her credit, Andrew's companion made no sign she'd noticed as she entered the chamber, where Loveday sat reclined in a rocking chair, eyes closed, a blanket on her knees, her baby sleeping in a nearby cot.

Florence approached her mother and gave the rocking chair a gentle push. "Ma."

Loveday stirred and frowned, a low groan reverberating in her throat.

"Ma!" Florence said, tugging at her mother's hand. "Vicar's here."

Loveday let out a cry, and her eyes snapped open. She withdrew her hand, and Andrew caught sight of a dark mark on her wrist before she tugged her sleeve over it. He glanced at Etty, who was staring at Loveday's hand, frowning.

Loveday teetered to her feet, letting the blanket fall to the floor. "Vicar! Oh, sweet Lord, what must you think of me not receiving you. I…"

She stumbled forward, losing her balance. Before Andrew could react, Etty dropped her basket, rushed toward Loveday, and caught her in her arms.

"There!" she said. "I have you, Mrs. Smith. You mustn't get up on our account when you're unwell."

"Oh—no!" Loveday shook her head. "Ma'am, no, you mustn't—" She broke off with a sob, moisture shining in her eyes.

"Here, let me sit you back down," Etty said. "What must you think of us, intruding when you're taking your rest?" She helped Loveday into the chair, then crouched at her feet, gathering the blanket before placing it over her knees.

"You must be wanting tea," Loveday said. "Florrie, love, see to it, would you?"

"What about the baby, Ma? You said I was to—"

"Never mind that, Florrie. We have guests."

"This is Mrs. Ward," Andrew said, gesturing toward Etty. "She very much wanted to meet you today."

"Oh." Distress and shame lined Loveday's features. "Oh, ma'am. I-if I'd known you were comin', I'd have…"

"There's no need to do anything, Mrs. Smith," Etty said, glancing about the chamber. "We're not in need of tea."

Andrew flinched inwardly. What must she think of the place? Would she deign to spend an afternoon here, or would she turn her pretty nose up at the filth and restrict herself to the charitable efforts Lady Fulford favored, such as tossing a coin or two at the needy without sullying her hands?

He placed a hand on her shoulder, and she turned and met his gaze. The compassion in her eyes stirred his heart.

We're guests *here,* he mouthed.

Etty glanced from Loveday to Andrew, and understanding flickered in her gaze. She drew up a chair beside Loveday, sat, and pulled a package out of the basket.

"I trust it's not too much of an imposition, Mrs. Smith," she said. "I've been looking forward to spending an afternoon with you. Do you like fruitcake?"

Loveday eyed the package. "I-I had some once," she said. "Leftovers, from one of Lady Fulford's garden parties." She winced, and Andrew's heart ached at the fear in her eyes.

"Well, this one's for you," Etty said.

"Oh no, ma'am—I couldn't possibly take it."

"It's only fair that I bring you a gift if I'm a guest in your home, Mrs. Smith, particularly if you've invited us for tea. Frances baked it."

"Frannie Gadd?" Loveday asked.

"Yes—all by herself!" Etty laughed. "I'm hopeless in the kitchen, I'm afraid. I do my best, but I know when to concede defeat in the presence of a more accomplished cook. Frances sends you her best wishes, Mrs. Smith."

"Oh, ma'am!" Loveday cried. "I'm quite overcome—I don't know what to say…"

"There's nothing to say," Etty said, placing a light hand on her arm. A flicker of pain crossed Loveday's expression. "May I look at your hand, Mrs. Smith?"

Loveday glanced at Andrew and shook her head.

"Mr. Staines," Etty said, "might you perhaps assist Florence with the tea? I know how men dislike listening to ladies prattling on, and I'd like to get to know Mrs. Smith better, if you'd be so kind?"

Andrew glanced at Etty, at the compassion in her eyes and the tender way she cradled Loveday's hand in hers.

Loveday was, perhaps, in safer hands today than she had ever been. He nodded, then ushered Florence out of the chamber.

BY THE TIME Andrew returned, the sun was well past its zenith. He should have been back at the vicarage hours ago—that sermon wasn't going to write itself. He would have already been home had Etty not insisted on prolonging each of their visits today. She'd taken the plight of his flock to her heart—young Matthew and Kitty Dodd, who'd struggled to make ends meet ever since Matthew's accident at Whittington Farm, and old Mrs. Penfold, who was determined to retain her home and her independence, but who suffered with the pains in her hands and feet. Mrs. Penfold was known in Sandcombe for her irascibility, but Etty had ignored her short-tempered jibes, rewarded her frowns with smiles, and even joined ranks with the old widow in her lamentations about the inequalities of the world and the faults of men—including Andrew himself, after which Mrs. Penfold regaled Etty with tales of her late husband's mishaps.

And now, laughter could be heard in Loveday Smith's house. Holding the tea tray in his hands, he followed Florence inside to find Loveday sitting upright in her chair, her eyes sparkling with mirth, and Etty standing in the center of the room, holding the baby in her arms.

"Florrie, love, would you see to Anna?" Loveday asked. "It's time for your walk."

"There's no need to remove the child on my account, Mrs. Smith," Etty said, then she cooed to the baby. "You're such a sweet girl, aren't you?"

"I always take Anna for a walk in the afternoon, ma'am," Florence said, holding out her arms. "She likes to see the sea."

"Then perhaps you can all join me for a picnic by the sea," Etty said, handing the baby to the girl. "I'm taking Frances, and I'm sure she'd like the company. She speaks of you often, Mrs. Smith."

"A picnic?" Loveday's eyes shone with delight. Then she

shook her head. "I can't possibly. My Ralph wouldn't permit it."

"I fail to see why not—the fresh air would be good for you, and there's much to be said about the benefits of sea bathing."

"I…" Loveday began, then flinched as a door opened and slammed shut downstairs. The baby in Florence's arms began to wail. "Florrie, love, take Anna outside, there's a good girl."

The child nodded and exited the chamber. Shortly after, voices echoed from downstairs—Florence's tone pleading, placating, alongside another, deeper voice, its surly tones thickening the air.

Loveday gripped the arms of her chair and struggled to her feet. Andrew set the tray on a table and took her arm, but she pulled free.

"Vicar, you should go," she said.

Then the heavy tread of footsteps drew near and the door opened to reveal a thick-set man with thinning brown hair and close-set, pale-brown eyes. He glanced about the chamber, giving Andrew a cursory nod before settling his gaze on Etty, a flare of lust in his eyes.

Andrew wrinkled his nose at the stench of stale sweat.

"Husband!" Loveday cried.

Ralph turned his attention to his wife. "What's goin' on?"

"The vicar's come to visit, Ralph," Loveday said. "Isn't that kind of him?"

"Busybody more like, pokin' his nose where it's not wanted." He gestured toward Etty. "Who the bleedin' hell's *this*, then?"

Etty approached the man. "Mr. Smith, I'm—"

"I didn't ask *you*, woman," he sneered. "I asked my wife."

"I'm your wife's guest," Etty said, her voice sharpening. "I have every right—"

"Get out!" he snarled. "I'll have none of that nonsense in my house! We don't need some fancy woman pokin' her sharp little nose in our business, thinkin' she's better than us merely because she sits on her arse all day drinkin' tea."

"Mr. Smith, there's no need—"

"Vicar, control your woman before I do it for you. I'll not have fancy women puttin' ideas into my wife's head."

"Ralph, the vicar only came to see the baby," Loveday said.

"The girl's taken the brat outside, so there's no reason for the vicar or his tart to stay, is there?"

Etty stepped toward Ralph. "How dare you refer to your daughters in such a manner? Is this how you treat your wife, also?"

"Mrs. Ward, please!" Loveday cried. "Ralph, forgive me. Mrs. Ward didn't mean to say such things—did you, ma'am?"

"I most certainly *did*," Etty said.

"Why you…" Ralph raised his fists and took a step toward Etty, but she stood firm, defiance in her eyes.

"Go on, Mr. Smith," she said. "Do your worst—unless, of course, you prefer to beat women behind closed doors with no witnesses present."

"Mrs. Ward, no, ma'am, please!" Loveday said. "I told you, it was my fault—I slipped on the stairs. Ralph, I told her, honest I did. Mrs. Ward, I think you should go—it's best if you do."

"Not before I have your husband's assurance that he'll not lay a finger on you."

"He won't, will you, Ralph?" Loveday said. "You're due at the Sailor, aren't you? And I'll have a nice bit of stew waiting for you when you get home tonight. Your favorite."

"I think we ought to go, Mrs. Ward," Andrew said.

Etty turned her gaze on him, anger in her eyes. "You *what*?"

"We can visit Mrs. Smith tomorrow." He turned toward Loveday's husband. "And we can check on your wife's wrist—make sure she's had no more accidents."

Ralph shrugged. "It matters not to me," he said, retreating. "I've got work to do. Someone's got to now Loveday's landed me with another mouth to feed."

"That's no way to talk about your—" Etty began, but Andrew stopped her.

"Mrs. Ward, we should let Mr. Smith get to work, then we

can go. Come, sir, I'll show you out."

"I know the way to my own front door," Ralph growled.

"Nevertheless, I insist." Andrew gestured to the chamber door. "After you."

Ralph stared at Loveday for a moment, then turned and exited the chamber, muttering.

"Mrs. Smith…" Etty began.

"Please go, ma'am," Loveday said quietly. "And I'm sorry I'll not be able to come to your picnic."

"But—"

"That's enough, Mrs. Ward," Andrew said, taking her arm. "It's time we left. A vicar must never outstay his welcome."

Ralph let out a snort as he descended the stairs. "If that were true, the vicar would keep himself to his bleedin' self. Woman, make sure my supper's on the table when I return!"

Loveday followed them out of the chamber, clinging to the doorframe. "Yes, husband, just how you like it."

Without a backward glance, Ralph reached the foot of the stairs, plucked his cap from a hook on the wall, and rammed it onto his head before opening the front door and exiting.

"Close the door after you, vicar," he sneered before he turned his back and set off toward the inn.

Andrew ushered Etty outside, bade Loveday farewell, then closed the door. Before she could protest, he took Etty's arm and steered her onto the path in the opposite direction.

"Vile man!" she cried.

"Hush—he'll hear you," Andrew said.

She withdrew her arm, and he caught a blur of movement before pain exploded in his face as she delivered a stinging slap to his cheek.

"No—I meant *you*!"

CHAPTER THIRTEEN

ETTY'S HAND SMARTED with the impact. *Heavens!* She hadn't expected it to hurt so much—by rights it should hurt him more than her, surely?

He stepped back, rubbing his cheek.

Good. Perhaps it *had* hurt him more.

"What in the name of heaven's wrong?" he asked.

"You dare ask such a question after what happened in there?" she cried. "We have to go back."

"No, Etty, we—"

"It's *Mrs. Ward* to you."

He flinched at her tone, but she ignored the hurt in his eyes. What right had he to be hurt after what they'd witnessed—a brute threatening that poor, gentle soul?

"Mrs. Ward, it's not as simple as what you see," he said.

"It's perfectly simple," she said. "Or did you not notice the bruise on her wrist? Loveday Smith is being terrorized by her husband—a man who pledged to honor and cherish her."

"Yes, and she pledged to honor and obey him."

"Ugh!" she cried. "With that argument you've lost the right to even *speak* to me."

"Etty…"

The pleading tone in his voice grated on her senses, and she turned her back on him and marched along the path toward Shore Cottage. A couple approached, arm in arm, and she recognized the proprietor of the haberdashery next to the inn.

"You've forgotten your basket!" the vicar called after her.

"I don't give a damn about my basket!"

She heard a sharp intake of breath from the approaching couple, and she held her head high and marched past them.

"Good afternoon," she said. "A fine day for a stroll, is it not? What splendid weather we're having."

The stared at her open-mouthed. At length, the woman shook her head.

"Well, *really*," she said, before turning her attention to the man following Etty. "Ah, vicar. It's pleasant to see *you*, at least. Have you been visiting Mrs. Smith? She's fortunate to have you to keep her on the path to righteousness."

Etty fisted her hands and increased the pace. The sooner she removed herself from these judgmental, self-righteous arses, the better.

Arses…

Were poor Loveday's situation not so dire, Etty might have laughed at her use of such a crude word. If nothing else, folk who lived beneath her in station possessed a far more descriptive vocabulary.

By the time the vicar caught up with her, Shore Cottage was in sight, and Etty's heart lifted as it came into view. Tiny and cramped it may be, but it was hers. Neither she nor it belonged to another.

How blinkered she had been as a debutante in her desperation to snare a husband! Failing to secure a match may have led to her ruination and disgrace, but what of women such as Loveday Smith? She had secured a husband, and the only outcome was her loss of freedom.

"Damn him—damn them all!"

"I quite agree with you," a male voice said. A familiar voice, which, to her misfortune, she was growing to love, even after today.

"Damn *you* most of all, vicar," she said, increasing the pace.

"Could you at least slow down?" he called after her.

"Can't you keep up the pace, vicar? I thought men were supposed to rule the world because they were stronger, faster, and better at everything. Or is that only when it suits you in your quest for the subjugation of women?"

"I'm not on a quest for the subjugation of women!"

He caught her sleeve, and she spun round to face him. "Then what *are* you for, vicar? What is the point of you? You deliver sermons about the need to be kind. You tell your parishioners to help those less fortunate rather than merely attend church and wallow in self-satisfaction for a hymn well sung. And yet when it comes to helping those people yourself, you're content to turn your back and ignore the suffering of the innocent."

"Loveday Smith is not..." he began, but trailed off as she raised her hand.

Then she lowered it. Striking him only placed her on a level with brutes such as Ralph Smith.

"Please don't insult me by arguing that Loveday is not innocent," she said. "The poor girl cannot be older than eighteen at most, yet she has already been seduced by a lecher and sold in marriage to a beast who, instead of caring for his wife, resents her children and no doubt punishes her for the sins of her seducer."

"Holy mother of God," he whispered. "How did you know..." He shook his head. "Did she tell you? She can hardly speak of it to me."

Etty folded her arms. "And I wonder why that might be, *Mr. Staines.*"

"She knows she can trust me," he said.

"Perhaps not enough," Etty replied. "Clearly she can't trust you to remove her from her miserable life."

"And you can?"

"I can give her, and her children, a home. She'd be safer with me."

"Oh, *would* she?" He shook his head. "Well meaning as you are, surely you don't believe that you, a lone woman, can defend her against her husband! He's acting within his rights by marriage. If you took Loveday in, her husband would hammer down your door and drag her back the same day, and there would be nothing you could do to stop him. He's her lawfully wedded husband, and you cannot fight the law."

"Then the law is an arse!" she cried. "Why can you not *do* something? Do you care so little for Loveday and her kind? I hadn't thought you to be so unfeeling, but perhaps you are—more content to take tea with Sir John and Lady Fulford than sully your hands with the young women whose lives they destroyed. Or is that why you continue to visit Loveday—out of guilt?"

"For heaven's sake, woman, will you desist?" he roared, his eyes blazing with fury.

She shrank back, and he closed his eyes, then drew a hand across his forehead. When he opened his eyes, the pain in them tore at her soul.

"Oh, Etty—Etty," he pleaded, his voice cracking. "Do you not think I'm doing all I can to help these people? Much as I'd wish to, I have no means of my own—nowhere to keep them safe. And so I must be content with the next best thing."

"Which is?"

"To ensure that they can survive their environment." He let out a sigh. "I know what I do is woefully inadequate. But it's the best I can do within my capabilities. Loveday is not alone. There are many more like her—the world is filled with such women. I cannot help them all. But in helping each one a little, I am making a difference, however small, to many. I would rather ease the suffering of many than leave them unattended."

He turned to face the sea, tilting his head toward the sky.

"I understand your anger," he said. "But I am but one man trying to make a difference—a lone man among those who are content to perpetuate their superiority. And so I do what little I can. I cannot remove Loveday and take her to safety, for the world is not a safe place for a woman in her position. All I can do is remain close by. Her husband is less likely to treat her ill if he knows I am to visit tomorrow. It may not be much, but it's what I can afford to give when there are so many others also in need of my services."

He thrust his hands into his pockets and continued to stare out to sea, as if searching for something—his faith, perhaps.

"You ask what is the point of me," he said quietly. "That is a question I ask the Almighty each and every night as I kneel beside my bed. And do you know what He says in answer?"

He turned to face her then, his warm brown eyes clouded with misery and moisture.

"What does He say?" she whispered.

"Nothing," he said. "My prayers are answered with nothing but silence."

She took a step toward him, and her ankle turned on a stone. She stumbled forward, and he caught her arm. A shock of need coursed through her as he drew her close, and she shivered as the sea breeze caressed her skin.

"You're cold," he said. "We need to get you home. It's getting late—the sun's almost below the horizon. I'm already in line for a dressing down from my housekeeper."

He gave a watery smile. "I sometimes wonder whether the life of a vicar isn't akin to that of a schoolboy. Here…" He offered his arm, and she took it before they continued along the path.

"A schoolboy?" Etty said.

"I'm given weekly compositions to complete, and I must stand up at the front of the class and recite them to my fellow pupils, who often don't even bother to pretend to pay attention." He glanced at her. "With a few notable exceptions, of course. The bishop is the housemaster, ready to punish me if I fail to conform to the rules. My patron…" He frowned. "He's the head boy who bullies the weaker pupils and languishes in his study while I do all his schoolwork. As to my housekeeper…"

"Yes?"

The flicker of a smile played on his lips. "Mrs. Clegg is always ready to admonish me if I'm late for tea. In her eyes, a man who lets his supper go cold has committed the very gravest of all transgressions."

"Then perhaps you should return to the vicarage forthwith," Etty said. "I have no wish to be accused of furthering your transgression. I suspect I'm viewed as enough of a sinner in this village as it is."

"On the contrary," he said. "To those who matter, you are held in high regard. And none more so than myself."

Her cheeks warmed at his gentle praise. "Are you saying that you matter, vicar? And, in any case, you know so little of me to be in a position to present an informed opinion."

"You impugn my judgment, Mrs. Ward," he said as they reached her front gate. With his free hand he unlatched it, then led her to the door.

"If you knew me better," Etty said, "I'm sure you'd—"

She drew in a sharp breath as he pressed a finger to her lips, and a sliver of need threaded through her body.

"Hush," he whispered. "I am not one to form judgment on another through their appearance, and the length of an acquaintance bears no relevance on the credibility of an opinion over another. There are those I have known in this village for years about whom I cannot give you an honest opinion, for they reveal so little—they *do* so little. There are others whom I might like, or dislike, based on their actions, their conversation, and whether I enjoy their company. There are those who delight in telling me what my opinion of them must be—who are so caught up in their own self-opinion that they care little for the independent opinion of others."

He paused, then brushed his thumb across her lips in a gentle caress before placing his palm on her cheek.

"And then," he said, his voice quieting, "there are those such as yourself. Those rare souls that no ordinary man expects to encounter in his lifetime. The purest of souls who express their opinions directly and openly, no matter the consequences—the bravest souls who possess that degree of integrity that drives them to challenge that which they see to be wrong, no matter the consequences to themselves. They are the rare souls placed upon this earth who are ready to fight the evils of mankind—not by wielding swords and claiming glory for themselves on a battle-field, but by standing up to wrongdoing."

He leaned toward her until their foreheads almost touched, and she tilted her head up, brushing her nose against his. His chest rose and fell in a sigh and he closed his eyes, a soft groan escaping his lips.

"Forgive me, Etty," he said. "I want nothing more in this world than to be worthy of your acquaintance—and your friendship. For, undeserving as I am, I hope, and pray, that for all my flaws, you see me as your friend—your very good friend."

She lifted her hand to his face, then caressed his cheek, running her fingertips over the stubble on his chin. He opened his eyes, and she was met with the full force of his gaze—the warm chocolate color of his eyes deepening with need, revealing the most honest of pleas.

A plea not to be hurt.

"Andrew," she whispered, and his nostrils flared as he inhaled, his eyes darkening. "Oh, Andrew—how wrong you are!"

He stiffened. "I-I'm wrong?"

"Yes, my dear friend," she said. "You are so wrong if you believe that you are just one man, alone, trying to make a difference to the world. Perhaps you were alone before, but you are no longer."

A flicker of hope sparked in his eyes. "You mean…"

"You have me," she said. "I will not sit idly by while there is so much to be done. Neither will I permit you to question your value in the world. Forgive me for speaking so harshly just now."

"Your anger is justified, Mrs. Ward."

"Etty, please," she said. "Are we not good friends?"

He blinked, and a film of moisture shone in his eyes—eyes filled with hope.

"I would not have you tell me you're unworthy, Andrew," she said, "for there's none rarer than a good man—a man ready to right the wrongs of the world, the very imbalances that have given him power over others. But you are not a good man."

The hope in his eyes died. "A-am I not?"

"No," she said gently, tilting her head and offering her lips. "You are the *best* of men."

"Oh, Etty!"

He let out a cry and crushed his lips against hers. Raw need ignited in her body, and she drew her arms around his neck, pulling him close. A groan of need reverberated in his throat, and he thrust his tongue between her lips, curling it around her own and claiming ownership. A ripple of pleasure ran through her body, pooling between her thighs, where a hot, thick pulse of desire began to swell.

Sweet heaven! Was this what it felt like to have pleasure at a man's touch? Not the pain, nor the humiliation at the hands of another, but the warm whisper of delights to come.

Innocent he may be, with his tentative touches and uncertainty in his eyes, but she found him all the more desirable for it. He was no rake seeking his own pleasure, or on a quest for another victim to seduce so he could regale his friends with stories of his conquests at White's and congratulate himself on his virility. No—he was a gentle soul, seeking a pleasure he was yet to understand.

And her heart was in danger of succumbing to the notion that he sought such pleasure with her.

She flicked her tongue against his, and, with a low growl of pleasure that reverberated in her bones, he deepened the kiss. Her breathing grew ragged as her body opened itself to unfathomable sensations—an ache in her center that begged to be eased. She arched her back, and his breath caught. He pulled her hard against him.

His length, hard and insistent, pressed against her thigh, and she froze, beset by the memory of another—the rush of cold air on the skin of her thighs as fleshy, sweaty fingers clutched at her skirts, followed by a searing pain…

She let out a cry, and he froze. Then he broke the kiss and stepped back, his eyes filled with horror.

"S-sweet Lord, Etty—forgive me!" He shook his head, retreating. "I-I didn't mean to…" He lowered his gaze to the bulge in his breeches and shook his head. "I-I know not what came over me. What must you *think?*"

"Andrew…"

"No—do not make excuses for me, Etty. I had no right to treat you in such a manner. Please believe me when I say I'm nothing like…"

She raised her hand, and his voice trailed away. Then she reached out. He stared at her hand for a moment, then took it, sliding his fingers between hers.

"Do not be ashamed, Andrew," she said. "You did nothing I did not want."

"B-but I saw it," he said. "For a brief moment—in your eyes— I *saw* it."

"Saw what?"

"The fear," he said. "The fear all women carry. And more than anything, I want you to trust me, Etty—if you feared me, I could not live with myself."

She curled her hand around his. "I could never fear you, Andrew," she said. "I might admonish you in the most appalling manner—but that does not mean I don't trust you. I cannot admire you any less than I do now."

"Then…"

"I was beset by a memory," she said, "by something—and someone—I'd rather forget. And you help me to forget, Andrew. I want to make new memories, to conquer the old."

His eyes widened and she caught the flare of desire reigniting. Did he, in his innocence, know what she was asking—what she offered him?

Then a voice called out, and he froze.

"I say, vicar!"

Etty flinched at the familiar, sharp tone and turned to see Lady Fulford standing beside the front gate, elegantly attired in a dark-green gown. Beside her stood three similarly attired figures, their pale faces all turned toward her, sporting identical sneers.

"Lady Fulford." Andrew straightened his jacket and smoothed the lapels, then strode toward the gate.

"I was on my way to see you, vicar," Lady Fulford said. "Elizabeth has an invitation, don't you, daughter?"

One of the younger women nodded. "Yes, Mama," she said. "I am to sing at a soiree, to which you're invited."

"How delightful," he said in a tone that conveyed anything but delight.

Etty smiled to herself. Andrew had mentioned the Fulford twins and their voices, which he'd said reminded him of crows scrapping over a carcass in the road.

"And I wanted to discuss the church flowers with you," Lady Fulford continued. "They're in a disgraceful state—I fear they've been quite neglected. You shouldn't entrust them to Mrs. Lewis, though she's a particular friend of mine. My Sarah here is very accomplished in the art of arranging flowers—are you not, my dear?"

"Yes, Mama," another daughter—who was clearly Elizabeth's twin—nodded, and smiled up at Andrew.

Heavens, could the woman be any more obvious in her desperation to foist her offspring onto him?

But how did that make her any different to Etty's own mother? What made the Fulford girls any different to Etty herself?

Lady Fulford then turned her attention toward Etty, who nodded in recognition—but rather than acknowledge her, the woman curled her lip in a sneer again.

"I see you've been visiting the needy, vicar," she said. "Very charitable, I'm sure. But I would counsel you not to spend too much of your time with those who rank so far beneath you. It's unbecoming in a man of your station. Sir John would object."

"But—" he began, but she raised her hand.

"Now, now, vicar, you know better than to contradict your patron's wife," she said, her voice pleasant yet carrying an undertone of threat. "As Sir John was saying to the bishop only last month, a vicar must lead by example when it comes to the moral fiber of the village, and while visits to the needy are a necessary evil of a vicar's vocation, he must always observe propriety when it comes to social calls. And he must never neglect his duties when it comes to tending to the church. Now, I insist you take tea with us now. I wish to discuss the village fete."

"Can it not wait?" he asked.

"I *beg* your pardon? Sir John would have much to say if he learned of your refusal."

Andrew glanced toward Etty.

"Go," she said. "I'll see you tomorrow."

At that moment, the door opened, and Frances appeared in the entrance.

"I thought I heard you, ma'am. You're back ever so late, I…" She caught sight of Lady Fulford, paled, and dipped into a curtsey.

"Oh, is that the Gadd girl?" Lady Fulford said. "Very charitable taking her on, Mrs. Ward. Though I must say I'm disappointed in *you*, vicar. I hear you promised her to Mrs. Ward before consulting my housekeeper on the matter."

"Why should the vicar consult your housekeeper?" Etty asked.

"It's the custom," Lady Fulford replied. "My housekeeper always gets first refusal when the girls in the village go into service." She cast a spiteful glance at Etty. "I trust you're not taking undue advantage of our vicar, Mrs. Ward. He's much respected among the villagers, as well as those among my acquaintance. We quite consider him to belong to us. But then, perhaps we should make allowances, given that you're an incomer and not one of us. Never mind, I'm sure you'll soon learn."

She stared pointedly at Andrew. "Vicar—would you be so

kind?"

Andrew bowed to Etty. "Forgive me, Mrs. Ward," he said. "Thank you for all your help today."

"It was a pleasure," Etty said, her gaze fixed on Lady Fulford, who wrinkled her nose. Then she retreated into the cottage.

Once inside the parlor, she glanced out of the window to see Andrew returning to the village, flanked by two of the Fulford daughters, the matriarch and the third daughter in front.

As she watched them, one of the daughters turned to glance over her shoulder toward the cottage, and Etty's gut twisted at the expression of hatred in the young woman's eyes. She shrank back from the window.

What had Lady Fulford said? *We quite consider him to belong to us.*

Etty had a rival—most likely three rivals—against whom she couldn't hope to compete. Sir John Fulford might be the monster who had caused such misery in the village, but he was merely a lecher, a man driven by base needs. His wife, being a woman with sharp cunning and a desire to destroy her rivals, was infinitely more dangerous—and Lady Fulford was the very last person in the world Etty wanted for an enemy.

CHAPTER FOURTEEN

"**I** WAS MOST astonished to see you with that woman, vicar."

Andrew set his teacup aside. He'd barely had time to sip it before his patroness fired her first arrow.

"I was visiting my parishioners, Lady Fulford," he said, "as is my duty as vicar of the parish."

She set her teacup onto the saucer with a sharp clatter. "Vicar, I feel it only fair to counsel you with regard to your behavior."

"My behavior?" He leaned forward. "Madam, if you wish to make unfounded accusations, I—"

"I wish nothing of the kind," she said, ice in her tone. "Please refrain from raising your voice in front of my daughters."

He glanced toward the trio, who sat with identical attitudes—backs stiff, holding their cups in their right hands, their little fingers crooked as they raised the tea to their lips in unison.

"Vicar, is it of *you* I am thinking," Lady Fulford continued. "You are responsible for the moral welfare of the village, and, as such, you set the example all must follow, and not be led astray."

"I assure you, I'm in no danger of being led astray."

"Ah, but therein lies the danger, my dear vicar," she said. "I only speak out of concern for you—and Sir John would say the same. Even the most steadfast of men can be led into sin by the very worst sort of temptress. In fact, the most steadfast of men is at greater risk, for he is less likely to notice the danger before it is too late." She turned toward her eldest daughter. "Elizabeth, serve the vicar a slice of cake. I wouldn't want him thinking you a poor hostess."

"Yes, Mama."

"I have no need of cake," Andrew said. "My cook would never forgive me if I were unable to finish my supper tonight."

His attempt at a joke was met with a cold stare.

"I insist, vicar. Would you refuse an offer from your patroness? Elizabeth, stop staring and see to it."

The young woman rose from her seat and approached the table, where she cut a slice of cake, casting sly glances in his direction, before placing it on a plate, together with a fork. Then she handed it to Andrew, a hopeful smile on her face—the sort of smile unattached young ladies made in an attempt to appear alluring to prospective suitors.

Ugh. Could the girl be any more obvious? On their return from Shore Cottage, she had clung to his arm with the strength of a drowning man, and he'd only been able to extract himself from her possessive grip when they reached Sandcombe Place and her mother instructed her to take charge and order the tea.

Today wasn't about discussing the village fair—it was about demonstrating the eldest Miss Fulford's prowess as a hostess.

And as a prospective wife.

Andrew suppressed a shudder at the notion, then he glanced up and met Lady Fulford's gaze.

No, Lady Fulford, I assure you, I am quite capable of noticing the danger before it's too late.

And the danger was here, in this very room.

"Your cake, vicar." Lady Fulford gestured to Andrew's plate.

He took a bite, wincing at the texture, which seemed to suck the moisture from his mouth, and the hard lumps of dried fruit that stuck to his teeth. After chewing for a moment, which seemed to make little difference, he conceded defeat, took a mouthful of tea, and swallowed.

"Delicious," he said.

He'd have to include a plea for forgiveness for uttering a

falsehood in tonight's prayer. But a falsehood seemed the safest option with four pairs of eyes focused on his every move—one stern and judgmental, the other three simpering and hopeful.

The eldest Miss Fulford let out a self-satisfied sigh, and her mother patted her arm.

"Quite so, Elizabeth, my dear," she said. "My daughter is accomplished, is she not, vicar? Quite the paragon, though I say it myself. I daresay she would be heralded a jewel if she were to be presented at court."

The daughter, if not the mother, had the grace to blush.

"I flatter myself that our society here is just as elegant as that in London," Lady Fulford continued. "And you, vicar, are a part of that society. We very much consider you as being within our social circle." She arched an expectant eyebrow.

Andrew nodded. "Thank you, Lady Fulford."

"Which is why I find it necessary to remind you of your position here. After what I witnessed today, I fear for your moral welfare."

"My moral welfare is in no danger, Lady Fulford," Andrew said. "A vicar is expected to spend much of his time visiting those of his flock whose need is greater than others'."

"And did you visit those in the greatest need today?"

"I visited most of the cottages in the back lane," he said. "Matthew Dodd and his wife—old Mrs. Penfold. And"—he fixed his gaze on her—"Mrs. Smith."

Her eyes narrowed. "Mrs. Smith—am I expected to know who she is?"

"She was your scullery maid for three years."

She made a dismissive gesture. "Mrs. *Smith*, indeed! Doubtless the world is littered with thousands of *Mrs. Smiths*. What can she have to do with me?"

"You may have known her as Loveday Ford."

Recognition flared in Lady Fulford's eyes. "Vicar, I commend you on your charity, but I must ask you to refrain from mentioning that little slut in front of my daughters. The woman is a hussy who trapped a respectable young man into marriage."

"How did she do that, Mama?" the youngest Miss Fulford asked.

"Caroline, you shall speak no more of the matter!" Lady Fulford cried. "This is not an appropriate topic of conversation for respectable young women." She turned to Andrew. "You see the danger now, vicar? While I applaud your charitable activities, you ought to confine them to something more respectable."

"You believe your daughters to be tainted by association with the more misfortunate souls of the village?" Andrew asked.

Particularly the young women whom your husband seduced to ruination…

Oh, if only he had the courage to utter that last remark out loud, to her face! But what good would it do? He'd merely find himself looking for another parish, given Sir John's penchant for wreaking vengeance on anyone who insulted his wife.

Etty would have no such qualms. Were she here, she'd rise to her feet and open the eyes of Lady Fulford and her preening daughters to the wrongs of the world.

"And as for that woman at Shore Cottage," Lady Fulford continued, "*there's* a den of immorality if ever I saw one!"

"Etty?" Andrew's hand shook, and hot tea splashed into the saucer.

"I *beg* your pardon?"

"I mean…Mrs. Ward."

"Oh, *vicar!*" Lady Fulford said, shaking her head. "It's worse than I feared. Do you not comprehend the danger you're in?"

"Danger?"

She glanced at her daughters. "Girls, would you leave us, please? What I am about to say is not for your ears."

"But Mama—"

"Elizabeth, do as I say. Have I not raised you to obey your elders and betters?"

The eldest Miss Fulford scowled, and Andrew caught a flash of the spite she'd leveled at Etty earlier that afternoon. There was no doubt that she was her mother's daughter. Her veneer of respectability barely concealed a soul defined by entitlement, resentment, and malice. Then she directed a simpering smile at Andrew, rose, and exited the parlor, her sisters in her wake.

After the door closed behind them, Lady Fulford leaned toward Andrew and placed her hand over his. He suppressed a shudder as she gave it a possessive squeeze. What had she said to Etty when she'd encountered them earlier that afternoon?

We quite consider him to belong to us.

"Vicar," she said, "what I'm about to say is out of kindness, and a concern for your moral welfare."

"My *moral welfare* is in safe hands, Lady Fulford," Andrew replied. "I am, after all, a man of the cloth."

"It's precisely that which places you in danger," she said. "I have been concerned for some time, but after what I saw today, it's worse than I feared."

"And what do you fear, Lady Fulford?"

"That you're being tempted from the righteous path, by a"—she leaned closer and lowered her voice—"by a harlot."

"Of whom do you speak?"

"Of Mrs. Ward, of course!" She glanced toward the door. "You may say it's not my place to interfere, but as your patron's wife, I have that right. Do you think I didn't notice what the two of you were doing on her doorstep? In broad daylight?" She shook her head and sighed, as if overcome with horror. "And *in full view of my daughters?*"

Andrew's cheeks warmed with shame. Beset by a powerful need, he'd succumbed to the call of his body, the feel of Etty's soft form against his. Had she not withdrawn from his embrace, he would have taken her, there and then, against her front door. And then she had invited him inside…

No.

Etty was not a temptress. She was merely a good, kind woman—with whom he was falling in love.

"Mrs. Fulford," he said, his voice strained as he struggled to control the desire simmering in his body at the memory of Etty in his arms, "I was merely—"

She raised her hand. "Do not attempt to explain yourself, vicar. You suffer—of course you do. I see it in your eyes, and I hear it in your voice. You are young, and the young are weak. But I consider you blameless in the matter. I know you well, and you have served us faithfully and honorably here at Sandcombe. As to *her*"—she wrinkled her nose—"we know so little of her. But a woman who arrives, unannounced and shrouded in mystery, is not a woman to be trusted. Consider the last woman to take residence in that very same cottage, the one masquerading as a widow. Miss Howard, was it?"

"You mean the Duchess of Whitcombe."

"Duchess she may be, having snared herself a titled husband," Lady Fulford said, "but she came to our village a ruined woman—living among respectable folk, with her head held high as if she were better than the rest of us. She carried a false name and deceived the honest, God-fearing people of Sandcombe. I cannot forgive her for having deceived *you*, vicar—we all noticed your partiality toward her. There is no greater evil than a hussy leading a good man into temptation. I only speak now because I have no wish for you to fall again."

"Mrs. Ward is no hussy, I assure you, Lady Fulford," Andrew said. "She's been very kind, helping me visit the poor in the village."

"And yet she is *another* mysterious woman, arriving unannounced in the village, living apart from the rest of us, styling herself as a widow." She leaned back, shaking her head. "My poor vicar—we are very fond of you here, and hate to see you deceived. But how can you be certain that she is a widow at all?"

"Because she told me so, Lady Fulford."

"As would any woman in her position."

"What are you implying?"

"Oh, my poor, dear young man," she said, sighing. "I am implying nothing. I only tell you this because I am—no, we *all* are—so very fond of you, and have no wish for you to be injured a second time."

"I'm in no danger of injury, Lady Fulford—certainly not by Mrs. Ward."

She lifted her hand to her chest and let out an exaggerated sigh. "Oh, vicar! You know not how relieved I am to hear that. It will make my telling you all the less painful."

"Telling me what?"

"That Mrs. Ward has been entertaining *gentlemen callers.*"

"Gentlemen callers?"

"Hush! It pains me to even speak of such things, much less hear the words fall from your own lips."

"It cannot be true," he said.

"It's to your credit that you refuse to think ill of her, vicar, but I saw him with my own eyes. As did Mrs. Lewis, if you have cause to doubt *my* word."

She arched an eyebrow and tilted her head to one side in the manner of a disappointed nanny on the brink of delivering a punishment.

"Of course I don't doubt your word, Lady Fulford," he said, "but perhaps there's an explanation."

"He arrived at the cottage on horseback, late in the afternoon," she said. "Sir John passed him on the road. Very well turned out, he was—he looked a man of means. I happened to be passing Shore Cottage while out for an evening constitutional..."

"*Happened* to be passing?" Andrew asked.

Her voice took on a sharp edge. "I am at liberty to take a stroll whenever and wherever I choose, vicar, and I often take the path by the sea. The air is beneficial for one's health, as you've said in many a sermon. But that's not the point. The point is, when I passed, I saw a horse at the cottage."

"Mrs. Ward is entitled to receive visitors, Lady Fulford."

"But a gentleman—when she's alone in the house? We're a respectable village, vicar. But that's not the worst of it." She shook her head. "I really don't know whether I ought to tell you—you'd be quite shocked, and I don't know if I'm able to voice the words."

Who the devil did the woman think she was, trying to turn an innocent visit into a scandal? Most likely the gentleman was a physician for Gabriel.

In which case, why hadn't Etty told him? In fact, she had remarked earlier that day that she'd had no visitors.

"I'm sure it was merely a passing visit," Andrew said, ignoring the whispers of doubt in his mind. "A stranger asking for directions, perhaps."

"Would she invite a stranger inside? When I passed the cottage, I saw the two of them in there…*embracing*."

"You must be mistaken, Lady Fulford," he said, "unless you were right outside the cottage with your nose pressed against the window."

"Mistaken?" she said. "I assure you, I was *not* mistaken when I passed by the cottage the next morning and saw the same horse tethered outside."

Andrew jerked back as his chest constricted as if an invisible fist had punched him in the heart.

"Y-you mean…"

She placed her hand over his. "You have no idea how much it pains me to be the one to tell you, vicar," she said. "And I'll not pain you further by speaking more overtly of what I saw. But any reasonable, respectable soul would draw the same conclusion that I have with regards to the status of Mrs. Ward—or whatever her name may be. It must be plain to even the meanest intelligence that the man who visited her was not her husband, but instead, he's her"—she made a random gesture in the air—"*protector*, I believe, is the name for it."

Andrew closed his eyes, willing his mind to deny what he'd heard. But everything Lady Fulford said made sense. Few women hid themselves away in obscurity if they were not running from something, some past sin. And Etty carried a secret—he had seen it in her eyes.

And had she ever said to him outright that her son's father was no longer alive?

No—instead, she had said that Mr. Ward was "no more." A rather strange turn of phrase that Andrew had paid little attention to at the time. Perhaps she had phrased her answer deliberately to avoid uttering a falsehood.

But was not deception a form of falsehood? Why had she not entrusted him with the truth?

And why had she been willing to lead him to believe that she cared for him? Or perhaps she hadn't deliberately deceived him, believing him to be a man of experience, as she was clearly a woman of experience herself. But he *was* inexperienced—untouched and unused to the wiles of women, and more easily deceived because of it.

But though Etty may be the sinner, Andrew couldn't blame her. No, he blamed *him*, whoever he was—the gentleman who had claimed her body in exchange for cash, and therefore believed he had ownership rights over her. The man who, no doubt, had a family living in London while he'd exiled his mistress to the countryside to indulge in conjugal visits when the fancy took him.

But Etty had made no promise to Andrew. Perhaps that was why she withdrew when he'd kissed her—because she had no wish to hurt him. After all, she was only playing the same game that men played when they toyed with the hearts of women.

Except he was not like most men. He was not his brother, a man responsible for a sackful of broken hearts who, when deceived by a woman, drank a toast to a worthy adversary before moving on to the next conquest. Neither was he the Duke of Whitcombe—or the lover Etty welcomed into her home.

How could I have been such a fool?

"You've not been a fool, vicar."

He opened his eyes to see Lady Fulford staring at him, the sympathy in her eyes marred by the undertone of triumph.

"Some women are cunning," she said, "but not all of us. And

never fear—you have friends in Sandcombe, and we'll do our utmost to ensure that you find a wife who deserves you."

He heard footsteps outside and glanced across the parlor to see a shadow on the floor beneath the door.

"Elizabeth!" Lady Fulford called out.

The door opened after a suspiciously short pause to reveal the three Fulford sisters. "Yes, Mama?" the eldest said.

"Girls, would you attend the vicar, please?" Lady Fulford said. "Elizabeth, a brandy, I think."

Before Andrew could protest, the eldest Miss Fulford approached a side table, unstoppered a decanter, and splashed a generous amount of brown liquid into a beveled glass. Then she thrust it in his hand and sat beside him, her wide-eyed gaze fixed on him.

"Our poor vicar has had a nasty shock, girls," Lady Fulford said. "But we'll take care of him, won't we? He deserves so much better, don't you agree?"

"Oh *yes*, Mama," Elizabeth said, leaning closer to Andrew.

Cringing at the expectation in the young woman's gaze, Andrew raised the glass to his lips and swallowed a mouthful of brandy. The acrid liquid stung the back of his throat, and he caught his breath. He took another mouthful, and another, until he'd drained the glass. Then he held out the empty glass for more.

He might have to add yet another plea for forgiveness in his nightly prayers for being a toper—but perhaps the Almighty would forgive him, given that the pain in his heart was punishment enough.

CHAPTER FIFTEEN

ETTY LAY ON the blanket, relishing the warmth of the sun on her skin. She drew in a lungful of fresh sea air while the waves whispered as they danced across the shore.

What could be better than a picnic by the sea? Particularly on a day such as today, where the heat would have rendered the air oppressive were it not for the breeze.

"More lemonade, Mrs. Ward?"

"Mmm?"

She opened her eyes and rolled onto her side, wincing at the soreness in her right leg. Frances sat cross-legged on the blanket, a glass in her hand, while Gabriel sat beside her, his fat pink fist clutching a slice of fruitcake.

"I made it special—Ma's recipe." Frances drew a stoneware bottle from the basket, and Gabriel let out a cry of joy and reached for it.

"Me! Me!"

"No, sweetheart, you must let your mama have some first," Frances said.

The boy let out a wail. "I want some!"

"You don't like it, sweetheart," Frances said. "Don't you remember the last time I gave you some?"

Etty smiled at the memory. Her son had unceremoniously spat a mouthful of lemonade into Mrs. Gadd's face. Then he'd collapsed into a fit of giggles and Mrs. Gadd had followed suit.

"Bot—bot," the boy said, stretching toward the bottle. He lost his balance and fell face forward onto the blanket. Etty braced herself for the tears, but he merely giggled, and Frances tickled his neck.

"Funny boy!" she said affectionately. "How about I give you the bottle when we've finished the lemonade? You could fill it with water from the sea—though mind you don't drink it. Seawater's bad for you."

"Yes," Etty said, ruffling the boy's hair. "The sea is for bathing in, not drinking."

"Would you like to paddle in the sea, Gabriel?" Frances asked. "Chase the waves and see if they catch you?" She pointed toward the sea. "Look—the waves are dancing in and out, asking you to play with them."

"Sea! Sea!" Gabriel scrambled to his feet and teetered across the sand.

"I think that's a yes," Etty said, smiling.

"He's a lovely boy," Frances said. "I adore him. And he takes such pleasure in everything."

"That he does." Etty sighed.

Unlike his mother at his age.

Etty's pleasure in life, even as a child, always seemed to be marred by the expectation of perfection. Mother had always said it wasn't done for a young woman of her rank to merely enjoy what she had. She must always strive for more. But a wish to better oneself was only to be admired if it came without a sense of disdain for everything.

Gabriel, with his innocent enthusiasm for everything placed before him and his joy in everything he saw, was everything Etty wasn't—and everything she wished to be.

To think—had she not had Gabriel, she'd never have known the simple joy of feeling the sand beneath her feet. No matter the path her life had taken, she had much to be grateful for. Most of all, her son.

Gabriel rushed toward the water, tripped, and toppled over.

He let out a wail, and Frances leaped to her feet.

"Oh, sweet boy—have you taken a tumble in the sand?" She laughed. "Just look at that big footprint you've made. Or should that be a Gabriel-print?"

The boy giggled and reached for her hand.

"Would you like to take a paddle?" Frances asked. She turned to Etty. "Perhaps your mama might join us."

"Mama—Mama!" Gabriel reached toward Etty. She stood and took his free hand. Then, between them, she and Frances walked him to the edge of the water.

"One, two, three…" Frances said, then Etty joined her in a final flourish of "Up we go!" and they swung the little boy into the air while he giggled with mirth.

"Shall we go again?" Etty asked.

"Yes, Mama, yes!"

Between them, Etty and Frances swung him up again, and this time he landed in the water, catching the edge of a wave. The boy jumped up and down, sending splashes of water sideways, which soaked Etty's dress.

"Oh, ma'am—your gown!" Frances cried. "I'm ever so sorry."

"There's nothing to be sorry for, Frances," Etty replied. "I can't remember enjoying myself as much. In fact…" She gazed out over the sea, the shades of blue and green, the coolness beckoning to her as respite from the heat. "Is it wicked of me to want to bathe in the sea?"

"Why would it be wicked, Mrs. Ward?" Frances asked. "And it would be good for your leg. That was a right nasty graze you got when you fell off that ladder yesterday. Beggin' your pardon, ma'am, but I did tell you to wait until our Jimmy could come over and prune that rose."

"I don't need a man to take care of me, Frances," Etty said. "And I certainly don't need a man to prune the roses around the door."

"I'm not saying you couldn't climb the ladder, ma'am—only that I didn't want you hurting yourself."

"It's nothing, Frances," Etty said.

"But it hurts, doesn't it, ma'am?" Frances said. "I can see it in your eyes. And there's nothing better than seawater to help with cuts and grazes. That's what my ma says, anyways. Vicar says it also, and he's *never* wrong."

An expression of devotion filled the girl's eyes. Heavens—was there nobody in the village who *wasn't* smitten with Andrew?

Etty gazed at the water, striving to conquer the longing. "I don't know…"

"Well, I do," Frances said.

Etty smiled inwardly at the girl's newfound boldness. Frances had blossomed into a confident young girl after a month in her employ. Perhaps, released from the shadow of her origins, she was now able to express herself more freely and no longer suffer guilt for merely existing.

"Folk rarely come to this part of the beach if that's what you're worryin' about, ma'am," Frances said.

"I've nothing to dry myself with," Etty said.

"There's the blanket."

Yes, there was—and Etty's undergarments were thin enough to dry quickly on such a hot day. Which only left…

Etty reached behind her gown and unknotted her sash. Moments later, she stood in her undergarments, her dress hooked over Frances's arm.

"Mama swim!" Gabriel cried.

"Yes, darling boy," Etty said. "Your mama's going for a swim."

"*Me* swim!"

"Perhaps another time, sweetheart."

"Swim! Swim!" the boy cried, his voice rising.

"Not here, Gabriel," Frances said. "The currents are strong and might pull you under. But I can teach you to swim in the lake by my pa's farm. How about that?"

"Lake! Lake!"

"Not today, my love," Etty said. "You say the currents are

strong here, Frances?"

The girl nodded. "Only at certain times. Along this part of the beach there's a current that can pull you out to sea. You can see it sometimes—a patch of water calmer than the rest of the sea, stretching outward, like a column."

"Is it dangerous?"

"Only if you can't swim and don't know what to do."

"And what do you do?"

"You have to swim *across* it," Frances said, "to one side, rather than back toward the beach, until you can no longer feel the current. Then it's safe to swim back."

"Has it happened to you, Frances?"

The girl shook her head. "Jimmy got caught in it once, but the vicar was there and told him what to do. He's ever so kind, isn't he, the vicar?"

"Yes," Etty said, "he is."

The memory of Andrew's kiss still lingered on her lips. Only last night she'd woken from a dream where he'd claimed her, bringing her to pleasure—but it was a pleasure she couldn't quite understand. In the dream she'd cried his name, but for what? Some unfathomable, imaginary sensation.

What *was* pleasure?

She shuddered at the memory of Dunton's words.

Pleasure is for the man to savor and for the woman to give.

A hand caught hers.

"Ma'am?"

Etty blinked and glanced toward Frances, who stared at her with compassion in her eyes.

"You'll feel better after your swim, I'm sure, ma'am," she said. "It'll help your body to heal—and perhaps"—she blushed and hesitated—"if I may be so bold, it'll help your heart to heal also."

Such insight for a young girl—a village child whom Etty would never have deigned to notice before. Meek, mild, an outcast from society.

A misfit, like me.

But, perhaps, the world misunderstood misfits at its peril.

Etty strode into the water.

"Mama!" Gabriel jumped up and down, laughing, while Frances held his hand.

"What's it like?"

"Wonderful!" Etty laughed at the tickling sensation on her skin as the waves crashed against her feet, moving toward the shore, then retreating, forming a plume of water against her calves. She winced at the sting of the salt water on her grazed skin.

"Too cold to swim?" Frances asked.

"If I were a man, I'd consider that question a challenge," Etty said. "And we're as good as men, are we not, Frances?"

"We're better!"

"That we are."

Before her courage failed, Etty rushed forward to meet an oncoming wave, then plunged into the water.

Her chest constricted at the cold, and she drew in a sharp breath, but she struck out with her arms and swam beyond the wave where the water was calmer, shifting up and down in a gentle swell. At length, the shock of the cold subsided, and she let out a cry of joy.

"Look, Gabriel! Look at your mama!"

Etty turned, treading water, to see Frances on the shoreline, a laughing Gabriel in her arms. She raised her hand in a wave, then turned over to float on her back and look up at the sky. Such an extraordinary shade, rich and pure. Perhaps it reflected the color of the sea. It was so unlike the skies of London, which had always carried a note of gray, as if the town drained the world of its natural beauty.

She drew in a deep breath, the air rushing in her ears, then closed her eyes. Her son's far-off laughter was punctuated by the cries of the seabirds circling above the cliffs and the rushing of the water. The sounds of nature.

Then another cry rose—a distant voice roaring, as if in pain.

Frances stood by the shore, Gabriel clutching at her skirts, the wide expanse of sand and the cliff rising beyond.

Then Etty saw it—a figure stumbling down the path, arms waving.

What was he doing?

A voice cried out, then the figure lost balance and tumbled to the foot of the path.

Then Etty heard Frances calling something, but the rush of the water in her ears obliterated the words. She kicked out and swam toward the shore.

"Frances!" she cried. "I'm coming!"

The figure in black struggled to its feet and continued running toward the shore, and Etty's heart stuttered as she recognized the vicar.

He wasn't running toward Frances. He was running toward her.

"Out!" he cried. "Get out!"

"What's wrong?" she called.

She continued to swim toward the shore, but he gave no sign of stopping. As the water grew shallower, she reached out with her feet and, gaining purchase, stood, the water reaching her waist.

"For the love of the Almighty—get out of the sea, you foolish woman!"

His voice hoarse and laced with fury, he shouted once more, then ran straight into the sea, the waves crashing about his legs, soaking his breeches.

"Andrew, don't be a fool!" she cried as he bore down on her.

"I'm not the fool!" he yelled. "Dear God, what were you *thinking*?" He lunged forward and grasped her arms. "How could you be so reckless?" he cried. "Do you *want* to drown?"

She winced as he tightened his grip. "Of course I don't want to drown!" she retorted. "I *can* swim, you know."

"But you don't know about the currents here." He glanced

over his shoulder. "Why didn't you stop her, Frannie? I never took you for a simpleton. You know about the currents, foolish girl!"

"That's enough!" Etty cried. "You may insult me all you like, but leave Frances alone. I chose to swim. Frances told me about the currents—and what to do."

He thrust his face close, an inferno of fury and fear in his eyes. "It's too great a risk to take, Etty," he said. "You have a child— would you abandon him? Do you care so little for him that you'd leave him motherless?"

"How dare you!" she cried. "I love my son more than any-thing. Do you think I'm so reckless as to ignore my son's needs— the needs of others?"

"But you *are* reckless," he said. "You have no comprehension of what you have done in coming here. Sandcombe is not somewhere you can toy with when you've grown bored of your former life. It's a living entity—a community of real people with real lives. I was content in my life before you arrived. Of all the places in the world, why did you have to come *here?*"

His voice cracked, and the initial anger gave way to pain. He drew in a shuddering breath.

"Andrew—" she began.

"No!" he cried. "Do *not*. I…" He shuddered then lowered his gaze to her neckline and drew in a sharp breath, his nostrils flaring. "Dear God—why must I be tempted so? What have I done to deserve such torment?"

Then he let out a groan and pulled her close.

Etty glanced down and let out a cry. Her undergarments clung to her body, revealing every curve, every outline. The water had rendered the material transparent, to reveal the pink swell of her breasts, and two peaks pressing against the material.

"Oh, Etty…" he rasped, lifting his hand to her breast. A fizz of need rushed through her as he brushed his knuckles against her nipple, which beaded against his hand. "Sweet Lord…" He flicked his tongue out, running it along his lower lip.

Like a starving man ready to feast.

"Andrew," Etty said, "your breeches—you'll ruin them."

She lowered her gaze, and her breath caught at the bulge in his breeches, his manhood straining for release.

"No…" he groaned, his voice laced with pain. "I cannot endure it—such torture…"

He closed his eyes, his body shaking. When he opened them again, they glistened with moisture, and Etty's heart ached at the agony in their depths.

He tilted his head to the sky. "What punishment is this?" he cried. "What have I done to deserve such torment? I have served you well, have I not? You cannot ask more of me!"

A tear splashed onto his cheek, and she reached toward him, but he slapped her hand away.

"No! Do not touch me!" He retreated, the waves crashing about his feet, and she followed, but he raised his hand. "Don't come any closer!"

"Andrew, I—"

"Do *not*!"

She froze at the fury in his voice. Then he glanced toward Frances, who stood by the water line, Gabriel clutching her hand. He let out another cry, then turned and fled.

"Vicar!" Frances said, but he ignored her, sprinting toward the cliff path before ascending. Halfway up, he stumbled, and his cry echoed across the air, but he struggled to his feet and toiled on until he disappeared over the top of the cliff.

"Oh ma'am!" Frances wailed. "I'm sorry. It's all my fault—it's *always* my fault! What must he think of us?"

Etty approached the quivering girl and drew her into her embrace. "It's *not* your fault, Frances, sweetheart," she said. "You are not to blame. Not for this or anything else. And it matters not what he—or any other man—thinks of us."

"Ma will be ever so angry when she finds out."

"She won't find out, Frances. Besides, there's nothing to tell. I went for a swim and the vicar suffered some sort of fit of hysterics."

"But Ma said I can be a bad child sometimes. She said—"

"Then she's *wrong*," Etty said, gritting her teeth, "and if your mother, or anyone else in the village, says anything bad about you again, they'll have *me* to answer to."

She clung to the young girl and her son. Three outsiders in a village filled with secrets—dark secrets and injustices that it preferred to bury.

And she would always be an outsider, unwelcome and unwanted. Why else would he have uttered those words that pierced her heart?

I was content in my life before you arrived. Of all the places in the world, why did you have to come here?

CHAPTER SIXTEEN

"I MUST SAY, vicar, that was a most...*unusual* sermon."

Lady Fulford stopped in the doorway and fixed Andrew with a stare, oblivious to, or most likely not caring one jot for, the rest of the congregation waiting behind her to exit the church.

Sir John stood beside her, the expression on his fleshy face conveying indifference, save the gleam of spite in his eyes.

"There is much to say about the sins of men, Lady Fulford," Andrew said.

"But considerably more about the temptation of women, vicar," Sir John said. "I would advise you not to instill an excess of modernity in your sermons."

"Modernity?"

"Quite so," Lady Fulford said. "The world thrives under a state of order, and on everyone knowing their rightful place."

"Including women?"

"*Especially* women," Sir John said, his vehemence releasing a droplet of spittle that settled on his chin.

"We are all weak in the eyes of the Almighty," Andrew said. "The greatest attribute we can possess is the humility to recognize our own failings and the willingness to atone for them."

"Granted, those of us with failings must recognize them—but it's up to those of us *without* such failings to restore order." Sir John stepped aside to let the rest of the congregation pass, ignoring most, but giving the occasional curt nod to those he deemed worthy, such as Mrs. Lewis, and Mr. and Mrs. Ham. "Look at them all," he said, a sneer in his tone. "Where would they be without men of my station? Is it not godly to know one's place in life?"

At that moment, Loveday Smith filed past with her husband. She drew in a sharp breath, glanced up at Sir John, and stiffened.

"Come along, woman," her husband growled. "Don't be makin' a show of me."

"Forgive me, Ralph," she said quietly, and clung to his arm as he steered her along the path to the lychgate.

"Now *there's* a man who knows his place," Sir John said. "And he knows to keep his woman in line, lest she stray."

Andrew's stomach churned, and he caught his breath to temper the rise of nausea in his throat.

"Of course, some men are less able to withstand temptation," Sir John continued, fixing his gaze on Andrew. "Perhaps your sermon was directed at them. But you must warn the weak minded against those who seek to tempt the unwary—sirens who draw men to their ruination by playing on their baser needs."

At that moment, Etty crossed the threshold.

Their gazes met, and Andrew's body tightened at the memory of last night, when, alone in his chamber, he'd succumbed to the same *base needs* that Sir John spoke of.

A faint blush colored her cheeks, and her eyes widened. The intensity of the blue only served to increase his shame. Did she know his thoughts, his desires? Surely she must after he'd conveyed them so plainly yesterday. Not with words, perhaps, but the violence of his body's reaction was such that even the most innocent of creatures would be in no doubt of the sinful urges that had raged through his blood.

Ye gods—had Frannie not been standing beside the shore, he'd have been unable to stop himself. He would have thrown Etty to the ground and taken her among the waves to ease the torrent of lust in his soul. His manhood had surged in his breeches, yearning to be buried inside that delectable body bared to him through those flimsy petticoats. His mouth had watered at the sight of those perfectly rounded breasts with their dark pink nipples beckoning to him.

What had begun as an almost paralyzing fear when he'd seen her swimming, exposing herself to those treacherous currents—a fear so potent that his body ached with it—had morphed in an instant to the most powerful, uncontrollable lust. His senses had been beset by the most primal of needs—a need that his rational mind had been unable to conquer.

The need to mate.

He—an educated man, in a trusted position where he set the moral standard that elevated him above the ordinary—was nothing more than a beast. The ugly stains in his breeches were evidence enough of his savagery. But, not content with that, he'd stroked himself to pleasure while he lay alone in his cold bed last night, crying her name as he came to completion—only to wake to the cold light of dawn, beset by shame and self-loathing as he caught sight of the stains on his bedsheets.

But he could not bring himself to pray for forgiveness. Not because he feared that the prayer—as every other prayer he'd uttered—would go unanswered, but because a wicked little corner of his soul had relished the pure bliss of completion. That dark essence inside him believed that there was nothing to forgive.

And what was the merit in seeking forgiveness for a sin that he was bound to repeat, seeking satisfaction at his own hand as some small compensation that he could never seek pleasure at hers?

"Vicar!"

Lady Fulford's voice returned him to the present, and he swallowed his shame at the realization that he'd been staring at Etty. "Yes, Lady Fulford?"

"I was saying that I require you to visit this afternoon, to discuss the village fete. I'm not satisfied that the new tenants at

Newford Farm are making enough of an effort, and there's barely a fortnight before the event. And Mrs. Dodds is making an awful business of the cake stall. She seems to have forgotten that the success of the village fete reflects upon us."

"Can you not speak to them?" Andrew asked.

"You're the vicar," she replied. "It's your duty to manage these things, and not be distracted by temptation."

"I assure you, Lady Fulford, I'm not so distracted by temptation that I cannot undertake my duties properly," Andrew said.

"Good. Then I shall see you at three o'clock." The edict delivered, she turned her attention to her husband. "Well, Sir John?"

"Yes—yes, of course, my dear. Vicar." He gave Andrew a curt nod, then escorted his wife away. The rest of the congregants parted to make room, leaving Etty standing in the doorway, Frannie beside her, holding Etty's child in her arms.

"Mrs. Ward, might I have a word—in private?" Andrew asked, glancing toward Frannie.

"You have nothing to say to me that Frances cannot hear," Etty replied, her voice tight.

"Nevertheless, I ask."

She sighed. "Very well. Frances, sweetheart, perhaps you'd like to spend some time with Freda? I'm sure Gabriel would enjoy a little walk."

"Yes, Mrs. Ward."

"You can tell Freda about the vicar's sermon," Etty added. "Particularly the passage about the responsibility of men and how those in a position of power must not be permitted to abuse it."

Andrew's cheeks warmed. Could she make him feel any more ashamed?

After Frannie had disappeared around the side of the church, Etty fixed her clear blue gaze on him. "Well?"

"I-I wanted to apologize," Andrew said.

"What for?"

"For yesterday."

She tilted her head to one side. "Much happened yesterday,

Mr. Staines. If I am to appreciate and accept your apology, I must at least understand the transgression you believe yourself to have committed."

"I-I fear I may have acted inappropriately toward you."

She folded her arms.

Heavens—this is going to be harder than anticipated.

"And…I wish to convey my apologies and promise that I will not do so again."

"What part of your behavior yesterday did you deem inappropriate?" she asked.

For a brief moment, her gaze flicked toward his breeches before she resumed her attention on him, and he shifted his legs to ease the ache in his groin.

"A man cannot be blamed for…"

"For responding to the temptations of women?" she said. "Are those your words, vicar, or Sir John's?"

"I-I was afraid," he said. "I was angry with you, but that anger came from fear."

Her expression softened and his heart ached as she placed a hand on his sleeve. "Afraid of what?"

"Afraid *for* you," he said. "When I saw you in the sea, I couldn't help myself. The thought of you, in danger, in those currents…"

"I was in no danger, vicar," she said. "I'm a strong swimmer. But I thank you for your concern." She smiled. "I confess, I've raised my voice at Gabriel many times when he's placed himself in danger. Anger is a natural reaction when you fear for someone about whom you care."

Why must she say such a thing? Did she not realize the pain it caused, knowing that she was attached to another?

"I-I will not plague you again," he said. "I have no right. Not considering…" He was unable to articulate the words. Voicing it would only confirm the reality.

"Considering what?" she asked softly.

He shook his head.

"Andrew?"

The tenderness with which she whispered his name breached his defenses.

"Considering that you love another," he said.

"I… *What?*"

"I don't blame you, Etty," he said. "I'm not like Sir John. I'd never blame a woman for the position she's placed in. The man must shoulder equal responsibility, if not more."

He paused, but she said nothing, her gaze fixed on him.

"A-and I know we're friends," he added. "Just friends. I'm *content* for us to be friends. It's unthinkable of me to assume…" He shook his head.

Bloody hell, I'm making a mess of this.

He lowered his gaze in shame, wincing at the profanity, even if only uttered in his mind.

"Andrew?"

His heart ached at her soft voice, filled with compassion, if not the love he'd hoped and prayed for.

"Andrew, there's no shame in—"

"No!" he interrupted. "Please do not say it, for it can never be unsaid. I only feel shame for what my feelings have been. But I shall always admire you, no matter your circumstances. I shall always be your friend—your very good friend. A woman must survive in the world in which she's placed. She can never wholly be mistress of her fate. And therefore I will not blame you, nor judge you."

She withdrew her hand, and he glanced up to see her staring at him, her face pale.

"Judge me for what?" she asked. "For Gabriel?"

"For Gabriel's father."

She flinched. "Y-you know…"

He nodded. "He was seen. Your…"

"My *what?*"

He leaned toward her and lowered his voice. "Your protector. Mrs. Fulford saw him—as did Mrs. Lewis."

Her brow furrowed. "Since when do you trade in gossip, vicar?"

"I didn't relish the account, believe me," he said, "and you can trust me not to tell others."

"Oh, *can* I?" she said. "That's so benevolent of you."

"I don't blame you," he said. "I never would."

"Your benevolence has no limit."

He flinched at the hard edge to her voice. "I'm not criticizing you, Etty," he said, "and I will defend you against those who do."

She stared at him.

"Do you have nothing to say?" he asked.

"Only this."

He caught a blur of movement as she raised her arm, then pain exploded in his cheek as she delivered a slap across his face. His head snapped sideways with the force of her blow, and he staggered back, rubbing his skin.

"How *dare* you!" she cried. "What right have you to judge me?"

"I told you I'd never judge—"

"It matters not what you *tell* me, vicar," she snarled. "In my life I've learned that I can never trust another soul based on what they tell me—I can only trust what they *do*."

"I'm not judging you, Etty."

"Then how would you define *this*?" She gestured toward him. "Your sanctimonious lecture about the sins of men and how us weak women are to be pitied when we succumb to the need to tempt your sex. And so, you believe the first story you hear about me—from the village busybody—that I am some man's mistress? Did she perhaps tell you that I've established a bawdy house in her precious village?"

"Do you deny that a man visited you?" he asked.

"I deny nothing."

"And…that he stayed the night?"

Her eyes flashing with outrage, she looked every part the lady of dignity, venting her disappointment at the unworthy soul who'd caused offense.

"I deny *nothing*," she repeated. The anger had gone from her voice—replaced by cold, hard ice.

"Then who…" He trailed off as she arched an eyebrow in the manner of a disappointed schoolmistress. "I have no right to ask."

"On *that*, if nothing else, vicar, we are in agreement," she said. "Nobody has the right to poke their noses into my affairs— not Mrs. Fulford, nor Mrs. Lewis, nor anybody in this accursed village. And especially not you."

"Etty, I—"

"You have said quite enough, sir," she said. Then she turned toward the churchyard. "Frances, sweetheart! Are you ready?"

"Yes, ma'am," a voice called, and shortly after, Frannie appeared, Gabriel at her side. Etty rushed forward and embraced them, and Andrew's heart ached at the love in her eyes, a love she had for her child, for the girl she'd taken in—and, most likely, for the man with whom he could never compete. Then, without a backward glance, the three of them retreated down the path and through the lychgate. He watched them toil along the road until they disappeared out of sight.

Chapter Seventeen

COULD THE FATE of Loveday Smith get any worse? Not only had her mother died in the night, but Loveday herself had sustained another injury—this time a graze to her side. Yet she continued to blame her clumsiness rather than the real perpetrator.

It was so unfair. The world was so *unfair!*

Etty's only consolation was that the poor creature's brute of a husband was away from home until the end of the harvest—no doubt wielding his thick arms and gruff words at Newford Farm.

With luck he'll have an unfortunate encounter with a scythe.

Then she checked herself. There was little virtue in lowering herself to Ralph Smith's level. Hateful as the man may be, it was not up to Etty to ensure he reaped the rewards of his sins. All she could do was protect his wife from further harm as far as she was able.

But were a handful of bandages and a jar of salve sufficient to keep Loveday safe—not to mention those poor children of hers?

Darkness had descended, though it couldn't have been far past noon, and Etty shivered as the wind penetrated her shawl and clawed at her bonnet, picking up dust from the road, which swirled around before dissipating in the air. The trees seemed to lean at an unnatural angle, their leaves turning to reveal silvery undersides, giving the landscape an eerie glow despite the fading light.

Etty adjusted the basket on her arm and continued along the path, nodding in acknowledgment to Mr. Ham as she passed the Merry Sailor. The innkeeper touched his cap.

"Afternoon, Mrs. Ward. Been to see Mrs. Smith again, have ye?"

"Yes, Mr. Ham," Etty replied. "Frances has been baking fruit-cakes for the fete, and she made one extra. But don't tell Loveday we made it specifically for her or she'll insist I take it back."

"You're a good lass," he said, "always visiting Mrs. Smith—and on a day such as this, when there's a storm coming."

"A storm?"

"Aye." He gestured to the trees. "See that? My ma always said that's the trees givin' their warning—like a rabbit's scut."

"A *what*?"

He let out a chuckle. "Ye're a Town lass, all right! It's the rabbit's tail, which he flashes to his kin when there's danger afoot, to tell them to take shelter. The trees do the same, my ma says, with their leaves, flashing their pale undersides to warn us folk of an oncoming storm. Some folk pass them off as old wives' tales meant to frighten incomers, but most of them hold true. Loveday all right, is she?"

"She's a little frail today, Mr. Ham."

He nodded. "Aye, poor lass, what with her ma passin' and all, she's got no one to take those girls off her hands. She's always ailing for something, and daughters are always such a handful."

"And I suppose sons aren't?" Etty said, swallowing her irritation.

"Fair dos, Mrs. Ward," he said good-naturedly. "Our Tom was a right tearaway when he was young Florence's age. But my Mary is a strong 'un and knows how to handle twenty boys. She can handle *me*, all right." He grinned. "Not that I mind—she's a fine, strong lass, is my Mary. Always has been. As for Loveday Smith, she was never a sickly child, but some women fade when they become mothers—takes it out of them, it does. Now, as for my Mary, she was as hale and hearty as ever she could be after our Tommy arrived. Mind you, that's not to say Tommy wasn't a handful. Mary had a lot to say about him when he was a little 'un. 'Jim,' she used to say, 'Jim, I swear that boy's going to be more trouble than all the lads in the village combined.' But he's a good lad, really. We thought he might do for Loveday before she married Ralph, but she'd already gone into service at the big house, and Mrs. Fulford's housekeeper was very strict about gentleman callers. In fact—"

"Forgive me, Mr. Ham, but I'm rather cold," Etty said. "I really should get back. I don't want to leave Frances on her own."

Heavens! Whoever said women were the purveyors of gossip while the men stayed silent had clearly not met Mr. Ham.

"Oh, beggin' yer pardon, Mrs. Ward," he said, chuckling. "I do prattle on so—my Mary is always pulling me up for it. 'Jim,' she says, 'Jim, you've a tongue on you as long as—'"

He broke off at the sound of thunder in the distance.

"There's the storm," he said. "Best get yerself home before it takes hold. If you're fit to wait a bit, I can hook Bessie up to the cart and take you over meself."

"You're very kind, Mr. Ham, but I'll be all right," Etty said, glancing at the sky.

"Hurry yerself, then, lass," he said. "Storms are known hereabouts for coming in quickly. You'll not want to be caught in it." He removed his cap and bowed his head, then returned inside the inn.

The sign over the door creaked as it swayed to and fro in the wind. Then another rumble echoed in the air, and Etty drew her shawl about her shoulders and set off, quickening her pace as droplets of rain spattered on her face.

By the time she passed the church, the rain was falling more steadily, soaking through her shawl and dripping off the brim of her bonnet. She shivered as she caught sight of the red rooftop of the vicarage—but it wasn't due to the cold.

How could Andrew have said such wicked things to her? How could he believe her to be a harlot, a woman who sold her body such that she might live under a man's protection, a kept whore living in obscurity, servicing a man old enough to be her...

She shuddered. Even the thought of it could not be borne.

But could he blamed for having made such an assumption? After all, she had been deceiving him, and the rest of the village, from the day she arrived. They believed her a respectable widow, when in fact she was a ruined woman with the natural child of the man she'd attempted to seduce into matrimony.

Which made her no different to a harlot—worse, because she hid behind a veil of respectability.

Not to mention her act of spite against her sister. Whereas a woman's desperation for security in a man's world might justify her ruination, nothing could justify Etty's deliberate attempt to ruin Eleanor.

What might her life have been like had she taken a different path?

I only feel shame for what my feelings have been.

What had Andrew meant? Had he loved her, only to retreat in shame at the notion of her ruination?

The rain began to fall more steadily now, blurring the air and turning the road into a quagmire. A dark shape shifted by the side of the road, and Etty's stomach clenched with fear. The shape seemed to increase in size, and she stumbled back. Her foot slipped on a stone and she turned her ankle, almost losing her balance. She tipped her head to the sky, letting the rain assault her face.

"Oh, what have I done?" she cried. "Must I be punished forever?"

The shape moved toward her, seeming to float in the air, and she leaped back with a scream. Her feet slipped and she tumbled backward, bracing herself for the impact.

But it never came.

A solid body collided with hers and pulled her hard against a broad male chest.

"Steady there!" a voice cried. "I have you."

She looked up into a pair of chocolate-brown eyes, their warmth in sharp contrast to the storm—a pair of eyes in a face she had grown to love, even though its owner had branded her a whore.

Her gut twisted with shame, and she struggled in his arms, but he held her firm.

"Leave me be!" she cried.

Another rumble of thunder filled the air, and she winced at the sharp crack overhead, as if the sky were tearing in two.

"I can't leave you out in the storm!" he said over the thunder. "Come inside."

"No—I must get home."

"You'll catch a chill if you remain outside much longer," he said. "You're soaked already, and the storm's right overhead."

"Andrew," she sobbed, "I—"

"No," he said, "I'll *not* see your life in danger a second time. I care not what you say, I'll brook no argument. Etty, trust me to take care of you."

His kindness had more power to breach her defenses than his sanctimoniousness, and she yielded, clinging to his greatcoat. He swept her into his arms as if she weighed no more than Gabriel and carried her toward the vicarage, yelling for his housekeeper.

With gentle hands and soft words, he tended to her, wrapping her in a blanket and placing her by the fire, issuing orders to his housekeeper, then absenting himself from the room while the older woman helped Etty remove her wet clothes and helped her into one of her gowns before settling her into a chair. Finally, he returned with a tray bearing a steaming bowl of soup, a plate of sandwiches, cheese and cold meats, and a pot of tea.

"Oh, vicar, you should have left me to do that!" the housekeeper scolded him.

"Mrs. Clegg, a bachelor is quite capable of taking care of himself," Andrew said, placing the tray on a table.

She let out a huff. "Not in my experience. But seeing as you'll not listen to reason, I'll leave you to it." She straightened the blanket around Etty's knees. "Is there anything else before I leave, sir?"

"Yes," Andrew replied. "Send Samuel to Shore Cottage to tell Frannie Gadd that her mistress is safe."

"There's no need," Etty said.

"There's *every* need," he replied, taking her hand.

The housekeeper arched her eyebrows, then nodded. "I'll see to it," she said before exiting the parlor.

Andrew released Etty's hand, then picked up the soup bowl.

"Andrew…"

"Indulge me," he said, ignoring her protest. "You're cold, yes?"

She nodded.

"Then this is the best medicine to ward off a chill. My cook would be most put out if I returned with an untouched soup bowl."

"Then why don't you drink it yourself?"

He frowned, and she swallowed her guilt at her sharp tone.

"Forgive me," he said. "I seem incapable of saying the right thing. When I strive not to hurt those dearest to me, I only succeed in causing more pain."

He dipped the spoon into the soup and lifted it, a plea in his eyes. A simple act of appeasement.

"Sorry," he whispered.

She reached toward his hand, and his eyes narrowed, as if he expected her to slap it away. Instead, she took his hand, guided the spoon into her mouth, and swallowed.

The flavor of beef, rich and warm, burst on her tongue.

"Do you like it?"

Her heart melted at the eagerness in his voice—reminiscent of a child who'd brought a gift to an adult whom he was desperate to please.

She nodded. "It's delicious. Please pass my thanks to your cook."

His mouth curved into a grin and his eyes sparkled with

pleasure. "I'm so glad you like it!" he said. "I warmed it up myself."

She suppressed a laugh at the notion of a man taking pride in something so simple as warming up a broth—a broth that, given the depth of flavor, his cook would have been simmering overnight, before straining it to remove the impurities.

Then she checked herself and smiled. Two years ago she wouldn't have even deigned to enter a kitchen, let alone learn the art of making a good broth. She had no right to laugh at his ignorance.

After she finished the soup, he took the bowl from her hands, then poured the tea, handed her a cup, and sat in a chair opposite.

She glanced toward the window, where the sky was already beginning to lighten.

"The storm seems to have passed," she said.

He nodded. "Storms come and go quickly here."

"So Mr. Ham said when I passed him earlier."

"When was that?"

"Just before the storm came."

"And he left you to walk home?" He let out a huff. "Foolish man!"

"Your concern is gratifying, but unfounded," Etty said. "Mr. Ham offered to drive me home in the cart, but I refused."

"I speak not out of concern, but out of…" He hesitated.

"Friendship?"

He colored and averted his gaze. "Can you ever forgive me for what I said?" he whispered. "I didn't intend to insult you. It was only that I was surprised to learn…"

He shook his head. "It matters not. It's my sin to deal with. I cannot excuse it—all I can do is tell you why."

She set her cup aside.

"Envy is the worst of the seven sins," he said. "For it causes a man to lose his reason. The other sins can be attributed to the natural urges of a beast. Any man can rise above those urges, and if he fails, the only one to suffer is himself. But envy…" He shook his head. "Envy is the root of all the evils of this world. Envy is the one sin that drives us to harm another, to take that from another which we feel we have greater claim to—whether that be happiness, a physical possession, or even a life."

His voice faltered, as if he were in pain.

"What can give you cause to be envious, Andrew?" she asked.

"Sweet heaven, Etty—don't you know?" He shook his head. "When I heard about your...*protector*, I was consumed with envy to learn that another had claimed your affection and not I. I thought only of myself. I was angry at first, then I realized that perhaps you had little choice, that you were the plaything of another. Then I was angry on your behalf, that you have been forced to live in deceit and obscurity as if you're a dirty secret, while *he* no doubt enjoys a gentleman's life elsewhere, being lauded for his respectability."

She opened her mouth to respond, but the words failed her. Was this what had tormented him the day he encountered her on the beach?

He pressed a finger against her lips. "Please, Etty—permit me to finish, for my courage will fail if I stop now. I have never known what it is like to have a rival, for I have never loved or wanted a woman. But I will say this. I know my brother—and men like my brother—who believe their worth in the world is measured by the number of women in their power. When Robert regaled me with tales of his mistresses and his exploits, I'm ashamed to say that I laughed with him. But no more. And do you know why? Because, in you, I see the consequences of a man's folly. I see a good woman imprisoned by circumstance, forever beholden to the man who owns her. I do not blame you—the father of your son must always hold a place in your—"

"Andrew, stop."

"No, I must—"

"Stop, please!" she cried. "Do *not* speak of Gabriel's father!"

"But the man—"

"The man about whom Mrs. Fulford is spreading gossip is *my* father, not Gabriel's."

He jerked backward, his mouth agape.

"I have no protector," she said, "I chose to come here of my own free will, to live a quiet life with my son. My income comes from a stipend my father's solicitor settled on me after the birth of my son. My father came to visit on his return from a business trip overseas—to meet his grandson."

"Oh sweet heaven!" he cried, his voice filled with relief. "What must you think of me? Can you ever forgive me?" He reached forward and caught her hands, lifting them to his lips. "Sweet, sweet woman—how I have misjudged you, when you are perfection itself."

"I am not perfection," she said. "You have every right to think ill of me. I deceived you—I've deceived everyone. Perhaps if I'd been honest with you from the start, you might not have formed the conclusions you had, which were valid under the circumstances."

"How can you speak so, my love?"

My love…

Almost as soon as he'd uttered the words, he gasped and stiffened. His cheeks reddening, he lowered his gaze and tried to withdraw his hands, but she held them firm.

"You…*love* me?"

His color deepened, and he grew still.

"Andrew?"

He lifted his gaze, and her soul seemed to sigh at the clear expression in his eyes—neither lust, nor need, but a deep regard, as if he valued her happiness above all else, including his own life.

The purest form of love.

She curled her fingers around his hands, caressing the skin with her fingertips, and he trembled.

"Then you deserve to hear the truth," she said.

"I have no need to—"

"Gabriel's father is alive."

He stiffened. "Then—you're still married?"

She shook her head. Realization filled his expression, but, rather than the judgment and condemnation that came with such understanding, she saw only compassion.

"Sweet heaven!" he cried. "Did he seduce you? You cannot be held accountable for that."

She shook her head. "It was me," she said. "I-I gave myself to him."

"You *what?*"

He stiffened, and she released his hands.

"I wanted a title," she said, "and the recognition and security that came with it, such that I could never be considered inferior again. I wanted it so badly that I was prepared to offer the only real thing of value I had. My…"

He drew in a sharp breath, his color deepening.

"My maidenhead," she whispered.

He winced and leaned back.

"As to Gabriel's father, he took what I"—she swallowed her shame—"what I offered. Then he abandoned me."

"Is he aware of the"—his brow furrowed—"*the child's* existence?"

A cold hand brushed the nape of her neck.

The child.

Not *your son*, or *Gabriel*, but *the child*. An impersonal thing— an unwanted creature to be tucked away, rather than a beloved son for whom she would do anything.

"I told him I was carrying his child," she said, "in the hope that it would force his hand. But my plan failed."

"What did you do?"

"I left London in disgrace," she said, "to have my child in secret. Of course, there were those who tried to persuade me to give him away—hand him over to some childless couple who would give him a proper family life where he could live without the stain of being some man's bastard…" Her voice caught in her throat as she uttered that vile word—the word her mother had used to punish her with, that Dunton had thrown in her face as he threw her out of his townhouse.

"You considered it?" he asked.

"Not for a moment," she said, rising. The blanket slipped off her knees, and he stooped to retrieve it. "I think I should be going now."

"But it's still raining."

"The storm has passed," she said, "and I don't mind the rain. I've weathered far worse in my life than a few raindrops."

"At least let me accompany you home."

She shook her head. "I have survived this far by looking after myself. And I wish to return to my son." She leveled her gaze on him, and he flinched, discomfort in his eyes. "He needs me," she said, "as I need him. And I won't let a little rain come between us. In fact, I won't let anything—or *anyone*—keep me from my son."

"Then I shall confine you here no longer," he said, folding the blanket and draping it over the back of the chair.

He rang the bell, and shortly after a maid appeared, bobbing a curtsey.

"Ah, Jane, please find a shawl for Mrs. Ward—and have her clothes sent over to Shore Cottage once they're laundered."

"Yes, vicar." The maid bobbed another curtsey and disappeared, returning shortly after with a thick woolen shawl. Etty took it, then Andrew escorted her to the door.

As she stepped outside, he caught her hand. "Etty."

She turned to face him. "Yes?"

"I promise I won't breathe a word of what you've just told me to anyone."

"Thank you."

He hesitated then dipped his head, his gaze falling to her mouth. She parted her lips, waiting for him to claim them, then he withdrew.

She searched his eyes, seeking the love that had filled them earlier. But all she could see was sorrow and disappointment.

She had taken the risk of entrusting him with her secret—and even then only part of it—yet he'd crumpled under the burden.

Just as Papa had said he would.

But she would not succumb to the burden. No, she'd spoken the truth when she said she'd let nobody come between her and her son.

Not even the man she loved.

CHAPTER EIGHTEEN

"M RS. WARD—MRS. WARD!"

Etty glanced up from her mending as Frances dashed into the parlor, her cheeks flaming.

"What is it, sweetheart?"

"It's Lady Fulford!"

"Fwannie!" Gabriel, who had been amusing himself with his toy boat, set it aside and reached up toward the girl.

"Lady Fulford often walks the cliff path," Etty said. "Most likely she does it so she can peer through my windows to see whether I have any more *gentleman guests* about whom she can spread her gossip. Well, I'll be delighted to disappoint her. And she needn't bother us."

"No, she's coming—" Frances broke off at three loud knocks on the front door. "She's here!" she whispered. "Quick! We must tidy the parlor."

"I'll do no such thing," Etty said. "If Lady Fulford wishes to impose herself on me, then she must take us as she finds us."

Frannie's eyes widened, then, as the knocking came again, this time more insistent, she fled from the parlor.

As soon as Etty heard the front door open, Lady Fulford's sharp tones cut through the air.

"Do you know how long you've kept me waiting, girl?"

"B-beg pardon, ma'am," Frances said. "W-would you like to come through to the parlor?"

"What a ridiculous question—of course I would!"

Moments later, Frances appeared at the door, her shoulders tensed as if she anticipated a blow.

Lady Fulford appeared beside Frances and looked about the parlor, taking in the pile of mending in the corner and the books on the floor. Her gaze lingered on Gabriel, who grew still, as if he recognized the danger, before settling on Etty.

For a moment, the two women stared at each other. Then Lady Fulford arched an eyebrow and dipped her head—the haughty expression of one who considered herself the principal inhabitant of the village, demanding deference from a subordinate.

With a slow, deliberate motion, Etty rose to her feet.

"Lady Fulford. To what do I owe the pleasure of a visitation?"

Her guest frowned, then wrinkled her nose. Etty gestured toward a chair at the opposite end of the room.

"Please, take a seat."

Lady Fulford approached the chair. She stood beside it for a moment before bending forward to brush the seat. Then she inspected her glove, making a show of flicking dust from her fingers, before, at length, she sat.

"Some tea, Frances, I think?" Etty said.

"I'm not here for *tea*," Lady Fulford said.

"But *I* would like tea," Etty replied.

Lady Fulford let out a sharp sigh. "Oh, very well, if you insist," she said. Then she gestured toward Gabriel. "What's *that* doing here?"

"*He* is my son," Etty said. "And he's playing."

"In my opinion, children have their place, and they should be in it at all times." Lady Fulford fixed her cold blue stare on Etty. "Particularly when their parents have guests."

"Even uninvited guests?"

Frances drew in a sharp breath, but Lady Fulford merely raised her eyebrows a little further. Then she cast her gaze on Gabriel once more. The boy continued to stare at her, then he let out a wail.

"Frances, would you take Gabriel to his chamber?" Etty asked. "I think he'd be happier there."

"We'd *all* be a great deal happier," Lady Fulford said. "The parlor is no place for a child."

"Particularly where the child does not feel safe," Etty replied.

"Are you being deliberately uncivil, Mrs. Ward?"

"I'm merely stating a fact, Lady Fulford," Etty said. "My son cries when he does not feel safe."

"In my experience, children that age cry when they seek attention for their own ends. Any competent parent would not yield to their wiles."

Etty let out a snort. Most likely, Lady Fulford had spent as little time as possible with her children as soon as she'd birthed them, foisting them onto nannies as soon as they drew their first breath, and onto governesses before they uttered their first words.

"Such cunning little creatures children are, Lady Fulford," Etty said. "But I thank you for your counsel, and will ensure I have my wits about me in future."

She turned to Frances, who stood open mouthed in the doorway.

"Frances, dear, please take Gabriel to his chamber. And there's no need to make tea. I have a feeling Lady Fulford will not be staying long."

"Why, I've never been so insulted—"

"I mean no insult, Lady Fulford, I assure you," Etty said. "I'm thinking of your welfare. A woman of your…*particular sensibilities* can find little enjoyment in spending time in a home that is so decidedly beneath that which you're used to. I'm afraid I can never exist on the same level as yourself, and have no wish to prolong your discomfort by insisting you stay a moment longer than is necessary."

Frances watched the exchange, her gaze flitting from Etty to her guest. The fear in her eyes lessened and a smile curved her lips.

"Come along, Gabey," she said. "How about we play sailors with your boat?"

Gabriel reached out toward Frances, his gaze still fixed on Lady Fulford in the manner of a rabbit watching a fox. Frances swept the boy into her arms.

"Shall we play pirates?"

"Yes—pirate!" he cried, clutching the toy boat as Frances took him out of the parlor.

Etty rose to her feet to close the door, then remained standing.

"Now my son is safely out of the way, perhaps you'd be so good as to tell me why you're here," she said. "Are you perhaps come to discuss the village fete, or to ask my assistance?"

Lady Fulford curled her lip into a sneer. "Don't be a fool!"

"I see no folly in my assumption," Etty said. "I can see no other purpose for your visit,"

"Unless you're a simpleton, you cannot be at a loss as to the *purpose of my visit.*"

Etty winced at the spite in Lady Fulford's tone. "On the contrary, Lady Fulford," she said, smiling, "that's why I asked."

"You are extremely frank for a woman in your position," Lady Fulford said. "It is a degree of frankness that borders on insolence."

"Would you rather I spoke an untruth? Or—better still—if I didn't speak at all?"

Her guest let out a sharp huff. "You must consider my position, if nothing else."

"A position we very much share," Etty said. "We are both women, are we not—and mothers?"

"Must you always answer back?"

"I'm merely responding to your remarks, Lady Fulford."

"Insufferable creature!" Lady Fulford said. "I'm referring to my position of *rank*, Mrs. Ward." She leaned forward, her eyes glittering with spite. "That is…if your name really is *Mrs. Ward.*"

Etty's stomach clenched in apprehension. Did the woman

know something, or was she merely speculating based on gossip?

"Why would you assume my name is anything other than that which I have told you, Mrs. Fulford?" Etty asked. "What purpose would I have in deceiving you?"

A gleam of triumph shimmered in Lady Fulford's eyes. "I find it unfathomable that a woman of your circumstances would ask such a question of a respectable, titled woman such as myself."

"I understand the title belongs to your husband, Lady Fulford," Etty said. "And I fail to understand how the wife of a knight can claim superiority over the daughter of a baronet."

"A…baronet?"

"Yes, that's right, Lady Fulford," Etty said. "The gentleman about whom I understand there has been a great deal of speculation among your particular set of acquaintances is, in fact, my father. Though why a father visiting his daughter and grandson is such a topic for gossip, I cannot fathom—unless you have nothing better to talk about."

Lady Fulford let out another huff. "I see little point in discussing our relative positions of rank when my superiority is evident even to those of the meanest intelligence. Perhaps I should explain the purpose of my visit now we have dispensed with niceties." Her face wrinkled into an expression of disgust. "Leave the vicar alone."

"I beg your—"

"Don't play the simpleton with me, *Mrs. Ward*," Lady Fulford snarled. "You may have fooled the vicar, and most of the halfwits in the village, but *I* am not so easily deceived."

"Lady Fulford, are you calling the vicar a halfwit?"

Lady Fulford leaped from her chair, her eyes glittering with loathing. "Insolent girl!" she cried. "How dare you speak to me so! Of course I'm not calling the vicar a halfwit, though he's been tempted by your wiles. I am calling *you* a *whore!*"

Etty's composure almost faltered, and she recoiled at the hatred in the other woman's eyes. "Unfounded accusations will not—"

"I thought I told you *not* to attempt to deceive me," Lady Fulford said. "Do you think I'd stand by and do nothing while you tainted this village with your presence, seeking to seduce the vicar as no doubt you seduced another before him?"

"I never—"

"Oh, don't be a fool!" Lady Fulford let out a harsh laugh. "It's plain to see that your son is some man's bastard. No doubt you lifted your skirts for the brat's father for your own gain."

Etty opened her mouth to deny the accusation, but she couldn't. Hadn't she confessed the very same to Andrew only last week?

Her gut twisted with shame. Perhaps, in his judgment of her, he'd related her history to Lady Fulford.

Andrew, I trusted you...

"Ah!" Lady Fulford gave a bark of triumph. "I'm right, am I not? Does the vicar know?" She shook her head. "No—of course not. A man of his morality would have run you out of the village had he known. Perhaps I ought to tell him."

"Then tell him and be damned, Lady Fulford!"

"Ah, the true harlot reveals herself," Lady Fulford sneered, stepping toward Etty until she towered over her, her thicker frame dominating the space. "Well, hear this—Mr. Staines will not become your next victim. He's an honorable, moral man, destined for greatness in the church. An association with you would ruin him. If you had the merest smattering of decency in that black heart of yours, then you'd leave him well alone—for *his* sake."

"Should he not be permitted to make up his own mind?" Etty asked.

"In matters such as this, when a man is being tempted by the devil's work, he needs guidance from the righteous. The poor man is, I'm afraid, in sore need of such guidance. He almost fell into temptation before—in this very house—and I shall not see him succumb a second time."

"A *second* time?"

"The previous occupant of this little hovel was a temptress such as yourself. She came here also, masquerading as a widow—the facade of a whore, it seems. In fact"—she fixed her stare on Etty—"you remind me a little of her. I wonder why I didn't notice it before."

"I know nothing of—" Etty began, but Lady Fulford continued.

"Does it not seem something of a coincidence that two young women of similar age, both masquerading as widows, would hide themselves away in the same cottage?"

"Of course it's a coincidence!" Etty said.

"You seem a little too eager to make that claim. What connects you to her, I wonder?" Lady Fulford tilted her head to one side, her brow furrowing in concentration. "Miss Howard—that was her name, though she passed herself off as Mrs. Riley, if I recall. She married a duke, though not before seducing our poor vicar. But Mr. Staines, in his naiveté, continued to defend her honor, claiming that she was the daughter of a baronet. A claim you have made today."

Etty caught her breath at the sharp pain in her chest as her body constricted with fear. Her secret was out—or on the brink of exposure.

A slow smile curled Lady Fulford's lips. "Ah—there we have it," she said. "Another harlot come here to hide her shame."

"I have done nothing I'm ashamed of," Etty said.

"And still she tries to deceive me!" Lady Fulford let out a laugh. "Your shame is evident—I see it in your eyes and I hear it in your voice. But let us put it to the test. With regards to the vicar, you instructed me to tell all and be damned. Do you stand by that sentiment?"

Etty's gut twisted with fear. She met her opponent's gaze, but the triumph in Lady Fulford's eyes only increased.

At length, she nodded.

"I see we understand one another, *Miss Howard.*"

Etty suppressed a shudder, but Lady Fulford's smile broadened and she gave a nod of self-satisfaction.

"Excellent," she said, stepping back. "I'm so glad we had this opportunity to get to know each other a little better. But I think the time has come to cease further revelation, do not you agree? For the vicar's sake—and yours, of course."

She extended her hand—thin, bony fingers, adorned by a multitude of rings, each jewel glittering with malevolence. Etty took it, and Lady Fulford curled her fingers around her hands in a claw-like grip, digging fingernails into Etty's flesh.

"Good," she said. "Very good. I trust you'll not trouble yourself with the inconvenience of attending the village fete. It is, after all, for those of us who belong to the village and who strive to preserve the moral fiber here. I cannot comment on whether you feel the need to continue to attend church, but I would counsel you on the folly of placing yourself in a position where our vicar is faced with further temptation. There are those us of here willing to undertake whatever is necessary to keep his soul safe. Do I make myself clear?"

She tightened her grip, and Etty suppressed a cry at the sting of pain.

"Perfectly so, Lady Fulford," she said.

"Excellent. Then I shall intrude on your time no longer."

Etty opened the door, and Lady Fulford swept out of the room, almost knocking Frances over.

"Out of my way, girl!"

Frances dipped into a curtsey and rushed toward the front door to open it. Once Mrs. Fulford was safely outside, Etty leaned against the wall, her defenses crumbling.

She knows.

Perhaps not everything, but a woman such as Lady Fulford would make it her business to sniff it out.

And, armed with the full history of Juliette Howard and the sins she had committed, Lady Fulford could command Etty in any manner that she liked. For if Andrew was to learn her true identity, then he would justifiably—and irrevocably—hate her.

CHAPTER NINETEEN

ANDREW CAST HIS gaze over the swelling crowd—Mr. Dodd hobbled across the field supported by his wife, while the Newnhams set out a blanket by the duck pond, watching their constantly increasing brood of children splash about by the water's edge. Sammy Legge stood more quietly at the opposite edge, throwing bread into the pond, on which the ducks descended like a charging battalion. At the largest stall, surrounded by a throng of villagers, Mr. Ham served ale to the men, while Mrs. Ham served lemonade to the women and children.

Andrew smiled as he caught sight of Sammy snatching a mug of ale. The lad met his gaze, and Andrew folded his arms and arched his eyebrows. Sammy's cheeks turned red and he scrambled away, dropping the mug, which bounced on the grass before settling beside Mrs. Ham's foot.

And, of course, among the noise and laughter, Mrs. Fulford could be heard barking orders at anyone who cared to listen.

Mr. and Mrs. Gadd wandered about, their son by their side, though Frannie was nowhere to be seen.

And there was no sign of the one person he sought.

Where are you, Etty?

Since their last encounter, she'd attended church each Sunday, but always slipped out of the building before Andrew had the chance to speak to her, to apologize for both his forwardness the afternoon of the storm, and his lack of compassion when she'd revealed her past.

In truth, he did not blame, nor judge, her for her actions. In fact, he admired her honesty. Only a woman of the utmost integrity would make such a full and frank confession, with no guarantee of the listener's understanding.

And he was determined to tell her the next time he saw her. Only the last time he'd gone to Shore Cottage, he'd received no answer, though he was sure he saw a curtain move on the upper floor.

But she was certain to come to the fete. *Everybody* came to the Sandcombe fete.

Little Gabriel would like the flags Mr. Fossett had set out on his stall. Mrs. Fossett had spent the past month making flags for the children, and Andrew had determined to buy one for the boy. He'd even picked it out—a rectangular flag of blue cotton, decorated with stars. Each time he spoke to Etty, he seemed to distress her even more than the time before. But with a gift, however trivial, perhaps he might be able to regain her trust and show that he was not like the others—that he cared not who Gabriel's father was.

The boy couldn't help the circumstances of his birth. Neither could his mother, the warrioress who protected and loved her son with a ferocity that Andrew could only admire.

It might not be much, but buying a flag for Etty's son was the first step in rebuilding their friendship. It was an innocent act, a gift for a child, neither conveying emotion, nor risking Andrew's heart. An olive branch—an offer of peace to symbolize the end to his judgment of her. If she didn't take it, then he'd lost nothing, for it was not unreasonable to refuse an offer of a gift, and he could preserve his dignity without having revealed his heart again.

But if she took it…

You're a coward, little brother.

He shook his head to dissipate his brother's voice. Robert would have known what to do, most likely would have taken what he wanted—claimed Etty for his own, silencing her protests until she yielded, after which he'd have grown weary of her and moved on to the next woman.

Perhaps that was what Gabriel's father had done—preyed on the desperation of a woman's lot in life, promised her security, perhaps even marriage, merely to satisfy his carnal lust, then discarded her, abandoning the woman he'd claimed and the child he'd fathered.

What man would do that to a child of his own flesh?

Most sins could be forgiven—except those committed against one's flesh and blood. Against sons, daughters…and sisters.

And wives. Andrew shivered as he caught sight of Ralph Smith standing on the edge of the field, a mug of ale in his hand, a dark scowl on his face. There was no sign of Loveday or her children, but if Ralph was occupied with the ale stall and his wife and children were at home, then they were safe from his bad temper—at least for today.

Perhaps that explained Etty's absence, if she was with Loveday. She had quite taken the poor woman into her care.

Andrew could slip away and pay Loveday a visit, just to check whether she was well—whether they *both* were.

"Vicar!"

Damn.

Andrew recognized the voice. The last thing he needed was for Mrs. Fulford to appoint him as her foot soldier in her quest to assert her dominance over the entire village—which, for all her professions of raising funds for the needy, was her true purpose in running the village fete.

He caught sight of Mrs. Swain and her pupils. A gaggle of twenty schoolchildren would provide more than adequate cover for a lone vicar seeking sanctuary from a predatory female and her daughters of marriageable age.

But Andrew hadn't considered the tenacity of a determined woman. Before he reached the schoolchildren, Mrs. Fulford appeared before him, out of breath, her eldest daughter by her side.

"Oh, *there* you are, vicar. Did you not hear me calling?"

I suspect they heard you all the way to Cromer.

"I'm afraid not, Mrs. Fulford."

"Well, never mind that. I'm in need of you—or rather, my daughter is, aren't you, Elizabeth?"

"Yes, Mama."

"How may I be of assistance, Miss Fulford?" Andrew asked.

"Elizabeth is in need of a companion. I cannot have her spend the day without one."

Andrew glanced across the field to where Elizabeth's sisters were wandering about, arm in arm. Mrs. Fulford followed the line of his gaze.

"Sarah and Caroline are undertaking something very particular, vicar," she said. "I'm afraid Elizabeth is on her own, and we cannot have a young woman unaccompanied, can we?"

"Miss Fulford is quite safe here, Lady Fulford," Andrew said.

"But it wouldn't seem right, would it?" she said. "Sir John would say the same, and, of course, I'm sure the bishop would agree."

I'm sure the bishop would agree. Six words that, put together, formed a thinly veiled threat to remove Andrew from office if he were to disobey his patron's orders.

One day I'll call you out on that, Lady Fulford.

But today was not the day. He could endure the eldest Miss Fulford's company for the fete. And it would do the conceited little miss a world of good when she bore witness to his paying Etty attention when she arrived.

If she was coming.

He offered his arm to Miss Fulford, but before she took it, a scream rang out.

"Help—help us!"

A figure was running toward the field from the direction of the cliff path, arms waving.

"Help!"

"Frannie!" Mrs. Gadd cried, pushing through the crowd. "Dear Lord—it's Frannie! William, Jimmy—come quick!"

Andrew began to move, but Elizabeth caught his arm. "Vicar, it's just that Gadd girl. There's no need—"

He shook off her hand. "There's every need, Miss Fulford. Please unhand me."

"Well, *really!*"

Ignoring her, he set off toward Frannie, overtaking Mrs. Gadd, who was already beginning to slow.

"V-vicar!" Frannie cried as Andrew approached her and took her hands.

"What's the matter?"

"I-it's L-Loveday," Frannie said, panting. "It's all my fault!"

"What is?" Andrew asked. Frannie burst into tears as Mrs. Gadd arrived, wheezing. Shortly after, her husband and son appeared.

"Fran—" Mrs. Gadd broke off, coughing.

"Now then, Peg, you'll do yerself an injury," Mr. Gadd said, taking his wife into his arms. "What's all this about somethin' being your fault, Frannie, love?"

"I-I've killed Loveday!" Frances cried. "Why do I kill everyone?"

"What nonsense is this?" Mr. Gadd said. "Frannie, love, you've never killed anyone."

"I-I killed Freda," she said. "Y-you all think it—and now I've killed Loveday."

"*Freda?*" Mrs. Gadd shook her head. "Frannie, love, you never—"

"You never say it, but you *think* it—I know you do!"

"What about Loveday?" Andrew asked. "Frannie, what's happened to her?"

The distressed girl turned her attention on him. "Sh-she's drowned in the sea, vicar—and it's my fault, because I told Mrs. Ward it was safe to swim."

"Was Mrs. Ward with her?"

"She went in after her, and they've disappeared."

A cold hand clutched at Andrew's heart. "Etty—in the water?"

"Loveday was swimming, and the bad current came, b-but she tried to swim against it, rather than across, then she disappeared under the water. I wanted to go in after her, but Mrs. Ward told me not to. She said to stay out of the water while she went in. B-but now she's gone also. I didn't know what to do!"

"Where's Gabriel?"

"Florrie's with him—she's minding him and baby Anna. It's all my fault!"

"No," Andrew said, drawing the trembling girl into his arms. "You did the right thing, coming to get help. Mr. Gadd, come with me. There's not a moment to lose."

"Right you are, vicar," came the reply. "Jimmy, son, go and find Loveday's husband."

"Not *him*," Andrew said. "He's—"

"He's her husband, vicar, and has more right than you. Jimmy—go, now!"

"Yes, Pa." The lad sprinted back toward the field.

"Where are they?" Andrew asked.

"Near the headland," Frannie said, "wh-where you saw us swimming before."

"Very good," he said. "You've done well. Now, look after your mother—and don't worry. I'm sure they'll be fine."

Frannie nodded, and Andrew sprinted toward the cliff path. Finally free of the obligation to assure others of that which he did not believe, he was able to succumb to the fear that gripped him when he'd first seen Etty swimming in the sea.

"Why?" he cried. "Dear God—why did it have to be her?"

As he approached the cliff top, he caught sight of three small forms on the beach below, by the water's edge. Wails of despair echoed from below—three children in fear for their mothers' lives. If for no other reason, he had to stem the tide of his own despair so he might give those poor children a sliver of hope.

He made his way down the path, stumbling halfway but picking himself up, ignoring the tear in his breeches. Then he sprinted across the beach, his feet sinking into the sand.

Florence Smith stood clutching her baby sister, little Gabriel clinging to her skirts, his mouth wide open in an *O* as he wailed into the air.

"V-vicar!" Florence cried. "My m-mama!"

"Where did you last see them?" Andrew asked.

She pointed out to sea. "In that direction."

Andrew's heart sank. Florence pointed toward the center of the current—a patch of dark water, clouded with churned-up sand that formed a break in the waves. Not even the strongest swimmer could have fought against it. But if there was the slightest chance they were still fighting for their lives, then he had to take it.

He unbuttoned his jacket and dropped it on the sand.

"Vicar, no!"

He turned at Mr. Gadd's voice, to see the man stumbling toward him, Ralph in his wake.

"Papa!" Florence cried.

"What the bleedin' hell have you been doin', you foolish brat?" Ralph said.

"There's enough of that, Smith," Mr. Gadd said. "We need to find your wife."

"The stupid slut will 'ave drowned herself by now—leavin' me with them two brats to feed," Ralph growled. "What am *I* supposed to do now?"

"Just what you've always done for them," Andrew snapped. "Nothing."

"Why you…" Ralph approached him, fists raised, but Jimmy Gadd interrupted him.

"Look! Pa, vicar—look over there!"

He was pointing out to sea, where an object bobbed in the water along the shoreline.

"What's that?" he asked.

"Nothin' but flotsam, son," Mr. Gadd said.

The object moved, splitting into two, then Andrew caught the white flash of an arm.

"Etty!" he called, sprinting along the beach. "Over here!"

He reached the water line and splashed into the sea, the waves rippling around his feet. Then she rose from the water, a sea goddess, her mouth set in a determined line as she clung to Loveday's limp form.

"That's it, sweetheart," she said. "We're safe now."

"Ma'am?" Loveday's eyes fluttered open.

"Hush," Etty said. "You need to rest."

She stumbled forward, and Andrew rushed toward her, breaking her fall and drawing her into his arms.

"Etty!" he cried. "Oh, Etty—you have no idea how relieved I am to see—"

"Take care of Loveday," she said.

"But you're exhausted."

"I'm not the one in need of help," she said, panting. "I'll be fine. Loveday needs you more."

Andrew lifted Loveday into his arms, his heart aching at her slight frame, then he waded back toward the shore, glancing over his shoulder to ensure Etty followed. Loveday clung to him as he set her down on the beach, but before he could return for Etty, Mr. Gadd had waded in and was already placing his jacket over her shoulders, ignoring her protests.

"Foolish lass," he said. "But brave, goin' in after Loveday in those currents."

"Anyone would have done the same, Mr. Gadd."

"That's where ye're wrong, lass," he said. "Jimmy, give Loveday yer jacket, there's a good lad."

"Oh no you don't," Ralph growled. "Get yer filthy hands off my wife." He gestured to Loveday. "Woman, come here—ye've caused enough trouble."

"Mr. Smith, I don't think—" Jimmy began, but Ralph struck out and clipped the lad around the ear.

"That's enough, boy!" He grasped Loveday by the arm and yanked her toward him. She stumbled against his chest and gave a cry, cowering. "Foolish little slut!" he snarled, "And to think—everything I've done for you!"

"What *have* you done for your wife, Mr. Smith?" a sharp voice asked.

Despite her fatigue, Etty was striding toward him, determination in her expression.

"Not enough by the looks of it, if she's tempted into sin by the likes of you," Ralph spat.

"Tempted into sin?" Etty said, tilting her head in the manner of a duchess. "What nonsense! Unless you believe taking a picnic by the sea to be an act of debauchery."

"Don't play the high-and-mighty with me, woman," Ralph growled, releasing Loveday and approaching Etty, his brutish, thick-set body towering over her. "I know all about you—the village harlot, ye are, inviting all manner of men into yer home. Disgusting, it is, and now ye're tempting my wife to stray from the path again."

"Again?"

"Aye," he said. "I always knew my wife was a slattern, but I took her on nevertheless. Much good it did me, being saddled with her brats."

"Ralph, no—" Loveday began.

"Silence, slut!" Ralph roared. "So help me God, when I get ye home, I'll—"

"You'll what?" Etty interrupted. "Beat her again? Throw her against the door then terrify her into telling the world she fell, thus concealing your savagery?"

"She's my wife—I'll do what I fucking well want with her!"

Andrew flinched at the profanity.

Etty curled her hands into fists and stepped toward Ralph until she had to tilt her head back to meet his gaze. "You think just because you're bigger than your wife that you can brutalize her?"

"She's *my* wife! She vowed to obey me."

"And did you not vow to keep and protect her?" Etty asked. "Do you think beating her into submission is protection, Mr. Smith? Or is it merely the act of a coward, a man who has failed in life, who seeks to improve his sense of self-worth by crushing that of another?"

"My wife is a whore. She needs correction."

Etty let out a snort. "Your wife is no more of a whore than any other woman."

"Aye," Ralph said, "and all women are whores."

"Including maidservants who are raped by their master?"

"Mrs. Ward!" Mr. Gadd said. "I hardly think that's—"

"You hardly think that's *what*?" she replied. "A subject for polite conversation? Why not? Is it perhaps because men such as Sir John Fulford hide behind the veneer of polite conversation so that they can force themselves onto vulnerable young women in their power then throw them out, leaving them to die in childbirth, or worse—surrender to marriage to a brute who spends their entire married life blaming her for the actions of another?"

She reached toward Ralph and grasped his lapels. "Men like you disgust me," she snarled. "Rather than lay the blame at the feet of the perpetrator, you content yourself with wallowing in self-pity, blaming your poor wife for having been violated by another. And yet you—and others like you in this godforsaken village—see fit to fawn over Sir John, touching your caps and bobbing curtseys as he passes by. What's it to you if he violated your wives, or your daughters? You see it as a necessary sacrifice so that you might continue to live your lives in peace—sending a virgin to be slain by the dragon."

"Mrs. Ward—" Mr. Gadd began, but she interrupted him.

"And as for *you*, Mr. Gadd, do you consider yourself blameless? Your own daughter Freda was destroyed by the very man you serve, and though you profess to love the child she bore, in your heart, you blame her. You might not tell her, but she feels it.

Frances is your granddaughter—and yet you also see her as the child of your daughter's rapist."

"You evil woman!" Ralph said. "Spreading your poison around the village. You're not proper Sandcombe—you weren't born and bred here. You're not one of us and you never will be."

"If being 'proper Sandcombe' means permitting violation, rape, and brutality, then I am glad to be a misfit!" Etty cried. She gestured toward Andrew and Mr. Gadd. "*All* of you share the blame for the sins in this village. You may satisfy yourselves that you are not the perpetrators, but turning a blind eye when you know something is wrong is the worst sin of all—because you should know better. You should *all* know better!"

What a warrior she was! A lone woman, slight of frame, standing up to a brute with a ferocity unmatched. A champion for those for whom nobody else spoke, freely and without agenda. Fearless and honest—with no thought for her reputation, or safety, in her quest for justice.

Andrew was never more in love than at that moment.

Then she swung her arm and punched Ralph in the jaw. He staggered back under the force of her blow, lost his balance, and fell into the sand.

Etty blinked and stared at her fist, incredulity in her eyes.

Then a wail rose. Andrew turned to see Frannie standing beside her mother, her face ashen.

She had heard every word.

"Frances…" Etty whispered, her hand flying to her mouth.

"Mama," Frannie said, "i-is it true?"

Mrs. Gadd stood trembling, tears spilling onto her cheeks. "Frannie, love…"

"Are you satisfied, Mrs. Ward?" Mr. Gadd said. "Is this what you came for, to unearth secrets which are none of your business—secrets that destroy families?"

"Your family was already destroyed by Sir John," Etty said. "And he'll continue to destroy it. Is that not why you were so desperate for Frances not to go into service? For fear that she'd suffer violation at the hands of her—"

"No!" Mrs. Gadd sobbed. "Do not say it!"

"Why, because you wish to deny it?"

"No! Because I cannot bear it! Why must you speak of such things?"

"Because it's better if the truth were not kept hidden!" Etty said. "Deception only leads to misery."

"Then what would you have us do, Mrs. Ward?" Mr. Gadd asked. "You may come and go as you please—you're an outsider. But those of us who have lived in the village all our lives, and our parents and grandparents before us, where can *we* go?"

"You fight the injustice," Etty said, "and you protect the innocent, even if that comes at the price of hardship to yourself. Not because it's the easy thing to do—but because it's the *good* thing to do." She glanced toward Andrew, a plea in her eyes.

"Mrs. Ward is right," he said. "We have all failed innocent young women such as Loveday and your Freda, Mr. Gadd. Perhaps it's time we stopped concealing the truth and did what was good."

"Vicar, there's nowt you've done wrong," Mr. Gadd replied.

"Isn't there?" Andrew said. "I have delivered sermons, pontificated on the morals of the world. I might have delivered a gift or two to the needy. But what does that all achieve? All I am doing is easing the suffering of a few souls in the village, rather than striving to put an end to the cause of their suffering. If I act within the boundaries set by my patron, am I not perpetuating the wrongdoing? I have no right to remain in this village if I stand by and do nothing."

"Ye're a fool, vicar."

Andrew turned to see Ralph struggling to his feet.

"No doubt you've been tempted by the village whore. It's not you who should leave Sandcombe—it's *her*."

Ralph curled his hands into fists, then he cocked his arm back and advanced on Etty.

"No!" Andrew rushed toward him and grasped his wrist.

"Leave me be, vicar," Ralph growled, wrenching himself free. "It's time someone taught this interfering tart a lesson."

"Do it, then!" Etty said. "Flatten me with your fists and show the world what you really are!"

Ralph grinned and flew toward her, fists raised. But before he could strike her, Andrew stepped between them. Fueled by anger and his fear for the woman he loved, he thrust his fist upward and connected with Ralph's jaw. Ralph's eyes widened, surprise in their expression. Then, with a sigh, he crumpled to the ground.

Etty let out a groan, and Andrew turned to see her nursing her fist. He approached her and took her hand, and she let out a low cry as he brushed his fingertips over her knuckles where the skin was broken and already darkening.

She drew in a sharp breath and began to tremble.

Andrew pulled her into his arms, and she softened in his embrace while a sob escaped her lips.

"Oh, Andrew, forgive me!" she cried. "I-I shouldn't have said such things. Poor Frances—I-I didn't know she'd returned. I'm so sorry!"

Mr. Gadd approached his wife and embraced her. Then he crouched beside Frannie and drew her into his arms.

"I'm sorry, sweet lass," he said. "Your ma and I love you, no matter what. Isn't that right, Peg?"

Mrs. Gadd nodded, then burst into tears. "Oh, Frannie, my sweet child!"

"B-but you're my—"

"I'm your *ma*," Mrs. Gadd said. "And don't let nobody tell you otherwise. I may not be yer real ma, but I love ye every bit as much as if ye were. It matters not if ye're a child of my flesh. What makes a family is them that love each other. We love you, our Frannie. And our Freda would have been ever so proud of you!"

Sobbing, she drew Frannie into her arms.

Mr. Gadd approached Andrew and Etty, his mouth set in a firm line.

"Don't blame Mrs. Ward," Andrew said. "She's the best of all of us. If you wish to harm her, you'll have to come through me. She has saved a life this day, and for that, she must be honored."

"Aye, she's saved more than one life today, I'll reckon," Mr. Gadd said. He placed a light hand on Etty's shoulder, and she blinked, her eyes glazed with fatigue. "Aye, ye're a brave lass, all right. A good lass. Credit to the village, ye are, for all that brute Smith might say."

Andrew glanced at Ralph's limp form.

"Never you mind *him*, vicar," Mr. Gadd said. "We'll take Loveday and her girls in tonight. He can rot in the sand, for all I care. I reckon ye need to get Mrs. Ward home."

"Gabriel…" Etty whispered.

"Your son's fine," Mr. Gadd said. "Loveday's Florrie's got him."

Etty glanced toward Loveday, who had joined her children and was clinging to them as if her life depended on it.

"Sweet heaven—what have I done?" she whispered. "Those poor girls. I had no right to say such things."

"You said nothing that was untrue," Andrew said, dipping his head to kiss her hair.

"Andrew, I…"

"Hush, my love," he said. "You were right in that it's best not to deceive."

She lifted her gaze to him, her eyes filled with love, and his heart soared. To think—together they could change the world, if only she would accept him.

He brushed his knuckles against her cheek, and he winced at the sharp sting. She caught his hand, her eyes widening.

"Your poor hand!" she said. Then she dipped her head and brushed her lips against his knuckles. "Is that better?"

"Oh yes, my love," he whispered. "You make everything better, my darling."

"Mama!" a voice cried, and he turned to see Gabriel toddling toward them. Andrew stooped to lift the boy in his arms.

"I think ye'd better take Mrs. Ward and young Gabriel home, vicar," Mrs. Gadd said. "We'll take care of Loveday and her young 'uns. And I hope ye'll not object if Frannie comes home with us tonight, to be with her family. I think, today, Mrs. Ward has shown us what a family should be. Them that love each other."

Holding Etty's son in one arm, Andrew held out his free arm to her, and she took it. Without protest, she let him steer her onto the path heading toward Shore Cottage.

Mrs. Gadd was right. It was time to learn what a family should be.

CHAPTER TWENTY

W HAT MUST HE think of her? What must they *all* think of her, revealing secrets that weren't hers to tell?

But as Etty glanced at the man cradling her son in his arms as if he were the most precious being in the world, she saw nothing but kindness, compassion—and love.

As they reached Shore Cottage, she pushed open the door and ushered him in. By rights she should have sent him on his way—she was only giving the gossipmongers in the village more material with which to tell tales about her.

The village whore…

That was what Ralph Smith had called her.

Gabriel stirred in Andrew's arms, then let out a yawn before nestling against his chest.

"Well, young sir, I think it's time you had your rest." Andrew glanced toward Etty. "Shall I take him to his chamber?"

She opened her mouth to protest, but he continued.

"You're exhausted," he said. "And don't try to deny it; you could barely walk. Make yourself comfortable in the parlor and I'll see to your son."

He reached for her hand, and a delicious warmth licked across her belly as his fingers curled around hers.

"Trust me, Etty."

He met her gaze, his warm brown eyes filled with tenderness, and she nodded as her soul slid into place.

Yes—she *could* trust him, as she could trust no other.

"Let me take care of your son," he whispered, "as I wish to take care of you both."

He dipped his head and brushed his lips against hers.

Gabriel stirred and opened his eyes. "Da." He let out another yawn. "Da—da."

Merely the babbling of a child still learning to speak, but Etty caught her breath at the syllable, and all its implications.

The man cradling her child closed his eyes and lowered his head to bury his nose in the boy's hair. When he opened them again, Etty was met with the full force of his gaze, and her heart swelled at the raw, unbridled love in his eyes.

She'd seen such an expression only once before—when her father had visited to make his peace with her at last.

It was the love that only the best of adults had for a child…

A father's love.

Her son—and, finally, herself—in safe hands, she let Andrew steer her into the parlor, where she wrapped a blanket around her shoulders and sank back into a chair, succumbing to fatigue and slipping into oblivion.

WHEN ETTY WOKE, a fire was crackling, casting a warm orange glow about the parlor. Andrew was nowhere to be seen.

Casting the blanket aside, she rose to her feet and approached the fire. She still shook with fatigue and teetered sideways before kneeling beside the fireplace, plucking a log from the pile and adding it to the fire. The flames flared and crackled, sending out a spark that landed on the carpet in a tiny burst of orange before it died.

Footsteps approached and the door opened to reveal the vicar.

"I thought I heard movement," he said. "Are you warm

enough?"

Nodding, she struggled to her feet, and he rushed toward her, taking her arm and steering her back to the sofa.

"You're still here," she said as he placed the blanket over her knees.

"I'm here for as long as you wish it, but you only need say the word and I shall leave."

She reached for his hand. "I don't want you to leave," she whispered. "Not ever."

Hope flared in his eyes, and he leaned toward her. She let her gaze fall to his mouth—his soft, full lips, always curved in a gentle smile.

She parted her lips in invitation, and he moved closer, his breath a warm caress on her skin.

Then he withdrew, and she swallowed her disappointment at the sense of loss.

"Tea," he said.

Then he stood and exited the parlor, returning with a tray laden with tea things.

"You made tea?"

He smiled, setting the tray on a table. "I thought you might be in need of some."

"B-but it's not…"

"Not what?" he asked. "Not a task for a man? I am not such a man as to be incapable of making tea. Please do not think any less of me for knowing how to navigate my way around your kitchen."

"On the contrary, I assure you, vicar," she said. "It makes you more of a man in my eyes—the best of men."

"Then my life is complete."

"How so?"

He approached her and kneeled beside the sofa, taking her hands. "For you to consider me the best of men—I can ask for nothing more, except…"

He colored and lowered his gaze.

"Vicar?" she said, then curled her fingers around his. "Andrew?"

"I-I dare not hope to ask, for it is my heart's desire."

Her own heart swelled with hope, and she dipped her head to kiss his knuckles. He winced as she ran her lips over his bruised flesh—the evidence of his courage in defending her.

"Have you not said in your sermons, vicar, that those who are prepared to risk a loss to themselves must always consider the merits of such risks if the rewards are bountiful?"

He let out a soft laugh and shook his head. "Do you recall *everything* I've said from my pulpit, Etty? Am I so fortunate as to have secured your attention and interest? Might I dare to ask that I have secured your heart also?"

She caught her breath at the intensity in his eyes. "Why yes, vicar," she whispered. "I believe that you may dare."

Doubt clouded his expression, as if he still feared her refusal. So unlike he was to the hard, impenetrable men of her previous acquaintance—the bright, shining lords who ruled over the *ton*, who thought nothing of crushing hearts and ruining reputations, who considered the women desperate for marriage to be their playthings.

But in being the very last man at whom the *ton* would look, he was the only man with whom she could entrust her heart— and her life.

"Etty, I…" He hesitated, and she placed her finger on his lips.

"Hush, my love," she said. "There's no need to ask—nor is there need for me to give you my answer in words. Why tell you that I return your feelings when I can *show* you?"

She ran the tip of her thumb across his lips, and he parted them to capture it in his mouth. His tongue, soft and gentle, caressed her thumb, and she let out a low groan as a lick of desire curled in her belly.

He withdrew, uncertainty clouding his gaze. "Etty, are you well?"

"Oh, yes," she whispered. "I am very well. Can you not tell?"

"I-I'm afraid… I have never—" He broke off, his cheeks flaming.

Sweet Lord—he was nervous!

She placed her hand on his cheek, and a fizz of pleasure ran through her veins at the feel of the stubble on his chin against her skin.

"I trust you," she whispered.

"But I have seen the fear in your eyes," he said.

"I have never had occasion to fear *you*, Andrew."

"That time we kissed, in this very room," he said, "I saw your fear—only for a moment, but it was long enough. I c-cannot touch you if I make you afraid."

She shuddered at the memory that kiss had elicited—Dunton's fleshy face leering at her while he claimed her body, while she parted her thighs like any whore, selling her maidenhead for the promise of a title…

He stiffened and retreated, but she caught his hand.

"No, Andrew," she said. "It was not you I fear, but a memory."

He blinked, slowly, then let out a sigh.

"I should have known," he said. "When you confessed your secret. I only feel ashamed that even for the briefest moment I judged you for giving yourself to another. But in trusting me with your secret, you have shown yourself to be a better person than I could ever be. All that remains for me to do is a apologize on behalf of my sex for the blackguard who harmed you—and to promise that I shall spend every day, until I breathe my last, striving to ensure that none shall harm you again."

He took her hand and kissed it. "I shall honor you now by leaving you in peace until we can make the necessary arrangements."

The necessary arrangements…

She smiled at his words. Like a nervous pup, he was unable to refer to their marriage, to ask her outright. But it was not because he valued her any less—it was because he valued her too much that the fear of her rejection prevented him from risking his heart.

But it mattered not. As he'd pledged to spend the rest of his life keeping her safe from harm, she would spend the rest of her days teaching him to trust her, as she trusted him.

And what greater expression of trust was there than to give herself wholly to him? Not to secure her position, or to coerce him into marriage—but a true gift of herself.

The greatest gift a woman could bestow on the man she loved.

She took his hand and kissed his knuckles. Then, meeting his gaze, she placed his hand on her breast.

His nostrils flared as he drew in a sharp breath, and she caught the flare of desire in his eyes.

"Sweet heaven…" he whispered. Uncertainty filled his gaze, while she remained still, smiling her encouragement. Then he shifted his hand, and a spark of desire flared as her nipple beaded against his palm. He flicked his tongue out, running it across his lower lip as if in anticipation of the feast to come. "Wh-what do I…"

"Anything you like, my love," she said, arching her back to press her breast against his palm.

He let out a low whimper, and, swallowing her shame at her wantonness, she grasped her neckline and lowered it to reveal the swell of her breast, the skin flushing a deep pink.

"Anything at all…"

Slowly, he dipped his head until she could feel his breath caressing the skin of her breasts. Then he placed a kiss on the top of one.

"Yes…" she breathed, tipping her head back.

He peppered her skin with tiny kisses while she murmured encouragement, then he flicked his tongue out again until the tip reached her nipple. He stiffened, as if uncertain, and she remained still, anticipation swelling within her. Then he curled his tongue around her nipple and drew it into his mouth.

She let out a soft cry at the wicked pulse of need in her center and shifted her legs to ease the rising ache between her thighs. He withdrew, and her skin tightened as cool air rippled across her breast.

"Am I not doing it right?" he asked, his voice hoarse. "Does it not please you?"

She smiled up at him. "I have never felt such pleasure before."

"B-but it's not your first—"

She placed her finger on his lips once more. "Hush, my love," she said. "Let us not speak of that. Today might be your first time, but in essence it's mine also. We must find our pleasure together."

"Then…" He lifted his eyebrows in question.

"You must do what gives you pleasure."

"And your pleasure?" he asked.

"I will take pleasure in knowing that you are taking yours."

She reached behind to unlace her sash, but he caught her hand.

"No, my love," he whispered. "I believe I may take pleasure in undressing you myself."

He rose to his feet and pulled her to hers. Then slowly, reverently, he unlaced her gown and peeled off her garments until she stood before him clad only in her stockings.

"Might I return the favor?" she whispered.

His answer was a low whimper, and she leaned toward him to remove his jacket, her breath hitching as her nipples hardened against the rough woolen fabric. She hesitated before fumbling at the buttons of his breeches. His hardened manhood strained against the material, then sprang free as his breeches fell to the floor, seeming to thicken under her gaze.

He took her hand and led her to the sofa, pushing her back until she lay before him.

He claimed her mouth, gently at first, slipping his tongue between her lips, then more insistently, a groan reverberating through his body as he curled his tongue around hers, drawing it into his mouth before sweeping across her mouth, as if he sought to devour her.

Then he withdrew and kissed the corner of her mouth, flicking his tongue along her skin until he reached her chin, where he left a trail of kisses along her throat, toward her collarbone, and, finally, the tops of her breasts.

"Does that give you pleasure?" he murmured.

"Yes," she breathed. "Oh…yes!"

She let out a cry as he clamped his mouth over her nipple and suckled deeply, drawing it into his mouth. He grazed his teeth over the bud, and she cried out again, arching her back as the exquisite nip of pain sent a bolt of pleasure through her.

"No! Do not stop!" she cried as he moved to withdraw, and she buried her hands in his hair to hold his head to her breast.

He let out a groan, like a man starved. As he laved her nipple, his hand gave her other breast the same loving attention, flicking the bud to a throbbing peak, until the twin sensations drove all rational thoughts from her mind, leaving only pure, base instinct.

The ache in her center continued to build, forming a dull, thick pulse, and she shifted her legs to ease it, but to no avail.

He shifted position, and her body sighed as he eased himself on top of her.

"M-may I…?" His voice, though thick with lust, bore a note of shyness that cleaved her soul in two.

"Yes," she cried. "Please!"

He relaxed, molding his body against hers, caressing her form with his hands, running his fingertips across her exquisitely sensitized nipples. Pleasure threaded through her as he swept his hands across her flesh, and her body tightened, as if it knew what it wanted. She shifted her thighs apart, her flesh slick with moisture, as his fingertips moved toward the center of her need, where the thick nest of curls concealed that secret place she'd dared not touch.

Then she felt him—iron hard and hot, pulsating against her thigh.

Shame threatened to overcome her at how she'd once bared herself to the man who disgusted her, for her own gain—for his title. But the beautiful man before her now, who was worshipping her—*loving* her—did not merely seek his own gratification. He sought a union of their souls.

His breathing grew shallow as he slipped his fingertips into her curls, toward the center of her need, and her body clenched in anticipation, shuddering and trembling, as if holding back a huge wave of...

Of what?

She shook her head, seeking the words, but none came. Her mind on the brink of dissolution, she could only surrender to pure sensation—as if, on the brink, she ceased to be Etty and instead was nothing more than a female driven by pure need, a mare presenting herself before the stallion.

"Andrew..." she panted. "I need... I want..."

"What, my love?" he asked, his voice strained.

She shook her head. "I d-don't know—but I need something. I—Oh!"

He dipped his finger through her curls and slicked it along her flesh. The ache sweetened and intensified, and she arched her back, opening her mouth to strain for air.

Then he withdrew his hand, and she let out a scream of frustration as the pleasure faded. "No!"

He grew still at her plea, and she opened her eyes to see him staring at her, his brow furrowed in pain, his eyes glistening, the tendons on his neck protruding, jaw taut.

"Etty..." he rasped through gritted teeth. "Etty—am I hurting you? I-I cannot stop..."

"No!" she cried. "Please—I *need* you!"

She thrust her hips upward, chasing the pleasure, and he closed his eyes, his breath stuttering. A low growl escaped his lips and he shook his head.

"I have no wish to hurt you," he said. "I—"

"You cannot hurt me, Andrew," she said. "I am no maiden."

"But how will I—"

He broke off with a long, low groan as she reached down and circled him with her hand.

"You cannot hurt me, my love," she whispered. "You can only give me pleasure—sweet, sweet pleasure."

She caressed him, running her fingertips along the soft, silken flesh, relishing the potent strength within. Her breath hitched as she reached the tip of him, slick with moisture, to match the slickness between her thighs, and he let out a cry as she gave a gentle squeeze.

"Sweet heaven—what you do to me!" he said. "Can I be dreaming?"

"No, my love—this is real," she replied. "The love we share is real."

She parted her thighs and guided him toward her center. His eyes flew open, and she smiled up at him. They stilled for a moment, then she nodded, giving her consent.

He tensed for a moment, then, with a quick thrust, he entered her. Pleasure flared, and as he sheathed himself fully inside her, his eyes filled with wonder.

Etty shifted her hips back, withdrawing. His lips curved into a smile, and he eased himself out of her. Then he inhaled sharply before plunging into her once more, and she lifted her hips to meet him.

Pleasure flared again, and she let out a low mewl.

"Is that..." he said, his breathing hoarse, and she nodded.

"Yes, Andrew," she said, "oh...yes!" She let out another cry as he withdrew and plunged in once more, setting a steady rhythm. He increased the pace, and the wave of pleasure swelled with each movement, pushing back and forth, a treacherous current that claimed her soul—to which she would gladly surrender.

With each thrust, her body swelled and pulsed, until, with a shattering explosion, she disintegrated, pulling him deeper inside and crying out his name.

"Andrew!"

He threw back his head and continued to pound inside her, while pleasure ripped her body apart. Then the wave crested. His thrusts grew more frenzied, until he let out a hoarse cry. Then he pulled her to him, shuddering and trembling while he clung to her as if his life depended on it.

The ripples in her flesh subsided while he sighed and murmured her name, his thrusts weakening until he lay on top of her, holding her close, his breath coming in quick, hard puffs beside her ear. At length, his breathing slowed. He lay still, his heartbeat a thick pulse against her chest, beating in unison with hers, and, a smile on her lips, Etty drifted into a doze.

WHEN ETTY WOKE, the fire was almost out. Andrew still lay on top of her, their bodies molded into one.

How joyous to have him hold her and cherish her, rather than merely take his pleasure and leave without a backward glance. How different he was to…

No—do not *think of him!*

She stiffened, and he lifted his head. His eyes had darkened to a deep mahogany, with sparks of light in their depths, glistening with moisture.

"D-did I hurt you?" he asked.

She lifted a hand to his cheek and brushed away the moisture there. "No, my love," she said. "It would be impossible for you to hurt me."

"It was what I feared the most—hurting the woman I loved when I…"

He colored and eased himself off her, then crossed the floor to the pile of clothes on the rug. Etty relished the sight of him— his lithe body glowing in the firelight, which cast shadows across the planes of his muscles.

He pulled his breeches on, then stood, buttoning his shirt.

"Robert told me that a woman's first time was always painful," he said. "I could never understand why a woman must feel pain, when a man…"

Her cheeks warmed and she reached for her undergarments. "Forgive me," she said, slipping on her chemise.

"What for?"

"For not being a maiden. For another taking me first."

"Oh, sweet love!" He caught her hand. "Do you think that matters? I care not about *him*. He wanted neither you nor Gabriel, and that is his greatest misfortune. Let us never think of him again."

"He's the Duke of Dunton," she said quietly.

He pulled her close and claimed her mouth. "I care not whether he's the regent himself," he said. "I care nothing for him. He has no claim on you—or on that sweet child. You are what matters, Etty, my love. What happened in your past is exactly that—your past. There are no secrets between us now. Let us therefore forget the past, move on, and build our future. Together."

He kneeled before her and took her hands. Then he lifted his head, his eyes filled with love and trust.

There are no secrets between us now.

"Let me, at last, voice the question I have wanted to ask you almost from the moment I set eyes on you in the back of my church."

"Andrew…"

"No, my darling Etty, I must ask you properly."

"I know, my love, but you must permit me to make my final confession."

"Your final…?"

"There must be no secrets between us."

"And there are none," he said, then gave a wry smile. "Unless the man Mrs. Fulford saw here was not your father after all—but I am more inclined to believe you than her."

"He is my father," she said.

"Then what secret do you carry still?"

She dipped her head and kissed his hands. "Have you never wondered what Etty was short for?"

"Henrietta, I presume?"

She shook her head. "No," she said quietly. "It's Juliette."

He nodded slowly. "Very well. Juliette." Her conscience pricked at her as he continued to smile. "It's a pretty enough name, but I must say, Etty suits you better."

"My father—his name…" She cast her gaze down, summoning the courage, then looked back up again to see doubt in his eyes. "His name is Sir Leonard Howard."

He frowned, the doubt turning into confusion. Then a spark of recognition glimmered in his eyes.

He shook his head. "Then…"

"My name is Juliette Howard," she said. "M-my elder sister is…"

He jerked back, rising to his feet, the recognition turning into horror.

"Eleanor," he whispered, shaking his head. "Dear God— Eleanor! So you're the sister who…"

She took his hands, curling her fingers around his. "Yes, Andrew," she said. "I am she. I am the one who, out of jealousy and spite, sought to ruin my sister by humiliating her and exposing her debauchery in public. I wanted the man she was engaged to for myself."

He withdrew his hands. "The Duke of Whitcombe," he said flatly.

"Yes."

"It seems you have a penchant for dukes. May I remind you that I am merely the second son of an earl?"

"How can you speak so?"

"With great conviction," he said. "Did you attempt to ruin Eleanor before, or after, you gave yourself to the Duke of Dunton?"

She flinched at the coldness in his voice.

"During."

"*During?*"

"I-I had already given myself to Dunton—but he rejected me." Her gut twisted at the memory of his words, and the revulsion she had suppressed at the notion of his hands on her flesh. "S-so I sought to teach Eleanor what it felt like t-to be…"

She caught her breath as the sob welled in her throat.

"Humiliated?" he offered, his expression hardening. "Demeaned?

"I'm sorry for it, Andrew," she said, "truly I am."

He shook his head. "*Truly I am,*" he muttered, a faintly mocking note in his voice. "The words of a sinner who seeks forgiveness even though she can never repent."

He retreated and rose to his feet, then glanced down at his shirt hanging loose. His lip curled in disgust and a flicker of shame crossed his expression—as if he'd recently engaged in a sin so unsavory that he deserved to burn.

"What have I done?" he whispered.

"Andrew, please…" She reached toward him, but he jerked back.

"No, madam!" he cried. "Say no more. I know not who you are."

The anger in his eyes fueled her indignation. "And who are *you*, vicar? A man who claims to be so righteous that he is incapable of sin?"

"I have never claimed to be free of sin, madam," he said. "I pray each night for forgiveness—"

"Only to commit those very same sins the next day? Or do you assuage your own guilt by convincing yourself that you have been led astray by a temptress? A whore?"

He flinched and lowered his gaze.

"What, vicar?" she said. "Are you so missish that you cannot bear to hear the word? And yet you are willing enough to rut—"

"*You* were willing enough," he said. "Nay, you *offered* yourself to me, parting your thighs like…"

He hesitated, then shook his head.

"Like what?" she asked. "A whore? A doxy? Or a slut? Fear not the words, sir—for the whole of your sex takes great pleasure from claiming the bodies of the women you revile. You blame us for the sins of the world, yet you are incapable of turning your own judgmental eyes on yourselves. I should have known better than to seek forgiveness from one such as you—a man incapable of forgiving another living soul."

"I *am* capable of forgiveness! Even for those deserving of none!"

Her anger burst and she lunged forward, striking his cheek with her hand.

"How *dare* you! Do not lie to me—did you not say there were to be no secrets between us?"

He stepped back, rubbing his cheek, then let out a cold laugh.

"I was wrong in that, was I not?" he sneered. "*I* harbored no secrets—it's a pity you cannot say the same yourself. But do you know what the most pitiful thing is—that which I hate myself for the most?"

"Do tell, vicar," she snarled. "One final sermon—for after today, I intend never to set foot in this godforsaken village again, where the principal inhabitants have no more morals than rutting dogs, and the only man I believed worthy of goodness himself turns out to be the embodiment of the *devil!*"

He recoiled at her words, his eyes filled with pain. He closed them, and her heart swelled with compassion.

Heaven help her—she still loved him. Even though he'd condemned her and uttered his disgust, still she loved him and could not bear the notion of his pain.

Then he opened his eyes once more, and she recoiled at his expression. All trace of emotion had gone.

"The one thing I hate myself for the most," he said, "is that I would have forgiven you for what you did to Eleanor. The woman who tried to destroy that pure, innocent soul—the woman who sought to bring an angel down to her level in the dirt…" He curled his hands into fists. "I would have forgiven you, Juliette Howard—if only you had trusted me enough to tell me the truth from the beginning."

Etty's heart shuddered at the toneless manner of his delivery.

"You're fooling yourself, vicar," she said. "You made your hatred of—of Juliette plain."

"Aye, I did," he said, "and I prayed nightly for forgiveness. But I would have grown to love her—to love *you*—regardless of your past sins." He let out a sigh and shook his head. "I did love you."

Did…

A knot of pain tightened in her body.

He stooped to retrieve his jacket, which he put on, securing the buttons with a measured, methodical movement. Then he tied his cravat and smoothed back his hair, adjusting his jacket and making a show of removing a speck of dust from his sleeve.

"Andrew…" she began, her voice a hoarse whisper, but he raised his hand.

A wail rose from elsewhere in the cottage.

"Your child is crying," he said.

"My—"

"*Dunton's* child."

She swallowed the spike of pain at his words, and for a moment, regret crossed his expression.

"Forgive me," he said. "I have taken up too much of your time."

"Yes," she said coldly. "You most certainly have. I am a fool for not having realized that weeks ago."

"Then we are both fools."

"Fool no more," she said. "Get out."

"With pleasure," he replied.

She retreated to the front door and opened it. He approached and brushed past her at the entrance. He drew in a sharp breath, and the expression in his eyes softened. Then he wiped them and the softness was gone.

"Good day, madam."

"Good riddance—*sir*," she snarled.

He issued a stiff bow, then turned his back and strode along the path. Etty watched his retreating back as he headed toward the village. Only when he'd disappeared out of sight did she close the door and surrender to her sorrow.

Choking with sobs, she stumbled along the hallway until the sharp cries of her son pierced the air. She rushed up the stairs and into his chamber, where she came upon Gabriel in his bed, his little body racked with sobs.

"Ma-ma!"

"Mama's here, my love," she said, sweeping him into her arms. She held him to her breast while he sobbed, soaking her gown, his little hands curling into fists as he clung to her with a ferocity born of a son's need for his mother.

"My darling," she whispered, rocking him to and fro. His cries subsided as he nestled against her and placed his soft head on her shoulder. "My sweet love—I'm here, and I promise I will never leave you. Mama loves you so much."

And she did. Her love for her son was not born of her own needs or desires, or her selfishness. It came without condition, without a need for forgiveness. She loved him no matter what he might do, or say, or keep hidden from her.

It was a love that no man could measure up to.

Clinging to her son, she approached the window and looked out across the landscape, the path leading toward the village hidden by trees, save the church spire, which towered over everything. A seemingly tranquil world where she had once believed that she might find peace.

But there was no peace to be found—not here.

Sandcombe was not her home. It never had been. Gabriel was her home—and wherever she went, as long as she had her son, her life would be complete.

"It's just you and me now, my darling," she whispered.

CHAPTER TWENTY-ONE

It is therefore toward men where we must cast the eye of judgment before condemning the sins of a woman.

Andrew dipped his quill into the inkpot, then dabbed the nib against the side before continuing.

Power without accountability is the root of all evil. All of us are guilty. Even myself. Even

He paused, his hand shaking. Dare he speak of the one who considered himself above sin?

Sir John Fulford… a voice said in his mind—as if his conscience compelled him to speak.

Then he set the quill aside. He had not the courage.

Only one soul in the village possessed the courage to speak of the sins being committed locally—sins permitted by the law and the church and given free rein to exist due to the parishioners' worship of the upper classes. But Andrew hadn't even the courage to speak to her after their last encounter.

At first his anger had prevented him from returning to Shore Cottage. Then, as he'd recalled the hateful words he'd said against Juliette Howard—not once thinking the very woman he'd voiced his loathing for had been standing before him all the time—shame replaced the anger. In accusing her of betraying his trust, he had committed an act of greater treachery.

She had opened her heart to him, given him the chance to prove his quality.

And he had failed at every level.

"Sir John!" a voice cried.

Andrew turned as footsteps approached. The study door flew open and the familiar, loathsome figure strode into the study brandishing a silver-topped cane, followed by the red-faced housekeeper.

"Oh, Mr. Staines, sir, forgive me, I couldn't stop—"

"Cease your prattle, woman!" Sir John cried, exuding a mist of spittle. "It's not you I'm here to see. It's him." He pointed the cane at Andrew as if brandishing a sword.

Andrew rose from his seat. "Thank you, Mrs. Clegg. Some tea, perhaps?"

"I don't want tea," Sir John sneered.

"Nevertheless, it's what I offer my guests—even those that come uninvited."

Sir John's face turned a deeper shade of red, and he let out a volley of coughs. Andrew's stomach churned. Why couldn't the man at least cover his mouth?

For a moment, an image violated Andrew's mind—Sir John's ungainly body overpowering a young maid while he sought his gratification, his smile broadening as his victim struggled in a futile attempt to escape.

Then a ball of nausea rose in his throat and he caught his breath and looked away.

"Take a seat," he said, gesturing to a chair.

"I'm not here to discuss pleasantries," Sir John said, his voice a hoarse wheeze. "I'm—"

He broke off in another round of coughing. Andrew approached him, but Sir John raised his cane and blocked his path.

"Do not touch me! I should have known you were wrong for this parish. From the moment you started to incite insurrection with those sermons of yours."

"Insurrection?" Andrew let out a laugh. "Sir John, you cannot seriously—"

"Do not tell me what I can and cannot do!" Sir John spat. "Gossip has reached my ears. Vile, sordid gossip, the like of which I should never have to hear."

"Then don't listen to gossip, Sir John."

Andrew's guest let out an explosive noise of rage, and his face darkened until it was almost purple.

"Nor should my wife have to hear such evil words."

"So, Lady Fulford has been spreading gossip."

"How *dare* you!" Sir John said. "I…" He bent forward, his body racked with spasms as he coughed, his chest rattling.

"You should see a doctor," Andrew said. "Shall I call for—"

"No!" Sir John said. "I'm in no need of a doctor! What I need is for evil to be cleaned from this place—starting with the principal agent of the devil. That"—he wrinkled his nose—"that *slut* has caused nothing but trouble since she came here— claiming to be a respectable widow when the meanest of souls could see that she's merely some whore with a filthy bastard clinging to her skirts."

Andrew's chest tightened at the hatred in his patron's voice, hatred directed at the sweetest, most innocent little boy—the little boy he had taken into his heart.

The boy who, only a few days ago, he'd resolved to call his own.

"If you mean Mrs. Ward—" Andrew began.

"*Mrs. Ward*, indeed!" Sir John yelled. "And you were fool enough to fall for it. But this time you've gone too far, letting her spread her poison, while you stand by and do nothing."

"Sir John, I'm afraid I have no idea of what you are speaking."

"Ralph Smith came banging on my door—at the front entrance, I'll have you know!" Sir John replied. "Bloody peasants. He came looking for that little slut he married. It seems she's run off—no doubt with some man—after your whore poisoned her mind with tales about me." He stepped toward Andrew, thrusting his face forward. "Me! To think—such a creature deigns to speak about me, when *I* rule this village."

"Mrs. Ward is no whore," Andrew said. "She's—"

"Oh, *spare* me! I know a fallen woman when I see one. And I know the look of a man too weak to resist the temptation. Was it worth it?"

"Worth what?"

"She spread her legs for you—yes?"

Andrew opened his mouth to deny it, then closed it again.

A smile of triumph crossed Sir John's lips.

"I *knew* it. A weak man will commit any sin if there's the prospect of a bloody good fuck at the end of it."

Andrew winced at the man's profanity. "Did you come with the express purpose of insulting me, Sir John?"

"I came to ask you to do the honorable thing and leave," came the reply. "I've already written to the bishop with my recommendation that you be defrocked. But, if you have a shred of honor, you would relinquish your living voluntarily. If not, you'll regret it."

"Oh, *will* I?" Andrew said, meeting Sir John's gaze. The man's expression faltered, as if he believed it impossible that another living soul would stand up to him.

"You do not want me for an enemy, *Mr. Staines.*"

"Then I shall bear the misfortune as best I can," Andrew replied.

Sir John's eyes widened, and his body shook with another coughing spasm. "I could have you thrown out of here in an instant!"

"I believe that power lies only with the bishop," Andrew said, "and until I hear it from his lips, I shall consider myself the incumbent of this parish. And now, given that you have not come for a social call, I must ask you to leave."

Sir John shook his head. "Would you risk your vocation— your living—for a whore?"

"Etty is not a whore!"

"*Etty,* eh? Such a telling lack of propriety. Is that the name you cry when you rut her?"

"Why, you…" Andrew balled his hands into fists and took a step forward.

"Do it!" Sir John snarled. "Go ahead. Show the world the savage you really are—the base beast willing to gratify his lust at the expense of his duty. It will only strengthen the case against you."

"And what about *you?*" Andrew said, shaking with the effort to restrain his fury. "Do you think I don't know why you hate Mrs. Ward so much? It's not because you believe her to be evil. It's because she's the one living soul in this cursed village who had the courage to reveal the extent of your sins and speak that which the rest of us know to be true!"

Sir John's eyes widened and he stepped back.

"Now, get out," Andrew said. "And know this—if I receive an edict from the bishop, I shall tell him the full truth of the matter."

"He'll not believe you," Sir John said. "We were at Eton together."

"I shall tell him nonetheless. Can you guarantee that he'll not at least wonder if there's a shred of truth in what I say? The truth always reveals itself eventually."

A flicker of doubt shimmered in Sir John's eyes.

"Do you know what I also believe?" Andrew continued. "I believe that a man will always receive retribution for his sins at the end, whether in life or beyond it. You may relish the retribution that you believe I am owed, but I would counsel you to look at your own ledger before commenting on that of others."

Sir John curled his hand around the top of his cane.

"Mrs. Clegg!" Andrew called out.

The door opened—a little too quickly—to reveal the house-keeper.

"My guest is leaving," Andrew said. "Please be so kind as to show him out."

"Very good, sir," the housekeeper replied, but Sir John pushed her aside.

"I can see myself out." He hobbled toward the front door and pushed it open. In the road was a barouche in which Lady Fulford sat. She turned toward them, a scowl on her face, and as Andrew raised his hand in greeting, she tilted her nose in the air and looked away.

Beyond the barouche, a figure was running toward the vicarage, and Andrew recognized Jimmy Gadd. He approached the doorway, and Sir John raised his cane and struck the boy in the chest.

"Out of my way, peasant!" he snarled.

"Jimmy, what's wrong?" Andrew asked.

The boy cringed, clutching his chest, his face twisted in pain. "It's Frannie!" he cried. "She's run away!"

Sir John curled his lip in a sneer and raised his cane again. An expression of determination filled Jimmy's eyes as he turned to his tormentor.

"You know Frannie, Sir John," Jimmy said. "She's my sister Freda's daughter."

"What does that have to do with me?" Sir John asked.

"She's *your…*" Jimmy began, but Andrew caught the boy's hand and, his eyes on Sir John's cane, shielded the lad with his body.

"It matters not, Sir John," Andrew said, "though you would do well to remember my warning about your ledger."

"You'll regret crossing me, *vicar*," Sir John said.

Andrew smiled. "I very much doubt it."

Sir John let out a snort, then stumbled toward the barouche, yelling at a footman who leaped down and helped him in, where Lady Fulford fussed over him, casting a look of hatred in Andrew's direction. Sir John barked an order then fell back into his seat with yet another coughing spasm, and the barouche drove off.

"Let's get you inside, Jimmy," Andrew said. "I must take a look at where that man struck you. Are you in any pain?"

"No—but we must find Frannie."

"Do you know where she's gone?"

"No." Jimmy sniffed and wiped his nose on his sleeve. "We've been looking for her all morning, then I saw Mrs. Penfold on the lane, and she said she saw Frannie climb into the most enormous carriage not half an hour earlier."

Andrew's gut twisted with fear. "Willingly?" he asked.

"Aye. Mrs. Penfold said that she called out, and Frannie waved back before climbing in."

"Was there anyone else in the carriage?"

"A woman, Mrs. Penfold thought, but it was dark inside, and she couldn't see who. It was a very fine carriage, she said."

A woman.

It cannot be a coincidence…

"Sir John told me that Loveday's husband was looking for her."

"Do you suppose they've run off together?" Jimmy asked. "Oh, Frannie! Why did she run?"

Why indeed? Perhaps Etty had the answer—Etty, who was able to understand the guilt poor little Frannie suffered merely by being born, and the shame Loveday had endured through being violated.

"Was it the mail coach?"

Jimmy shook his head. "Mail coach doesn't come by on a Friday, and it only stops at the Sailor, not the end of the lane. I-I hoped you might know, seein' as you're so fond of Frannie."

"And…Mrs. Ward?"

"I was goin' to try Mrs. Ward next. She might know where Frannie's gone."

"Then let us go together."

Jimmy nodded, and they set off for Shore Cottage.

As the isolated little building came into view, Andrew's skin tightened with apprehension. It seemed to exude an air of abandonment. He shook his head, cursing his folly. But he quickened his pace nevertheless.

As he approached the cottage, he glanced at the chimney for

the telltale wisp of smoke, but there was none. He grasped the door handle and turned it. It yielded with ease and swung inward.

The hallway was empty. The little seascape that adorned the wall opposite the parlor door had gone, leaving a nail where it had hung. He approached the parlor, his footsteps echoing, and his heart fluttered as he opened the door.

The furniture had been covered in sheets. The bookshelves were full, save for the bottom shelf where she'd once placed the teapot that Frannie had broken—the teapot he'd helped her to mend. The thin layer of dust was broken by a round mark, where the teapot had once been.

Andrew exited the parlor and brushed past Jimmy, making his way upstairs to Gabriel's chamber.

The room was empty. Even the cot was no longer there.

His heart rate increasing, he approached the door to the other chamber—her chamber—and turned the handle.

It, too, was abandoned—empty save for a bed and a chair covered in dustsheets.

"Vicar!" Jimmy called from downstairs. Andrew flew down to see the lad standing by the front door, a note in his hand. "I found this on the floor. It's for you." He held it out, and Andrew took it, his breath catching as he read the inscription on the front in familiar handwriting.

Mr. Staines.

So formal an address! But what could he expect after the way he'd spoken to her at their last meeting?

His fingers trembling, Andrew tore open the envelope and read the note.

Dear Mr. Staines.

I have returned home, to where I have the greatest chance at finding happiness.

You will not see me again.

Yours etc.

Miss Juliette Howard.

Her words, delivered in such a cold, impersonal manner, did more to strike at his heart than any angry recrimination or accusation. It was as if she no longer cared for him.

Or perhaps she never had.

Juliette Howard had returned to Society—and much good it would do her.

As for Etty—*his* Etty…

She no longer existed.

CHAPTER TWENTY-TWO

Rosecombe Park, Hertfordshire, October 1817

"THERE IT IS, look! My heaven, I've never seen anything so large in my life!"

Etty turned to the window and caught her breath as the building came into view.

Rosecombe. The seat of the Duke of Whitcombe—and her sister's home.

The last time Etty had laid eyes upon the building, she had been beset by jealousy and a determination to make Eleanor suffer for having gained what Etty had considered to be *her* right.

She clasped her hands together, palms slick, as a ball of guilt tightened deep in her stomach.

What if Papa had been wrong about Eleanor? He had assured Etty that her sister had forgiven her, but surely not even the kindest soul could forgive her for what she had done.

Andrew certainly couldn't forgive her—he'd made his contempt plain. He'd...

No. Do not think of him.

"Mrs. Ward, are you well?"

A slim hand caught Etty's, and she turned her attention to her companions—Frances leaning toward the window, vibrating with enthusiasm as she held Gabriel in her arms, and Loveday, apprehension in her expression, her eldest child staring out of the window, and the baby asleep in her lap.

Loveday squeezed her hand. "Mrs. Ward?"

Etty shook her head. "It's Miss Howard now," she said. "I'm sorry I deceived you."

"You've nowt to be sorry for, ma'am."

Loveday glanced toward the building, and Etty caught a flicker of fear in her eyes. She lowered her gaze to Loveday's bandaged wrist.

"You'll be safe here," she said. "I promise."

Loveday remained silent, while Frances pointed out the building to Gabriel.

"Big house!" he cried.

"It's like a palace," Frances said. "What do you think, Florrie?"

Loveday's eldest nodded, then she resumed her attention on her mother. "You look tired, Ma. Shall I take baby Anna?"

Etty's heart ached at the understanding in the little girl's eyes. Florence was a child—younger than Frances—yet the concern for her mother in her expression spoke of a life lived, and horrors witnessed, that no child should ever have to endure.

Loveday nodded, and winced as she handed the baby over.

"Does your wrist still pain you?" Etty asked.

"It's nothing, Miss Howard. I've had worse."

"Nevertheless, I'll ask my sister to send for a doctor."

"The duchess?" Loveday asked. "Oh no—I can't. What would the duke say if he found out?"

What would he say, indeed? Etty's father had assured her that Eleanor would welcome her with open arms. But as for Eleanor's husband, the man renowned for his impenetrable demeanor and cold heart…

Her gut twisted with fear. Perhaps this hadn't been such a good idea. But Papa had insisted that the time had come to face the consequences of her sins and not spend the rest of her life running from them.

The carriage rolled to a halt, and Etty caught sight of two female figures standing at the foot of the steps leading to the main doors of the building. Then the carriage door opened and a footman appeared, offering his hand.

"Miss Howard."

Trembling, Etty took the proffered hand and climbed out. She stumbled on the bottom step, and the footman caught her arm.

"Steady there, miss."

Then he released her, and she found herself standing before her sister.

Etty recognized the woman standing beside her—the black-clad housekeeper with her iron-gray hair set in a severe style. But had it not been for the intense expression in her emerald eyes—which had always disconcerted Etty, for she had always believed her sister could penetrate her soul with a single look—Etty would not have recognized Eleanor.

Gone was the awkward, shy young woman, the misfit who had weathered the taunts of Etty and her friends with quiet distress. Eleanor had been transformed into a duchess—not the glittering diamond to whom Society looked for inspiration, but a genteel creature, understated and dignified. Her gown, a pale-green silk, was elegant in its simplicity, accentuating her soft curves.

Etty stared at the sister against whom she'd once relished the comparison in her favor, but who now outshone her in every aspect. With the goodness that radiated from her soul, and the sheer happiness of her countenance, Eleanor was a woman who had found peace and fulfilment.

Next to her sister, Etty was nothing more than the spiteful creature who had tried, and failed, to ruin the kindest soul to have walked upon the earth.

How she must hate me.

Eleanor stepped forward, and Etty fought to conquer her shame, moisture stinging her eyes as she braced herself for the recriminations.

But none came. Instead, a pair of soft arms drew her into an embrace.

"Welcome, sister."

"Eleanor, please forgive—"

"Hush, Juliette," Eleanor whispered. "Let us not pursue it. You are here, which is all that matters."

"But what I did to you—"

"It's forgotten."

Etty let out a sob, and Eleanor kissed her cheek.

"Come now, sister," she said, smiling. "It's a day to be happy, is it not? For you've come home."

"Home?"

Eleanor nodded. "Yes, Juliette. This is your home, for as long as you wish it."

"B-but your…your husband—"

"Gives me free rein to direct the household as I see fit," Eleanor interrupted. "Besides, he's in London with his sister, and is therefore not here to plague us for the next few days at least. Now, where is my nephew?"

Etty turned toward the carriage. "You can come out, now, Frances."

The girl stepped out, Gabriel in her arms, and approached. Eleanor extended her hand, and Frances stared at it.

"Welcome, Frances," Eleanor said. "And this must be my nephew!"

Gabriel turned away and buried his head in Frances's shoulder, and Eleanor withdrew her hand.

"Forgive him, Your Grace," Frances said. "He's shy of strangers."

A stricken look crossed Frances's expression as Eleanor's smile slipped.

"I understand," she said quietly. "I am not fond of strangers myself."

Frances blushed. "He's friendly enough when he gets to know you, Your Grace."

Eleanor nodded. "My nephew is a fortunate young man to

have such a champion in yourself, Frances."

Gabriel stirred in Frances's arms and turned to face Eleanor, a serious expression in his dark eyes.

"I hope we'll become well acquainted, young sir," she said. "Do you like gardens?"

The boy nodded.

"We have a lovely garden, just right for a young man to explore and to have all sorts of adventures in. And how about cake? I've never known a boy who does not like cake, especially fruitcake."

A broad grin spread across his face.

"He loves fruitcake," Etty said. "Frances here makes an excellent fruitcake."

"You must all have a slice at tea," Eleanor said. "Then perhaps, young man, you can tell me whether it's as good as that which you're used to."

The boy grinned and reached out toward Eleanor. She took the boy's hand. "Pleased to meet you, little man," she said. "I'm your Aunt Eleanor."

"Ant," the boy said. "Ant. Ell."

Eleanor let out a soft laugh. "Ant Ell it is, then!" She turned to Etty. "I should have invited you and Gabriel earlier. I never wanted us to be strangers. Please forgive me."

"You're the last person needing forgiveness," Etty said, choking back a sob.

"Then let us never be strangers again," Eleanor said. "I… Who's this?"

Her eyes widened as the rest of the party climbed out of the carriage—Loveday first, followed by Florence holding baby Anna. Then she turned to the housekeeper.

"Mrs. Adams, I think we'll be needing two more guest chambers prepared."

"Oh, no, ma'am!" Loveday said. "Pardon me—I mean, Your Grace… We're not guests. We're…"

"If you're friends of my sister, then you're my guests," Eleanor said.

"But Your Grace—" the housekeeper began, but Eleanor raised her hand.

"Mrs. Adams, these ladies will be tired from their journey. Miss…?" She glanced at Frances.

"Frannie Gadd, ma'am."

"Very good. Miss Gadd, and…?" She looked toward Loveday, who dipped into a curtsey.

"Loveday Smith, ma'am—a-and my eldest, Florence, and baby Anna."

Eleanor cast her gaze over Loveday and her children, and Etty flinched. Now her sister was a duchess, would she consider herself too grand for Loveday and her kind?

But Eleanor's gaze settled on Loveday's bandaged wrist. Her nostrils flared almost imperceptibly, and she stiffened and glanced toward Etty, a flicker of pain in her eyes. Then she blinked, and the pain disappeared as she smiled brightly at Loveday.

"I am determined," she said. "One chamber for Miss Gadd, and another for Mrs. Smith and her children—I think the blue room would do for Mrs. Smith, if you'd see to it, Mrs. Adams?"

"Of course, ma'am." The housekeeper dipped her head. "I'll send Tilly and Sarah to tend to them."

Eleanor placed a hand on the housekeeper's arm. "Thank you," she said, smiling. Then she took Etty's hand once more. "Mrs. Adams will show you to your chamber, then, when you've taken your rest, I hope you'll join us for tea."

"*Us?* I-I thought you said your husband wasn't at home," Etty said.

"He's not, never fear," Eleanor said. "But it wouldn't matter if he was. You're my guest, and he must accept that. But I have another guest who is eager to see you again."

"Who?"

Eleanor smiled, mischief sparkling in her eyes. "You'll have to take tea with us to find out," she said. "And you must bring Gabriel so he can give his expert opinion on my cook's fruitcake."

She turned to Frances and Loveday. "You are welcome also. The drawing room has a wonderful view of the gardens."

Loveday's eyes widened, and she stepped back. "Oh, no, Your Grace, I couldn't possibly—"

"You could," Eleanor said, "but I shan't impose on you if you'd rather take tea in your chamber." Her gaze dropped to Loveday's wrist once more. "You are quite safe here, Mrs. Smith—and free to do as you please."

She offered her arm to Etty. "Come, sister," she said. "Let us get you inside. We've been apart for two years, and I intend to make up for that."

Etty took the proffered arm and let her sister lead her into the building.

On one count, her sister was wrong. The two of them hadn't been apart for two years. They'd been apart for a lifetime— separated by their differences in character and the rules of Society that set women, even sisters, against each other.

But no more.

⇛⇚

ETTY STEPPED OUT of her bedchamber with Frances, who carried Gabriel in her arms. A clock struck four in the distance, followed by another, then another, until a chorus of chimes filled the air, before falling silent, leaving a faint echo that clung to the air before dissolving into the walls.

Etty descended the stairs, where a footman stood waiting.

"Miss Howard," he said, bowing. "The duchess awaits you in the drawing room in the east wing. If you would follow me?"

He led the way along a hallway, his feet clicking against the polished stone floor. Etty followed, Frances beside her, the girl's footsteps at a more hurried pace.

At length, he stopped outside a pair of doors. Voices came from the room within. Etty recognized her sister's voice, accompanied by that of another woman, and a deep male voice.

Eleanor's other guests.

Seeking comfort, Etty reached for Frances, her hand shaking. Her sister might have forgiven her, but the rest of their acquaintance was not likely to match Eleanor's generosity, however naïvely Eleanor might believe others to be as kind as she.

The footman opened the door. "Miss Juliette Howard," he called.

Etty flinched at the announcement, as if it proclaimed her guilt to the world. Summoning her courage, she entered the room.

Eleanor rose to her feet. "Sister! I trust you're well rested." She gestured to the woman sitting on the sofa. "You already know Lady Arabella, of course."

Etty drew in a sharp breath as she recognized her sister's guest.

Lady Arabella Ponsford. Her former friend—and the woman who had triumphed over Etty's disgrace and secured an offer of marriage from the Duke of Dunton.

But the man with Arabella was not Dunton. Tall, muscular, with an unruly mop of dirty-blond hair, brilliant blue eyes, and huge hands, he looked the very antithesis of the portly, lecherous duke. He was dressed in a tailored jacket of dark blue, with a waistcoat embroidered in formfitting silk breeches and polished boots. But he did not wear them well. He rose to his feet, moving with the awkwardness of a man in an environment he deemed hostile—as if he believed he did not belong there.

He reached for Arabella, and she rose too, revealing her rounded belly, and the two exchanged a smile before resuming their attention on Etty.

Arabella's smile disappeared, and Etty took a step back.

Then the man approached Etty, hand outstretched.

"Lawrence Baxter, at your service, Miss Howard," he said, and Etty found her hand swallowed up in what could only be described as a great paw, the skin roughened and calloused. A broad grin stretched his face, and his eyes twinkled with warmth and kindness.

With his country accent and ungentlemanly air, he was the very last man with whom the Arabella she knew would have associated. But Etty couldn't help warming to his lack of pretension and the raw honesty that came with it.

From the corner of her eye she saw Arabella watching her, her brow furrowed into a frown. Then she resumed her attention on the giant.

"Mr. Baxter, a pleasure," Etty said.

"You know my Bella, of course. She's been wantin' to see you ever so bad. She's told me so much about you."

"Oh, dear, forgive me. I—" Etty began, but Mr. Baxter interrupted her by throwing his head back and bellowing with laughter.

"Ha! You told me she'd not like it if I said you'd been talkin' about her, didn't you, Bella? Women are so funny sometimes. No, Miss Howard, my Bella's only ever said good things about you. And I can see for myself she spoke the truth."

Etty glanced at Arabella, whose cheeks had turned a shade of rose. "What did my friend say?" she asked.

"That you were the most beautiful creature in the whole of London," Mr. Baxter said. "Now, seein' as I think my Bella is the most glorious creature to walk this earth, I found it impossible to believe that any other woman could measure up to her. But I'll grant that you're a very pretty thing, and were you to grace London with your presence, you would indeed be declared the most beautiful."

"Lawrence, I'm sure Juliette hasn't come here to be *flattered*," Arabella said. "Nor has she come to listen to your nonsense. Talk sensibly, lest my friend think you a simpleton."

Etty flinched at the sharpness in Arabella's tone. "Lady Arabella," she said, dipping her head. But before Arabella could reply, Frances entered, Gabriel in her arms.

Lady Arabella stared at the boy and drew in a sharp breath.

She glanced from Etty to Gabriel, understanding and recognition filling her eyes, then her mouth settled into a firm line.

Etty braced herself for her former friend's contempt as Arabella approached Etty's son—the bastard son of the duke who'd offered Arabella his hand.

"Yes," she said, at length. "I see the likeness."

Etty swallowed her shame and awaited Arabella's condemnation.

Then Arabella reached out and touched Gabriel's cheek.

"What a beautiful child," she said softly. "A credit to your mother. And let nobody tell you otherwise, young man."

Gabriel stared at Arabella, then reached up and caught a curl of her glossy black hair in his fist. Etty caught her breath.

But Lady Arabella took Gabriel's hand and smiled. "Sweet boy," she said. "Perhaps you'd like to sit with me for tea, if your mama has no objection?"

She met Etty's gaze, a plea in her eyes, and Etty understood the peace offering for what it was.

"You'd like that, Gabriel, wouldn't you?" she said.

The boy nodded.

"Excellent!" Arabella said. "Eleanor tells me you like gardens, Gabriel. Did you know that my husband here is the finest gardener in the country?"

Etty's heart warmed at the pride in her friend's voice. It was not the selfish pride Arabella had once possessed in abundance—pride in her beauty, or her title. It was the pride in another, in the husband she so evidently loved.

Gabriel turned his wide-eyed expression toward Mr. Baxter.

"I'm sure he'd love to give you a tour of the gardens here, Gabriel," Arabella continued. "He designed them himself. Perhaps he could show you after tea—then your mama and I can catch up on the past." She glanced at Etty. "Or, perhaps, we can forget the past and reforge our friendship for the future."

She took Etty's hand, the tightening of her grip conveying more than any words.

"Yes," Etty whispered. "I should like to reforge friendships—and to look to the future."

"Excellent!" Arabella patted the couch next to her. "Come sit beside me, Juliette. Lawrence can make room."

Etty glanced toward Frances, who stood beside the doors, discomfort in her eyes.

"Come and sit with me, Frances," Eleanor said. "Then you can tell me what you think of my cook's cake."

The young girl hesitated, then took a seat, after which Eleanor began to serve the tea, issuing instructions to the footman, who sliced the cake.

Etty relaxed into her seat, relishing the air of friendship and informality. Eleanor and Frances laughed together while they discussed the merits of soaking fruit in wine before baking, and Arabella shared her cake with Gabriel, fussing over him while he sat on her knee as Mr. Baxter regaled the boy with tales of the finest wonders of the world—ancient palaces and exotic gardens that he had re-created in the grounds of Rosecombe.

For the first time, Etty was able to shed the façades she had striven to wear all her life. Her secrets now exposed, she no longer had need to deceive, and nor had she the need to atone for past sins. She was with friends, and family, who accepted her for who she was and what she had done.

Perhaps, at last, she was truly home.

CHAPTER TWENTY-THREE

Sandcombe, Lincolnshire. October 1817

THE CHIEF BENEFIT of liquor was its ability to dull the senses and numb the pain. But, as all topers must come to learn, an excess of liquor placed a man in danger of acknowledging the absolute truth.

"Foolish nonsense," Andrew muttered as he refilled his glass then took another mouthful of brandy. The liquor burned the back of his throat and he swallowed quickly. Then he tipped his head back, drained the glass, and slammed it on the table.

The *absolute truth* of the matter was that *she* didn't deserve him.

He filled the glass once more, then clicked his tongue in frustration as he tipped the now-empty decanter up, shaking the last droplets out.

He took another mouthful.

I'm well rid of her.

He swallowed once more and winced at the sharp spike of pain between his eyes.

"I'm better off without her!" he declared to no one.

No, you're not—and well you know it.

Bloody hell—liquor was supposed to *dull* the senses. But where his conscience was concerned, it only seemed to sharpen with each mouthful until it jabbed at his mind in its relentless determination to thrust a mirror before his soul.

He lifted the glass to his lips, then set it aside. An empty glass was a sign of a man who lacked self-control. Whereas a man capable of leaving a glass half full demonstrated that he did not need liquor to survive the day.

He needed nothing to survive the day.

Not even *her*.

Curse it! Could he not have a single waking thought unviolated by her? His dreams he'd long since surrendered to, with her soft voice whispering to him while he slept, tempting him, deceiving him…

But she had left him, abandoned him, taking Frannie Gadd and Loveday Smith with her, leaving the Gadds without their daughter—and leaving Andrew to deal with the fury of Ralph Smith and the outrage of Sir John Fulford, who had suffered a seizure shortly after he visited Andrew, for which Lady Fulford and most of her acquaintance placed the blame on Andrew's shoulders.

Any moment now, a letter would come from the bishop ousting him from his position.

Let it come.

He reached for his quill and knocked over the decanter, which fell to the floor with a crash.

"Shit!"

He winced at the profanity. Another sin to pray forgiveness for at night. Not that any of his prayers were ever answered. Had his prayers been answered, then *she* would not have…

Curse it! There she was again. And now his head hurt.

The door opened, and he jerked upright, wincing at the pain in his head, to see the blurred outline of his housekeeper standing in the entrance, holding a cup in her hand. Her keys jangled on her belt, and the grating metallic sound pulsed in his head.

"What is it, Mrs. Clegg?"

She tilted her head sideways.

"*Must* you do that?" he snapped.

"Do what?"

"Look at me like I'm a belligerent child and you're my nursemaid."

He blinked, focusing on her, his head throbbing. She lowered her gaze to the remnants of the decanter, then resumed her attention on him, her expression that of a disappointed parent.

"Why should I not look at you as one might a *belligerent child*?" she said. "I see not the actions of a man." She gestured to his half-empty glass. "A man who loses himself in liquor is no man at all."

"Got that from the Bible, did you?" Andrew sneered, wincing with regret almost as soon as the words left his mouth.

"From my father, actually," she replied tartly. "He spoke a good deal of sense, he did. You've only to look about the village to see the creatures who call themselves men who have turned to liquor. Men such as Ralph Smith, Sir John Fulford. But you, vicar—I thought *you* better than that."

"Then I'm sorry to disappoint you."

"You don't sound sorry," she replied. "At least not for *that*."

Another spike of pain pulsed behind his eyes, and he lifted his hand to his head, pressing the fingertips against his temples.

She approached the chair opposite his desk and sat—without asking for leave, but he hadn't the strength to admonish her.

"You're hurting, vicar," she said. "And I'm not referring to your headache—for which, truth be told, I have no sympathy, given that it's self-inflicted."

"I'm fine."

"If you say so. There's no shame in regret, you know."

"Regret?" he asked. "I've no regrets."

The lie clung to the air, and she let out a sigh. "To heal our pain, we must first accept the truth."

"And the truth is?"

"That not all sins deserve punishment," she replied. "When we're entrusted with a sinner's confession, we must show compassion for the sinner and honor their trust."

"What nonsense you speak, Mrs. Clegg," he said. "Where did

you hear *that* from?"

"From one of your sermons," came the reply. "The very same sermon where you declared that a woman's misfortune is to shoulder the blame in a world ruled by men." She leaned forward and placed the cup on the desk.

"You brought me a cup of tea?" Andrew asked.

"Coffee, actually."

"What for?" He peered into the cup at the black, steaming liquid within. "I don't take coffee at this hour."

"Neither do you reduce yourself to a state of inebriation," she replied. "But needs must. You have a guest, and judging by the look of him, I'd recommend receiving him with at least a semblance of sobriety."

"A guest?" Andrew gestured toward her. "Send him away. He can wait."

"I wouldn't advise it."

"Why? Who is he?"

His stomach spasmed and he swallowed a bolt of nausea. Was it Sir Leonard Howard, come to challenge him to a duel for dishonoring his daughter?

The housekeeper pulled a card out of her pocket and placed it on the desk. Andrew picked it up, his head throbbing as he focused his gaze on the inscription.

Gerard Turnbull

Watkins, Turnbull & Grimley

Chancery Lane, London.

"He said you'd know who he was," she said.

Andrew nodded slowly. "He's my father's solicitor."

"I thought as much. I took the liberty of giving him tea while he waited." She pushed the cup toward him and gave a soft smile. "I told him you were resting after a busy day visiting the poor of the village."

"An untruth, Mrs. Clegg?"

"With the most noble of motives, vicar. And you have engaged in several busy days visiting the poor of the village, so it's not a complete untruth. Mr. Turnbull was happy to wait. As long as need be, he said. He's taken a room at the Sailor for the night."

So, it wasn't a fleeting visit. Apprehension churned in Andrew's gut, and he picked up the coffee cup and took a sip, then wrinkled his nose.

By heaven, that was strong!

"I told him you'd be with him in thirty minutes. Will that be enough time to make yourself presentable?"

Andrew nodded meekly. There was no defense against a strong-willed, determined woman—particularly if she was in the right.

"Good," she said. "I have some feverfew tea infusing, which I'll bring along in a moment. For your head."

"Yes, Mrs. Clegg," he said, fighting the urge to say, *Yes, Nanny*.

She arched an eyebrow, then gave a smile of indulgence. "You may try my patience, Mr. Staines, but I shall miss you when you leave the parish."

"I'm going nowhere," he replied.

"Perhaps." She rose and approached the door. Then she turned and fixed her gaze on him. "May I speak out of turn?"

"When do you not, Mrs. Clegg?"

She rolled her eyes. "Very well. I just wanted to say that you were wrong."

"Wrong?"

"When you said you were better off without her."

He winced. "Eavesdropping at my door, were you?"

"When one's employer makes a declaration at the top of his voice, one cannot help but hear it," she said. "You may have believed the liquor to assist you in securing your conviction when your heart speaks to the contrary, but I'll wager all it has given you is a sore head. Perhaps the time has come to take heed of your own sermons. The trust of another soul is a gift—a precious gift to treasure."

"I don't know what—"

"Now, you're not going to disappoint me again, are you?" She folded her arms. "Have you never stopped to consider the amount of courage it takes to defy convention and stand up for what is right? A woman—with little power over her fate—must choose her battles wisely. You may view her as an incomer who disturbed the peace of the village, but that peace came at a price. That price was innocent souls such as Freda Gadd and Loveday Smith. And Mrs. Ward was the only one of us brave enough to stand up and put a stop to the payments. Yes, it's come at a cost to those who believed in the perfection of village life. But that cost is better borne than the suffering of innocents."

He stared at her—the prim housekeeper always ready to maintain convention and order. Where had that impassioned speech come from? Did every woman conceal a warrioress beneath her subservient exterior?

He swallowed another mouthful of coffee.

"Good," she said. "Now, drink it all up, and I'll be back with your infusion."

He drained the cup, and she gave a satisfied nod.

"Men!" she huffed. "They never know what's best for them."

"I don't know how I'd manage without you, Mrs. Clegg," he said.

"Perfectly fine, I assure you," she replied. "When faced with adversity, the finest of characters will always find the resources to survive."

"And you think me a fine character?" he said. "You've never said as much."

"I'm not a flatterer, vicar. But perhaps what you should ask yourself is if another exists without whom your life is incomplete."

"Is that—"

"From one of your sermons?" She shook her head. "No. But it's the best advice I can think of to give to a man in love."

He opened his mouth to deny it, then closed it again. Mrs. Clegg was the kind of woman who had the ability to sniff out an untruth as a pig sniffed out a prize truffle—though doubtless she'd clip his ear at the analogy.

She smiled, then nodded and exited the study.

BY THE TIME Andrew approached the parlor, his headache had lessened a little, though whether that was due to the restorative properties of feverfew or the distraction brought about by its bitter taste, which still lingered at the back of his throat, he knew not.

He pushed open the door. A small, neat, balding man sat in an armchair beside a round table laden with tea things. As Andrew entered, he rose, clicked his heels together, then issued a stiff bow.

"Mr. Turnbull," Andrew said. "A pleasure. Forgive me for not waiting on you when you arrived."

He extended his hand, but the man merely stared at it. Then he bowed again. "Viscount Radham."

Andrew froze. "Wh-what?"

"Forgive me, your lordship. May I be the first to—"

"No," Andrew whispered. He stumbled forward, and the lawyer grasped his hand. The strength of the man's grip belied his diminutive appearance. Perhaps he was in the habit of propping up clients at risk of swooning, given that much of his occupation would necessitate the imparting of bad news.

Viscount Radham.

Shit.

That meant only one thing.

Robert...

Andrew's gut twisted with horror, and he drew in a deep breath to swallow the ball of nausea sticking in his throat. "I— I..."

The lawyer tightened his grip, then steered Andrew toward a chair. "I deemed it appropriate to tell you in person, your lordship," the lawyer said. "Forgive the manner of my intrusion. I came as swiftly as I could. Your father asks that you return with me posthaste."

"I-is my father well?"

"As well as can be expected under the circumstances. But the earl, naturally, is in need of you, given that you are now his—"

"Yes, yes," Andrew interrupted. He had no wish for the man to voice it.

His *heir*.

"I quite understand, your lordship."

Andrew winced. Must the man address him so?

"You don't look at all well, your lordship," Mr. Turnbull said. "A brandy might be in order, if you have any?"

Andrew shook his head. More liquor was the last thing he needed right now. No, what he needed was now irrevocably beyond his reach.

His freedom.

"What happened?" he asked.

"Your brother was involved in a riding accident."

"In the country?" Andrew asked. "I cannot believe that. Robert always detested the country."

"It happened in London," the lawyer said. "Hyde Park. He was racing his carriage and it overturned."

"Sweet Lord!" Andrew whispered.

"I have it on good authority that he didn't suffer," Mr. Turnbull continued. "Broke his neck, apparently. Killed instantly."

Andrew drew in a sharp breath and lifted his hand to his mouth as the nausea threatened to spill over. "When?"

"Two days ago. Just before dawn."

"Was he alone?"

Mr. Turnbull's cheeks reddened. "Your brother's—ahem— *companion* was in the carriage with him. She survived only a few hours after the accident. The gentleman he was racing came to his aid, but it was too late."

Companion. Mistress, more like, given the expression in the lawyer's eyes.

"The gentleman he was racing?" Andrew asked.

"His Grace, the Duke of Sawbridge."

Definitely a mistress, then—or, more likely, a whore.

Sawbridge—a man whose reputation as the most profligate womanizer alive had reached even Andrew's ears. Sawbridge and Robert had been at Eton and Oxford together. He had a reputation for spending a veritable fortune on women, liquor, and wild parties, and he was the man whom Robert had always aspired to be—the epitome of the soulless, amoral rake.

"When he has recovered, His Grace will be writing to you to offer his condolences," Mr. Turnbull said.

"I'll bet he bloody will," Andrew muttered.

The lawyer's eyes widened at the profanity.

"Wait, what do you mean—when he's recovered?" Andrew asked.

"The duke broke his leg in the accident. *His* companion survived unscathed."

"Well, I'm glad for *that*, at least."

Mr. Turnbull raised his eyebrows but had the sense not to ask Andrew whether he was glad that Sawbridge's doxy had survived, or glad that Sawbridge had broken his leg.

I bloody well hope it hurts him. A lot.

"What about my brother's…companion?" Andrew asked. "Has Sawbridge sent her family his condolences?"

"I believe she has no family, your lordship," Mr. Turnbull said, his cheeks reddening further. "I believe she is—was—a woman of…" He made a random gesture, his blush extending to the tips of his ears.

"I understand," Andrew said.

Given Sawbridge's—and, if Andrew were honest, his brother's—reputation, Robert must have indulged in a drunken carriage race after a night's drinking and whoring.

Sweet Lord Almighty! Pain hammered at Andrew's mind, and he leaned forward and placed his head in his hands.

"I trust you understand the necessity of attending your father," Mr. Turnbull said. "I have taken a room at the inn here and shall await your instructions when you are ready."

Andrew nodded. "Yes, of course."

"Then I shall trespass on your time no longer." Mr. Turnbull rose to his feet and extended his hand once more, and Andrew took it. "Please accept my condolences for your loss, Lord Radham."

Ignoring the pain in his head and his heart, Andrew took the proffered hand. "Thank you. If you would be so good as to remain at the inn for another day to give me time to settle my affairs here, I shall be ready to depart this time tomorrow."

"Very good, sir." The lawyer gave a neat bow. "If I may be so bold as to venture an opinion, I believe that the viscountcy will be in good hands."

After Andrew had ushered the neat little man out, he returned to the parlor. His gaze fell upon the decanter, its rounded belly filled with dark brown liquid—and with it, the potential to bring forth oblivion.

He picked it up.

Please accept my condolences for your loss, Lord Radham.

A mirthless laugh rose in Andrew's chest, and he surrendered to it. His voiced swelled with a crescendo until, with a final roar, he threw back his arm, then flung the decanter at the door, where it shattered on impact, exploding into shards, issuing a thick mist of brandy that clung to the air momentarily before falling to the floor.

"Loss!" Andrew cried. "You cannot comprehend what I have lost!"

That bald-headed harbinger of doom had uttered all the appropriate words in the appropriate place. But Andrew had lost more than a brother. He'd already lost the woman he loved. And now, he had lost his vocation. All hope for a quiet life away from the demands of Society had gone—and with it, his freedom.

He sank to his knees, shaking as he fought to conquer his despair. Only now, as everything he valued had been stripped from him, did he fully understand the despair that *she*, his Etty, must have felt, the fortitude with which she had fought against her fate, the strength with which she had fought for those whom she loved.

He'd been waiting all his life for a sign from the Almighty, an answer to his prayers for peace and salvation. And today, he finally understood that an answer would always be forthcoming at the end.

Even if that answer was *no*.

CHAPTER TWENTY-FOUR

Rosecombe Park, Hertfordshire, October 1817

"*OH MIO CARO dolce amore…*"

Etty had forgotten the pure joy to be had from a love song. The soft music from the pianoforte filled the drawing room, stilling its occupants while they listened, enraptured, as Lady Arabella's fingers caressed the keys, providing a gentle backdrop to Etty's voice.

At first she'd shied away from Eleanor's insistence that she sing for the company after dinner. But, encouraged by her sister's gentle touch as she led Etty to the pianoforte where Arabella had already set aside the music, Etty finally relented.

"Possa trovare l'amore."

As she sang the final words, the music trailed away, followed by silence punctuated by the ticking of the clock on the mantelshelf. Giving Arabella a quick, tight smile, Etty moved toward her seat, but Eleanor caught her arm.

"You sing well, sister. I trust you will sing for us every night while you're here."

"Oh, I-I did not think you'd want me to…"

"To what? Accept your sister's hospitality?" Eleanor said. "You are welcome here for as long as you like. Having you here is a joy."

"You flatter me," Etty said, then regretted her words as Eleanor narrowed her eyes and looked away. She took her hand. "Forgive me, sister—I did not mean to imply that you were insincere. It's just that I am unused to—" She broke off, her cheeks warming.

"Unused to praise that is genuine, as opposed to mere words from another who wishes to ingratiate themselves?"

Etty met her sister's gaze, wincing at the intensity of Eleanor's expression. "I always used to fear your insight," she said. "Instead I should have welcomed it. I suppose the choice of song was yours?"

"Bella's, actually," Eleanor said, gesturing to Etty's friend, who was rising from the pianoforte, a protective hand over her belly. Etty's heart ached as Arabella's husband leaped to his feet and gently guided his wife back to her seat.

"Lawrence, I'm perfectly capable of walking to a chair," Arabella huffed.

"Yes, love, but I'm incapable of watching you struggle without feeling like an arse," he replied. Arabella swatted him on the arm, and he winced and nodded toward Etty. "Beggin' your pardon, ma'am, for cursing. That song were lovely, though I'm afraid I couldn't understand a word of it. What was it?"

"'*È degna di amore,*'" Arabella said.

"It means, 'She is worthy of love,'" Eleanor added, slipping her arm through Etty's. "Bella and I thought it appropriate under the circumstances. Now, sister, I think you've earned a rest. I—" She broke off and tilted her head to one side, a smile curving her lips. "Is that…?"

Footsteps approached, and the doors were flung open to reveal two men. The first, tall and broad shouldered, strode into the room, and Etty caught her breath as she set eyes on him—on the savagely handsome face that had claimed the hearts of every eligible debutante—and their mothers. With thick, dark hair that curled rakishly at the ends and brilliant blue eyes, the Duke of Whitcombe was the handsomest man to have ever walked upon the earth. But he had eyes for none but his wife.

"Monty!" Eleanor let out a cry and ran toward him while he pulled her into an embrace, lifting her off her feet to spin her around, before claiming her mouth for a kiss.

"I didn't hear the carriage," she said, breathless. "We did not expect you before Saturday."

"Ah, but, my love, when the opportunity presents itself to return to you early, I'd be a fool were I not to take it. And to return to such sweet music only convinces me that the duration of my absence has been too long."

"Have you brought Olivia with you?"

"I believe my sister will enjoy the trappings of London more without her brother getting in the way," he said. "But I've ensured Olivia's virtue is safe by bringing *this* reprobate home with me."

He gestured toward his companion, who limped toward Eleanor and dipped his head in a bow. Etty recognized the Duke of Sawbridge—a committed rake whose piratical good looks had secured his position as Whitcombe's main rival for female attention, but who was renowned for spending his considerable fortune contributing to the profits of London's most notorious gaming hells and bawdy houses.

But, judging by the splint bandaged to the lower half of his right leg, his profligate lifestyle must have caught up with him. Perhaps a cuckolded husband had met Sawbridge at dawn and he now sported a bullet hole in the leg.

I hope it gives you much pain.

As if he'd heard her thoughts, Sawbridge glanced toward Etty. "Well, I'll be damned!" he cried.

Whitcombe approached Etty and extended his hand. "The songstress, I presume," he said. "For as much as I love my wife, I know that her talent lies in drawing, not singing. Forgive me, I don't believe we've been..."

He froze, his voice trailing away. Then he glanced toward Eleanor before resuming his attention on Etty, his expression hardening.

"For what purpose are *you* here, madam?"

Etty flinched at the harshness in his tone.

"Monty, I invited my sister here," Eleanor said. "Forgive me. I meant to—"

"*You've* done nothing to forgive, my love," he said, his gaze still fixed on Etty. "As to this creature"—he gestured toward her—"no reasonable man could ever forgive her for what she did. And to prey on your good nature by slithering her way into our lives once more… Madam, what right have you to disturb our peace? Were you not content with destroying your sister's life the first time that you seek to ruin her again?"

"Your Grace, I—"

"No!" he barked, raising his hand. "You have no right to address me in my house, as if you are my guest when you are come to spread your poison. You are not welcome here."

"Montague, please!" Eleanor cried. "My sister is here at *my* invitation."

"Then why was I not told?"

"Must I ask your permission every time I wish to invite a guest here?"

"Eleanor, you know you may do as you please," he replied, "but—"

"She's my *sister*, Monty," Eleanor said. "We have made our peace. Can you not therefore make your peace with her also?"

He shook his head. "I cannot forget what happened," he said. "You fled London in disgrace, alone, and friendless, your life *destroyed*."

Eleanor placed a hand on his cheek, and his expression softened. "Not destroyed, my love," she whispered. "I suffered pain, yes…"

"Pain that *she* caused."

"But that pain gave me understanding, Monty. I may have lost my reputation, but I gained so much more—the confidence to express myself, and to live on my own terms."

She caressed his cheek, and Etty's heart ached at the love in her sister's eyes.

"That pain taught me that I could survive, no matter what trials were placed before me," she said. "I learned to be strong, and to love myself for who, and what, I am, not for how the world perceived me. Can you not see what a gift that was? I have much to be thankful as a result of what happened. As do *you*, my love."

Her eyes shining with moisture, Eleanor turned toward Etty and extended her hand. Etty took it, and gentle fingers interlocked with hers.

"That is the gift my sister gave me, at such a cost to herself. All I ask is a little generosity of heart from you, Montague—enough to forgive my sister."

He placed a kiss on Eleanor's lips. "You make me a better man, my love," he said. "For your sake—and yours alone—I shall endeavor to forgive your sister."

He pulled his wife into an embrace, then looked toward Etty. "I am, however, not the type of man to forget."

"Your Grace—" Etty began.

"For my wife's sake, I'll forgive you, Miss Howard, though it would be hypocritical of me to welcome the prospect of your staying in my home. I take it you're residing with Sir Leonard and this is merely a passing visit to convey the apology due to my wife?"

Etty's gut twisted with shame. What a fool she'd been to think the duke would suffer her company in his home! A man with his reputation for harshness could never bring himself to forgive a woman—especially not the woman who had publicly tried to ruin his wife. His reputation would not weather it, despite Eleanor's assurances to the contrary. The dear woman believed the world was as forgiving as her. But the harsh man she'd married had only the capacity to love one other without condition—Eleanor herself.

What might it be like to be loved so completely by one so fierce?

"Sawbridge, Your Grace," Arabella said, rising to her feet and gesturing toward Whitcombe's companion. "It seems you are somewhat indisposed. I take it the other fellow came off worse?"

Sawbridge colored. "I know not of what you speak, Lady Arabella."

"Come now, sir," she replied, "a man of your…*experience* of the world should understand me perfectly. May I be so bold as to suggest that your injury took place at dawn?"

He winced and shuffled toward a chair.

"Leave my friend be, Lady Arabella," Whitcombe said. "He's had a rather unfortunate time of it."

"So has *my* friend," Arabella retorted, glancing toward Etty, "but I'll warrant you'll cast less judgment on your friend than on mine. I wonder why that might be?"

"Bella, love," Mr. Baxter warned.

"No, Lady Arabella is right," Eleanor said. "Sawbridge, were you engaging in a duel?"

Etty winced at her sister's directness, and Sawbridge's color deepened.

"As a matter of fact, I wasn't," he said. "Though I might as well have been, seeing as the outcome was the same."

"You mean—a man was killed?" Eleanor asked.

Sawbridge winced. "How did you know? Surely the gossip hasn't reached here yet."

"I see it in your eyes, sir."

"See what?"

"The shame."

Sawbridge closed his eyes and sighed. Then he opened them and nodded slowly. "A man was killed, yes—and a woman. It was Viscount Radham."

"*Radham!*" Lady Arabella cried, rolling her eyes. "May God preserve his soul, but he was the most prolific toper to disgrace London's drawing rooms. And the lady?"

"Mrs. Delacroix."

Eleanor glanced at her husband, who shifted position like a

child fidgeting when brought before his nanny for admonishment.

Mrs. Delacroix, the renowned courtesan who had warmed the beds of most gentlemen of the *ton*—Whitcombe among them.

"I see," Eleanor said, her tone sharp. "Mrs. Delacroix is well known to my husband, and yet he still believes that my poor sister is undeserving of our friendship."

"I parted company with Mrs. Delacroix before I met you, Eleanor," Whitcombe said.

"And I have long since forgiven you. All I ask is that you give my sister the same courtesy."

Whitcombe nodded and sighed. "You are right, of course, my love."

Eleanor turned her attention to Sawbridge, who'd taken a seat, beads of sweat glistening on his forehead. "Your Grace, may I fetch your something?" she asked.

"No brandy for him," Whitcombe said. "Coffee. Strong."

"See to it, would you, Gillingham?" Eleanor said to the footman circulating around the room. "I fear His Grace will faint if he's required to stand again."

The footman issued a quiet bow, then poured a cup and offered it to the duke.

Sawbridge took it with a nod, then lifted his gaze to Etty. "Come sit beside me, Miss Howard," he said. "I've heard much of you."

"Sawbridge," Whitcombe growled. "This is hardly the time nor the place."

"Miss Howard and I have a friend in common," Sawbridge said. "We saw him in Town—didn't we, Whitcombe?"

Etty's stomach churned.

"He's not the man he was," Sawbridge said, "but then, losing one's fortune can do that to a fellow. Radham will soon find that out."

"I thought you said Radham had died," Eleanor said.

"I meant the *new* Viscount Radham. He's almost as badly off as—"

Eleanor raised her hand. "I'd stop if I were you, Your Grace," she said. "You may be my husband's friend, but that doesn't give you the right to—"

"—Dunton," Sawbridge finished.

Etty's stomach tightened, and she drew in a sharp breath, willing her body to move. Her legs crumpled beneath her and she pitched forward, closing her eyes in anticipation of the fall.

But it never came. A pair of thick, strong arms caught her.

"Steady on, love—I've got you."

Etty opened her eyes to find herself in the arms of Lady Arabella's husband. Arabella herself had risen and fixed Sawbridge with a hard stare, the kind of withering look that had seen off suitors who'd dared approach her—the look that was the precursor to a put-down.

"I think it's time you and I retired to the library, Sawbridge," Whitcombe said. "I didn't bring you here to insult my wife's guests. In fact, I'm beginning to wonder why I bothered to bring you here at all. I should have left you in that ditch you fell in—or better still, thrown you in the Serpentine."

Sawbridge opened his mouth to reply, but Whitcombe approached him, a flash of steel in his blue gaze, and the other man struggled to his feet. They approached the doors, and before they exited, Sawbridge glanced over his shoulder at Etty. He gave a wink, then let Whitcombe lead him outside.

Etty withdrew from Arabella's husband's grip.

"You all right, love?" he asked. "Don't take no notice of that man."

"I'm quite all right, Mr. Baxter," Etty replied. "I just didn't expect to hear…"

"I know," Lady Arabella said. "And we need not mention *his* name again. There's no need for him to touch our lives anymore. We have both suffered at—"

"Dunton," Etty said, wincing. "I must speak his name, for if I am afraid to, then I'll never be free of him."

Arabella took her hand. "Dunton," she said. "You and I have both suffered at his hands—but he cannot hurt us again." She squeezed. "Why don't you come and live with Lawrence and me?"

Etty glanced at Mr. Baxter, whose eyes had widened. "Bella, are you sure?" he asked. "What with the baby…"

"Of course I'm sure!" Arabella huffed. "Etty is my best friend. You know what Dunton did to her."

He nodded. "Of course, love. That man has much to answer for. Miss Howard, our home is yours, if you wish it. The children will adore your Gabriel—and it'll be good for him to have young 'uns to play with."

"B-but, Frances…Loveday…" Etty said. "I cannot abandon them."

"We wouldn't expect you to," Arabella said. "We have plenty of room at Longford Hall. You *and* your friends could have a new life—a fresh start."

"But I've given my sister a new life *here*," Eleanor said. "Juliette, you're welcome at Rosecombe as long as you wish. Monty will come around, eventually."

Etty took her sister's hand. "Dear Eleanor, you are too good," she said. "Your one failing is that you assume everyone else to be as forgiving and openhearted as yourself. I cannot stay where I am a problem to be solved, or a burden to be shouldered."

"You're no burden."

"Or a sinner to be forgiven." A sob rose in Etty's throat, and she wiped the moisture from her eyes. "I have faced my sins—and asked forgiveness from those whom I have sinned against. And now I wish to find peace. But how can I find peace if I am to be forever reminded of my sins? I will never look upon you, Eleanor, without knowing what I did. Your husband…"

"Monty will grow to love you as I do," Eleanor said.

Etty shook her head. "Your husband will never be able to look upon me without remembering what I did to you. Perhaps he can forgive, but he'll never forget. And neither will I. If I am to begin again, I must leave."

Eleanor drew Etty into her arms. "Dearest sister!" she cried. "I only want you to be as happy as I."

"The difference is that you deserve your happiness, Eleanor," Etty replied. "But don't judge your husband too harshly. He acts out of love for you. And until I can find another to love me as fiercely as he loves you, then I can never find your happiness."

"You will find love," Eleanor whispered. "But you must find a man to *deserve* you. Such a man is rare."

"That he is," Etty said. A tear splashed onto her cheek, and she wiped it away. "But I didn't deserve him."

She choked as her throat tightened, and Eleanor placed a hand on Etty's cheek. "Sister?"

"You see—I know that I can never truly begin again with a clean conscience, with others who have borne the brunt of my sins. Not even those who professed to love me in spite of everything could truly forgive me for what I did to you."

Eleanor's eyes widened. "You mean—you fell in love?"

Etty nodded.

"With whom?"

"Can you not guess?"

Eleanor shook her head, then understanding flowed into her eyes. "You stayed at Sandcombe," she whispered. "So you met…"

Unable to speak, Etty nodded.

Andrew.

"And…?" Eleanor said.

"He rejected me when he discovered that I was your sister."

"Oh, Juliette!" Eleanor held her close. "My poor, darling sister! How can you ever forgive me?"

"There's nothing to forgive," Etty said, shaking.

"There's *everything* to forgive! I should not have told him what you'd done. I did so out of selfishness, seeking the sympathy of others. But I had thought better of *him*."

"Don't judge him too harshly, Eleanor," Etty said. "He, like your husband, acted out of his love for you. And therefore he couldn't have truly loved me."

"Then he did not deserve you," Eleanor said, her voice hardening. "Nor does any man who professes to do the good thing, yet lets himself be ruled by his own self-importance. 'Tis a wonder why the world does not turn to ruin, ruled by men as it is."

Etty glanced at Mr. Baxter, who had chosen that moment to take a great deal of interest in a vase on a plinth by the window.

"Perhaps we should retire," Lady Arabella said. "Etty, my dear, shall we seek out Frances and Loveday so they can be ready to leave in the morning?"

Etty glanced at her sister, then nodded. "Yes, I'm certain. I must begin a new life unencumbered by my sins."

"Then I wish you well, sister," Eleanor said. "And I pray that, one day, you will find the forgiveness you seek."

"I don't deserve his forgiveness."

"I didn't mean Andrew," Eleanor said. "I meant the one person who judges you more harshly than any other. And before you can begin to accept the forgiveness of anyone else, you must seek forgiveness from them."

"From whom?"

Eleanor brushed her lips against Etty's forehead in a soft kiss.

"You, dearest Juliette. The time has come to look into your heart and forgive yourself."

CHAPTER TWENTY-FIVE

London, October 1817

THE FRONT FAÇADE of the building reeked of ostentation. A flight of stone steps led to the main entrance—a thick, dark door with a polished handle. Andrew tilted his head to cast his gaze over the rest of the building—three stories that gleamed bone-white in the afternoon sun, with tall, arched windows that reflected the light. On the first story, to the left of the main doors, an enormous, bowed window looked out over St James's Street, in which a foppish young man sat, his jacket an eye-wateringly bright shade of pink, one hand raised in a gesture that might have implied he was on the brink of sneezing, while he held an embroidered lace handkerchief aloft.

Sweet Lord—if this was what gentlemen were supposed to do with their time, it was a wonder they had not all gone insane.

"Welcome to White's," Andrew's companion said.

Andrew fidgeted with his jacket, then fumbled at the top button. Why did the tailor have to make the thing so damnably tight?

"No, Radham, leave it," his companion said. "You want to create a good first impression as you enter the club."

Andrew eyed his companion. Adam Hawke, the Duke of Foxton, was an old schoolfellow—if a boy he'd known fleetingly at Eton could be called a *schoolfellow*. Foxton had been three years above Andrew and head of Godolphin House, issuing sanctions for transgressions among the more boisterous inmates, most of whom had grown up to be rakes such as Robert.

Robert…

"I don't understand why the first thing I had to do upon entering London was purchase a new suit," Andrew said.

"You're in mourning, therefore are required to dress appropriately."

"Robert wouldn't have cared what I wore," Andrew replied, "and spending further funds—of which the estate has very little—at Weston's establishment doesn't seem appropriate."

"Ah, but surely by now you should understand that in Society, we do not do what is appropriate, we do what gives the *appearance* of propriety."

"And indulging at White's gives the appearance of propriety?" Andrew let out a snort. "Look at that dandy in the window, Foxton! What in the name of the Almighty does he think he's doing?"

"Attempting to emulate Beau Brummell," Foxton said. "Brummell made quite a name for himself occupying that window at all hours. Rumor has it he never wore the same jacket twice. Several aspiring leaders of men's fashion have been seen posturing in that window since Brummell fled to France."

"And do they aspire to the same levels of debt?" Andrew asked.

Foxton shrugged. "Following the heights of fashion is a costly exercise."

"At least being in mourning excuses me from spending a fortune on such gawdy colors," Andrew said, tugging at his cravat. "I intend to extract my money's worth from this ridiculous attire."

"If it's funds you're concerned about, Radham, I've already said I'll stand your ledger, given that you're my guest. But I cannot guarantee congenial company here, though I'll wager you'll have a marginally less miserable time than you would with your father in Grosvenor Place."

Which was true. The death of his favorite son had turned Andrew's father into a bitter shell of a man, content to nightly imbibe brandy and wallow in self-pity about how the legacy of the earldom was doomed.

An earldom Andrew had wanted nothing to do with and considered himself free of, until Robert had chosen to destroy everything by indulging in his selfish desires.

Then a bolt of shame twisted Andrew's gut. Robert had lost his life.

Whereas I've only lost my freedom.

Which perhaps was worse. But it was not the done thing to voice such an opinion aloud, particularly given that the members of White's would consider inheriting a viscountcy and becoming heir apparent to an earldom something to celebrate.

Foxton led the way up the steps, and the door opened to reveal a liveried footman, who issued a deep bow.

"Welcome back, Your Grace." He settled his gaze on Andrew. "And your friend…?"

"Viscount Radham," Foxton said.

The footman's eyes widened, then his mouth twitched into a smile. "You are most welcome, Lord Radham. Please, come inside."

"I'll have my usual, please, Grantchester," Foxton said. "And my friend will have the same."

"Of course, gentlemen. Your table will be ready for you to take luncheon at your leisure, Your Grace." The footman nodded toward Andrew. "Lord Radham, you are most welcome."

"Yes, yes, you've already said that," Foxton said, waving his hand at the man. "Just show us to the dining room."

"Very good, Your Grace."

The footman bowed again, then led them into a high-ceilinged room adorned with a thick, deep-red carpet, ornate gilded carvings, and an enormous chandelier suspended from the ceiling that cast droplets of light about the room in myriad colors.

A few of the diners looked up and acknowledged Foxton with a nod. They cast curious glances toward Andrew, then resumed their attention on their luncheon.

After the footman had helped him into a chair and disappeared to fetch their drinks, Andrew leaned across the table to his companion.

"He seemed very congenial. I thought you told me they were very particular here about guests—even those with titles."

"Ah, but you are Viscount Radham," Foxton said. "Your predecessor left a legacy of debts to rival Brummell's. I'll wager Grantchester is at this moment informing the secretary of your presence here."

Andrew moved to stand, but Foxton raised his hand.

"Never fear, my friend. The secretary wouldn't be so vulgar as to discuss *commerce* while you're taking luncheon."

Nevertheless, Andrew watched the footman as he returned with two glasses of dark liquid. "Luncheon will be served in five minutes, gentlemen," he said, eyeing Andrew.

"To your good health, Radham," Foxton said, raising his glass after the footman disappeared once more.

"I say, Foxton!" a voice cried. "I never thought to see you here."

Foxton narrowed his eyes and set his glass aside, and Andrew turned to the owner of the voice—a portly man with thinning gray hair and the kind of complexion that, though ruddy, signified sickness born of overindulgence.

"I thought you'd been exiled to the country," Foxton said.

"Something of an exaggeration, dear boy." The man paused by their table and raised an eyebrow as he cast his rancid gaze on Andrew.

An odor of stale liquor reached Andrew's nostrils, and he lifted his glass to his lips to smother the stench. The newcomer's jacket might have been fashionable some ten years before, but such an excess of frills was beyond even Mr. Weston's style of tailoring. Most likely the jacket itself was several years old, given the fraying ends of the cuffs.

"Retirement, then," Foxton said. "But out of necessity."

"*By choice, dear boy*," came the reply.

"And…the duchess?" Foxton asked.

The man grimaced. "My wife is in poor sprits."

The duchess? Good heavens—surely this fellow wasn't a *duke*?

The man resumed his attention on Andrew. "Who's this fellow, then? A new member?"

Not if Andrew could help it—there seemed little merit in wasting funds merely to be granted the right to spend one's time in the company of dandies. *Respite from women*, Foxton had said— a haven of peace where a gentleman could indulge in the company of his peers without the incessant chatter and demands of the fairer sex. Assuming, of course, he could afford the membership dues.

Which the porcine newcomer couldn't, judging by his ap- pearance.

"Lord Radham is my guest," Foxton said.

"Radham, eh? So you must be the brother. Damned foolish business that was, if you ask me."

"What business?" Andrew asked.

"Radham making such an arse of himself in the park—and taking the delicious Danielle with him."

"Danielle?"

"Mrs. Delacroix. I mean, if a man is foolish enough to risk his neck racing carriages in London, that's his lookout, but to risk the neck of the finest doxy in Mayfair—well, that's just plain selfish."

"Selfish?" Andrew asked.

"Danielle was the best fuck in town."

A ripple of coughs threaded through the dining room.

"Though she was a little grasping," the man continued. "Cost me a bloody fortune, she did."

"I say, Dunton," Foxton said, "that's not the done thing to—"

Andrew pushed his chair back and rose. "*What* did you say,

Foxton?"

"I said it was not the done thing—"

"No, I mean this…*man* here. Is he…"

"Oh, I'm sorry," Foxton said in a tone that meant he was anything but. "I quite forgot. Radham, this is the Duke of Dunton."

Dunton inclined his head in a bow. "At your service, I—"

"*You!*" Andrew cried. He cast his gaze over the man once more—the huge belly that strained against the buttons of his waistcoat, thick hands with swollen fingers adorned with rings that glittered malevolently in the afternoon light, the wisps of unkempt, thinning hair framing his fleshy face, and his eyes…

Cold, pale-blue eyes, gleaming with inebriation and self-satisfaction.

"What are you doing here, *Dunton?*" Andrew asked.

"Taking luncheon."

"Who's standing your ledger *this* time?" Foxton asked, a lick of cold amusement in his tone.

Dunton huffed with indignation. "Sir Heath Moss, if you must know. At least a man has *some* friends he can rely on."

Foxton let out a snort. "I suppose when a man's exhausted his credit with every tradesman in town he must resort to his friends—what few he has remaining."

"Careful, Foxton, or you'll be mistaken for a tradesman yourself with all this talk of funds," Dunton said. "If I were you, Radham, I'd choose your friends wisely. Half the election committee at White's are personal friends of mine."

"And how would you define a *friend*, Dunton?" Andrew asked. "Someone from whom you take what you want before casting them aside? Much like a woman?"

Dunton frowned, his weak eyes glazing with confusion. "A man is a fool if he considers a woman to be his friend. Women are to be enjoyed then cast aside."

"Such as innocent maidens? Debutantes?"

Andrew caught a flicker of recognition in Dunton's eyes

before the man shook his head and let out a laugh. "I say, Foxton, I'd think carefully if you wish to sponsor this fellow's membership. You wouldn't want your reputation tarnished by association."

"A man's reputation is almost impervious to ruination, no matter what he does," Andrew said. "Even *yours*, Dunton."

"I say, Radham, there's a time and a place," Foxton said. "Do you know Dunton?"

"Only by reputation."

Dunton laughed. "Gossip, more like, if there was a woman involved."

"Not *any* woman," Andrew replied, bile rising in his gut. "Miss Juliette Howard."

"Oh, you mean a *whore*."

"Miss Howard is no whore!" Andrew cried, and another volley of coughs rippled through the dining room.

"Radham," Foxton warned, rising to his feet. "Dunton, perhaps the two of you should settle your disagreement elsewhere."

"It's no disagreement," Andrew said. "This fellow here debauched a young woman then abandoned her."

"Now, old chap, I've never—"

"She bore your child!" Andrew cried.

Tutting filled the air, and a voice muttered, "For shame!"

"For shame indeed," Andrew said, and Dunton curled his lip in a sneer.

"I think they're referring to *you*, old chap. Disturbing our peace—it's simply not done."

"But violating a respectable young woman is?" Andrew said. "Then you're hypocrites—all of you!"

"Ha!" Dunton replied. "Violating, eh?" He leaned toward Andrew and lowered his voice. "That little slut was only too eager to spread her legs for me. Begged for it, she did, offering her cunny in the hope it would earn her my hand."

"Why you…" Andrew began, but the footman approached and raised a white-gloved hand.

"Gentlemen, if you please," he said. "I am compelled to remind you to observe club rules. You must desist or I shall be required to remove you from the premises."

"I trust you're not referring to *my* behavior," Dunton said. "I was merely passing on my way to luncheon when this bounder insulted me."

"Sit down, Radham," Foxton said. "There's nothing to be gained from this."

"Other than personal satisfaction," Andrew snarled.

"Drunken beast!" Dunton said, gesturing toward Andrew's glass. "Brandy at luncheon—I should have known. Your brother was just the same, and much good did it do him. If you wish to accuse me of debauchery, I suggest you look to your own house. Who knows how many bastards your brother has littered over the countryside? As to that Howard whore…"

Andrew fisted his hands as his stomach churned at the stench of sweat and stale liquor. Then Dunton lowered his voice to a whisper.

"How does it feel to know that *I* got there first? Who knows? With your brother's reputation, I'd not be surprised if he dipped into that well himself. Next time you fuck her, think on that—think on how she squealed like a sow in heat as I took her from behind."

Dunton stepped back, a broad grin creasing his fleshy face, triumph glittering in his eyes, and a swell of anger coiled in Andrew's chest—an over-wound spring.

"I wish you joy of her," Dunton said. "Many a man has had to content himself with my leavings, and you can at least console yourself with the thought that I broke her in nicely for you. At very little cost to myself, I'll add. She might not be the best fuck in town, but she was the cheapest."

The spring snapped. With a roar of rage, Andrew lunged forward and slammed his fist into Dunton's face.

"Vile bastard!" he cried as pain exploded in his knuckles. He drew back his arm and again struck Dunton, who toppled backward and crumpled to the floor. Andrew flew toward him, both fists raised, and landed another punch in the man's gut while Dunton curled up and wailed.

But before Andrew could secure another blow, he was pulled back and found himself restrained by two footmen.

"Stop!" Foxton cried. "That's not how we settle our differences."

"Then what do we do?" Andrew replied. "Tut loudly at each other? Stand each other a round of drinks then agree we'll say no more on the matter? Cordially shake hands while the sin goes unpunished?"

"Yes," Foxton said. "It's called being a gentleman."

"If that's the case, then I want no part of it."

"You're no gentleman," Dunton said. "You're…" He broke off in a fit of coughing, spattering droplets of blood on his jacket. "Damn you, Radham—that'll have to be cleaned."

"Is that all you care for? Your damned *jacket*?" Andrew stepped forward, but the footman tightened his grip.

"That's enough, sir," he said. "This behavior is not to be tolerated." He turned to Foxton. "Forgive me, Your Grace, but if you do not show this man out, I'll have to evict him."

"Then evict me!" Andrew said. "If you'd rather protect creatures such as Dunton, then I have no wish to set foot inside this cursed building again!"

"Very well, sir. You give us no choice." The footmen tightened their grips, then marched Andrew toward the main doors.

"I can see myself out," Andrew said, but the expressions of satisfaction on the footmen's faces told him that they'd relish the opportunity to forcibly throw an undesirable out of their establishment. The door opened, and Andrew found himself pushed down the steps, where he lost his footing and fell to the pavement just as a man and woman approached, arm in arm.

"Well, really!" the man said, raising his eyebrows. The lady said nothing, until Foxton appeared at the top of the steps and a sheen of desire colored her expression.

"Oh, Your Grace," she said, and her husband frowned. Ignoring them, Foxton helped Andrew up and brushed the dust off his jacket. Then he steered Andrew along the pavement, leaving the couple open mouthed at the foot of the steps.

"There goes luncheon," Foxton said, sighing.

"Sorry about that," Andrew said.

Foxton snorted. "No matter. I'll wager there's several fathers who'd applaud you for giving the fellow a shiner. But you'll never be able to show your face at White's again."

"You think I care?"

"And…Miss Howard?"

"It matters not," Andrew said. "I doubt I'll see her again."

Foxton shook his head. "Look for the source of a man's misery and you'll always find a woman," he said. "When a man drives himself to ruination, invariably a doxy sits at the root of it. Women are not to be trusted—instead they are to be enjoyed. In that, if nothing else, I find myself in agreement with Dunton."

"That's rather a bleak view of the female sex."

"But realistic, Radham. It's a lesson you must learn if you are to survive. You're not a country parson anymore. You're a gentleman about town—a viscount, heir to an earldom."

"And?"

"And therefore, dear chap, you are prey in the eyes of every woman you encounter. There is only one way to survive. You must become the predator."

"And if I have no wish to become a predator?"

"Then you must remove yourself from Town. What did you come here for, other than to settle your affairs with your lawyers? Did you hope to see this Miss Howard?"

Andrew flinched. Perhaps he *had* hoped to see Etty. Where else would she have fled to if she intended to go "home"? But since he'd arrived there had been no sign of her—though London was a big place, and Etty was hardly likely to be parading around, given her status as a fallen woman. He'd been a fool to think he'd stumble over her the moment he set foot in Town.

"No," he said quietly. "I doubt I'll see her again."

"All the better for you," Foxton said. "If you want my advice, settle your affairs, then leave London. Contrary to popular opinion, gentlemen with titles don't spend the entirety of their time at White's, or with their mistresses—at least, gentlemen in your financial position don't. With a title comes responsibility and, in your case, a neglected estate in need of restoration. What better way for a man to purge a woman from his soul than by devoting himself to his duty? And as a vicar…"

"Vicar no more," Andrew said bitterly.

"As a *former* vicar, then, you should at least have a better understanding of duty than most men thrust into your position."

Andrew sighed. His friend was right. He'd viewed his title as akin to a slave collar, binding him to a life of servitude. He'd lost everything else. But with the estate came a building, grounds, in need of restoration—not to mention servants and tenants in need of a lord to care for them. Radham Hall was no different to his church at Sandcombe, and the souls dependent on the estate were no different to the parishioners.

They were now his flock.

There was one thing that even the most brokenhearted man could commit himself to. And that was his duty.

CHAPTER TWENTY-SIX

Longford Hall, Sussex, November 1817

STRAINS OF LAUGHTER filtered through the air. Etty glanced across the lawn to a gap in the hedge clipped into the shape of an arch. Four children emerged, brandishing sticks.

Mr. Baxter, who was clipping the hedge at the far end, glanced up, smiled, then shook his head and resumed clipping.

"He's after us—quick!" one of the children—a girl, though she wore breeches—cried. "What shall we do, admiral?"

"We stand and fight!" another child yelled.

"At arms!" called a third.

The fourth child, Florence, stood apart from the rest, holding her stick awkwardly.

"Come on, Florrie," the girl in breeches said, placing an arm around her shoulders. "We must defend ourselves from the captain of the enemy ship."

Arabella, who sat beside Etty, looked up from her embroidery. "Roberta, sweetheart, maybe Florence doesn't want to fight. Not all girls like to play sailors."

"She's not Florence, Mama," the girl replied. "She's Captain Edward Berry!"

A fifth child emerged through the archway—Etty's son, holding a stick aloft as he ran toward the others.

"Gabriel!" Etty cried.

"He's not Gabriel—he's Captain Thomas Foley," the girl said.

"Roberta!" Arabella said. "That's no way to speak to our guest."

The girl blushed and lowered her stick. Gabriel continued to run toward her, then he tripped and fell forward onto the grass. He looked up, his face wrinkled with distress, and Etty leaped to her feet, anticipating the screams. But the girl ran toward him and scooped him up into her arms. He burst out laughing, his little body shaking with mirth.

Arabella placed a hand on Etty's arm. "Your son's fine, Juliette. Roberta will ensure he comes to no harm. She quite adores him. Come, sit."

Etty resumed her seat. "Who's Captain Thomas Foley?"

Arabella shrugged. "Something to do with Admiral Nelson. The children are playing Band of Brothers."

"Band of what?"

"Band of brothers, Miss Howard," the girl said, approaching Etty.

"Mama!" Gabriel cried, his cheeks pink with exertion, a broad grin on his face. He wriggled free from the girl's grip and rushed toward Etty, stumbling into her arms.

"Are you having fun, sweet boy?" she asked.

"I'm taking care of him, Miss Howard," the girl said. "Come along, Gabriel, we need to induct you into our band if you want to be a brother. Then we can give you your command."

The boy wriggled free from Etty's grip, and she swallowed the sense of loss as he ran toward Roberta and took her hand.

"Thomas Foley is captain of the *Goliath*," Roberta said. "We thought it fitting, given Gabriel's size."

Etty glanced at her son, over whom the girl towered, and let out a soft laugh. "You may live to regret that, Roberta. You're taller than Gabriel now, but when he's older he'll tower over you."

"Was Gabriel's father very tall?" the girl asked.

Etty stiffened, and Arabella took her hand.

"Roberta, why don't you take the children into the kitchen? Mrs. Brown said she'd be making iced buns for tea today. Tell her I said you could have one each."

"Yes, Mama."

"That's *one* each, Roberta—I don't want you overindulging, then claiming you cannot eat your supper tonight."

The girl grinned, then tugged on Gabriel's arm. "Come along, captain. Mrs. Brown makes the finest buns in the whole of England."

The children trooped inside, laughing together, and the youngest of Arabella's stepchildren—a freckle-faced lad with a mop of red hair—took Florence's hand.

"You come with me, Florrie," he said. "Mrs. Brown will give you an extra bun for your sister, and maybe your mama would like one also."

Their animated chatter faded as they disappeared inside the house, and Etty leaned back into her chair.

"Exhausting, aren't they?" Arabella laughed. "But the key to managing children is ensuring that they tire each other out."

"Your Roberta seems a sensible child," Etty said.

"That she is. She terrified me at first, but I love her as if she were my own. No—she *is* my own."

"Does she fear that when…" Etty trailed away as she glanced at Arabella's swollen belly.

"That when the baby comes I'll love it more than her and her brothers?" Arabella caressed her belly and smiled. "It was the first thing she asked me when Lawrence and I told the children that I was expecting."

"You told them together?" Etty asked, glancing across the garden. Mr. Baxter had stopped clipping and was standing back to admire his handiwork. "I must say, your husband is a most unusual man."

A soft smile curved Arabella's lips. "That he is, and I wouldn't have him any other way. He's even insisting on being present for my confinement. I know it's not proper, but I have to admit to some relief in knowing that he'll be with me."

A ripple of fear flickered in her eyes, and Etty took her hand. "You will be well, Bella," she said. "You'll be surrounded by people who love you."

Whereas I was alone.

Etty shivered at the memory of the pain, the ripples of agony that gripped her body until she couldn't breathe, tugging at her insides until she feared she would burst…

And the screams—shrill and desolate, they had filled her mind while she prayed for them to stop. Until she'd realized the screams were hers.

And then, finally…

The plaintive cries of a helpless creature—unwanted and reviled, the cause of her ruination; cries that, instead of inciting the disgust she'd expected, had unlocked her heart until her body and soul were consumed with a single need.

The need to protect the one she loved.

Etty blinked, and a tear splashed onto her cheek.

A hand caught hers. "Juliette! Oh, forgive me. I didn't mean to distress you with my concerns. I should have realized."

Etty shook her head. "It wasn't your fault."

"Nor was it yours," Arabella said. "It was *his*." She squeezed Etty's hand. "But there's no need to speak of those who should be confined to the past. You and your son are here now, which is all that matters. He's an adorable child. I see much of you in him."

"You do?"

"He has your kindness."

"I am not kind, Bella. When I think back to how I was in London, before…"

"That wasn't the real you," Arabella said. "And what of myself? *Harpy of the Ton*, they called me. We were a pair, were we not? But we were a product of the world in which we lived."

Arabella glanced across the lawn to her husband and raised her hand in greeting. He responded in kind, and she smiled softly.

"Lawrence showed me that another world existed outside of

Society," she said. "A good world—a world where a woman can be honest about her needs and desires, and not be ruled by a man."

"Not even a husband?"

"Not if she finds the right husband."

"I don't want a husband," Etty said. "I have no wish to be owned."

"What about being *loved*?"

"You cannot expect me to place myself on the Marriage Mart again. Not after…"

"Heavens, no!" Arabella said, laughing. "I wouldn't send my worst foe into that nest of vipers. But a wider acquaintance might ease your melancholy."

"I'm not—"

"I'm your friend, Etty," Arabella said, the laughter dying in her eyes. "I know you well enough to recognize your unhappiness. You've had your heart broken."

"A fitting end for she who was called *Heartbreaker*."

"Etty, you have as much right to be happy—and loved—as any other."

"I'm not looking for a husband."

"Friends, then."

"I have all the friends I need, Arabella," Etty said, "but I have no wish to trespass on your hospitality for too long. I've already been here a month."

"Is it that long?" Arabella asked. "Though it matters not, it feels as if you've been here forever."

"Gabriel and I can leave as soon as you wish it."

"Oh, no, dearest Etty!" Arabella said. "You're welcome here for as long as you wish. I only meant that I already feel as if you're part of the family."

"And Loveday?" Etty asked.

"Mrs. Smith is proving invaluable," came the reply. "My housekeeper told me only yesterday that she doesn't know what she'd do without her. She's turned into a confident young woman, fulfilled in her occupation. Nothing like the poor, timid creature who first came here. Her Florence is getting on so well with the children, and you wouldn't want to remove her from her home, would you? As to young Frances, my own maid Connie quite dotes on her. The life of a lady's maid can be rather lonely when she has only her mistress for company. I've never seen Connie so animated. You wouldn't want to deprive her of her new friend, would you? Frances has the makings of an excellent lady's maid, and who better than Connie to teach her?"

"You make a good argument."

"What's this about arguments?" a deep male voice said.

Mr. Baxter appeared, a pair of shears in his hands, his large frame silhouetted against the low afternoon sun.

"Is my wife plaguing you, Miss Howard?" He chuckled. "Bella, love, you might consider yourself within your rights to order your poor husband about, but your friend must be permitted to think for herself."

"Lawrence, you're a beast!" Arabella replied.

"Ah, but I'm *your* beast, love," he said, kneeling before his wife and taking her hands.

A pang of envy tugged at Etty's heart at the easy manner between a couple so evidently in love.

"I must apologize for my manners, Miss Howard," he said. "Our life here is somewhat different to what you're used to. Please forgive me."

"There's nothing to forgive," Etty said, "and everything to admire."

"I was about to ask Juliette whether she'd object to our hosting a house party," Arabella said.

Etty's gut twisted with apprehension. "A house party?"

"Just a small one, with a few close friends," Arabella said. "You have naught to fear—our parties are nothing like those you've experienced in London."

"But they're parties nonetheless," Etty said, cringing at the notion of members of Society—the very same individuals who'd once admired her for her beauty—now looking down on her and basking in their own superiority over the fallen woman in their midst.

"We select our friends very carefully," Arabella said. "People who have something interesting to say."

"Provided they can get a word in when Bella's talking, of course," Mr. Baxter said.

Arabella gave him a playful slap. "You're supposed to be encouraging my friend, Lawrence, not putting her off. I shall have to admonish you later."

"You may admonish me all you like, love, after supper."

Etty's cheeks warmed as she caught the glint of desire in his eyes as he smiled at his wife.

"Lawrence!" Arabella chided, though desire flickered in her eyes too.

"Forgive me, Miss Howard," he said. "I'm afraid you must be unused to my uncouth manners. My wife was right when she said I am a beast. But our friends are liberal enough to endure my company, and I know they'd find you charming. You'll have nothing to fear. And if any of them give you cause to complain, I can always throw them into the ditch."

Etty eyed the giant of a man with broad shoulders and thick muscles that strained at his jacket—and his huge, rough hands, covered in callouses, with traces of dirt under the fingernails.

"I daresay you would," she said, smiling.

"So that settles it," Arabella said. "You'll find our friends somewhat different to the acquaintances we shared during our Season. Here, we prefer people who have something interesting to say."

"Such as?"

"Your sister, of course," Arabella said. "Then there's Lady Marable. She's a poet—writes the most extraordinary verse. Some might say her work is a little scandalous, for it certainly stirs the blood."

"Doesn't it just," her husband said, a wicked grin twisting his lips.

Arabella gave him another playful swat, and he rose to his feet.

"I'll leave you ladies to it," he said. "I fear the conversation will soon turn to discussions about menus and after-dinner entertainment—something I'd rather indulge in at the time than discuss the preparations for at length. Besides, talk of Lady Marable's verse is rendering me in need of a cold bath, and I fancy a dip in the lake."

He bowed to Etty and winked at his wife, whose cheeks had turned a shade of crimson, before leaving.

"I must apologize for—" Arabella started.

"It's not necessary," Etty said. "Your husband is an extraordinary man, and I find his…*natural* style of address refreshing."

"Our friends are quite in awe of him," Arabella said. "He says what he thinks with no concern for propriety. And if he takes a dislike to someone, he makes it perfectly clear."

"That must be challenging."

"Ah yes, but at least it means I can trust him. He speaks highly of *you*, Etty."

"Of me? I'm of little consequence to him."

"Ah, my friend, that's where you are wrong. He admires your defense of Mrs. Smith."

"I merely removed her from a violent husband."

"You speak as if that were nothing, but it was everything to Mrs. Smith. Few people will stand in defense of others if they have nothing to gain themselves. Lawrence dislikes men and women of Society who only wish to further their own cause."

"Isn't that how most members of Society behave?"

"Not all of them," Arabella said. "And my husband has the good fortune to be in a position that has given him a better understanding of men than I."

"How so?" Etty asked.

"Lawrence works in trade," Arabella replied. "And you can always tell a man's honesty by how he treats his paid subordinates. Some of Lawrence's clients would faint at the notion of associating themselves with us—which suits me just fine, as I am not so desperate to gain a ticket to Almack's. So you see, my friend, you are safe with us."

"Is that because those who would associate themselves socially with a common gardener and his wife are more likely to tolerate my company?" Etty asked. "A fallen woman who was evil enough to ruin her own sister and debauched enough to bear a bastard child?"

Etty regretted her words as soon as she spoke them, but Arabella gave no sign she'd taken offense. She merely took Etty's hand.

"Etty, my love, you must cease to say such things about yourself. Gabriel is a delightful child. Surely you don't think…"

Etty shook her head. "No, of course not," she said. "Gabriel is my world, and I love him more than life itself. But what chance do I have of finding someone to love me for who I am, someone who'd accept Gabriel for who—and what—he is?"

What chance have I of finding another man such as him?

But even Andrew, the man who had professed to love her and Gabriel, could not bring himself to love Etty for herself—her true self, with all her past sins.

"You have as much chance as any of us, dearest Etty," Arabella said. "Better, in fact, now that you're not required to parade yourself around the Marriage Mart. There's plenty of eligible men among our acquaintance. There's Lord Devereaux, who, despite his eccentricity, has secured my husband's good opinion."

"His eccentricity?"

"He doesn't talk."

"As in gossip?" Etty asked.

"As in at all. He comes across as a little standoffish. But perhaps he's merely shy. Lawrence won't hear a word against him."

"Why not?"

"Because he has one defining characteristic that sets him apart from most men of the *ton*."

"Which is?"

"He settles his accounts on time," Arabella said with a smile. "Lawrence told me that no sooner had he shaken hands with the fellow after completing the works on his garden, Lord Devereaux sent his steward to the bank to deposit the funds in his account. You can always tell a man's virtue by how quickly he settles his debts."

"And you intend to invite this Lord Devereaux to your house party?"

Arabella shook her head. "Sadly, he's something of a recluse. But Lawrence has secured another client—a new viscount about whom I have high hopes. I'm minded to invite him."

"Because he's a viscount?"

"Oh no, my dear—because he's already issued a down payment for the work. It seems as if his estate was left in disrepair by the previous incumbent and he's eager to restore it."

"A man concerned with appearance, no doubt."

"And concerned about his tenants. Lawrence told me that while he was there, the fellow was engaged in a discussion with his steward about restoring the tenants' properties. And he was very insistent that if Lawrence were to undertake the works, he must employ men from his estate and pay them a fair wage."

"A veritable paragon, then," Etty said.

"You jest, but you'd be surprised at how many of my husband's prospective clients spend much of the first meeting justifying why they should pay a lower fee than everyone else. You recall Heath Moss—or rather, *Sir* Heath Moss now he's inherited the baronetcy?"

Etty shuddered at the memory of the golden-haired Mr. Moss, who'd always thought a little too much of himself, and thought nothing of ruining the women he preyed upon. "What of him?"

"He refused to even speak to Lawrence," Arabella said. "Instead he sent his steward to convey the message that the privilege of having Sir Heath as a client was worth more than any fee."

"And did he pay the fee?"

"My husband refused the work. He said that as a commoner, he was unworthy of that privilege. But this new fellow—Viscount Radham—offered my husband tea and apologized for the state of the house."

"Radham?" Etty asked. "I've heard that name somewhere."

"He's the one with the profligate brother," Arabella said. "Eleanor's husband mentioned him—he recently inherited the viscountcy, poor fellow."

"Why poor fellow?"

"Because he's short on funds, and there's only one way by which a titled man can restore his fortune. A rich wife. If he went to London for the Season, he'd be devoured by desperate debutantes."

"Women such as us?" Etty shook her head. "Bella, I have no intention of throwing myself at the feet of a titled man. You saw how Eleanor's husband spoke to me. In the eyes of any respectable person, I'm nothing but a—"

"No, you're *not*, Etty, and well you know it," Arabella said firmly. "And though you may never be admitted into Society again, is that so much of a loss? Whitcombe was insufferably rude toward you, but his behavior came from the ferocity of the love he bears your sister. Not all men will think badly of you because of your past. And my husband tells me that Radham had a profession before he inherited the title. In fact, Lawrence told me that had the man not introduced himself as a viscount, he'd have believed him to be a perfectly ordinary man. Coming from my husband, that is the greatest of compliments."

"A perfectly ordinary man in search of a rich wife to purchase his title," Etty said. "What would he say to a fallen woman with a natural child?"

"I'll not invite him if you don't wish it," Bella said, "but you must appreciate the benefits of a wider acquaintance. You weren't born to be tucked away in obscurity—you were born to be admired." She squeezed Etty's hand. "Admired for your disposition and your kindness, rather than your beauty and fortune.”

“I don’t know…”

“Would you trust me?” Bella asked. “I only want you to be happy. You liked Mr. Ryman, did you not?”

“Ah, Mr. Ryman,” Etty said, smiling at the recollection of the thick-accented man who’d arrived in the garden last week in search of Arabella’s husband—who, on being asked whether he’d had a productive day, said it would have been a good deal more productive “had the fucking horses not escaped again.”

Bella let out a laugh. “The poor man! I thought he’d have a fit of apoplexy when he caught sight of us and realized we’d overheard his rather *interesting* greeting to my husband. He didn’t speak a word all afternoon after your unfortunate introduction, for fear of offending you. But you liked him, nonetheless.”

“I did, but he’s smitten with your maid.”

“Ah yes,” Bella said, smiling, “and Connie is quite in love with him. But there are plenty of men like Mr. Ryman, hardworking souls capable of making you happy—as you deserve.”

“I suppose so,” Etty said. “Gabriel took to him immediately.”

“There! You see? Is your son not the best judge of character?”

Etty nodded, recalling the way her son had nestled into the shoulder of another man in the little cottage at Sandcombe.

But *he* was long gone. No doubt he’d live out his days as a respectable vicar, preaching goodness to those who came to his church to be seen rather than to listen.

He would never have been happy with her. The stain of her past would have tarnished his reputation and stunted his prospects. Lady Fulford and her acquaintance with the bishop would have seen to that. At least, free from association with Etty, he might ascend to the position of bishop himself and fulfil his dreams—his destiny.

As to my *destiny…*

“Very well,” Etty said. “You are right—it’s time I looked to my future. And Gabriel’s.”

“Excellent!” Arabella replied. “I’ll issue the invitations. And have no fear, my dear. One word out of place with regards to your past, and they'll have me to reckon with. That is, if they can survive a pummeling from my husband. Marriage to a beast has its rewards, you know."

She smiled the smile of a woman well satisfied—in every respect.

But it wasn't merely Mr. Baxter's looks and manner that Bella took such enjoyment from. It was the fact that she had found a man to love her exactly as she was. And that made him unique among men. The chances of another such man existing were slim at best. Only one had come close to measuring up.

But Etty would never see him again.

CHAPTER TWENTY-SEVEN

Radham Hall, Surrey, October 1817

ANDREW SET HIS teacup aside. Had he heard his guest right?
"An *invitation*, Mr. Baxter?"

"That's right, Lord Radham," the gardener said. "My wife was most insistent. She's hosting a house party next month and wishes you to be among the party."

"But she hasn't even met me." Andrew shook his head. "I don't know if it would be proper."

"It's just a house party, not an intimate family dinner. There'll be other guests. My Bella says that's the done thing for a new acquaintance. And it'll give you a chance to see my handiwork. Give you a feel for what your garden might look like. There's a sunken garden just like the one I'm planning by the east wing."

"The one the morning room will overlook?" Andrew asked.

"Aye, sir, that's the one. And my wife's a lady, if that's what ye're hesitatin' over."

Andrew let out a laugh. "I wouldn't care if she were a milkmaid. If she's clever enough to have produced such detailed garden designs, then I confess I'm intrigued by the prospect of meeting her."

"She's right clever, is my Bella." Baxter grinned, and his heavy-lidded eyes narrowed as if he were on the brink of swooning. Clearly the man adored his wife—he'd spoken of little else over tea.

"A paragon of womanly virtue," Andrew said.

"You don't know the half of it, sir." Baxter's expression took on a faraway look.

Yes, the man was utterly smitten. But Baxter didn't look like a fool. In fact, for all his uncouthness, he had a sharp intelligence—greater than that possessed by any member of White's, certainly.

"You must call me Radham, not *sir*," Andrew said. "If I'm to accept your invitation then it must be on equal terms."

Baxter set his cup aside and glanced out of the window toward the small group of tenants who were digging into the soil. "If I am to justify my fee," he said, "I shouldn't be lingerin' here takin' tea. Not while it's still light outside, and not while others are workin' so hard themselves."

"I admire your industry, Baxter," Andrew said. "In my experience, a man in your position is always ready to issue instructions to his subordinates, but is never prepared to carry them out himself."

"What sort of man would I be if I stood idly by and watched while others toiled so that I might be enriched?"

Andrew laughed. "You'd be a *gentleman*, Mr. Baxter. And yet, if your wife is a lady, that's precisely what you are. I must confess you are something of an enigma. Perhaps I will come—after all, my acquaintance is somewhat limited."

"You must have friends in London."

"Hardly any, I'm afraid. I've discovered that London Society is not really to my taste."

"Ha! In which case, you *must* accept my invitation. You'd fit in our little circle perfectly. My Bella has secured the most extraordinary set of friends—poets, artists. And if you'd rather discuss business than the arts, Trelawney's always good company."

That name was familiar. "The wine merchant?" Andrew asked.

"The very same."

"I believe Trelawney has made a tidy profit from the Radham estate over the years, if my ledgers are anything to go by," Andrew said. "Not that I hold it against him, of course," he added, as Baxter frowned. "I fear my late brother indulged in wine to excess."

And women.

"Oh, forgive me," Baxter said. "I quite forgot—you're still in mourning for your brother."

"No matter," Andrew said. "Robert lived life to the fullest, most likely treating each day as if it were his last—until, of course, that day finally came. He'd not have wanted me to hide myself away and wallow. Besides, I have my father for that. But Father prefers to remain in London mourning his favorite son. And so I find myself here—defined by my title, an indentured servant, if you will, slave to a viscountcy and heir to an earldom."

What a sorry creature I am.

Most would sneer at his self-pity, arguing that thousands of men would envy his position. But Baxter nodded, sympathy in his eyes. "Do you miss your profession?" he asked. "Beggin' yer pardon if I'm speaking out of turn."

Baxter *had* spoken out of turn, but his open honesty, delivered with a thick country burr, rendered him worthier to be called friend than any other living soul Andrew had encountered.

Except perhaps…

Stop it!

There was little point in thinking about *her*.

Andrew nodded. "I do miss it," he said quietly. Then he rose and gestured toward the window overlooking the garden. "But I have a new profession now."

"That of a gentleman?"

"Being a gentleman is a matter of perspective," Andrew said. "Many would define a gentleman as one who lives off an inherited estate without having to lift a finger, idling his way from day to day while others tend to his whims. By virtue of possessing a title, I am considered by many to be a gentleman. But with the title comes an estate, with servants and tenants, all needing someone to care for them. An estate is like a living, breathing entity, much like your business, Mr. Baxter."

"But my business is a *trade*, Lord Radham."

"Yes, but you have employees, do you not, who work for you in order to earn a wage? Your business yields a profit from which you pay your employees, much as my estate yields a return from which I pay my servants and maintain the homes of my tenants. You intend to pass your business on to your sons, and I am bound by duty to furnish the earldom with an heir. So far, you and I are equal. Or, at least, we will be once my estate is solvent once more."

"Then perhaps you stand to gain from accepting our invitation, Lord Radham," Baxter said. "You'd find our acquaintances are of a similar mind to yourself, and a wider acquaintance can only be to your advantage—in one respect, at least."

"Such as?"

"My Bella has a number of interesting friends. There's one in particular who's our guest at the moment. Charming creature she is, and though I'd never advocate marrying for money, she has a sizeable dowry. She—"

Andrew interrupted, his gut twisting with revulsion. "Mr. Baxter, I'm certain your intentions are good," he said, "but I am *not* in search of a wife. If your wife's invitation is for the purpose of matchmaking, then I must decline. My title is not for sale, Mr. Baxter—*I* am not for sale."

"My apologies," Baxter said, rising from his seat and approaching the door. "I ought to be getting on."

"Wait," Andrew said. "Forgive me—I meant no offense, and I know you meant none yourself. I just… I wasn't meant for all *this*. I was meant to be a country vicar, not the heir to an earldom."

"I understand," Baxter said. "I wasn't born to live in a grand house with the daughter of a duke, but love happens in the strangest of places. My Bella and I were never meant for each other—our marriage was one of convenience—but we grew to love each other."

Andrew shook his head. "How in the name of the Almighty did you enter into a marriage of convenience with the daughter of a duke?"

Baxter grinned. "*That*, my friend, is a story I'll save for when you honor us with your company. If that don't tempt you to come, I don't know what will."

Andrew held out his hand. "Then I'll gladly accept," he said, "if only to have sight of the most extraordinary woman in the kingdom. Your wife must be unique."

Baxter raised his eyebrows, then took Andrew's hand, enveloping it in his great paw. "An extraordinary woman may be the rarest of creatures," he said, "but I'll wager she's not unique. It's just a matter of finding *your* extraordinary woman."

And therein lay the problem. Andrew *had* found her. Then, in his folly, he'd let her slip through his fingers.

Perhaps Baxter was right—a marriage of convenience was the only solution. It would raise funds for the Radham estate and enable Andrew to furnish the title with an heir. And, most importantly, it would not present any risk to his heart, given that he'd irrevocably lost that to another.

CHAPTER TWENTY-EIGHT

Longford Hall, Sussex, November 1817

THE PATH OPENED out into a clearing in the woods, where the sunlight, broken by the canopy of trees overhead, formed a dappled pattern on the ground. Clusters of ferns nodded in the breeze, their bright green fronds curling to form tight spirals at the ends. Etty reached out and caressed the tip of a fern with her fingers, letting out a soft sigh.

Though Arabella had assured her the forests surrounding the estate were perfectly safe, Etty shivered as shadows moved in the gaps between the thick, gnarled trunks.

Then light laughter filled the air, followed by footsteps as Etty's companions approached—Arabella's stepdaughter Roberta, hand in hand with Florence Smith.

"Here it is!" Roberta cried.

"It's so pretty," said her companion, "just like a fairy den!"

"See? Didn't I tell you, Florrie?" Roberta said. "Not that I'd call it a fairy den," she added, wrinkling her nose. "Fairies aren't real."

"But we can play at being fairies, can't we?"

Roberta let out a snort. "That's a game for *girls*."

"You're a girl, are you not?" Etty said, suppressing a laugh at the look of horror in Roberta's eyes.

"But I don't play silly make-believe, Miss Howard."

Etty placed her hands on her hips. "Didn't you declare yourself to be Admiral Nelson yesterday and make your brother walk the plank?"

"Yes, but Admiral Nelson is *real*."

"I doubt he made his lieutenant walk the plank," Etty said, "and nor did he tie Empress Josephine to the mast—or in your case a sapling—and threaten to feed her to the sharks."

Florence—also known as Empress Josephine—shivered, then slipped her hand in Etty's.

"You didn't mind our tying you up, did you, Florrie?" Roberta asked.

Florence glanced toward Etty, then shook her head. "I'm sorry, Bobby. I'm not a good sailor."

Frowning, Roberta stared at her new friend, and Etty steeled herself for an argument. Roberta was a bright, intelligent creature, but her forceful, assertive nature dominated the little group of friends, and Florence, having grown up in a home where her mother was repeatedly beaten, had learned the benefit of shrinking into the shadows when challenged by a more forceful personality.

At length, Roberta nodded and embraced the younger girl. "Not everybody has to be a sailor," she said. "For one thing, there's not enough ships to go round. I wouldn't be a good friend if I was horrid to you just because we like different things. That's not what being a friend is."

Etty smiled as Roberta—who couldn't have been much older than ten years—nodded as if she stood in a pulpit addressing a congregation while the sunlight illuminated her features.

Then she caught her breath at the memory of another who had stood in a pulpit, the sunlight on his face casting myriad colors from the stained glass windows, while he delivered his sermon to his parishioners before he settled his gaze on her.

"Miss Howard, is something wrong? You don't look at all well."

Roberta stared at Etty, a curious expression in her sharp blue eyes. Arabella had said her stepdaughter was one of the most insightful children she'd known. At first Etty had believed her friend's words were merely those of a doting stepmother, but there was no doubting Roberta's intelligence. Had she been born a boy, Roberta would have been destined to grace the colleges of Oxford, excelling over her fellow scholars. But her father had done the next best thing and engaged both a governess and tutor to school her in mathematics and history. A most remarkable man was Mr. Baxter.

Etty smiled to herself. To think—she had been raised to consider a man in trade not worth even *looking* at, let alone inviting into her acquaintance. And yet her best friend with whom she'd prowled the Marriage Mart in search of titled husbands—rivals for the attentions of a duke—had found her perfect match in a simple gardener with uncouth table manners and a perpetual layer of grime under his fingernails. But in place of the gentility that Mr. Baxter lacked, he had other qualities rarely seen in men of Society—loyalty, generosity, and a sharp intelligence. Together with a propensity to work hard for his loved ones, such qualities rendered him the best of men.

Or, perhaps, the second best.

Etty could never hope to encounter another such man. Perhaps Arabella was right in that it was time for her to settle—to aspire to peace and contentment, lest she be perpetually disappointed by her hopes for something more. A union of convenience where both parties negotiated the terms of the marriage contract might not promise a life of passion, or of love, but it would at least save her from disappointment and heartbreak. She had a dowry to offer, and, in reality, most prospective suitors cared for little else. In return, all she wanted was a home of her own, and a father for Gabriel. If a man existed who would accept her on those terms, then she could at least live out her life happier than she had been before.

Such as this Viscount Radham.

A marriage of convenience...

Etty shook her head and laughed inwardly. Most likely Lord Radham would flee back to his ancestral pile the moment he learned about her past. He'd certainly be disinclined to love her.

But what was a husband and lover compared to good friends? Arabella had those in abundance. Only that morning, she'd introduced Etty to the first guests to arrive: Lady Marable, with her extraordinarily *stimulating* verses, together with her sister-in-law, who worked as a physician despite being the daughter of an earl, and their husbands, who both supported and encouraged them in their careers. Such liberal ideas would have them chased out of Almack's, despite their titles. But here, in the country, Arabella had created a haven for souls who wished to engage in honest conversations and genuine friendships, far from the drawing rooms of the *ton*.

Yes—with good friends, a woman alone had no need of a man's love.

And I shall tell myself that each morning I wake.

A rustling noise in the forest caught Etty's attention, and she approached the edge of the clearing. But the denseness of the trees restricted the light and she could only make out a few blurred shapes where the trees receded into the distance and the darkness. For a moment, two pinpoints of light flickered in the depths of the forest—a pair of eyes. A beast, perhaps? Or a phantom?

Her skin tightened as a low snarl filled the air. Then the lights flickered and disappeared, leaving the darkness and the hush of the breeze sliding through the trees.

Laughter came from behind, and Etty turned to see the girls amusing themselves at the opposite end of the clearing. Then Florence placed something on Roberta's head.

"What do you think, Miss Howard?" she said. "Can you guess who Bobby is?"

Etty approached the girls. Roberta had a crown that seemed to have been fashioned from bracken leaves on her head. "Is she Titania?"

Florence's eyes widened. "How did you know?"

"Two reasons," Etty said. "First, Miss Evans has been reading Shakespeare's plays to you—I found a copy in the schoolroom when I was helping her clear up."

"You helped our governess clear up?" Roberta asked. "But you're Mama Bella's guest."

"Which means that I am creating more work for her household," Etty said. "It wouldn't be fair if I sat idly by and watched someone else work when I have arms and legs of my own to help."

"And the second reason?"

"That's easy," Etty replied with a laugh. "The look of horror on Roberta's face. But I commend you, Roberta, for accommodating your friend and wearing the crown of a fairy queen."

"What does 'accommodating' mean?" Florence asked.

"It means doing something you wouldn't usually enjoy doing, because you know it makes a friend happy," Etty replied.

"Like how you're helping the servants to make them happy?" Roberta asked.

"That's nothing more than showing them a little consideration," Etty said.

"But none of our other guests would be so helpful," Roberta replied. "Except Mr. Ryman. He's always helping Connie, but that's because he likes her so much. And Duchess Eleanor, of course."

"My sister helps out when she stays here?" Etty asked.

"All the time," Roberta said. "She's so kind. You're very like her, Miss Howard. She's helped Miss Evans with our lessons when she's stayed here. She showed me how to draw a tree trunk."

"Yes." Etty nodded, a memory drifting into her mind. "Eleanor used to love studying trees. I'm ashamed to say that I took little interest in her paintings when we were younger."

"I could show you some of my drawings if you'd like," Roberta said.

"I'd like that very much," Etty replied. "And your drawings also, Florence."

"Would you like to see them before supper?" Roberta asked.

"I'd love to," Etty said. "And I think perhaps it's time to return if we're to be ready before supper. Your mama would never forgive me if we were late."

"Mama Bella would forgive you anything," Roberta said. "She loves you as a sister."

"Roberta…" Etty began.

"Yes, she does," the girl said firmly. "She told Papa yesterday that you're one of the kindest people she knows but have had little chance to show it. She said that out of everyone in the world, you deserve to be loved the most."

Etty blinked as moisture blurred her eyes, and Roberta slipped a hand into hers.

"I hope you don't mind my saying that, Miss Howard."

"Of course not, my darling," Etty said, smiling. She extended her other hand, which Florence took, and the three of them set off on the path leading back to the road.

Before they emerged from the forest, a faint sound pulsated in the air. Etty's stomach clenched again. Was the beast—or whatever it had been—following them?

"Hurry along, girls," she said, quickening the pace. But the sound only increased, filling the air with a rhythmic tattoo.

Then she smiled to herself, cursing her folly.

It was a horse—traveling at speed, from the sound of it. But nevertheless, her heart rate steadied as the trees thinned out and she caught sight of the road leading toward the house. With a final glance over her shoulder toward the darkness of the forest, she stepped out onto the road, flanked by the children.

The hoofbeats increased in volume, reverberating in her chest until she could almost believe the ground vibrated beneath her feet.

Then the rider emerged at the turn at the far end of the road—a man on an enormous black horse, approaching them at a gallop. The horse's mane rippled with the motion as man and beast claimed the path, riding as one. He leaned forward in the saddle, urging his mount on, and Etty tightened her grip on the girls' hands as the rider swallowed up the path, moving closer with no sign of slowing.

Florence let out a whimper and Etty stepped back, drawing the girls to her, lest they be trampled.

Then the rider stiffened and straightened his back. "Whoa there!" he roared, and leaned back, grasping the reins. With a neigh that split the air in two, the horse reared up and unseated the rider, who tumbled to the ground with a curse.

He made to stand, then collapsed back, his leg giving way beneath him.

"Damnation!"

His top hat had come off, and Etty plucked it from the ground and approached him. "Are you hurt, sir?" she asked.

"What in the name of the Almighty does it look like?"

Etty's gut twisted at the familiar voice. He turned to face her, and her voice caught in her throat. "I…"

Dark, expressive brown eyes widened as they recognized her.

"You!" he cried. "What are *you* doing here?"

"Helping you up," she said, offering her hand. He stared at it for a moment, then took it, curling his gloved fingers around her wrist as he struggled to his feet. "How do you come to be here, Andrew?"

"I-I'm a guest at Longford Hall."

"You're *Bella's* guest?"

He nodded. "Mr. Baxter issued the invitation."

"I didn't think…" Her voice trailed off as she cast her gaze over him, taking in the perfectly tailored jacket and cream breeches—albeit streaked with mud now. Then she turned his hat over in her hands, running her fingertips along the soft charcoal-gray felt exterior to inspect the inside, lined with cream silk, bearing a label embroidered with the inscription *Lock & Co. St. James.*

She ran her fingertips along the silk, and a nugget of pride swelled in her heart. Lock & Co. was one of her father's customers. Perhaps Papa had supplied the very bolt of silk from which the hat's lining had been fashioned.

"Why do you smile?" he asked, reaching for the hat.

"Because…" Etty hesitated as understanding slid into place. "You're Viscount Radham, aren't you?"

He nodded.

"But that's wonderful! I'm happy for you, Andrew."

His eyes narrowed. "Happy that my brother is dead?"

"No, of course not. I only meant—"

"I know what you meant, madam," he said. Then he shook his head and sighed. "I ought to have known—fool that I am. You're *the* woman, aren't you?"

"What woman?" she asked.

"The woman looking to purchase a titled husband," he said. "I ought to have known when Baxter made such a business of insisting I attend to meet his wife's *particular friend* that some stratagem was afoot. Tell me, madam—was the plot of Baxter's making?"

"No, of course not!"

He nodded, brushing leaves off his jacket. "I didn't think so. Baxter strikes me as an honest sort, though a determined deceiver is capable of making even the most cynical believe his lies. Or should that be *her* lies?"

She took a step back, clutching the brim of the hat. "Is that what your elevation to the aristocracy has done, Andrew?" she asked. "Turned the kind man I once knew into a misanthropist?"

"I have no war with humankind," he said, "merely those individuals who have done me wrong. No doubt you and Lady Arabella schemed to secure you a titled husband."

"Bella did nothing of the sort!" Etty cried. "She's merely inviting a few friends to widen my acquaintance now that I'm no longer welcome in Society. Had I known that *you* were Viscount Radham…"

"Ah, there we have it," he said. "From your own lips, you confess that you set your cap on a viscount. But I suppose given that in your last missive you informed me that you were *going home*—a return to the drawing rooms of Society and the Marriage Mart to secure the prize you'd failed the win before—I should expect nothing less. Tell me, did you and your friend also scheme to deceive your quarry about your history?"

"I've done nothing to be ashamed of," she said, but even as she spoke the words, her conscience stabbed at her and she lowered her gaze, unable to meet his eyes.

"Your friend, then. Is Lady Arabella Baxter nothing more than a scheming—"

"Do *not* impugn my friend's honor!" Etty interrupted. "You may say, and think, what you like about me—you've already made your disgust clear. But I will not give you leave to dishonor my friend. She invited you out of friendship because her husband thinks highly of you."

"And will you seek to correct his opinion of me?"

"No, sir," she said. "I have long since learned the cost of attempting to influence the opinion of others. I care nothing for his opinion of you—just as I no longer care for your opinion of me."

He opened his mouth to respond. She shook with the need to hear his soft words of love—the words that had plagued her every night since she fled Sandcombe with a broken heart and a determination to free two similarly broken women from misery.

But such a need was an exercise in futility. To succumb to it would only lead to heartbreak.

He snatched the hat from her grasp and rammed it onto his head. Then he limped toward the horse, which stood patiently in the middle of the path. He grasped the reins and hesitated.

"Do you need help to mount?" Etty asked.

He turned to face her. "No, I need nothing from you—including your dowry. Some men cannot be purchased."

He lifted his foot into the stirrup, then launched himself upward, grimacing. He swung his leg over the saddle, almost toppling over the other side, and muttered a curse. Then he righted himself and squeezed the horse's flanks. The animal veered toward Etty, and she leaped back into the verge, almost losing her balance. He cursed again, then urged on the animal on, which galloped along the road, disappearing at the far end where it curved toward the main house.

Moisture pricked Etty's eyes, and she bit her lip to stem the tears that he did not deserve. Then a small hand slipped into hers, and she looked down to see Florence staring up at her, the child's face streaked with tears.

"I-I d-didn't know the vicar could be s-so unkind," she said softly. "Do all men turn cruel?"

"Certainly not!" Roberta said, taking Etty's free hand. "My papa would never behave like that to a lady. Why was he so horrid to you, Miss Howard?"

Etty squeezed her hand. "He said nothing I did not deserve," she said quietly.

"*Nobody* deserves such incivility," Roberta huffed. "I can't think why Mama Bella invited such a horrid man to stay. And Papa's a fool if he thinks highly of him."

"He was always so kind," Florence said, sniffing.

"Well, *I* think he's horrid," Roberta said. "And I'll tell Mama how horrid he is."

"No, you won't," Etty said.

"Don't you want him punished?"

Etty shook her head. "He was only meting out the punishment that I deserve," she said. "You may think he behaved badly just then—but I've behaved much worse than he did, and for far longer."

"But you're not horrid now, are you?" Roberta said.

Etty sighed. "That's a matter of opinion."

"My opinion is that you're one of the kindest people I know," Roberta replied. "And even if you weren't before—well, the right thing is to forgive, isn't it? That's what Mama Bella always says."

Roberta was right, of course, but what she didn't know was

that Etty had deliberately set out to hurt a lot of people, including someone Andrew loved.

Which was a sin that no man could be expected to forgive.

CHAPTER TWENTY-NINE

"A H, *THERE YOU* are, Radham!" Mr. Baxter approached Andrew as he entered the drawing room and held out his hand. "I trust your room is to your satisfaction."

"Perfectly so, I thank you," Andrew replied, taking his host's hand. He cast his glance about the room, but other than his host and the rest of the gentlemen he'd spent the afternoon fishing with—a pleasant enough afternoon during which he'd bagged a trout—none of the other guests were present.

Mr. Baxter steered him toward a table where two footmen stood guard beside a row of decanters, and gestured toward them.

"Madeira?" he said. "Or we have sherry that my Bella tells me is a drink for ladies, but I'll confess having taken a likin' to it."

"Are the ladies joining us soon?" Andrew asked.

"Ha!" Baxter slapped Andrew on the back, and he almost lost his balance. "Eager to meet the marriage prospect, are you, my friend? What do you think of that, Marable?"

The tall, raven-haired Scot in the corner turned to face them, a smile on his face. "A bonny lass she is," he said, nodding, "though don't say that in front of my Carin or she'll chew my ballocks off."

Andrew flinched at the man's turn of phrase, but the rest of the party merely laughed. Longford House was unlike any London townhouse he'd visited—and any country estate, for that matter—with the easygoing manners of its inhabitants and guests. So unlike the stuffiness of Sandcombe Place, where Sir John Fulford had lorded it over his inferiors—until his latest seizure had rendered him an invalid. Now, the bitter old man resided in the gatehouse with his equally bitter wife and resentful daughters, while a merchant had purchased the main house. But it was no longer Andrew's problem to deal with—the present incumbent at Sandcombe vicarage could tend to the moral welfare of the village.

"I wouldnae touch the sherry, though," Marable continued. "Tastes like horse's piss."

He ambled over to Andrew, his burly frame towering over even their host, and slapped him on the back again. Andrew staggered forward. Since when had gentlemen taken to striking each other as a form of greeting?

"I'd recommend a good whisky," Marable said.

"Now that *does* taste like horse's piss." The slender man whom Baxter had introduced to Andrew as Major Axley, Marable's brother-in-law, approached, his scarred face puckering as he smiled. "I'd stick to madeira if I were you, Radham. It'll save you from being compared to a woman without rotting your insides."

"I thought you liked whisky," another guest, a tall, lean, dark-haired man, said.

Axley laughed. "It has its uses, Trelawney. Our housekeeper has employed it when polishing the silverware—gives it a proper shine, it does."

Marable rolled his eyes. "Take no notice of these weaklings, Radham," he said. "There's nothing to be compared to a good single malt. I'll send you a crate on occasion of your marriage if you like."

Heavens—were all the guests engaged in a conspiracy to have Andrew marched up the aisle? Had *she* engaged them to champion her cause and trick an unsuspecting titled man into matrimony?

Well, *he* wouldn't be purchased—and he'd told her as much when she accosted him on the road, fluttering her eyelashes, acting the savior as she tried to help him up after his damned horse had unseated him.

For a moment, the image of her face floated in the forefront of his mind—the concern in her expression as she rushed toward him, and the flicker of compassion in her eyes as she reached out to help him up.

But the compassion had morphed into sorrow when he rebuffed her offer of help.

You're a cad, Andrew Stiles.

Silencing his conscience, he gestured toward one of the decanters. "Maderia, if you please," he said.

"And a very fine one it is, too," Trelawney said, "though I say so myself."

"Cost me a pretty packet, it did," Baxter said, "but my wife has a fondness for it. As does Miss Howard."

Andrew's breath caught at the mention of her name.

Baxter had uttered it without a trace of anger or dislike. Did he know what she'd done—her crimes against her sister, her ruination?

"Have a care, Radham," Baxter said. "Trelawney here will have you spending a fortune filling your cellar with his wares."

"A married man needs a well-stocked cellar," Trelawney said.

"Only if his wife is a toper," Andrew replied.

"She has every right to be, if it's her fortune that pays for it," Baxter said, laughing, "though I assure you, Miss Howard is not the sort to imbibe every night. In fact, she hardly touches the stuff."

"She sounds a veritable paragon of womanly perfection," Andrew said, unable to keep the bitterness from his voice.

Baxter frowned, but Marable let out a belly laugh.

"Careful there, Baxter!" he cried. "If you're overly assertive when marketing the goods, your prospective buyer will flee. Miss Howard is a charming creature, but I doubt she'd welcome being described as 'a paragon of womanly perfection.'"

"Why not?" Andrew asked. "Don't all women wish to be praised?"

"In my experience, women only wish to be heard," Marable said. "And the very worst sort of woman a man can take for a wife is one whom Society deems to be perfect."

"So Miss Howard is *not* perfect," Andrew said.

"She is not a debutante in search of a title," Baxter said. "But she's a charming creature, and my wife quite adores her. She's suffered greatly yet carries not a trace of bitterness."

"Really?" Andrew flinched as he uttered the question.

"And she has the sweetest little boy imaginable," Axley said.

"That she does," Baxter added. "Of course, some men may be deterred from paying court to Miss Howard, given that she has a son. It's a rare good soul indeed who's prepared to love another's children as if they were their own. But Miss Howard may yet enjoy the same good fortune as me. I never believed I could find a woman to love my three little brigands—until my Bella."

Baxter gave a soft sigh and smiled.

"Here we go again," Marable said, rolling his eyes. "We all know how devoted you are to Lady Arabella—there's no need to hang your tongue out like a lovesick puppy every time you think of her."

"Leave him alone," Axley said, giving Marable a push. "We all know you'd crawl through broken glass stripped naked if it pleased my sister."

"Well, there is that," Marable replied, a smile of satisfaction on his lips. "I was never one to recommend marriage until I met my Carin. You must forgive us lovesick fools, Radham. Rest assured, we shall not tease you when the ladies arrive."

"You wouldn't dare," Axley said. "My sister would cut off your—what was it?"

"Ballocks," Andrew said.

"I beg your pardon?" a female voice cried, and Andrew turned to see four ladies in the doorway.

The woman who'd spoken must be their hostess, judging by the way Baxter stared at her with slavish devotion. With glossy black hair set in an elegant style, dotted with pearls, and eyes the color of sapphires, she was a striking creature.

Andrew's cheeks warmed, and he shifted from one foot to the other. One of her companions, a brown-haired woman with a determined set to her chin and dark, intense brown eyes, let out a laugh.

"Has my wayward husband been teaching you his particular style of cursing, Lord Radham?" she asked. "I assume you *are* Lord Radham." She approached Andrew and offered her hand. "Carinthia MacCallum," she said. "Lady Marable."

Andrew glanced toward the tall Scot, who nodded. "Aye, that's my Carin," he said, pride in his voice. "The love of my life and purveyor of the finest poetry in the land—even to rival Burns himself."

Andrew glanced at Axley, the woman's brother, then recognition slid into place. "Carinthia *Axley*? The poet?"

"The very same," she said.

Andrew took her hand and bowed over it. "A pleasure," he said. "My late brother kept a copy of your poems in his study. I happened upon them when I took residence at Radham Hall."

She smiled in response then glided across the floor toward her husband.

Lady Arabella gestured to her two remaining companions. "Mrs. Axley and Lady Alice Trelawney. Ladies, this is Lord Radham."

The ladies nodded in acknowledgment. Mrs. Axley smiled then joined her husband, but Lady Alice tilted her head to one side and cast her gaze over Andrew's form as if undertaking a critique, not only of his style of dress, but of his very nature. At length, she lifted her gaze. As her eyes met Andrew's, his skin tightened, as if cold fingers caressed the back of his neck. Her benign expression was that of any Society beauty, save for the flicker of pain simmering in her gaze. Though she was a young woman, small creases marred the corners of her eyes.

She hid her pain well, but nevertheless it shimmered around her, shifting the air as she moved.

He offered his hand, but she made no move to take it. "So you're Lord Radham," she said. "Accept my sympathy for your loss."

Her words, delivered in a flat, businesslike tone, sounded like an instruction rather than an expression of sympathy.

"Thank you," Andrew said.

"I met your late brother in London."

He waited for the usual bland words that everyone he'd encountered since Robert's demise had uttered—false declarations of how great a man he was, such a loss to the world, et cetera et cetera. But none came.

He blurted out bland niceties to fill the silence. "Were you a friend of his?"

She narrowed her eyes, the creases deepening, and the flicker of pain flared into a flame. "No," she said after a pause. "He reminded me of—"

"Alice, my love," Trelawney said, approaching her and offering his arm. She took it, and her expression softened. "I believe Radham here is a different creature to his brother," Trelawney continued. "He knows little of London Society—is that not right, Radham?"

Andrew nodded. "I am—no, *was*—a country vicar," he said. "I saw little of my brother after we left school. I find myself sailing in unfamiliar waters among London Society, though my father is fond of it. For my part, I wish to avoid Society as much as possible."

She smiled. "Then I am pleased to meet you, Lord Radham."

"Alice, come and take some sherry," her husband said, and he steered her toward the table where the footmen were unstoppering the decanters.

Lady Arabella approached Andrew and offered her hand. He took it and bowed.

"Do forgive me for not welcoming you on your arrival, Lord Radham," she said. "The ladies and I were engaged in a game of *pale-maille*. Do you play?"

Andrew shook his head. "I fear not."

"It is something of a tradition here at Longford Hall. The gentlemen attempt to relieve the occupants of our trout stream of their liberty, while the ladies play *pale-maille*—though some of our guests took to exploring the grounds this afternoon."

"Yes, I met one on my way here," Andrew said, wincing at the harshness in his tone.

She frowned. "How strange! None of them mentioned it, though Juliette seemed a little out of sorts this afternoon. That's Miss Howard, you know. I particularly wanted you to meet her—I had sat her next to you at dinner—but I'm afraid she's been taken ill."

"Ill?"

"A megrim, poor creature," Lady Arabella said. "I had warned her not to work so hard."

"Work?"

"She insists on helping about the house, despite being my guest. I had to almost push her out of the house this afternoon. I thought a walk and some air would restore her spirits, but she returned awfully discomposed. In fact…" She fixed her gaze on him. "Perhaps it was she whom you met on your way here?"

"I believe it was," Andrew said, his cheeks warming.

"I wonder why she neglected to mention it," Lady Arabella said. "Are you perhaps acquainted with her?"

"I know her sister, Duchess Whitcombe."

"Eleanor? You met Eleanor in London, perhaps?"

Andrew shook his head. "I-I knew the duchess before she married. I was vicar in the parish where she stayed for a while."

She took in a sharp breath, then withdrew her hand and frowned. "I see."

"You do?" he asked.

Her expression hardened. "I believe so—the vicar at Sandcombe. Tell me, Lord Radham, when a woman behaves improperly or commits what is generally believed to be a sin, do you place the blame on the woman?"

"The Almighty tells us to forgive the sinner," he said carefully.

"That's not what I asked. A man who forgives merely because he believes that his God has instructed him to do so is not demonstrating goodness. Rather, he is demonstrating self-righteousness, declaring himself superior to whomever he forgives."

"Then what must the man do, Lady Arabella, if he is witness to sin?"

"He should understand," she said. "Especially if the alleged sinner is a woman. We live in a world ruled by men. When a man sins he does so with the full knowledge that Society, the law, and the church permit him such liberties that legitimize the sin. When a woman sins, her reasons are often more complex."

"Sin is sin, is it not, Lady Arabella?"

"You speak the words of a man with little understanding, Lord Radham."

"Bella, love. Are you lecturing my friend?" Baxter appeared at his wife's elbow.

"Forgive me, Lord Radham," Lady Arabella said. "My unfortunate husband has married a harridan."

"You are entitled to your opinion, Lady Arabella," Andrew said.

"But perhaps I should not always express it so freely."

"I would rather be responded to with honesty than listen to niceties that are only spoken to maintain social convention, Lady Arabella."

She nodded, then gestured toward Lady Trelawney. "Alice in some ways is similar to Juliette. They both committed acts that they regret, and for which they have suffered. Some may call them sinners, but those who know and love them understand that they are guilty of nothing more than having committed acts of survival in a world ruled by men."

"Survival?"

"If two doves are caged together, eventually they will turn against each other to survive," she said. "But rather than condemn the doves, you should look to the man who caged them in the first place, and the world that enabled their incarceration. I myself was a caged dove—and until you have suffered such imprisonment, you cannot condemn the inmate for merely trying to lessen her own suffering."

"You make me quite ashamed, Lady Arabella," Andrew said.

"I did not intend to—" She broke off, a smile illuminating her features. "Oh, the children!" she cried. "How delightful. Gather round, my darlings, and say how do you do to our guests, then we can bid you good night."

Andrew glanced up to see a thin woman in a neat, crisp gown, surrounded by a gaggle of children and issuing instructions to her charges in a soft voice with a country burr. Her voice seemed familiar.

Where had he seen her before?

Then their eyes met and recognition slid into place. She let out a cry and stepped back. She collided with a footman, who dropped his tray, which fell to the floor with a clatter and explosion of glass.

It was Loveday Smith.

She stared at the mess on the floor, then grew pale as she lifted her gaze to the footman.

Baxter approached her and she flinched, her eyes widening with terror. She took a step back and he raised his hand.

"Stop!" he cried.

She cringed, hunching her shoulders as if in anticipation of a blow.

"Baxter!" Andrew said, leaping forward. "Leave her be! It was an accident."

"I know that, you numbskull," Baxter huffed. "But there's glass on the floor and I'm not wantin' Mrs. Smith to tread on it and hurt her feet." He resumed his attention on the shivering young woman. "Keep still, love, while Simon clears the mess up, You don't mind, do you, Simon?"

The footman shook his head and crouched to the floor, plucking shards of glass from the rug.

"Children, come here," Lady Arabella said. "Careful not to step on the glass."

Three of the children sidestepped the shards and approached Lady Arabella, who steered them toward the other guests. The fourth clung to Loveday.

Andrew approached them, offering his hand. "Here, let me help you."

Loveday shook her head.

"You know me, Loveday, don't you?"

"Yes," she said quietly. "I do. Miss Howard said she'd seen you today."

"Did she say anything else?"

"She didn't have to," Loveday said. "I saw how upset she was."

The child began to cry, and Andrew glanced toward her. "Florrie!" he said. "I didn't recognize you there."

"You didn't recognize me in the woods, vicar," the girl said.

Then he recalled them—two children standing by the edge of the road, eyes wide with fear, who had leaped back into the verge as he struggled to regain control of his mount.

Heavens—did they think he'd meant to mow them down with his horse? Did *Etty* think he'd intentionally tried to harm her?

"I-I'm sorry," Andrew said.

"'Tisn't us you should be apologizin' to," Loveday said, flinching again as if she expected a blow as payment for her words. "It's Mistress Juliette."

"But she—"

"I don't care what you think she did," Loveday interrupted, straightening her stance. "All I know is that Mistress Juliette is a good woman who doesn't deserve your condemnation."

Andrew couldn't help but stare at her in admiration. What had happened to the timid creature he'd known at Sandcombe?

"I admire your spirit, Loveday," he said. "It's good to see you flourishing here."

"I owe it all to Mistress Juliette. She saved my life."

Andrew nodded. "I recall it—the day she pulled you out of the sea."

"No, sir, I didn't mean that. I meant in every way possible."

"I don't understand."

"I expect you don't," Loveday said. "Florrie, darlin', why don't you go with Roberta?"

The child hesitated, then, with a glance at Andrew, darted across the floor, as if she expected him to deal her a blow. Loveday resumed her attention on Andrew.

"Do you know who Florrie's father is, vicar?"

Andrew felt his cheeks warm with shame.

She nodded. "Of course you do—like anyone else in the village who listens to talk."

Andrew lowered his voice. "Sir John Fulford seduced you."

"No, he didn't."

"You seduced *him?*"

She sighed and shook her head. "Seduction implies that the woman succumbed to temptation—that perhaps her head had been turned by the prospect of her master wantin' her."

Andrew glanced toward Florrie, who was engaged in conversation with Mrs. Trelawney, who'd lifted the girl onto her knees.

"Then..."

"He forced me," Loveday said flatly. "The first time I struggled while he beat me, until I could take it no more. The second time—"

She broke off as Andrew drew in a breath to dissipate the nausea swirling in his gut.

"Do you not wish to hear it, vicar?" she said. "In the end I learned that I had to survive, so I had a choice. Fight him until he took me, or go willing and spare the pain. So I went willing."

"And your husband?"

She flinched. "Ralph was courtin' me at the time. I didn't want to marry him, but when I quickened with child, I had no choice. I thought he'd keep me safe from Sir John, but after Florrie was born, we needed the money, so I had to go back. Until I fell pregnant with Anna, and then…"

She shook, and Andrew took her shoulders. She stiffened, but lifted her gaze to his.

"Ralph called me a whore, saying I'd sold myself—that I'd disgraced him. I was ashamed, tried to keep things nice for him, like, but when he'd come home from the Sailor after a drink or two, he…"

Andrew took her hand. "It's all right," he said, grimacing at the image of Loveday with her bandaged arm and the bruises on her face, which she'd tried in vain to hide.

"No," she said. "It's *not* all right. Mistress Juliette was the only one who wanted to help me. She didn't deliver a sermon, or tell me how to please my husband, or bring me her discarded dresses to indulge her desire to be seen as charitable. She saw what I needed and gave it to me."

"And what was that?"

"Freedom from the men who believed that they could own another person merely because they had employed them, or married them."

She froze at a low cry, and Andrew saw Lady Arabella staring at them, wide eyed.

"Oh, Mrs. Smith," she whispered. "I did not know…" She glanced toward Florrie. "Your poor child. Does *she* know?"

"That she came from…" Loveday hesitated, unable to voice it.

Rape.

An act of violence undertaken by only the most depraved of beasts—and if it bore fruit, that fruit was deemed to be rotten, fetid, beyond salvation.

"Sweet heaven…" Andrew closed his eyes, but he was unable

to deny that which he knew to be true.

Loveday Smith had not given herself to her master, nor had she been seduced. She had suffered an act of violence and violation.

Deep down, the whole of Sandcombe knew it to be true as well, and the whole of Sandcombe had turned a blind eye.

Except one. An outsider, a misfit, who, rather than *preach* of goodness and salvation and deliverance from evil, had been the only soul in the village to show what goodness truly was, and to effect that deliverance for those who needed it.

Etty.

Who could not help but love and admire such a woman who had defied the laws of Society—of the land—and followed a different law? That of right and wrong?

"Oh, Etty…" he whispered.

"Do you blame her for what she did—for saving us?" Loveday asked. "Is that why she was so distressed earlier?"

"No," Andrew said. "I don't blame her. I admire and love her."

"Mrs. Smith," Lady Arabella said gently, "I think perhaps you should see if Miss Juliette needs anything, then you must retire yourself." She glanced toward Andrew, her eyes darkening. "I think I now understand what discomposed my friend today."

"But the children, Lady Arabella…" Loveday protested.

"*I'll* see to it that the children are tended to."

Loveday nodded and slipped out of the room.

"Have you given her a home here?" Andrew asked.

"A home and a position," Lady Arabella replied. "But rest assured that we are not in the habit of exploiting the servants for our own gratification."

"I didn't think—"

"No," she said. "You *didn't* think. And neither did I. I must apologize."

"You have no need to apologize to me," he said. "Quite the opposite."

"Nevertheless, I apologize for wasting your time. I see now that you are quite unsuitable as a dinner partner for my friend. I have grown to admire her since her return from exile—a woman who has striven to make an independent life for herself and for her son. But Mrs. Smith's revelation has shown me how wrong I was. I have not admired Etty nearly as much as she deserves."

"Neither have I," Andrew said.

"Then perhaps you should have told her that before you broke her heart."

"How did you know—"

"A woman *knows*, Lord Radham," she said. "Do you think we do nothing but sit in silence and let our minds and bodies be ruled by our husbands? Or do we watch and listen, gaining an understanding of those we encounter? It was plain to see that Juliette had suffered greatly when she came to us. Not the ruination and disgrace that drove her into exile, for she has reconciled herself to that—nor the gift of her son, whom she loves more than her own life."

"Then what?"

"She has lost her *faith*, Lord Radham. For a woman in this world, faith is often all she has—faith that she will be loved for who she is, without judgment or expectation of reward, but for herself."

Lost her faith…

When a soul lost their faith, they often believed that the world was a better place without them.

A ripple of fear threaded through Andrew, and he glanced toward the door, willing Loveday to return, Etty by her side.

Hurried footsteps approached, and he caught his breath, buoyed by hope as Loveday appeared at the door.

But she was alone.

"Oh, your ladyship!" she cried, panting. "It's Miss Juliette!"

The murmur of chatter among the guests ceased.

"Has she been taken ill?" Andrew asked. "Loveday—take me to her."

"I-I can't do that, sir."

"She doesn't want to see me?"

"It's not that," Loveday said, "She's *gone!*"

"Surely she can't have gone," Lady Arabella said. "She'll be with her son if she's not in her chamber."

Loveday shook her head, her face streaked with tears. "I checked," she said. "Mistress Juliette has gone without her son—she's taken her cloak. Sh-she was so distressed when she came back from her walk, but I said nothing. What if she's had an accident? It's all my fault!"

Andrew's gut twisted with horror. It wasn't Loveday's fault.

It was *his*.

CHAPTER THIRTY

THE SHAME THAT had gripped Etty while she fled from the building and out into the night lessened as she toiled her way through the forest.

Sharp shadows sliced across the path, picking out the shapes of the stones, which glowed in the cold blue moonlight.

What must he think of her? What must they *all* think of her? A fallen woman with nothing to offer other than her dowry, on the hunt for a man so desperate for cash that he was willing to take on soiled goods with a bastard clinging to her skirts. Rumor had it that such women had to debase themselves in order to secure a husband—parading themselves in gaming hells where such matches were brokered.

She'd been a fool to think that even Bella's friends would look upon her with anything other than disgust. The ladies might perhaps have been persuaded. But as to their husbands…

Whatever Bella might say, it was men who ruled the world. Men such as Andrew, who, now he'd been elevated to the aristocracy, must have set aside his misgivings about adhering to the traditions of Society. Had he not inherited the viscountcy, he might have deemed her worthy of his notice. But now…

No viscount who didn't wish to be a pariah among Society would want to associate himself with her, let alone marry her. She would have to watch, from a distance, while he courted some respectable young woman. He would be a happier—and a better—man without her.

And Gabriel…

Her sweet, sweet boy, the innocent soul she had brought into the world through her own sins—her pride, greed, and envy, which had driven her to offer herself like a harlot.

Gabriel was far happier now than he had ever been—surrounded by people who loved him. He would also be a happier boy—and would grow to be a happier and better man—without the ruined woman who'd birthed him.

She slowed her pace, her breath misting in the night air, then glanced through the trees back toward the house. Its occupants would be sitting down to dinner now—dinner and gossip.

And what gossip there was to be had! She, the poor, wanton wastrel, the victim of her own jealousy and spite, whom Lady Arabella had taken in out of charity. How they must be laughing at her out of contempt and pity, reveling in their superiority…

And congratulating the newly anointed viscount on his lucky escape.

Silhouetted against the sky, the building's dark form rose above the horizon. A row of illuminated windows glared out into the night, almost as if they were eyes—watching her, judging her.

Condemning her.

The lights flickered, and she turned and resumed her flight, taking the path into the forest, where the malevolent lights would soon be out of sight and she would be free of them. The shadows deepened as the path grew narrower, until she could no longer discern the ground.

Then a low snarl filled the air ahead.

She glanced backward again, but the house was no longer visible. The lights had winked out.

The snarl came again, and she froze, her heart hammering at her chest.

What was it?

She paused, but the only sound was the soft hush of the breeze through the trees.

Then the skin on the back of her neck tightened as the sound of a twig snapping cut through the air. Two pinpricks of light appeared in the darkness ahead. A low growl sounded, and the lights blinked, turning a pale green.

She stepped off the path and slipped between the trees. A ghostly white form appeared in the air ahead, and she let out a scream that echoed through the forest. A high-pitched screech answered from behind, and fear coiled inside her body as the call of the night hunters filled the air.

The predators had surrounded her, beasts and otherworldly creatures alike.

Then a deep growl filled the air—low and sorrowful, until she could discern a name.

Juliette...

With a cry of terror, she broke into a run, stumbling through the undergrowth, ignoring the slashes of pain as the brambles tore at her skirts. Her foot caught on something and she tripped forward, reaching out to grasp a low-hanging branch, but she missed and crashed to the ground with a jolt. Tears stinging her eyes, she struggled to her feet, wincing at the spike of pain in her palm as she pushed herself upright.

She took a step forward and cried out at the burst of pain in her ankle. The wind whistled through the trees ahead, swirling into a roar, echoing her cries, mocking her terror.

She must get back to the path. But where was it? She stopped and looked around, but there was no sign of it—only the blurred shapes of the tree trunks fading into the distance with the deep darkness between them.

What lay in the darkness? Retribution, perhaps? Punishment for her sins?

Another howl joined the wind, and she limped forward. Her skirts snagged on the undergrowth, and she struggled to maintain her balance, wincing as the pain in her ankle throbbed with each step.

She tripped again and fell against a tree trunk. She clung to it, seeking comfort in its solidity, shaking with sobs.

What a fool I am!

Then she heard it—a faint rustle, its very quietness sending more terror through her soul than any roar.

It was a footstep. A deliberate footstep, nearby. Something was tracking her.

Her heart thudding against her chest, she straightened her stance and took a step back.

A rush of cold air brushed across her neck in a caress, and she bolted, stumbling through the forest. Then a thick, dark shape rose ahead, blocking her path.

She screamed and jerked back as the shape seemed to float toward her, claw-like fingers reaching out.

Sobbing, she fled, ignoring the slashes against her legs as she tore through the undergrowth, until she caught her ankle and groaned at the burst of pain. She reached forward to break her fall as the ground rushed toward her.

But it never came.

A hand caught her arm and thick, strong fingers curled around her flesh.

"No!"

A pair of arms snaked around her body, tightening their hold.

"Juliette!" a voice howled.

"Leave me be!" she cried, but her assailant was too strong, holding her firm while she sobbed and struggled. But no matter how violently she beat against the arms holding her, they remained still, neither tightening nor letting her go—as if they merely waited for her strength to ebb.

Her limbs aching, she slumped against the body holding her, shaking with sobs, while the roaring subsided.

Then the voice spoke again, cutting through the fog of terror.

"Etty."

Her heart ached at its gentleness and the memory it evoked— of a tender moment in a remote little cottage when she had opened her body and her heart.

"Etty, my love, be still."

"A-Andrew?"

"Aye," the voice said. Soft lips brushed against her neck, and warm breath caressed her skin. "It is I, my love. You're safe now. None shall hurt you again."

What must he *think* of her?

No—she couldn't face him after what she'd done.

"Please let me go," she whispered.

"No, my love. I let you go before and have regretted it ever since. I never want to let you go again."

"B-but you said…"

"Do not speak of what I said, my love," he said, his voice hoarse. "I said such cruel things, of which I am so ashamed. You have been nothing but kind, caring, and honest."

She shook her head. "I deceived you—I deceived *everyone.*"

He turned her to face him, and she lowered her gaze, unable to look into his eyes. A tear splashed onto her cheek, and he placed his palm on her face and brushed her skin with his thumb.

"It pains me to know that I'm the cause of your sorrow, Etty," he said. "You had every right to secrecy and privacy, given how the world had treated you. And my own behavior after you opened your heart to me showed that your fears were justified— that the weakest of souls would continue to judge you without understanding or kindness."

"You are not weak, Andrew. I am the one who is undeserving."

"Undeserving of what?" he asked. "Happiness, love? Or even—life itself?"

She flinched in his arms, and he drew her close, his body vibrating with anger.

"*Never* think you are undeserving, Etty," he said through gritted teeth.

"You're angry."

"Aye, my love," he said. "I *am* angry. Angry at the world. Angry that you believe that you always have to flee. When you were ruined…"

She flinched again as shame swelled within her, and he sighed.

"You carry the shame still, and I am sorry for it. You chose to flee then, and you fled a second time after you'd placed your trust in me and I betrayed that trust. And now you're taking flight once more. But you should never run away from anything, my love. Do you not understand that yet? You must always run *toward* something—not away."

Etty shook her head. "I have nothing to run to, Andrew."

"Oh, my love—you do!" he said. "As do I. I have always had something to run to, though, fool that I was, I did not fully understand it until now."

"Understand what?"

He took her head in his hands then brushed his mouth against hers. The instinct to reach out was too strong, and she yielded, parting her lips as he slipped his tongue inside to caress her before withdrawing.

"There is only one thing in this world I wish to run to, my beloved Etty," he whispered. "And that is you."

CHAPTER THIRTY-ONE

RELIEF COURSED THROUGH Andrew as he held the woman he loved in his arms.

Only moments before, he'd been paralyzed with fear. His blood had frozen at the raw terror in her scream echoing through the forest.

The merest thought of her coming to harm would destroy him—and it would have been at his hand.

When he caught her before she fell, she was stiff with terror, eyes wide like a rabbit transfixed in a predator's gaze. No wonder she hadn't heard him calling! Fueled by guilt and shame, she had done what he now realized she had always done—fled. But this time her shame had been so great that she had fled without her son, believing that his life would be better without her.

It was unbearable to consider what the world would be like if she were no longer in it—the sweet woman with a passion for justice, unafraid to champion the beset upon.

"Never run from your fears, my love," he said. "For you are strong enough to face them—stronger than most."

"No," she said, "I cannot—"

He silenced her protest with a kiss. "Yes, you can," he said. "Have faith in yourself."

She shook her head. "I have lost my faith."

"I have not," he replied. "My faith in you has only strengthened. And while I have done nothing to deserve your trust, I promise, here and now, that never more will you have to face your fears alone. For I will face them with you—to the best of my ability."

A screech tore through the night, and the ghostly shape of an owl glided across the air. Etty stiffened and shivered, and Andrew took her hands.

"You're freezing!" he said. "We must get you inside."

"N-no," she said, her voice rising. "I-I cannot. What must they think of me? Bella, her friends…"

"They think you're a wronged woman who's endured more than most."

"I-I can't—I can't face them. Bella must think I'm a fool."

"She doesn't, my love," he said. "Arabella knows and loves you as I do. And you'd be doing me a favor if you returned. Your friend has promised to cut off my manly parts with her letter opener and feed them to the pigs if I do not atone for my behavior."

"Is that what you want?" she whispered. "Atonement?"

"That, and an assurance of the safety of my manly parts."

The corner of her mouth twitched, and he planted a swift kiss on her lips.

"But I would gladly weather the loss of my manly parts if it atoned for my sins."

"And what of *my* sins, Andrew?"

"You committed no sin," he said. "You were sinned against. Come back with me—not for the sake of my manly parts, but for your sake—and for the sake of your son. Then, if you are generous enough to consider it, for my sake also. For I fear my life will never be whole without you."

She closed her eyes and leaned against him. At length, she nodded against his chest. He picked her up, cradling her body in his arms, his heart aching.

How had she got so thin? She weighed almost nothing—her body as fragile as a bird yet, within that slight frame was a heart as strong as a lion's.

The owl screeched again. But this time, Etty did not startle. Perhaps, if she felt safe in Andrew's arms, it was a sign that he could regain her trust.

»»»«««

As ANDREW APPROACHED the main doors, his hostess appeared, together with the other ladies.

"Lord Radham—you've found her!" Arabella glanced at Etty, taking in her disheveled hair, and the torn gown smeared with dirt and stained with blood. "What in the name of heaven has happened?"

"I'll tell you what's happened," Andrew said. "I've finally realized what a damned bloody fool I've been."

Mrs. Axley drew in a sharp breath at his profanity.

Lady Arabella gestured toward the footman. "Simon, send for Frances to tend to Miss Juliette in her chamber," she said. "Then have the fire lit and send for Dr. Long."

"No!" Etty stiffened. "No doctor—please. What will he think?"

"You're injured, Juliette," Lady Arabella said. "Just look at your legs. I must insist. Dr. Long is a ten-minute ride away. Lawrence can fetch him as soon as he's back."

"Back from where?" Etty asked.

"He's out looking for *you*, my dear," Lady Arabella said. "All the men went in search of you after we heard you'd fled. Mrs. Smith said you were very distressed. We've been terribly worried."

Etty let out a soft cry and buried her head in Andrew's chest.

"I think, Lady Arabella, we should trust Etty to know what's best for her," Andrew said.

"But she needs treatment," Lady Arabella protested. "It's no trouble if you're concerned about the expense."

"Etty?" Andrew whispered. She glanced up at him and shook

her head, and his heart ached at the raw plea in her eyes.

It wasn't the expense she was concerned about—but the diagnosis. In a world where women were judged, and a distressed woman judged most of all, Etty had every right to be afraid. She had run out into the night, believing the world would be a better place without her in it. What might some judgmental Society doctor make of *that*?

"Forgive me, but I must insist also," he said. "Etty went for an evening walk and had an accident in the forest. There is no reason for troubling a doctor merely for a few cuts and bruises." He turned to the footman. "Good man, be so kind as to fetch some bandages, hot water, clean cloths, and a jar of salve."

The footman looked at Lady Arabella, who sighed, then nodded. "Please do as Lord Radham says, Simon. Then would you find my husband and the rest of the gentlemen? Tell them that Miss Juliette has been found safe and well after taking a walk and there's no further need for concern."

"Lady Arabella, might you show me the way to Etty's chamber?" Andrew asked.

"I can walk by myself," Etty protested.

"No, my love," he said. "You have been taking care of others for too long. Let someone take care of you for once. Someone who loves you."

Lady Arabella's expression softened, and she placed a hand on Etty's arm. "Perhaps you might indulge a gallant man intent on being of service to you, Juliette," she said. Then, without waiting for a response, she led Andrew inside.

ETTY'S CHAMBER WAS in the east wing of the house, overlooking the forest. By the time Andrew arrived, his charge in his arms, the footman was already there, setting a tray on the table with a bowl of water from which wisps of steam rose, a jar of salve, and a roll of bandages.

A maid was crouched by the fire, poking the logs while flames curled over the wood, casting an orange glow in the chamber. She leaped to her feet as she saw Andrew, and he set Etty on her feet.

"Oh, sir! What's happened? Miss Howard, are you all right?"

"Perfectly so, thank you, Tilly," Etty said, her voice wavering.

"Shall I send for Miss Gadd to tend to you?"

Etty shook her head. "No, Tilly, dear—there's no need to disturb Frances. I can see to myself."

The maid bobbed a curtsey and exited the chamber.

"Lord Radham, shall I tell Lady Arabella that you'll be down presently?" the footman asked.

Andrew took Etty's arm and helped her into a chair beside the fireplace. "No," he said. "I must tend to Miss Howard."

The footman arched an eyebrow, but said nothing.

"Andrew…" Etty began, then she colored and glanced toward the footman. "I mean, Lord Radham—there's no need for you to stay. It's a few cuts, nothing out of the ordinary."

Nothing out of the ordinary! The woman he loved had injured herself while running from his anger and the judgment of the world—and she called that *nothing?*

He caressed her hand. "Let me help you, my love," he said. "For your sake—and mine."

She gave him a quick, tight smile, but made no protest as he drew a footstool before her, then lifted her injured foot onto it.

"I see I have no voice on the matter," Etty said.

Her words pricked his conscience—the words of a woman acknowledging her position in a world of men where her fate was dictated by others.

"Tell me to go, Etty, and I will," he said. "Nothing matters more to me than your happiness."

Her eyes widened, and for a moment he thought she would shoo him out. Then she relaxed into the chair and nodded.

"So be it."

Not the most encouraging of invitations, but he treasured it nonetheless.

"You may go," he said to the footman. "We'll call if you're needed again."

"Very good, sir."

"Thank you, Simon," Etty said. "You've been very kind."

The footman smiled and responded with a nod. Clearly, unlike many in Society, the residents and guests of Longford Hall thanked their staff on a regular basis and such civility came as no surprise.

As soon as Simon left, Andrew placed the tray at Etty's feet and kneeled beside it. She made no protest as he grasped the hem of her skirts and lifted it to reveal her legs. The stockings were torn and smeared with dirt and blood.

She caught her breath and stiffened as he grasped one stocking and slowly peeled it away to reveal her skin, and he glanced up to see her watching him, her eyes the color of sapphires. She gripped the chair, curling her fingers around the arms, but made no protest while he removed the stocking. Then he repeated the gesture with the other stocking, pausing where the silk was stained with already-drying blood, for fear of hurting her, and lifted his gaze to her, silently begging approval.

Her mouth curved into a smile and she nodded. His heart soared at the expression of trust in her eyes, and he removed the second stocking. A fresh pulse of blood glistened on her skin, but, brave soul that she was, she did not cry out. Then he dropped the stockings onto the floor.

"Poor Frances," she said with a sigh.

"Frannie?" he asked. "Is she hurt also?"

She nodded toward the stockings. "She'll think I've caused more work for her. And I dread to imagine the mending my gown will need. I tore it last week, and she mended it so beautifully."

"Frannie Gadd's always been a good girl," Andrew said. "Has Lady Arabella taken her in?"

She shook her head. "She's my lady's maid, and she's already very accomplished."

"Your lady's maid? Isn't she a little young for the position?"

"Perhaps, but she wanted the position—and how could I refuse the dear girl?"

He picked up a bandage and began winding it around her ankle, which was already swollen, and she flinched as he secured it with a knot.

"And Loveday?" he asked.

"Lady Arabella has employed her to help her housekeeper, who says Loveday is a very adept young woman. Which should come as no surprise, given what she's achieved, taking care of her home and her children under such circumstances."

Her expression darkened and she glanced toward the window, as if she feared the enemy outside.

"I only hope her husband doesn't try to claim her," she said, "but Mr. Baxter has assured me that he'll protect her until I have found a home of my own."

"And then?" Andrew asked.

"I shall be needing a housekeeper, shall I not?" she said. "I can think of none better."

He rinsed the cloth and pressed it against a long scratch on her leg, soaking up the dried blood, and she grimaced.

"Does it pain you?"

"It's a little sore, that is all," she said. "Nothing the salve won't fix."

"Or perhaps..."

He dipped his head and brushed his lips against her reddened flesh. She stiffened for a moment, then relaxed as he placed a gentle kiss either side of the wound.

"Better?" he whispered.

"Mmm..." She leaned forward and placed a light hand on his head. "Is that your remedy for wounds?"

"Only for the woman I love."

She leaned back. "I would never have imagined a viscount

performing such a service," she said. "Most men in Society, particularly those with titles, would consider it beneath them."

"Ah, but you forget that to you, I am merely a humble country vicar, dedicated to serving my flock."

"Viscount Radham has no flock," she said, her smile fading.

"Do you think that because I have lost my career, I've also lost my vocation?" He shook his head. "You're wrong, Etty. My responsibilities have increased a thousandfold."

"How so?"

"Instead of a village full of parishioners to serve, I now have an estate to run, with tenants and servants to care for. *They* are my flock. And though my life has changed in a manner that I could not have imagined, one constant remains. And that is you, my beloved Etty—you are the one whom I wish to serve the most."

Her expression clouded with doubt.

"You are the most remarkable woman I have met," he said.

She looked away. "You speak such nonsense sometimes, Andrew," she said. "I'm nothing out of the ordinary. In fact—"

"Forgive me for contradicting you, my love, but that is one subject on which I must disagree. Consider what you have done for Frannie and Loveday."

"That was nothing."

His heart ached at the conviction in her tone. Did she *still* believe she had no worth?

He took her hand and lifted it to his lips. "Was it nothing to take in Frannie Gadd—a young girl shrouded in scandal—into your home, merely at my recommendation?" He placed a kiss on the back of her hand. "Was it nothing to champion Loveday Smith and deliver her from her brutish husband when none else would come to her aid?"

"Andrew, I—"

"Was it nothing to give sanctuary to two young women whom the world viewed as merely the property of others, then furnish them with a purpose—giving them safety and the freedom to dictate their own futures? Would you truly call *that* nothing?"

He placed a kiss on her thigh, his body flaring with lust as he caught the faint aroma of female desire.

She wanted him. He only had to lift her skirts further and claim her as his—to pull her to the hearth rug and take her for his own.

But he was not his brother. Though desire flared in her eyes to match his, it was a desire born of her body's need. And he did not merely want to claim her body—he wanted her heart.

The door opened, and a neat young woman in a dark blue gown entered, holding a cup.

"Miss Juliette, I've brought you some hot chocolate. I—Oh!" she let out a shriek as she caught sight of Andrew, and he lowered Etty's gown and leaped to his feet.

"Frannie, is that you?"

"Vicar!" she cried. "What have you done to Miss Juliette?"

"He brought me back, Frances," Etty said. "He's been taking care of me."

"Has he, now?" Frannie asked, tilting her head to one side and eyeing Andrew with suspicion. "I'm the one to take care of you, miss. I can't think why Simon didn't send for me. But I'm here now."

"It's all right, Frances," Etty said.

"Is it?" Frannie glared at Andrew. "You were very distressed earlier on account of your encounter with…Lord Radham. I'll not have you distressed again, not by anyone."

The girl spoke with a confidence Andrew had never heard before. Gone was the timid farmer's daughter living under a cloud of disgrace. Before him stood an assertive young woman, taking care of her mistress and showing pride in her employment.

"You have my word that the very last thing I want is to distress your mistress," Andrew said. "I believe I have finally come to learn her true worth."

"Then I am glad of it," Frannie said, smiling. "Thank you,

vicar—forgive me, *Lord Radham*."

"You may call me what you like, Frannie," Andrew said. He gestured toward the cup, "Is that for your mistress?"

"It's hot chocolate."

Joy shone in Etty's eyes. "My favorite," she said. "How kind."

"Allow me," Andrew said, taking the cup from Frannie. "Would you be so kind as to give me leave to spend a little time alone with your mistress?"

"It's not proper, your lordship," Frannie said. "A lady's maid shouldn't let her mistress…"

"I think we can dispense with propriety," Etty said. "You may go. And thank you. I don't know what I'd do without you."

Frannie blushed, a shy expression in her eyes, then exited the chamber, closing the door behind her.

Andrew drew up a chair beside Etty then held the cup to her lips. "Here," he said.

"I can hold a cup by myself, Andrew."

He caught his breath as her fingers brushed against his. Her eyes widened and she lifted the cup to her mouth. When she lowered it again, he saw a bead of moisture on her lip.

"You've spilled some," he said.

She lifted her hand to wipe the droplet away, but he caught it, sliding his fingers through hers.

"No, let me," he said, leaning toward her until their lips met. He flicked his tongue out, running the tip along her lips until he tasted the chocolate. "So sweet," he breathed. "Does the rest of you taste as sweet?"

Desire flared in her eyes again, but before he could kiss her, she lifted the cup to her lips once more. Then she lowered it again, revealing a droplet of chocolate on her chin.

He needed no further encouragement. He placed a gentle kiss on her chin, tasting the chocolate, then claimed her mouth once more, slipping his tongue between her lips, relishing the smoky sweetness inside. He lowered his gaze to her neckline and the swell of her breasts where the skin had grown a delectable shade of pink to match her face. And just beneath the neckline…

He saw two little peaks beneath the material of her gown.

His manhood stirred at the prospect of their sweetness, and, unable to conquer his raw need, he dipped his head and brushed his lips against the soft skin at the top of her breasts. She drew in a sharp breath, lifting her breasts, and his senses were beset by the sharp scent of her need.

Then he caught her hand and withdrew. Disappointment flashed in her expression, and he lifted her hand to his lips.

Dare he hope that, despite the hurt he'd caused her, she still wanted him—still loved him?

He placed a kiss on each of her knuckles, then lowered himself to the floor. He closed his eyes momentarily, uttering a silent prayer to the Almighty, the one prayer—over and above all the prayers he'd uttered while alone at night—where his life depended upon the answer.

But it was not the Almighty's answer he depended on.

It was *hers*.

He lifted his gaze and summoned his courage to ask for the one thing in the world he desired above all else.

"Etty," he whispered, "I know I am not worthy, but I ask it anyway. I love you—I believe I loved you from that first moment I saw you in my church, illuminated by the light, cradling your son in your arms. Will you make me the happiest of men and do me the honor of becoming my wife?"

"You can't," she said quietly.

He clung to her hand and closed his eyes as his gut twisted with shame and loss. "Forgive me," he whispered.

She shook her head. "You can't want to marry *me*."

He opened his eyes and met her gaze. She had every right to doubt his worth—but to doubt *hers*?

"Would you want to marry a woman who has sinned?" she asked, moisture in her eyes. "A woman who committed a spiteful, selfish act on one of the purest souls who ever lived? A woman who offered her body like a commodity in an attempt to secure the hand of a duke? A whore—a woman who bore his bastard then hid herself away as if her innocent child were a dirty secret? A woman who ran from her troubles no matter whom she'd hurt?"

She caught her breath, then shook her head. "Who would want to marry such a woman?"

"*I* would," he said, lifting her hand to his lips. "I want a woman who was driven to act out of desperation by the cruel world in which we live—a mortal woman who has spent her life atoning for her actions. A loving mother to the sweetest little boy in the world, to whom I want nothing more than to be a father. A woman who survived in a world ruled by men. A woman who fought for the rights and safety of others—others whom no other living soul would fight to protect."

He kissed her knuckles again. "That is the woman I want to marry. A woman who thought nothing of her own life when she placed it at risk to save another. A woman I fell completely and utterly in love with."

The moisture in her eyes spilled over, and a tear splashed onto her hand. He brushed it away.

"Andrew…"

"Never again say that you are unworthy," he said. "In the eyes of those who love you, you are the most treasured soul in the world."

She took his hand and placed it on her breast, and his manhood hardened at the sensation of her stiff little peak poking insistently against his palm through the muslin of her gown.

She was his for the taking.

A knock came on the door, and the footman appeared. Andrew leaped to his feet, his cheeks warming, while Etty's blush deepened.

"Oh, forgive me, Miss Howard," the footman said. "Supper will be ready in an hour, and Lady Arabella wanted to know if Lord Radham would be joining the other guests. I can have your maid bring a tray up to you, miss."

"Thank you," Andrew said. "If it is not too improper, I'd like to take my supper here, with my…"

He glanced at Etty, uttering a silent plea. The clear blue depths of her eyes were filled with love.

A love he did not deserve, but would gladly cherish for the rest of his life.

She took both his hands in hers. "Simon," she said, "please be so kind as to tell Lady Arabella that I will be taking supper in my chamber with…my betrothed."

My betrothed.

The footman's eyes widened, then he bowed and exited the chamber.

Andrew pulled her toward him for a kiss.

"Would it be wicked to indulge in a little aperitif before supper?" she asked. "To celebrate our union?"

He glanced around the chamber. "There's no sherry here, but I can send for some."

"Oh, Andrew," she said. "I was thinking of a far more *pleasurable* means of celebration."

His heart leaped at the sparkle in her eyes, at the love—and trust—that had returned to them, rendering her more beautiful than she had ever been.

"We can't," he said. "What will Lady Arabella think if she finds out?"

"She'll think that her friend is the most fortunate of women." She glanced at the hearth rug. "Besides—we have the next hour to ourselves."

He needed no further invitation. He claimed her mouth in a kiss, then lifted her out of the chair and placed her on the rug, already eager in anticipation of sealing their union.

EPILOGUE

Radham Hall, Surrey, May 1818

E TTY CLUNG TO her husband, her body rippling with the aftereffects of her climax.

No matter how wicked such an act might be, nothing could surpass the pleasure to be had from making love out of doors—fully clothed, straddling her husband on a garden bench.

And, judging by the expression of satiation on her husband's face, he shared her opinion.

She shifted position, and his manhood twitched inside her. He drew in a sharp breath, and his eyes flew open, dark with desire. "Oh, Etty—what you do to me!"

She grinned and squeezed her thighs together, and his nostrils flared.

"Witch!" he cried. "You seek to torment me?"

"Ah, torment is it?" She pouted. "Then perhaps I should desist, for I have no wish to increase your pain."

She began to withdraw, but he placed his hands around her waist and held her firm.

"Torment it may be," he said, his voice hoarse, "but that does not mean to say it's not exquisite." He leaned forward and placed a kiss on her lips. "As exquisite as my wife is."

"You flatter me, Andrew."

He grinned. "Oh, flattery, is it, Lady Radham? Have you not

learned by now that I am no fop who seeks to ingratiate himself via flattery? Was it flattery when I cried your name as I came undone inside you?"

Her cheeks warmed at the raw hunger in his gaze.

"Was it flattery when I parted your thighs and feasted on—"

"Andrew!"

"That's it, my love," he said. "It gives me great pleasure to hear my name on your lips"—he kissed her again—"and to taste those sweet lips." Then he placed his palm on her stomach and caressed it, the warmth of his hand penetrating the material of her gown. "And to see your belly growing rounder each day with our child."

Desire fizzed through her. Lately her appetite for him had grown insatiable, and they'd made love in almost every room in the house, taking pleasure from all manner of adventures—up against the wall of Andrew's study, where she'd relished the feel of the hard wood panels against her back; over the mahogany dining table, after which she'd blushed at the butler's remarks about the scratch on the polished surface. And then last night…

Last night, they had indulged in the cook's chocolate sauce, when her husband had smeared a spoonful over her body before devouring it. Then, in a moment of wickedness, she had reciprocated, smothering the thick, sweet sauce over that part of him that gave her such pleasure.

"My wife is blushing."

His voice, a low growl, returned her to the present.

"Is she perhaps recalling her wantonness in feasting on her husband's—"

"Papa!" a voice cried in the distance, and Etty slid off her husband's lap to sit beside him, smoothing her skirts.

She cast her gaze over the walled garden with the array of rose and lavender bushes, set in a pattern that appeared random, but was specifically designed to give the appearance of natural beauty. "Mr. Baxter is a talented man."

"I believe we have his wife to thank for the design," he said. "I would say Baxter is the luckiest man in all England, but for one thing."

"Which is?"

He smiled, his eyes crinkling at the corners. "But for the fact that *I* am the luckiest man in the whole world." He placed his hand on her stomach. "Isn't that right, little one?"

The baby moved inside her—minute ripples resembling light fingertips tapping against her skin—and Andrew's eyes sparkled with joy.

"How did I deserve such good fortune?"

She took his hand and slid her fingers along his. "By being a good man."

"Papa!" the voice cried again, and Gabriel appeared at the entrance to the garden, cantering across the path with his toy horse. "Mama, Papa! See my horse?"

The boy reached them and lifted his arms toward Etty.

"Not so fast, sir," Andrew said, lifting the boy into his arms. "Your mother's in a delicate state. Come sit on your papa's lap."

Gabriel settled, and Etty blinked back a tear at the sight of her son nestling in the arms of the man he called father.

No—the man who *was* his father, in every aspect that mattered.

"Did you see me ride, Papa?" Gabriel asked.

"I did," Andrew replied. "And when you're older, I'll buy you a real horse to ride, then we can all ride together. Would you like that?"

"And Mama also?" Gabriel asked, turning his expressive blue gaze toward Etty.

"After the baby's arrived, my love," she said. "Until then I fear I'd be too ungainly for my poor horse to bear. My riding days are over for a while, I'm afraid."

"Oh, I don't know about that," Andrew said, a wicked glint in his eyes. "We've already enjoyed a good, long ride today."

"Andrew!" Etty cried, but could not suppress the laughter in her voice.

"But your horse has been in the stables today, Papa," Gabriel said. "Florrie and I have been feeding him.

"Quite right, son," Andrew said, winking at Etty. "Your papa is mistaken."

"Can we all ride when the baby comes?" Gabriel asked, looking to Etty's belly.

"Of course, my love," she replied. "Would you like a brother or a sister?"

"A brother!" Gabriel said. "All I want is a brother. And a sister. And another brother. And another…"

Footsteps approached, and Florence appeared, panting.

"There you are, Gabriel! Cook's been looking for you. She has a batch of biscuits fresh from the oven and has said we can have one each—you, me, and Anna. Those fruit biscuits that are your favorite."

"Fruit biscuits!" Gabriel's eyes lit up, and he scrambled off Andrew's lap and picked up his horse.

"Say goodbye to your mama, sir," Andrew said sternly.

Gabriel blushed and took Etty's hand. "Goodbye, Mama," he said. "Do you want a biscuit?"

"No thank you, my darling," Etty said, smiling at the formality with which her son bowed over her hand.

The boy ran toward Florence, and the two children disappeared through the archway in the hedge.

Etty's husband drew her into his arms. "Gabriel has the makings of a fine young man," he said. "I'm only sorry he cannot be my heir."

"He has your love," Etty said. "That's all he needs—and it's more than most boys are given. Besides, you heard him say that all he wants is a brother."

"And a sister," Andrew said. "And several more siblings, by the sound of it. My dear Lady Radham, we're going to be very busy fulfilling Gabriel's request. But I'm sure we'll find the work enjoyable, if a little exhausting."

She gave him a saucy smile. "Have I exhausted you already,

my lord?"

"You impugn my prowess, your ladyship," he replied. "I find I am ready for you again, and I'm eager to explore the delights of your body in a new location."

She squeezed her legs together to temper the thick pulse of pleasure. "Andrew, we have indulged in every room in the house, and almost every corner of the garden."

"*Almost,*" he said, a wicked grin on his lips. "Mr. Baxter has finished the work on the gazebo overlooking the lake, and I'm anxious to test its sturdiness. Have you ever taken pleasure in a gazebo?"

"I've taken *tea* in a gazebo."

He chuckled and placed a kiss on her lips. "I think I can promise you something hotter—and sweeter—than tea."

He rose to his feet and offered his arm. Smiling, she took it, and he helped her up.

"Then, my lord," she said, a thrill coursing through her veins at the prospect of the pleasure to come, "please escort me to the gazebo."

About the Author

Emily Royal grew up in Sussex, England, and has devoured romantic novels for as long as she can remember. A mathematician at heart, Emily has worked in financial services for over twenty years. She indulged in her love of writing after she moved to Scotland, where she lives with her husband, teenage daughters, and menagerie of rescue pets—including Twinkle, an attention-seeking boa constrictor.

She has a passion for both reading and writing romance with a weakness for Regency rakes, Highland heroes, and Medieval knights. *Persuasion* is one of her all-time favorite novels, which she reads several times each year, and she is fortunate enough to live within sight of a Medieval palace.

When not writing, Emily enjoys playing the piano, baking, and painting landscapes, particularly of the Highlands. One of her ambitions is to paint, as well as climb, every mountain in Scotland.

Follow Emily Royal
Newsletter Signup: subscribepage.io/RKBvRE
Facebook: facebook.com/eroyalauthor
Bookbub: bookbub.com/authors/emily-royal
Instagram: instagram.com/eroyalauthor
Amazon: amazon.com/stores/Emily-
Royal/author/B07NCBKJZ4
Website: www.emroyal.com
Goodreads:
goodreads.com/author/show/14834886.Emily_Royal
Twitter: @eroyalauthor

www.ingramcontent.com/pod-product-compliance
Lightning Source LLC
Chambersburg PA
CBHW060429310726
48977CB00001B/109